Time Travelers Never Die

continued . . .

Novels by Jack McDevitt

THE HERCULES TEXT
ANCIENT SHORES
ETERNITY ROAD
MOONFALL
INFINITY BEACH
TIME TRAVELERS NEVER DIE

The Academy (Priscilla Hutchins) Novels

THE ENGINES OF GOD
DEEPSIX
CHINDI
OMEGA
ODYSSEY
CAULDRON

The Alex Benedict Novels

A TALENT FOR WAR
POLARIS
SEEKER
THE DEVIL'S EYE
ECHO

Collections

STANDARD CANDLES
OUTBOUND
CRYPTIC: THE BEST SHORT FICTION OF JACK McDEVITT

TIME TRAVELERS
NEVER DIE

JACK McDEVITT

ACE BOOKS, NEW YORK

THE BERKLEY PUBLISHING GROUP
Published by the Penguin Group
Penguin Group (USA) Inc.
375 Hudson Street, New York, New York 10014, USA
Penguin Group (Canada), 90 Eglinton Avenue East, Suite 700, Toronto, Ontario M4P 2Y3, Canada
(a division of Pearson Penguin Canada Inc.)
Penguin Books Ltd., 80 Strand, London WC2R 0RL, England
Penguin Group Ireland, 25 St. Stephen's Green, Dublin 2, Ireland (a division of Penguin Books Ltd.)
Penguin Group (Australia), 250 Camberwell Road, Camberwell, Victoria 3124, Australia
(a division of Pearson Australia Group Pty. Ltd.)
Penguin Books India Pvt. Ltd., 11 Community Centre, Panchsheel Park, New Delhi—110 017, India
Penguin Group (NZ), 67 Apollo Drive, Rosedale, North Shore 0632, New Zealand
(a division of Pearson New Zealand Ltd.)
Penguin Books (South Africa) (Pty.) Ltd., 24 Sturdee Avenue, Rosebank, Johannesburg 2196,
South Africa

Penguin Books Ltd., Registered Offices: 80 Strand, London WC2R 0RL, England

TIME TRAVELERS NEVER DIE

An Ace Book / published by arrangement with Cryptic, Inc.

PRINTING HISTORY
Ace hardcover edition / November 2009
Ace mass-market edition / November 2010

Copyright © 2009 by Cryptic, Inc.
A complete listing of permissions can be found on page 387.
Cover art by Tony Mauro.
Cover design by Rita Frangie.
Interior text design by Kristin del Rosario.

ISBN: 978-0-441-01955-7

ACE
Ace Books are published by The Berkley Publishing Group,
a division of Penguin Group (USA) Inc.,
375 Hudson Street, New York, New York 10014.
ACE and the "A" design are trademarks of Penguin Group (USA) Inc.

PRINTED IN THE UNITED STATES OF AMERICA

10 9 8 7 6 5 4 3 2 1

For Barry Malzberg,
for his encouragement

Acknowledgments

My appreciation to Ginjer Buchanan, who's been an essential part of these projects for almost a quarter century; to Bert Yeargan and Joe Garner, who showed me the way around a dentist's office; to Sara and Bob Schwager, who made their presence felt to a degree previously unknown; to Ralph Vicinanza, for his continued support; to Athena Andreadis, who acted as guide and translator at Alexandria; to Robert Dyke, who kept me on track. And, of course, as always, to Maureen.

Lives of great men all remind us
We can make our lives sublime,
And, departing, leave behind us
Footprints on the sands of time.

—LONGFELLOW, "A PSALM OF LIFE"

PROLOGUE

THEY buried him on a gray morning, unseasonably cold, threatening rain. The mourners were few, easily constraining their grief for a man who had traditionally kept his acquaintances at a distance. The preacher was white-haired, feeble, himself near the end, and Dave wondered what he was thinking as the wind rattled the pages of his prayer book.

"Ashes to ashes—"

Shel had been the first time traveler. Well, the second, really. His father had been first. But of all the people assembled at the funeral, only Dave was aware of any of that.

He stood with hands thrust into his coat pockets. He'd buried friends before—Al Caisson after he'd been struck down by an aneurysm, and Lee Carmody, who'd fallen out of a tree at Scout camp. But neither loss had been this painful. Maybe because Shel had seemed so *alive*. Maybe because Dave and Shel had shared so much. It was true the guy had been odd, sometimes annoying, unpredictable. Selfish, even. He didn't have a lot of friends. But on that final day, Dave realized that he'd *loved* him. Had never known anyone like him.

"In the sure and certain hope—"

Dave wasn't all that confident about a resurrection, but he knew with cold clarity that Adrian Shelborne still walked the earth in other ages. Even up ahead somewhere. Shel had admitted to only brief jumps downstream, nothing beyond a month or so, just enough to satisfy his curiosity. But Dave had sensed recently that he was hiding something. Shel, he suspected, had gone deeper into the future than he'd admitted.

Not that it mattered anymore.

The preacher finished, closed his book, and raised his hand to bless the polished orchid-colored coffin. The wind blew, and the air was heavy with approaching rain. The mourners, many anxious to be about the day's business, bent their heads, queued up, and walked past, placing lilies atop the coffin. When it was done, they lingered briefly, murmuring to each other. Helen stood off to one side, looking lost.

Lover with no formal standing. Not even known to Jerry or the other family members. She dabbed jerkily at her eyes and kept her gaze riveted on the gray stone that carried his name and dates.

She looked his way, and their eyes touched.

The mourners began walking toward their cars, exchanging a few last words, starting the engines, driving away. A few seemed reluctant to leave. Among them, Helen.

Dave strode over and joined her. "You okay?"

She nodded yes.

Shel had never understood how Dave had felt about her. He used to talk about her a lot when they were upstream. How she'd enjoy Victorian London. Or St. Petersburg before the first war. And, of course, he'd never shared the great secret with her. That was always something he was going to do later.

For that matter, *she* had never understood how Dave felt. He'd introduced her to Shel and stood by while he walked off with her. Dumb.

It occurred to him that maybe he was getting a second

chance. The thought no sooner entered his mind than a flush of guilt ran through him. He pushed the idea away.

Still—

She was trembling.

Her cheeks were wet.

"I'll miss him, too," David said.

"I loved him, Dave."

"I know." He caught her arm. "Let's get out of here."

They started toward the road. Tears leaked out of her eyes. She stopped, tried to say something, tried again. "I would have liked," she said, when she'd regained a degree of control, "to have had a chance to tell him how much he meant to me. How glad I was to have known him."

"He knew, Helen. He was obsessed with you." She sniffled, wiped her eyes. "Are you going back to the house for coffee?"

"No. I think I've had enough."

"Why don't you let me take you home?"

"It's all right," she said. "I'll be okay." Her car was parked near a stone angel.

Linda Keffler, Shel's boss for a good many years, came over and expressed her condolences. "We'll miss him," she said.

She obviously had no idea who Helen was, so David introduced them. "They were close friends," he said.

"I'm so sorry, dear. To lose him like that—"

Helen didn't try to speak. She just stood, trying to control her emotions.

Linda looked a bit weepy herself. "Let me know," she said, "if there's anything I can do." Then she was striding toward her car, moving quickly, anxious to be away.

When she was gone, Helen started for her own car. Dave walked with her. "When you get a chance," she said, "give me a call."

He opened her car door for her. She got in, started the engine, and lowered the window. "Thanks for everything, Dave."

She raised her left hand in farewell and drove slowly away.

She had known so much about Adrian Shelborne. And so little.

JERRY was Shel's older brother. He wasn't much like Shel. He smiled more easily and was more aware of what was going on around him. He'd been staring down at the coffin, which waited on broad straps for the workmen who would lower it into the ground. When he saw that Helen was gone, he came over. "Dave," he said, "I appreciate your coming."

"No way I wouldn't have."

"I know. I know you guys were pretty close." He took a deep breath. "It's hard to believe."

"Yeah. I'm sorry, Jerry."

"You coming over to the house?"

"Yeah. I could use a drink."

They shook hands, and Jerry walked away. Dave thought how superficial the guy was. This was the first time he could recall that Jerry had actually seemed to care about anything important. If Shel's father had taken him into his confidence, had given him access to the converter as he had Shel, he wouldn't have known what to do with it.

Jerry ducked his head and climbed into his limo. He pulled out into the road and scattered a few pigeons.

Dave took a deep breath and turned away. Hard to believe. Gone now. Shel and his time devices.

They'd been destroyed in the fire. Dave had the only surviving unit. Safely hidden in his sock drawer. When he could summon the will, he'd get rid of it, too. Let it go.

ON the way home, he turned on the radio. It was an ordinary day. Peace talks were breaking down in Africa. Another congressman was being accused of diverting campaign funds. Domestic assaults had risen again. The economy wasn't doing well. And, in Los Angeles, there was a curious conclusion to an expressway pileup: Two people, a man and a woman, had broken into one of the wrecked vehicles and kidnapped the driver, who was believed to be either dead or seriously injured. They had apparently made off with him.

Only in California.

SHEL had never talked much about his father. But Michael Shelborne had been a Nobel candidate on two occasions, for work that Dave couldn't begin to understand. And he had found a way to travel in time, a feat that nobody except Dave even knew about. He recalled Shel's mentioning that his father had been disappointed at his career choice. Shel, like his dad, had become a physicist. But he apparently lacked Michael's genius and had eventually become the public-relations director for Carbolite, a high-tech firm. But if Michael had been disappointed in Shel, what must he have thought of Jerry, who'd become a lawyer?

Dave already missed Shel's voice, his sardonic view of the world, his amused cynicism.

He sighed. The world was a cruel and painful place. Enjoy life while you can. He remembered his grandfather once commenting that he should live life to the fullest. "While you can," he'd said, his intense sea-blue eyes locked on Dave. "You only get a few decades in the daylight. Assuming you're lucky."

Ray White, a retired tennis player who lived alone near the corner, was out walking. He waved as Dave slowed down and pulled into his driveway. Dave waved back.

He got out of the car, went inside, and locked up. He didn't usually drink alone, but today he was willing to make an exception. He poured a brandy and stared out the window. The sky, finally, was clearing. It would be a pleasant evening. In back somewhere, something moved. It might have been a branch, but it sounded inside the house.

He dismissed it. It had been a long day, and he was tired. He sank into a chair and closed his eyes.

It came again. A floorboard, maybe. Not much more than a whisper.

He took down a golf club, went into the hallway, looked up the staircase and along the upper level. Glanced toward the kitchen.

Wood creaked. *Upstairs.*

A hinge, maybe.

He started up, as quietly as he could. He was about half-way when the closed door to the middle bedroom clicked. Someone was turning the knob. Dave froze.

The door opened. And Shel appeared.

"Hi, Dave," he said.

PART ONE

ALL THE TIME
IN THE WORLD

CHAPTER 1

...Gone before
To that unknown and silent shore,
Shall we not meet?—as heretofore,
Some summer morning....

—CHARLES LAMB, "HESTER"

ADRIAN Shelborne, at an early age, fell in love with the ancient world. While most of the kids in his school went to the seashore or to theme parks during vacation, his father, Michael Shelborne, M.A., Ph.D., resident genius at Swifton Labs on the northwest side of Philadelphia, used his downtime to take him and his older brother, Jerry, to the Leaning Tower, the Great Wall of China, the Taj Mahal, and the Great Pyramid. They photographed the Sphinx, walked through the Parthenon, and visited the site of the Alexandrian Lighthouse. But Michael's interests were universal. The family also rode a cruise ship through the Panama Canal and peered down at the Colorado River from the lip of the Grand Canyon. They visited Victoria Falls when he was eight, and he flew past Mt. Fuji at ten. He'd pleaded with his father for a chance to climb Everest, but that, perhaps, in the elder Shelborne's words, might be better left for another day. Shel was, in most ways, a typical kid and would have loved to be able to say he'd thrown snowballs from the top of the mountain. But, as most of us do, he became more rational, more cautious, as he grew older. By the time he arrived at thirty, there would have been no way to coax him to undertake such a project. Or, for that matter, to venture too close to the edge of the Grand Canyon.

Everest became the end of the line for it all. Jerry had discovered girls and had never much liked the trips anyhow. He'd wanted to go to Wildwood and sit on the beach all summer. He claimed seniority to his brother in such matters. Consequently, Dad had grown tired of the carping, so the boardwalk took over for the Great Buddha and riding camels across the desert.

Shel's father had hoped his boys would follow in his footsteps but had given up early on Jerry, who made it clear that he was headed for law school. He'd tried not to put any pressure on Shel. Had told him any number of times, "Do what you want; find what's important to you." Still, Shel knew what his father hoped for. Knew he was disappointed in his older son. Moreover, Shel was interested in why people fall when they walk off rooftops, or whether the sky really did go on forever, and if it didn't, what was out there at the edge of space? So he'd gone to Princeton, majored in physics, turned in a mediocre performance, sweated out his doctorate, and come away with the knowledge that he would never be more than someone who confirmed other people's findings.

His problem with physics was that he could never quite visualize reality, never understood that space was made out of rubber. That he aged more slowly doing seventy than waiting for his car to warm up. He *knew* these things to be true, if somewhat exaggerated, but he couldn't *see* them.

Shel's mother had died in an automobile accident when he was four. He'd been with her at the time but had escaped without a scratch. She'd secured him in his car seat, but had neglected to belt herself in. He remembered vividly being thrown against his restraints and the screech of metal being wrenched out of shape and the desperate cries of his mother.

His father had not married again. "There's no way to replace her," he'd told his sons, who worried for a time that a strange woman would come into their house.

Then one day in October 2018, when both of his sons were out on their own, Jerry in a law office and Shel doing public relations for Carbolite Systems, Michael walked out of the world.

THE first indication that something unusual was going on came in the form of a late-evening phone call. It was his father, who'd been away for several weeks consulting on a government project. *"Adrian,"* he said. *"I wanted to let you know I'm home."*

Shel was surprised. "I didn't know you were coming."

"I didn't, either, until the other day. Listen, I've left a message for Jerry. Why don't we try to get together tomorrow for lunch? Are you available?"

There was something in his voice. "Dad, are you okay?"

"Sure. I'm fine."

"Okay," he said. "I'm glad to hear it. Where did you have in mind?"

"How about the Italian place?"

"Servio's?"

"Yes. Maybe eleven thirty, so we can beat the crowd."

"That's good." Shel had been watching the *Phil Castle Show.* They were interviewing someone who was trying to sell a new movie. He'd been about to turn it off when the phone rang. He did so now. "Are you home to stay? Or are you going back?"

"I'm going to take a couple of days off. Then I'm going back to Swifton."

"Well, I'm glad to hear it. We missed you."

"I missed you, too, Shel."

"And I'll look forward to seeing you tomorrow."

BEYOND a mild physical resemblance, Jerry Shelborne could hardly have been less like his brother. He was several inches taller than Shel and had for years enjoyed introducing his brother as "the other half of the comedy team." Jerry was trim and kept in good shape. He was one of those guys who worked out at his club every day.

The chasm that had opened between them came from Jerry's view that Shel was shuffling through life. That he'd caved in to his father's wishes instead of following his own muse—that was actually the term he'd used—and that consequently, Shel would be stuck selling electronics for the rest of his life unless he got his act together. There was, unfortunately, some truth to the charge. And that, of course, made it all the more painful.

Jerry saw his own career as a way to "leave a footprint." He argued that he was protecting those he called "the little people." "The corporations will take us all," he liked to tell prospective clients, "unless we're willing to fight back." And, to give the guy justice, he usually seemed to be on the right side of his cases. Though he was obviously collecting a substantial fraction of the money that was changing hands in the courtroom.

They were waiting for their father at Servio's, an upscale Italian restaurant near City Avenue. "There was a case last week," Jerry was saying, when Shel glanced at his watch and broke in.

"He's twenty minutes late."

"Not like him," said Jerry.

Shel took out his cell phone and made the call. A recorded voice responded: *"Dr. Shelborne is not available at the moment. After the tone, please leave your name and number."*

"Let's go find out what's going on," said Shel. He told the waitress, whom he knew, what had happened. "If he comes in," he said, "call me, okay?"

MICHAEL Shelborne lived on Moorland Avenue in a modest two-story frame with two big oaks in the front yard and a backboard Shel had used growing up, and which now more or less belonged to the neighborhood kids. Shel and Jerry pulled into the driveway in Shel's car. Michael's black Skylark was visible through the garage-door windows.

"So why isn't he answering his phone?" asked Jerry.

Lights were on in the kitchen and in the den. They walked up to the front door, and Shel rang the bell.

A squirrel wandered across the lawn, stopped, and looked at them.

Shel rang again. He listened to the chimes.

Jerry twisted the knob. It was locked. "You bring the key?" he asked.

Shel had been coming over from time to time during their father's absence to make sure everything was okay. A control unit turned lights off and on periodically to create the illusion someone was home. Still, the Skylark had been in New Mexico with their father. It wouldn't have been too hard to figure out no one was here.

"No," said Shel, "I didn't think I'd need it."

"Maybe one of the other doors is open." They tried the back, but it was also locked. The side door was located inside the garage, but the garage door was down, and it locked automatically.

Shel lived only a few minutes away. "I'll get the keys," he said. "Be right back."

THE door was chained. "Not a good sign," said Jerry. He stuck his head in as far as he could. "Dad, you here anywhere?"

"Maybe we should call nine-one-one."

"Let's wait till we see what's going on. We'd look kind of foolish if we get an ambulance in here, and he's just fallen asleep." He rang the bell again.

Shel tried a couple of the windows. They were locked, of course. No rocks were visible on the lawn, but there was a broken branch that had fallen into the driveway. He picked it up and came back. Jerry told him which window to break. It was one of the reasons he and Jerry didn't do much socializing.

Before going any further, Shel called Servio's. *"No,"* they said, *"he hasn't come in."*

He picked a different spot from the one Jerry had suggested

and rammed the branch through the glass. He reached in, turned the lock, and raised the window.

Jerry stood aside and waited for Shel to climb through and open the door. "Very good," he said, as if Shel had done an outstanding piece of work.

They called out again. Still no response. Shel hurried upstairs and looked into his father's bedroom. It hadn't been slept in. Two pieces of luggage, full but unopened, had been placed by the window. The other bedrooms were also empty. He returned downstairs, where Jerry was coming out of the den, shaking his head. "He's not here. His luggage is up there. It looks as if he just came in and dropped them."

"I can't figure it," said Jerry. He held up a wallet and a set of keys.

"Where were they?"

"On the dining-room table." He started going from window to window, trying to lift each one.

"What are you doing, Jerry?"

"The other doors, side and back, are both bolted." He turned and shrugged. "The windows are all locked. He has to be here somewhere."

Shel couldn't picture his father climbing down from the second floor. Nevertheless, he went back up and looked through the rooms, one by one. The windows were all locked.

He was not in the bathroom.

Not in any of the closets.

Not under the bed.

"He got out somehow."

"When's the last time you were here, Shel?"

"Wednesday." Five days ago.

"Chain wasn't on when you left?"

"How could it be?"

Jerry picked up the keys again. "He never goes anywhere without his car."

Shel went back outside. The neighbor across the street, Frank Traeger, was raking leaves. Shel went over.

"Shel," he said, "good to see you again. How you been doing?"

"Okay, Frank. Listen: Have you by any chance seen my father?"

"No," he said. "I assumed he was home, though."

"But you didn't see *him*?"

"No. Just the car."

Back at the house, Jerry was calling the police.

TWENTY minutes later, a car arrived. Two uniformed officers, both males, got out. They asked a few questions, whether their father had any health problems, whether he was prone to walk off without warning, whether anything like this had happened before. They conducted a search of the house. Then they asked some more questions. When Jerry mentioned that they had no idea how his father could have gotten out of the building, the shorter of the two, who seemed to be in charge, responded that the exit was really a secondary matter. "Let's find him first. Then we can worry about the details." When they'd finished, he said okay, they'd make a report. "We'll call it in," he said. He was overweight, African-American, and he would now have one more crazy story to tell his kids. Shel suspected he'd concluded this was a hoax, that their father was playing some sort of elaborate joke on his sons. "We'll need a description," he added.

Shel found some pictures. Several with both parents and their two sons. Another with Michael and his nearly grown-up boys standing under a tree. And several relatively recent ones, including a photo of the father and his sons raising a toast while they celebrated the opening of Jerry's law office.

"Okay," the smaller officer said. "If he gets in touch with you or if you find out what happened, we'd appreciate it if you'd let us know."

The officers went outside and walked around the perimeter of the house. They asked Jerry to open the garage door, and they looked at the Skylark. "Is that the only car he has?" they asked.

"Yes, sir," said Shel.

"It *is* strange," said the partner. "Do you know anybody who'd want to harm him?"

"Not that I know of," said Shel.

"Okay. If we turn up anything, we'll get back to you."

They got into their cruiser and drove away.

THEIR father maintained an office in back. Books were everywhere, mostly dealing with the joy of physics, the sheer ecstasy of the quantum world, the absolute unadulterated rapture of zero, and happy times with the gravitational constant.

Several volumes Shel hadn't seen before were piled on a desk. Petrarch's *Canzoniere*, *The Divine Comedy*, and *The Decameron*. He lifted the covers. All were in Italian. Also on the desk were two software packages: How to Learn Italian at Home and Speak Italian Like a Native.

Michael Shelborne had no facility with Italian. He'd picked up a little when they'd visited Rome and southern Italy years ago. But he had just enough to say "hello" and "good-bye" and, as he liked to joke, "You got a boyfriend?"

On a side table he found a copy of John Lewis's memoir, *Walking with the Wind*.

The walls held more family pictures, of him and Mom from their salad days. There was one of the four of them together, taken with Shel in his mother's lap, while Jerry stood cradling a baseball bat. And there was a picture of Clemmie, a cat they'd owned years ago.

Piled on a table were plaques and framed certificates recognizing his accomplishments. Thank you from Parker Electronics. Appreciation from Deercroft Oversight. Montgomery County Man of the Year. There was a team picture of last year's Phillies. (Dad, like Shel, was a loyal fan.) Centered over the printer was a portrait of Galileo, gazing soulfully at his telescope. His father's hero.

Shel tried the cell phone again. It rang, a few notes from Beethoven's Fifth. The phone was in the desk. He pulled the drawers open. Picked it up. Saw no record of calls other than the ones to him and to Jerry.

* * *

IT made no sense. Jerry went upstairs, and Shel could hear him walking around, opening doors.

"Shel." Jerry came out onto the stairway landing. "Did you see these robes?"

"What robes?"

"In the closet. Come on up here a minute." Jerry went back into one of the spare bedrooms. "Look at this."

Several robes hung side by side. They were the only clothes in the closet. Jerry took one out. It wasn't really a bathrobe. "It's more like a toga," said Shel.

It was dark scarlet, made of coarse material. Jerry laid it on the bed and took down another one. Mud brown, this time. Again, a rough fabric. "It's what you might wear onstage," he said. "You ever know Dad to be interested in acting?"

"Dad? I can't imagine it."

There were six of them. And, on the floor of the closet, three pairs of sandals. "I don't recall ever seeing him wear these, either," said Jerry.

Shel took a closer look. "They've been used," he said.

"WHAT do we do now?" asked Shel.

Jerry looked more annoyed than worried. He took a deep breath. Exhaled slowly. "Give up and go home," he said. "And wait to hear what's happened."

Shel stared at the house, at the big empty windows, at the chimney, at the front deck where he'd spent so many quiet summer evenings. The place was full of memories, of jigsaw puzzles and card games and essays that had to be written for next morning's class. Of old friends and girls he'd loved for a summer.

It had all gone away. The house felt strange. It had become a place he'd never known.

CHAPTER 2

One now finds scholarly analyses of time travel in serious scientific journals, written by eminent theoretical physicists....
Why the change? Because we physicists have realized that the
nature of time is too important an issue to be left solely in the
hands of science fiction writers.

—KIP THORNE, QUOTED IN *PHYSICS OF THE IMPOSSIBLE*
BY MICHIO KAKU

NEXT day, the police called Shel and asked him to meet
them at Michael's home, where they interviewed him for an
hour. Had he heard from his father? Had anything like this
ever happened before? Could Shel provide a list of friends and
associates? Did his father have any enemies that he knew of?
Had anyone ever threatened him?

Because the investigators could construct no easy explanation for the robes—there were six—they removed them.
They also boxed everything that had been on top of the desk,
including Michael's index cards and the Rolodex. Even the
pens went away.

A day later, Thursday, the *Inquirer* got the story. EMINENT
PHYSICIST MISSING, read the headline. There was no mention
of the locked doors and windows.

The FBI arrived Friday with a search warrant. "Strictly
routine," they told him. "But your father did some consulta-
tion work for the government, so naturally we're interested."
Had Shel ever noticed any unusual strangers talking to his

father? (That description fit at least half of those with whom his father routinely dealt.) Had he noticed people with foreign accents? They asked about the robes. Had he ever seen his father wearing one? Did Shel know what they were used for? Was it possible his father had been living some sort of double life? Was he gay? Did he belong to a secret society of some sort? They showed him photos and asked whether any of the faces were familiar.

Meantime, calls came in from friends and relatives. "Sorry to hear about your dad." "Everything'll be all right." "Let us know if there's anything we can do."

Nobody ever knows what to say at such times. In some ways, this was even more difficult than it would have been had his father died. His old friend Dave Dryden admitted there simply were no words.

Dave was a big, easygoing guy who'd been around since they were kids. While Shel had played baseball on the high-school team, Dave, who even then was almost six-four, had been strictly debating and chess team. Still, there'd been a chemistry between them, and they'd kept the friendship alive when most of the other people from that era had drifted apart. When Shel had arrived at a point at which he needed to talk to somebody, he automatically reached out to Dave.

Friday evening, they met at Lenny Pound's Bar and Grill. Dave was the biggest guy in the place, with red hair and green eyes. He moved with the fluidity of a natural athlete and, moreover, was left-handed. He taught languages and classics at Penn. "A wasted life," Shel had told him. "You could have played for the Phillies."

Dave was fascinated by the appearance of the FBI. "What kind of project was your father involved in?"

Shel shrugged. "No idea. He never talked about it."

"You mean he figured you couldn't handle the math?"

"Probably."

Lenny's was usually loud on Friday nights, and this was no exception. You had to project if you wanted to be heard. It wasn't the place Shel would have chosen for a quiet talk, but they'd gotten into the habit of going there because it drew a lot of women. The sound system was banging away, and the level of conversation was at about a thousand decibels.

There wasn't much to be said, though. Nobody had reported any progress on the search. The FBI had been interested in the locked doors, but they'd concluded that, whatever had happened, Shel's father had been a party to it.

Eventually, by unstated mutual agreement, they changed the subject: "Shel, are you still going to the show next week?"

He'd forgotten. They were members of the Devil's Disciples, a group of theater devotees. Shel enjoyed live theater, but that wasn't why he belonged to the group. Membership in the Disciples, for reasons he did not understand, drew an inordinate number of attractive young women. Tuesday night they'd be seeing *Arms and the Man*. Shel had never seen a play by Shaw that he hadn't liked. But this didn't seem like the right time. "I think I'll pass, Dave."

Dave showed disapproval. "You can't really do anything to help, Shel. I don't think it's a good idea to sit around in your apartment all night."

THE Saturday morning media turned up with details of the disappearance, primarily that there seemed no way Michael Shelborne could have gotten out of the house. Within hours, online news had found a deranged physicist who talked about quantum flux and how the government had a secret project that could lead to someone simply stepping into another dimension. *"If indeed that's what happened,"* he said, speaking on *WideScope*, *"we'll probably never see him again."*

When questioned further, he said that the experimentation, if it was in fact taking place, could lead to a space-time discontinuity.

"Is that dangerous?" asked the interviewer.

The physicist chuckled. *"We could lose New Jersey,"* he said, with dead seriousness.

The story translated into headlines. It led every news show and went national. Another rumor surfaced that Shelborne had been working on an invisibility device. The networks brought more physicists in, or maybe pretend physicists, and asked whether invisibility was possible. The answer was a resounding *yes*. Which led to off-the-wall questions about the kind of society we'd live in if people could make themselves, or their cars, invisible.

Sunday afternoon, more investigators contacted Shel and descended on his father's house. They asked interminable questions, none of which he hadn't already answered. Didn't these people talk to one another?

Shel was convinced there'd be a call. Or his father would walk in the door with an explanation. "We were trying an experiment for the Pentagon. A new device that allows secret agents to walk through walls."

CARBOLITE manufactured a range of household and work-place entertainment and communication devices. Their most popular unit was going to be the Showbiz, which would allow the owner to write his own screenplay, plug in a director, select a musical score, choose his cast, and watch the performance. Shel was working on the prerelease publicity when his secretary told him he had a call from a Mr. Joshua Jenkins.

"I'm busy," he said.

"He says he's your father's lawyer."

Shel didn't even know his father had a lawyer. "Get his number. Tell him I'll get back to him."

He knew what it would be. Provisions of the will. Complications since his father had disappeared and his actual status was unknown. At some point, if it didn't get resolved, he and Jerry would probably have to start proceedings to have him declared dead.

No, that couldn't possibly be what it was. It was too soon for anything like that.

He picked up a phone and punched in the number. Got a secretary at the other end. *"Washburn and McKay."*

"This is Adrian Shelborne. Returning Mr. Jenkins's call."

"One minute, please."

Clicks at the other end. Then a male voice: *"Mr. Shelborne?"*

"Yes."

"I was sorry to hear about your father. Have they found anything out yet?"

"Nothing as far as I know."

"Hard to believe something like that could happen. Well, let's hope for the best."

"Thank you."

"Mr. Shelborne, I wonder if you could find time to stop by the office? Your father left something here for you."

"Really? What's that?"

"I don't know. It's an envelope. My instructions were to give it to you in the event he died. Or became incapacitated. Or other circumstances occurred in which it seemed justified."

"Mr. Jenkins, none of those conditions applies."

"I know. If you prefer, I'll simply hold on to it. But I thought at least you should know of its existence."

JENKINS was an oversized man, a small rhino, bald, with a pointed white beard and sharp blue eyes. He was seated behind an equally oversized desk, scribbling in a folder, when the secretary showed Shel in.

He looked up. Smiled. Pointed to a chair. "I like your father, Dr. Shelborne," he said. "I hope they find him. And he's all right. But I guess you know the common wisdom about these sorts of things?"

"That if he's not found within a couple of days, the chances of his survival—" Shel sat down. "I know." By then, he'd been missing a week.

"I didn't want to say this over the phone because I just don't understand what's going on. But he told me there was a possibility he might disappear."

Shel had to run the remark a couple of times before he grasped it. "He *knew* this might happen?"

"Apparently."

"Why? What was he doing?"

"I don't know."

"Didn't you ask?"

"Of course. He refused to say any more. Only that it was a possibility. If it happened, you were to get the envelope." He looked embarrassed. "I wasn't very happy to hear it. I told him he was either to explain himself or get another lawyer."

"I see how that turned out."

"He can be a difficult man, Dr. Shelborne. He told me it was unlikely to occur, but just on the off chance—I think that was his exact phrasing—just on the off chance he dropped out of sight, I was to call you and put this in your hands." He opened a side drawer and took out an envelope.

"How long ago was this?"

"It was in June. Four months ago." He handed the envelope over. "I don't believe we've ever had a request quite like this before."

Shel's full name was printed on it. *Adrian George Shelborne.* He looked at the lawyer and opened it. Inside he found a metal key and a note in his father's handwriting.

Adrian, the key is for a rental mailbox at the local UPS. Inside you'll find three Q-pods. Destroy them. I don't simply mean you should throw them away. But take them apart. Hammer them flat. Throw them into a fire. Then weigh them down and drop what's left into the ocean.

Don't say anything to anyone about them. Even Jerry is not to know. Just destroy them and forget them. Nobody else knows they exist. Keep it that way.

You and Jerry are now the owners of Swifton, with about 70% of the stock. You guys will do what you want, but I advise you to keep it. Put Markeson in charge. You can trust him.

The two of you will also inherit the bulk of the estate. I've arranged for modest contributions to a couple of charities. Again, handle the details however you like. I want to thank you for being the son that you were. You've given me more pleasure over a lifetime than I could ever have hoped. I'm sorry your mother could not have lived to see who you became. Have a long and happy life.

Jerry will be getting a similar letter, but without the Q-pod details.

Love.

THEY looked like ordinary Q-pods. A little wider, maybe, than the standard devices onto which people loaded books and music and movies. Each had a power pack attached. One thing caught his attention: There was no corporate logo. The units had been assembled privately.

He took out a plastic bag and placed the Q-pods into it, then rolled it up so no one could see what was inside. He closed the mailbox, walked out of the UPS store and back toward the parking lot.

It was raining. Several people charged past, trying to get to a bus without getting wet. Down near the intersection, brakes screeched, and there was a burst of profanity.

If his father had wanted the Q-pods destroyed, why hadn't he done it himself? In any case, what the hell was on them that he was so worried about?

He pulled out of the parking lot, turned south on Cavalier Avenue, and hit the red light at the first intersection. The windshield wipers rolled back and forth, clearing the rain. A bus pulled up alongside. While he waited for the light to change, he opened the bag and removed one of the Q-pods. It did not impress him. More compact units were available. He was about to turn it on when the car behind him beeped. The light had changed.

He rolled through the intersection, steering with his right hand. With his left, he flicked open the lid. The screen glowed and black letters appeared: ENTER ID.

Best wait until he got back to the office. He laid it on the seat beside him and turned on the radio.

HE put the Q-pods on his desk. Picked up one. Went back to ENTER ID. Spaces for seven characters appeared.

He poked in *michael*.

The Q-pod blinked. INVALID ID.

He tried *swifton*.

INVALID ID.

What else? His father had gone through a phase of using their cat's name as a code word for everything. He tried it. *Clemmie*.

INVALID ID.

He kept at it until he ran out of ideas.

HE talked to Jerry that night. Jerry agreed they'd hold the stock, as long as the growth potential was reasonable. But he'd want to look at the earnings statements before committing himself.

In the morning, Shel visited Swifton Labs. His father's company. Everybody was jittery about the future. He informed Edward Markeson of his father's wish that he take over. "At least until Dr. Shelborne returns." Then he met with the staff and passed the news to them.

Afterward, he went through the building, reassuring everyone individually, as best he could, that the laboratory would continue as always.

He'd brought one of the Q-pods with him. He showed it around, despite his father's directions, to see if it rang any bells. But nobody was familiar with it. And nobody was able to suggest a code word to get into it.

BACK at Carbolite, Shel's distractions must have been showing because, toward the end of the afternoon, Linda called him in and advised him to take a few days off. She was a good boss, bright and easy to work for. "I know this thing with your father has been wearing on you, Shel," she said. "Go home. Come back when you're yourself again."

He argued that he was fine, but maybe he'd take the rest of the day anyhow.

He lived in a town house on Wallace Avenue. It was a

quiet area, with a park across the street. The town house was flanked by a pharmacy and a music store. There were a few trees, and a few kids, and he liked the place. He pulled into his garage and went in the side door and collapsed onto the sofa. That apparently set off his cell phone, whose ringtone was "Love in Bloom." (He and his father had watched a lot of the old Jack Benny shows when he was growing up.) It was the FBI again. *"Mr. Shelborne, do you have a few minutes? I won't take much of your time."*

They wanted more information on his father's associates. How well did he know Lester Atkin? Did your father have any connection with James Greavis? Had Shel ever seen *this* gentleman? And they e-mailed a picture of a guy with a mustache and dangerous eyes who looked like a hit man.

"No," he said. "I don't recall ever seeing him."

It took more than a few minutes. He didn't know any of the people they mentioned. When he asked whether the FBI was aware of a link between any of them and his father, they declined to respond. When it was over, they thanked him for his help and disconnected.

He picked up the Q-pod. Raised the lid and watched the light come on.

ENTER ID.

His father had never been big on security. He thought people worried too much, and there was a good chance he'd have written the code word down somewhere. Probably, if he had, it would be among the materials the investigators had taken from the house. In fact, he recalled seeing Clemmie's name on one of the cards. He called the police and identified himself. "I was wondering if you were finished with my father's stuff."

The person at the other end asked him to wait, then informed him that the case was still under investigation.

"I understand that. I was wondering, though, if my father's personal effects could be returned?"

That seemed to require a conference. A new voice, deeper, more authoritative: *"Dr. Shelborne? We'll need to keep them a bit longer, I'm afraid."*

"Would it be possible for me to look at them?"

"It's not part of the routine, Doctor."

"I'd be grateful." He made up a story about looking for a lost phone number. "Put a guard on me, if you want. I'll wear gloves. I'd just like to look at his Rolodex and note cards for a minute."

Another pause. Then: *"Okay. Come on down. We'll see what we can do."*

THEY led him into a side room and, while one of the officers watched, he flipped through the cards until he found the one with Clemmie's name. It was one of nine character groups on the card. But only two others consisted of seven characters. One was *Oscar14*. The lone Oscar Shel knew of had been a pet parrot owned by his now-deceased Aunt Mary. He had no idea where the *14* might have come from.

The final possibility was *XX356YY*. The digits sounded like someone's batting average, and knowing his father's passion for baseball, it wouldn't have surprised him.

He got up, thanked the officer, and left.

Out on the street, he fished out the Q-pod. Both code words came back invalid.

There'd been an aunt Eleanor, on his father's side. He tried that. And got nothing.

He drove home, made himself a scotch, and settled onto the sofa. It was a beautiful, warm day. Lots of kids playing across the street.

He went to Clement's for dinner, took the Q-pod along, and played with it while he waited for his meal. He entered various types of food and drink that his father had liked. *Chablis. Hotdogs. Pancake. NYstrip.* And some he *didn't* like. *Oatmeal. Lobster.* They'd often eaten there together, so he tried *clement.*

When the roast beef came, with mashed potatoes and coleslaw, he put the device away and concentrated on enjoying the food.

*   *   *

HE was back at his desk Tuesday. He took the Q-pod back to the lab and showed it around to the engineers. Nobody could tell him anything significant although they offered to do an analysis.

Shel wasn't comfortable allowing that after his father's insistence on destroying the things.

That night, Dave picked him up for the show. He immediately asked whether there'd been any more news.

"No," Shel said. "They're still looking." He showed him the Q-pod. "Ever seen one like this before?"

"I don't think so. Maybe. I don't pay much attention. What do you do? Play games on it?"

"Yeah," said Shel, as they set off for the theater.

Dave confessed he'd been looking forward to the night's show for months. Usually, the Disciples went over to nearby Bala-Cynwyd, where there was an amateur theater group. Tonight was special, though. A troupe of professionals were at Penn to perform *Arms and the Man*.

They got there about twenty minutes before curtain time and took their seats. Dave told him he'd seen the group in rehearsal that afternoon. "They're not bad," he said.

As is usually the case at a college performance, the auditorium was noisy as it filled up. Eventually, the houselights dimmed, the audience quieted, and the curtain went up. It revealed a young woman's candlelit bedroom.

The bedroom is, of course, Raina's. She is standing out on the balcony when her mother enters, sees her, and sighs loudly with exasperation. "You'll catch your death," she says. But she brings news of a major victory in the war. The two embrace over their good fortune. They talk politics for a few minutes to bring the audience up-to-date. Then Raina is left alone. She selects a book and goes to bed. The audience's attention is drawn back to the balcony. Something is moving out there. And they watch a male figure steal into the room.

If Shel needed anything that night, it was Bernard Shaw. Chocolate works better than bullets, one of the characters observes. And he came very close to forgetting, for two hours, the world outside.

When the show was over and the players had taken their bows, the Disciples gathered in a meeting room, where they were joined shortly by the cast and supplied with hors d'oeuvres and soft drinks.

The Disciples had two new members that evening. One was Helen Suchenko, with lush brown hair and eyes the color of seawater. The other Shel could never afterward remember.

Dave introduced Shel to her with a sparkle in his eye. "An old friend of mine. I've been trying to get her to join us for a year now."

"I heard about your father," Helen said. "I hope everything turns out all right."

Shel thanked her and said something about being pleased to meet her, and that was the substance of the conversation. He had a distinct impression there was a connection between her and Dave. How could there not be? The woman was a knockout. So he resisted temptation. In any case, making a pass at a stranger who was offering sympathy seemed in at least moderately bad taste.

IT was well after two when he got home. He turned his cell phone back on and saw that he had a message. *"Dr. Shelborne, we're finished with your father's belongings. We wanted to let you know that you can pick them up tomorrow."*

He got out of his jacket, removed his tie, and started again with the Q-pod. He tried every physics term he could think of. *Angular. Neutron. Quantum. Fission. Gravity.* He entered *virtual, thermal, nuclear, isotope,* and *kinetic.* He went online to look for more.

Eventually it told him to recharge the power pack.

He complied, grumbled, and stared at it. So what exactly do you do?

The Phillies had two players with seven-letter names. Neither worked. Then he remembered Galileo.

He poked it in. Hit ENTER.

The screen flickered. Replied: INVALID ID.

Damn.

Maybe it was just as well.

He wondered whether Galileo had had a title? *Professor*, probably. But that wasn't seven characters.

He did a search, but found nothing.

On the other hand, he *did* have a family name.

Galilei.

He tried it and pressed ENTER.

The screen blinked. DO YOU WISH TO TRAVEL?

He laughed. It was going to book a flight for him. Or a train.

He entered: *Yes.*

HERE?

Here? That made no sense to him. *No.*

DEST?

He tried to enter *Cairo.* But it repeated DEST? Then, after a delay: LAT/LONG?

He was getting spooked. What the hell was happening, anyhow? What were the local numbers? He shrugged. Punched in approximations. Latitude 41°40'N, longitude 79°03'W.

It gave him more blanks. Wanted him to narrow the target area. He added additional digits.

DATE?

He shrugged. Tomorrow? Why not? He entered October 24, 2018.

TIME?

What the hell? Get there for a late lunch. Three o'clock was as good as anything. He inserted it, checked P.M.

RESET DEFAULT?

Why not? Yes.

HERE?

Yes.

The screen read: READY.

A large black button was marked GO. He pressed it.

The lights dimmed and went out.

The sofa went away. The floor tilted and turned to grass. Lights came back on, and he fell on his face and began rolling downhill.

CHAPTER 3

Physics tells us what is impossible, no matter what we spend.
Engineering tells us what is possible, and how much it will cost.

—WALTER F. CUIRLE, NOTEBOOKS

SHEL bounced through a patch of brambles, picked up some thorns, and crashed into a tree. Overhead, a tangle of branches filtered sunlight. Birds sang, but other than that, the world was silent.

Sunlight.

He checked his watch. It said 2:35 A.M.

Where the hell was he?

In a bunch of trees. In the middle of the day. No. More like morning. The ground was still wet.

He picked himself up, struggling to maintain his balance on a grassy slope. A squirrel peeked at him from behind some shrubbery. It was *cold*. He was out here with no sweater or jacket. He began shivering. And not entirely from the temperature.

He couldn't see more than a hundred feet in any direction. The Q-pod lay on the ground. He picked it up and looked at it. The display read RETURN?

He fished through his pockets for his cell phone. But he

apparently didn't have it. That happens when you don't know you're going out.

"Anybody here?" he said. Then he tried again. Louder. "Hello! Anyone here? Help!"

The squirrel scrambled up a tree trunk.

The Q-pod was too big to put into his trouser pockets, so he simply held on to it. And, picking a direction at random, he began to walk.

HE kept going over what had happened, how he had come back from the show and had been trying various combinations on the Q-pod. And suddenly he'd been *here*. He hadn't awakened here. The place had simply shown up. As if he'd stepped out of his den into this forest. Into the sunlight.

He hadn't been drinking. So the only thing that made sense was that he'd suffered a stroke of some sort, or a mental episode. He'd blacked out, gone amnesiac, gotten into his car, and driven out here.

Wherever *here* was.

But that was ridiculous. He had no history of anything like that.

And where was the car?

He listened for the sound of traffic. But heard nothing other than birds. And wind.

The walking got his circulation going, which helped a little. He arrived at a brook. It was too wide to jump, and the last thing he needed was to get his feet wet. He turned right and walked along the bank.

He'd gone about a mile when he arrived at a place where someone had recently been camping. By then he was seriously cold. He looked at the charred wood. Maybe he should try to start a fire. But he had no matches. Never carried them. And how the hell did you start a fire without matches? Boy Scouts made a big deal of igniting a blaze by rubbing pieces of wood together. He'd been a Scout at one time, but Shel had never attempted to make a fire with a couple of sticks. Neither had anybody else. Except Tommie Barker, who'd always been a show-off.

He kept walking.

After a while, he parted company with the brook. The sun was rising higher in the branches, and he heard the sound of a plane. It passed overhead and droned on and droned on and finally began to fade. Moments later he came on a half-buried plow that looked as if it had been out there for a century. A fence appeared, and he followed it, but saw no buildings anywhere, no cows, no plowed fields, nothing.

Finally, he heard a car.

It was ahead somewhere, its sound receding. He broke out of the woods and stood at the side of a highway. The car was climbing a hill. It reached the summit and slowly dropped out of sight.

The road was a two-lane. A stretch about a mile long was visible. Over the hill in one direction, around a curve in the other. He wrapped his arms around himself and waited.

A pickup appeared. Coming around the curve. Shel waved. Please.

The pickup slowed while the driver looked his way. Thought about it. And elected to keep going. Their eyes met as the truck bounced past. The driver was bearded, with white hair, probably in his sixties. Shel watched it start up the hill. Two more vehicles passed, one going each way, before a Prince electric came over the rise and pulled off the road in front of him. Two guys were inside, both in work clothes. Each looked about twenty.

"Where you headed, pal?" asked the driver.

He had no idea. "Any town with a restaurant."

The right-side door opened and the passenger looked back. "Sheffield's about four miles ahead." He nodded toward the curve. "Hop in." He scrunched over to make room.

Gratefully, Shel climbed in and pulled the door shut. He closed his eyes momentarily as a wave of warm air engulfed him.

"You okay?" the passenger said. "You look half-frozen."

"Yes. Thanks. It's cold out there."

"Where's your car?"

"Broke down."

"Not the best weather for it."

THEY left him at a Chevron station with a convenience store that served hot dogs. And good coffee. But they didn't have a public phone. Probably nobody had a public phone anymore.

The only resource he had was the few bills folded into a pocket. About thirty bucks. He didn't have his wallet with him, so he had no credit cards, no identification, nothing.

"You all right, mister?" It was the clerk, an older, gray-haired woman, who doubled as a waitress. She looked at him with concern as she refilled his cup.

"Yeah," he said. "I'm good. Umm, where am I?"

"You mean where are we located?"

"Yes. Please. I've gotten lost."

"You're in the Allegheny National Forest."

"You're kidding." He wasn't sure where that was, but he knew it wasn't near Philadelphia. "This *is* Pennsylvania, right?"

"Sure."

A large wall clock, the kind you get at a discount store, showed 11:45. His watch read a quarter after four. "Miss," he said, "could you do me a favor?"

"Sure. What do you need?"

"Access to a phone. I need to make a long-distance call. I'll pay for it."

"Hold on a second." She left. The classified section of a newspaper lay on an adjoining table. He reached for it and checked the date. They'd gone to the show Tuesday evening. It was now Wednesday morning. He'd lost almost eight hours.

My God.

She came back and handed him a cell phone. He thanked her.

"It's okay," she said.

* * *

HE set his watch to the correct time and called Dave.

"You're where?" he asked.

"The Allegheny National Forest."

"What the hell are you doing out there?"

"It's a long story."

"I guess."

"Can you come get me?"

"Sure. Where are you, exactly?"

"Hold on." He asked the clerk.

"Sheffield," she said. "On Route 6."

He relayed the information. Dave said okay. Then: *"Your car break down, Shel?"*

"No."

"So why don't you tell me what happened?"

"I don't know what happened." He was angry, and the emotion had crept into his voice. The clerk was watching him, and he didn't want to say anything that would alarm her.

"You don't know?"

"I've no idea."

"You mean you don't remember anything?"

"Not since I got home last night."

"Shel, you should check into a hospital."

"I feel fine. Could you—?"

"Sure. But, look, I've got a class coming up. Two classes, really. I can get somebody to cover for the afternoon. But if you can hang on, the twelve o'clock class is ready to start. I can take off right after that."

"Okay. I'll be here."

"I'll get there as quickly as I can."

He called Linda. "I'm sorry I didn't show up this morning. My alarm didn't go off, and I was dead tired after—"

"Who is this?" she said.

"Shel."

There was a long pause. Then she hung up.

He tried again. "Linda—"

"Look, whoever you are, please stop. I don't have time for games." And she hung up again.

THE clerk came over periodically to see how he was doing. He asked how late they were open.

"Till eight," she said. "When will your ride be here?"

"He's coming from Philly."

Her face showed sympathy. "That'll be four, five hours, probably."

"I know." It occurred to him that Dave would be rushing around. Not a good idea. It wasn't as if Shel would be going anywhere. He should call again and tell him to take his time.

"Here's the phone," said the waitress.

But all he got was Dave's voice mail.

He gave the phone back. "If you don't mind," he said, "I'd like to wait in here."

"Sure." She smiled. "Make yourself comfortable."

Her name was Marilyn. When he got home, he'd send her a box of chocolates.

DAVE arrived at about five thirty. "I called Les before I left the office," he said, as they pulled out of the Chevron station and headed southeast on U.S. 6. Les was Shel's next-door neighbor, the guy who ran the pharmacy. "He tells me your car is in the garage."

"Yeah. Okay. By the way, I tried to call you. Ask you to take your time. All I got was your voice mail."

Dave felt his pockets and came up empty. "I must have left it in my desk. I don't take it with me into the classroom." He nodded. "Yeah. That's what happened. Because I came right from the room." He shrugged. "No problem." They were behind a tractor-trailer. Dave watched for his chance, pulled out, and passed. "Shel, you really have no idea what happened?"

"I was working at the house. Then I was out where you found me."

"And that's all?"

"Yes."

"What've you got there?" Dave was looking at the Q-pod.

Shel shrugged. "Don't know. Something my father had."

Dave shook his head. "You need to see a doctor, Shel."

"I guess."

On the long ride home, the conversation concentrated on brain tumors and amnesia and various neuroses, of which neither of them knew anything, but it didn't slow Dave's theorizing. After all, what else could it be? Shel squirmed the entire trip. "But even if I've got a tumor or something," he said, "how did I get way the hell out here? Walk?"

They had just connected with the Pennsylvania Turnpike in Harrisburg, when he realized he didn't have his keys. He'd have to break into the house.

IT was dark when they stopped at a roadside diner. While they ate, Shel figured it out. The Q-pod induced some sort of mental disruption. That would explain why his father wanted them destroyed. It was a weapon! Though that still didn't explain how he'd gotten to the Allegheny National Forest.

Dave shook his head. It still didn't make sense. "I think it has to do with the pressure you've been under. It's your father's disappearance, Shel. It's been eating at you. It can't be a coincidence that this happens just after you lose him."

"How did I get out there?"

"Maybe you caught a bus. Rode a taxi, for that matter."

Finally, desperate to change the subject, Shel asked about Helen Suchenko.

"She's pretty nice, isn't she?" Dave said.

"Yeah. She looks like a heartbreaker."

"She's a doctor."

"Really? Ummm—" He hesitated. "You introduced her as an old friend. How *good* an old friend, exactly?"

Dave smiled. "No problem," he said, with a touch of jauntiness. "Nothing serious between us."

Shel thought he detected a reluctance in the answer. "You sure?"

"Absolutely."

HE delivered Shel to his front door shortly before eleven. The outside lights came on as they pulled into the driveway. First thing they did was check the garage. The Toyota *was* there, just as Les had said.

Shel sighed. "Now we get to break in." He looked help-lessly at the house. "I keep an extra key at the office, but I have no way of getting in there, either."

"Why don't you stay at my place tonight?"

"That doesn't really work." He thought he saw movement in one of the windows. A face drawing back. "Wait. What's that?"

"What's what?"

But it was gone now. "I thought I saw somebody inside."

"Are you serious?"

"Right there. In the dining room."

Dave went over and looked in. "Don't see anything."

"Neither do I, now."

"There's a light on in there." The den.

"I had that one on last night."

"Shel, maybe we should call the police."

"I feel as if I'm in a rerun. But no. It was probably my imagination."

"So why don't you spend the night at my place?"

"Dave, I'd still have to come back here to change for work. I couldn't go in like this. Well, I could, but it's more trouble than it would be worth. No, it's okay. I'm getting good at break-ins." He was tired. Scared. Literally terrified about the possibilities of a brain tumor. Maybe he *was* coming apart.

Dave was still looking through the window. "I don't think you should take any chances. Let me take you to the hospital."

"Look, I'm okay."

"Best to play it safe, Shel."

"I don't need a hospital. I need a key."

He tried the side door. It was, of course, locked. "Thought I might get lucky."

Dave walked around to the front of the house. Climbed four steps onto the porch. And tried the knob.

It turned, and the door opened.

"That's odd," said Shel. He stepped past Dave, went inside, and listened. Air moved through vents.

Dave pushed in behind him.

"Who's here?" said Shel. Outside somewhere, a dog barked.

He turned on more lights. Looked around. Saw nothing. No sign of a forced entry anywhere. "I'm going upstairs," he said.

Dave went with him. They looked in the closets and under the beds. Checked all the windows. Everything seemed secure. He saw no indication anything had been taken. "Must have been my imagination."

His keys were downstairs in the wicker bowl where he customarily dropped them when he came in the door.

"It's been a long day," Dave said.

"Yeah."

"You want me to stay over?"

"No." Shel was feeling silly. "I'll be fine."

"Okay." Dave started for the door. "I'll call tomorrow," he said.

"All right. Good night, champ. And thanks."

Shel stood at the door while Dave walked out to his car. He got in, gave him a thumbs-up, don't worry, everything will be fine, and started the engine. Shel remembered he'd left the Q-pod in the backseat. "Wait," he said.

IT was good to be home. He sat down on the sofa and turned on the TV. He watched it for a while, not really paying attention, still thinking about the lost eight hours and the way Linda had responded on the phone when he'd tried to call in.

Eventually, he wandered into the kitchen and raided the chocolate chip cookies. It was almost midnight, but he was still not sleepy.

He turned out the lights, all except the lamp on the table beside the sofa, and of course the electric candle at the top of the stairs. The house felt very still. He sat down and picked up the Q-pod. On a whim, he raised the lid and the screen blinked on. It said: ENTER ID.

He poked in *Galilei*.

Then it asked a question: RETURN?

He stared at it.

RETURN?

Return where? The Allegheny National Forest?

The smart thing would be to leave it alone. Put it on the coffee table and forget it until tomorrow. But when he tried, when he shut the lid and set it down and closed his eyes, he couldn't get it out of his head.

Return where?

Okay. Settle it. He put on a jacket, just in case, and touched the YES key, just barely, thinking how cold it might be out in the woods.

Ridiculous.

He pressed ENTER.

The dim glow of the electric candle faded and went out. Then the lamps came on. Two of them. Including the one he'd turned off just a moment ago.

He felt himself lifted off the sofa and dropped immediately back onto it. He sat listening to the silence. Got up. Looked at the lamps. But he was still at home. Still in his town house. Thank God for that.

But it had happened again. *Something* had happened again. His heart pounded.

He hung on to the Q-pod. Hung on as if it were a lifeline.

The Q-pod was doing it. He didn't know how, didn't even know *what*. But the goddam thing...!

He sat, not moving. Whatever it was, at least it hadn't been a stroke.

Finally, he put the Q-pod down on the coffee table. Gingerly. Then he got up and made himself a rum and Coke.

CHAPTER 4

To see a world in a grain of sand,
And a heaven in a wild flower,
Hold infinity in the palm of your hand,
And eternity in an hour.

—WILLIAM BLAKE, "AUGURIES OF INNOCENCE"

THE sun was bright through the curtains, and the events of the day before seemed far away. Shel got up and looked at his watch, as was his habit. It showed 4:02. His alarm clock, which he hadn't bothered to set, read 7:12. He checked the TV. The seven o'clock shows were on. But why was the watch three hours behind? Fear settled in. He tried to push it aside, made the watch right, and went over to Maggie's for some pancakes.

Usually, he allowed himself time to relax and read the paper before going into the office, but he wanted to set his mind at ease and get back into his work routine, so after he'd finished his breakfast, he headed directly for Carbolite. He wondered what Linda's explanation was going to be for hanging up on him the day before. Twice. She wasn't exactly the most even-tempered person in the world, but that was way out of character.

When he arrived, she was in her office. "Hi," he said.

She looked up from her keyboard. "Good morning, Shel."

He sat down. "I don't quite know what happened yesterday," he said. "I got stranded. But anyhow, I'm sorry I didn't call earlier."

"Call about what?"

"About not showing up for work."

She gave her head a shake, as if a ghost had appeared in the doorway. "What are we talking about, Shel?"

"About my not being here yesterday. Or didn't you notice?"

She dropped her eyes to the floor, then came back to him. "Shel, you *were* here. At least until yesterday afternoon. Is *that* what you're talking about?"

"Yesterday afternoon?"

"You *do* remember, right? I suggested you take the rest of the day off, and you went home early."

"Linda, that was *two* days ago. I wasn't here at all yesterday."

"It was *yesterday*, Shel."

"No. We're confused here somewhere," he said quietly. "I spent the entire day yesterday trying to get home from western Pennsylvania."

Her eyes narrowed. "What are you talking about, Shel?"

"Just what I said."

"Western Pennsylvania?"

"Yes. A town called Sheffield. Dave came and got me."

"Dave?"

"Dave Dryden. I think you know him. He's been here a couple of times. But anyhow, that's where I called from."

"Sheffield."

"Yes. And you hung up on me. Twice."

Her jaw was sagging. She looked worried. "You're saying I hung up on *you*?"

"You don't remember that either?"

"Shel, I don't hang up on people."

"You did yesterday. I was stuck and I was trying to talk to you—" He stopped.

Linda got up and walked past him to the door of her office. "Sally," she said, "would you come in here for a minute, please?"

Sally was her secretary. Dark skin, black hair, glasses. A bit too serious, probably. Linda looked at Shel. "Sally, was Shel here yesterday?"

"Well, of course," she said. "He was here."

"All day?"

"As far as I know. Except that he left early, I think."

"This is crazy," said Shel.

"You want to ask around?"

HE promised he'd make an appointment with a psychologist. Linda urged him again to take some time off, take the rest of the week off, but Shel assured her he was fine. But when he sat down in front of his computer, he got another shock.

The Devil's Disciples had gone to see *Arms and the Man* Tuesday evening. Early Wednesday morning, around two thirty, he'd experienced the *event*, whatever it was. He'd spent all day Wednesday getting home. It was now Thursday morning.

Except that it wasn't. His computer indicated it was still Wednesday. He stuck his head in Bill Shanski's office, across the hall. "Bill," he said, "what day is this?"

"Wednesday," said Bill, with his usual vacuous smile.

"You sure?"

"All day long."

HE tried to bury himself in his work, assembling a sales presentation for a new data-control system. He'd never dealt with a therapist, always thought that therapists were for the weak-minded, that talking to an outsider about problems was a waste of time and money.

But he didn't have much choice. He opened the yellow pages, picked a psychologist, and made an appointment. *"You should come in tomorrow,"* said the female voice on the phone after he'd explained the problem, *"for an appraisal."*

He'd never really had a physical problem other than once going to a hospital after he'd crashed into an infielder chasing a fly ball. The possibility that he was suffering from a mental problem left a cold knot in his stomach. He went through a dozen cups of coffee. (He usually had about two.) And, as if the day hadn't produced enough shocks, Linda came in on her way out to lunch to tell him she'd just had a weird phone call. Two of them, in fact.

"About what?"

"A guy claiming to be you, Shel."

Shel was starting to get out of his chair, but with that news he slid back down. "What did he say?"

"He said he was sorry he hadn't been able to get to work today." She shook her head. "He sounded just like you."

Shel just stared at her.

"If this is some kind of joke, Shel, I don't appreciate it."

It was enough. He told her about his appointment with Dr. Benson. And then said he was going home.

"I think that's a good idea. Why don't you *stay* home until you're feeling better."

HE tried to call Dave, but all he could get was his voice mail. He'd probably be in class, so the phone was in his desk.

He skipped dinner. Had no appetite. He tried to read. Tried to watch some TV. Got on the computer for a while. But it was hard to think about anything other than what was happening to him.

He went back to the bookcase. Took down *Hands on the Past*, by C. W. Ceram. One of his favorites when he was growing up.

Hands on the Past.

It consisted of accounts of the early archaeologists. He thought of his father's passion for history. How he'd disappeared from a locked house. And Shel wondered if, somehow, he had in the same manner disappeared from *his* house Tuesday night?

The idea was crazy. But it was too coincidental not to have some validity. In any case, there could be no harm running a test. As long as he was careful.

He picked up one of the three Q-pods, sat down on the

sofa, opened the lid, and entered *Galilei*. When it asked where he wanted to travel, he hesitated. Keep it simple: *Here*.

DATE?

Today.

TIME?

On his Wednesday morning experiment, he'd asked for 3:00 P.M. It certainly hadn't been three o'clock in the afternoon when he'd opened his eyes in the Allegheny National Forest. It had been more like midmorning.

But it might have been three o'clock GMT.

Greenwich Mean Time? Maybe that was it.

He'd sat in this same sofa after Dave brought him back. The Q-pod had asked him RETURN? and he'd replied *yes*. Maybe the Q-pod had taken him back, not to *where* he started, but to *when*. Two thirty Wednesday morning. My God. Was that possible?

If it were true, then it had been Shel himself on the phone to Linda this afternoon, calling from the Sheffield Chevron. Or was it *yesterday* afternoon? His head was starting to spin.

He tried calling Dave again. Still got the voice mail. The whole idea was preposterous. But it was time to find out. Where did he want to go?

There was one way to settle it: He could stay in the town house, but take himself to the time when he and Dave were just getting in. Say, a quarter to eleven. Dave had brought him back Wednesday night. But then he'd pushed the RETURN key on the Q-pod. If he was right, it had taken him back to the point where he'd been early Wednesday morning. That was why it had still been Wednesday at the office. Or been Wednesday again, if that was more accurate. If he was correct, he and Dave were at that moment on the way home from the Allegheny National Forest.

A quarter to eleven Wednesday night translated to Thursday, 3:45 A.M. GMT. He set the time and date, and was about to push the big black button when it occurred to him that it wasn't a good idea to be sitting down. If it really happened, he'd want to arrive standing up. That way he wouldn't fall on his head.

He got to his feet. Took a deep breath. And hit the button.

The lights flickered and went out. One of the lamps came back on. He was still in his den. He hadn't moved.

He checked his watch. No change. But then, it wouldn't, would it?

He went into the kitchen. The wall clock showed ten forty-five.

Bingo. My God, I did it.

His father had invented a time machine.

Shel walked through the downstairs, wanting to scream it to the heavens, tell the world, *We can travel in time.* He knew that physicists had been saying for years there was no known reason it couldn't be done. But Shel had never believed it possible.

How long ago had it happened? When had his father developed the first working model? Had he possessed this thing for years? Or was it connected with the government project?

No. He knew the answer. The letter had gone to the lawyer a few months ago.

Why had he told no one? More to the point, why did he want the devices destroyed?

HE turned out the lights. He wasn't sure why. If David's car actually showed up, carrying both Dave and himself, he'd open the front door and charge out onto the pavement and shake his own hand. Explain to himself what was going on.

*In*credible.

But wait. That wasn't the way it had happened.

As much as he liked the idea of meeting himself, he decided caution would be a better policy. He couldn't have said why. Maybe he was driven by his father's secrecy. *Hammer them flat. Throw them into a fire. Then weigh them down and drop what's left into the ocean.*

The Shel coming back from western Pennsylvania, though, had no keys. He unlocked the front door. Save them from having to break a window. Then he picked up a spare key from the wicker bowl and put it in his pocket.

Minutes later, a car pulled up outside.

Shel was so excited he could hardly breathe. He went over to one of the dining-room windows and peered out through the curtain. Headlights swept across the driveway, and Dave's white Regal eased in off the street. It was dark, but Shel could just make out the passenger. A chill slithered up his spine.

The engine died. They got out of the car, and Shel—the one outside—stood looking around, wondering, of course, how he was going to get into a locked house. Shel watched, unable to believe what he was seeing, and, somehow, mildly disappointed in his appearance. He didn't look as good as he'd expected.

Abruptly the man outside turned Shel's way. Shel ducked back into the dark. The outside Shel stood staring for a minute. Then he shook his head, and said something to David. He remembered: *"Somebody's in there."*

Shel retreated from the dining room into the kitchen and stood near the side door.

They'd be coming in the front. When he heard them on the porch, he eased the side door open and slipped out into the driveway.

He went for a walk. Gave it an hour just to be safe. When he returned, the lights were out, and the Shel who had arrived with Dave had by then consented to the time machine's query: RETURN? It had put him back in the town house early Wednesday morning.

HE sat cradling the Q-pod in his hands. His father must have had a big time with this. The guy who'd lived to visit Urquhart Castle and the Palmengarten and the Hanging Gardens had extended his reach dramatically.

He wondered how far back he'd been able to go. A few days? Years? Was the Mesozoic within range? Had he been able to travel in the other direction? Into the future?

And that explained his disappearance. He'd gone somewhere, and, obviously, something had gone wrong. Maybe he'd landed in the middle of the Little Bighorn. If Shel could figure it out, he could follow him and, he hoped, do a rescue. If he was in time.

Wait a minute.

Shel had a time machine. If you have a time machine, there's never any question about the cavalry arriving on cue. If he was too late with the first attempt, he could just reset the clock and go back another hour. Or whatever it took. All he needed to do was figure out where his father had gone.

He visualized him on Lincoln's train to Gettysburg, or watching Washington cross the Delaware. Maybe he'd decided to tour the Renaissance. Hell, that would explain the robes! He *had* been going back pretty far.

But how to know where to look?

Then he realized how dumb he'd been: There was no need to follow his father into the past. Or the future. Whatever. He'd left from the house on Moorland Avenue a week ago Monday. All Shel needed to do was to show up at the house on Monday the fifteenth and say hello.

CHAPTER 5

We were the first that ever burst
Into that silent sea.

—SAMUEL TAYLOR COLERIDGE,
"THE RIME OF THE ANCIENT MARINER"

SHEL would have liked to transport himself directly into his father's house, or, failing that, onto Moorland Avenue. Why drive over there when he had, in effect, instantaneous transportation? But he didn't know how to do it. There were provisions for narrowing down the arrival site, but he had no idea of the precise location of the house in terms of degrees, minutes, and fractions of seconds.

So he waited until morning. Usually, breakfast was his big meal, but he got up with no appetite, settled for a cup of coffee and a piece of toast, wrapped the Q-pod in a plastic bag, and drove to Moorland Avenue. He parked in the driveway, got out, walked behind the house, where he was more or less out of sight, and set the converter to take him back to Monday night, October 15. With no change of geographical position.

Then he pressed the button.

The sun went out, and the sky filled with stars. The house remained dark.

He walked back out to the driveway. And voilà. Shel's car was gone. Now it remained only to wait for his father to arrive.

But, come to think of it, there was no need to wait. Time travelers don't have to wait for anybody. And there was the title for the book he would one day write about all this. My God, he felt good. The vast realms of past and future were opening up. And, more important, he didn't have to worry anymore about a tumor. Life had become a dream.

What time had he spoken with his father on that night? On *this* night?

He couldn't remember. He'd been watching the TV but wasn't sure what had been on. Okay. It was simple enough. The time at the moment was eleven minutes after nine. He set the Q-pod to take him forward to ten o'clock.

The darkness faded and came back. And he realized he was standing in the middle of the driveway. Time traveler run down by father.

But no car was coming, and the garage was still empty. He was sure the call hadn't come in after eleven, so he set the device to move forward one hour. This time he walked onto the lawn before activating.

And the black Skylark had arrived. Inside the house, lights were on.

Who said Shel wasn't brilliant? He congratulated himself and knocked at the front door. There was movement inside, the living-room lights came on, and the door opened.

His father's eyes went wide. "Adrian."

"Hi, Dad." They stood for a long moment staring at each other. "Did you want to invite me in?"

"Yes. Of course." He stepped back. "I just got finished talking to you."

"I know."

Michael Shelborne resembled Jerry more than he did Shel. Or would have had Jerry not picked up weight. His father was tall, lean, with thick black hair and the kind of face that would have allowed him to play Sherlock Holmes. "Adrian, were you in your car when we talked?"

"No."

"I thought not."

Shel showed him the Q-pod. His father acquired a distinctly unhappy expression. "Come in," he said, using a tone that one might adopt to a sixteen-year-old caught smuggling his girlfriend into the house.

They sat down while the elder Shelborne contented himself with glaring at one of the walls. Then the eyes, dark, penetrating, cool even when he was irritated, locked on him.

"Where are you going, Dad?" Shel asked innocently.

"Why does it matter?"

"That lunch tomorrow?" Shel made no effort to hide an accusing tone. "You never showed up. Or, rather, you *won't* show up."

"What happened?"

"That's what I wanted to ask you."

He'd settled into an armchair. Now he pushed back in it, licked his lips, and braced his jaw on one fist. "Is that why you're here?"

"Isn't it sufficient reason?"

"Don't tell me any more," he said.

"Why not?"

"Trust me." He indicated the Q-pod, which Shel had attached to his belt. "How long have you known about that?"

"A couple of days. To be honest, it's hard to be sure. What day is this?"

"Monday."

"Incredible. A few minutes ago it was Thursday."

Michael's eyes closed. "Look, Adrian, I know you're probably upset."

"Did you make this thing?"

"You were supposed to destroy it."

"I'm glad I didn't."

"I'm sure you are." Michael pressed his lips together. "Yes, I made it. Along with a colleague."

"Why do you want it destroyed?"

"Because it's dangerous."

"Why's that?"

"For a number of reasons."

"Tell me about them. I don't have a clue what's going on."

"I take it I haven't turned up since the lunch?"

"No. You've been missing nine days."

"Okay."

"Where were you planning to go?"

He laughed. "You wouldn't believe it."

"At this point, I'm ready to believe *anything*."

He smiled, casually, easily, like a man in charge of the world. "You know what the converters can do."

"A converter. Is that what you call it?"

"Yes. But the name's not important."

"I guess not. So where did you go? Where are you going?"

"I'd always wanted to spend some time with Galileo."

"Galileo."

"Or maybe Cicero. Or Ben Franklin." He managed a smile. "I haven't made up my mind yet."

"You've had this thing—what?—three or four months? It's part of that government project, right?"

"More or less."

"How do you mean, 'more or less'?"

"It was an accidental discovery. We were working on something else."

"Okay. So now the government has time-travel capability."

"No."

"No? Why not?"

"It's too dangerous to put in anybody's hands. Let alone a government."

"You keep saying it's dangerous."

"I don't think we would be permitted to change the past. Though there are people who'd want to. Hell, *I'd* want to. You could save Lincoln. Kill Hitler. Things like that. But I'm not certain what the result would be."

"I'm not sure I'm following."

"We had reason to believe that the time stream has a lot of flexibility. You can go back and do things, and the continuum will adjust. As long as you don't create a paradox. A loop. Something that can't be absorbed."

"What makes you say that?"

"The math suggests it. But we pushed it too far. We did an experiment."

"I'm listening."

"Adrian, my partner in the research was Ivy Klassen."

"Was?"

"She's dead."

"What happened?"

"The experiment."

"Explain."

"What happens if someone goes back and rescues JFK? Prevents his going to Dallas?"

"I don't know. We stay out of Vietnam?"

"I don't know either. What we *do* know is that it didn't happen. Look, Adrian, the standard theory is that if you go back and rescue Kennedy, you cause a split in the timeline. Another reality is created. That's nonsense, of course, but if it happened, there'd be diverging timelines. The one we live in, and the one in which he survives."

"And that's what you wanted to test?"

"Yes."

"What did you try to do? Post somebody at the Texas School Book Depository?"

"We did a different kind of test. We put a copy of a book into a briefcase."

"Why are you laughing?"

"Because of the book. Anyhow, we closed the briefcase. Left it alone in Ivy's office for fifteen minutes. Then we went in and opened it. The book was still there."

"I would think so."

"Then Ivy used the converter to go back five minutes, to a time before we looked in the briefcase. The intention was that she'd remove the book."

"So it should have been empty when you opened it."

"Yes. But had it been empty when we opened it, then Ivy would have done nothing. Either way, we'd have had a paradox. We would have changed reality."

"So what happened?"

"I found her dead in the office."

"What? How?"

"The doctors said it was a heart attack."

"My God."

"She was twenty-seven. In perfect health, as far as anyone knew." He sighed. "It was my fault, Adrian."

"Why do you say that?"

"I should have realized there might be a factor, something built into the continuum that prevents our screwing around with it. No paradox allowed."

"But we've both traveled in time. I did it tonight. This was a conversation that did not take place. And here we are."

"How can you say it didn't take place? It *is* taking place. I did not live through a variant of this evening in which I called you, agreed to meet you and Jerry at Servio's, and you *didn't* show up here with a converter.

"Listen, son, if we went back to watch the signing of the Magna Carta, then we *were* part of the event. If photographers had been there, taking pictures, they would have gotten us, as well as the other witnesses. There never would have been a Magna Carta event that we did not attend. I think—I can't be sure, but I *think*—it's only when we violate the time flow, when we create a situation we know could not have existed, that a corrective sets in."

"A corrective."

"Call it a principle that maintains chronological integrity. That prevents modifications to history. It disallows paradoxes. Negates contradictions."

"A chronological integrity principle."

"Yes."

"You mean a *cardiac* principle. Threaten the prescribed chain of events, and your heart gives out."

"It need not be so dire. I hope not. But yes, I think you're correct."

Shel sat quietly, trying to absorb it all. "What was the book? Why did you smile when you mentioned it?"

"It was one of my favorites. The Library of America edition of Tom Paine."

"Why's that funny?"

"The first essay is 'Common Sense.'"

"DAD, if you were actually to go back to talk to Galileo—"

"Yes."

"How's your Italian?"

"Not bad. I've been doing a crash course."

"Have you done anything like this yet? Have you actually been anywhere?"

"Only a couple of experimental trips."

"Nothing long distance?"

"No. But let's get to the point. You're here because I didn't come back from this, right?"

"Yes."

He pursed his lips. Not to worry. Everything's under control. "Okay."

"Dad, I don't think you understand. You're going back there to Renaissance Italy, or wherever, and something happened. Happens. Probably the Inquisition gets you, too."

"No," he said. "Nothing will happen."

"How can you say that?"

"Because when I'm done with my visit, instead of coming back here, I'll return in, say, two weeks."

Shel's head was starting to spin again. "Then the reason you disappeared is because I warned you you'd disappear."

"Sure." He grinned.

"Wouldn't it be simpler, and safer, not to go?"

"It's perfectly safe, Adrian. Because I know what I'm doing."

"What would have happened if I hadn't shown up here?"

"Pointless question, son. You *did*, and that's all that matters."

Shel listened to a car approach, slow down, and pull into a driveway across the street.

"Now, I'm still missing as of when? When did you leave your base time?"

"Base time?"

"Your present."

"Um. Thursday, the twenty-fourth."

"Morning? Night?"

"Morning."

"Okay. That's the day I'll come back. In the evening." He produced a Q-pod, a converter, and did something to it. "Make it nine o'clock. In the evening. I'll call you as soon as I get in."

"Okay," said Shel. "Good. That'll work." A sense of relief flooded through him.

"One other thing: You need to keep quiet about this, Adrian. Tell nobody."

"Okay."

Mission accomplished. Shel got up, as did his father. They embraced. "It's good to see you again, Dad. I thought I'd lost you."

He laughed. "Nice to know you care, son."

"So, where've you been, exactly? Where were the experimental trips?"

"I sat up front and watched Beethoven play the *Pathétique*. And I went to Broadway for *Over the Top*."

"*Over the Top*?"

"Fred and Adele Astaire."

"Who?"

"Before your time, lad."

"When was that? *Over the Top*?"

"Nineteen seventeen." He actually looked apologetic. "I probably shouldn't be doing it. But it's been hard to resist."

"How about if I come?"

"To talk to Galileo?"

"Sure. Why not?"

"How's *your* Italian?"

CHAPTER 6

> ...To the gods alone
> Is it given never to grow old or die,
> But all else melts before relentless Time.
>
> —SOPHOCLES, *OEDIPUS AT COLONUS*

SHEL returned to Thursday morning, October 25, retrieved his car from the driveway, and went home. He came away from the conversation with mixed feelings. An overwhelming pride in his father's achievement. Exhilaration at the knowledge that he, too, had traveled in time, had literally gone back into the previous week. Misgivings that his father was going ahead with his intention to travel to Renaissance Italy. Or wherever he finally decided to go.

He called the office and told them he'd be late. He stopped for breakfast at Maggie's and thought about calling Dave to tell him what had happened. But that meant flying in the face of his father's insistence that he keep the existence of the converters quiet. Anyhow, Dave would think he'd lost his mind.

When he arrived at the office, Linda didn't want to let him in. "Have you been to see the psychiatrist yet?" she asked. She tried to make it sound like a joke, but her expression clashed with that notion.

"He's a *psychologist*," Shel said.

"What did he say?"

"I'm supposed to be over there at eleven thirty."

"Okay. Good. Why don't you take the rest of the morning? Go to Starbucks or something. Relax. See the doctor, then come back."

"Linda," he said, "I'm okay."

"I know that, Shel. But I think maybe you've been under too much stress lately. I mean, something like this could happen to anybody."

In fact, Shel had forgotten about Dr. Benson. "I'll be fine, Linda," he told her. "Look, I've got work to do, and I'm not delusional."

"You're sure?"

"How long have you known me?"

"I'm sorry, Shel. But yesterday was a little scary."

"I know. Look, I'll sit quietly in my office and play with the computer for an hour. Then I'll go see Dr. Benson. Okay?"

BENSON must have been eighty. He wasn't much taller than his desk, and he looked as if he didn't eat enough. But he had a leisurely manner that put Shel, despite his reservations, at ease. "Why don't you tell me what happened?" he said.

The truth, Dr. Benson, is that I have a time machine. Got it right here in my briefcase. "Doctor, my father is Michael Shelborne, the physicist who disappeared two weeks ago." He gave a fictionalized account of the last few days. Stress over the loss of his father had left him confused, and he'd lost a day out of his memory. "But I remember it now. It came back to me."

Benson asked more questions. Had anything like this happened to him before? What sort of relationship did he have with his father? Was there a woman in his father's life? He asked what day it was. (He almost got Shel there.) Who was the current occupant of the White House?

Then it was over. "These things happen all the time, Dr. Shelborne," he said. "Nothing to worry about. You've undergone a severe shock, and sometimes, when that happens, people simply want to get away from it. So we push it out of our memory. Or, we may forget other things instead." He smiled. "You'll be fine."

Shel drove back to the office and described the conversation to Linda. She was relieved, and said, "See, that wasn't so hard, was it?"

DURING the afternoon, Shel's spirits improved. Linda seemed to have forgotten his odd behavior, and everything returned to normal. He spent most of his time thinking about the converter, where he'd like to go, what he'd like to see. The Wright Brothers, maybe. The "I Have a Dream" speech. And he'd like to go back and watch a couple of the ball games he'd played in for Teddy Roosevelt High School. They'd almost won a title one year. He'd cleared the bases late in the final game, the deciding game, with a double to right center. It gave the Rough Riders a one-run lead, but Lenny Khyber couldn't hold it.

Damn. It still annoyed him, remembering Lenny walking three guys in the seventh to give it all back. His father wouldn't like it, wouldn't approve, but in the end he'd give in. He had to, because he'd been doing it himself.

And there was also going to be the matter of explaining where Michael Shelborne had been the last eleven days. But, ultimately, it wasn't Shel's problem.

This would be a weekend to celebrate. Maybe with Helen. He hadn't asked for her phone number—should have done that—but he found it easily enough in the directory.

It was late in the week to call and try to set up a Saturday date. But another possibility suggested itself.

That evening, he took the converter into the park and, when he was alone, used it to return to the previous night. Wednesday. Then he called her on his cell phone.

She picked up on the fifth ring. *"Hello?"*

"Helen? This is Shel."

"Who?"

"Adrian Shelborne. From the Devil's Disciples."

"Oh, yes. Of course. How are you, Shel?"

"I'm fine. I hope I'm not disturbing you."

"No. I was just reading the paper."

"Helen, I enjoyed meeting you last night." Was that right? Had it only been the night before? "I was wondering if I could talk you into having dinner with me Saturday?"

"It's nice of you to ask, Shel. But I already have a commitment."

"Oh. I'm sorry to hear that." For a few moments neither spoke. Then Shel continued: "How about next week?"

"Sure," she said. *"I think I can manage that."*

AT twenty to nine, Thursday evening, he was parked in front of the TV, watching *Heavy Hitters*, a political show with people yelling at one another over, mostly, trivia. Whom could the ordinary people believe? Who was being inconsistent on the issues? Shel was grateful it was an off year for elections.

He imagined what time travel could do for the media. Take a camera crew back and record what a given candidate had actually done or said. (They'd probably need a court order for that sort of thing.) And for specials, they could record the Caesar assassination. Or Alexander routing the Persians and their war elephants at—Where was it?—Guagamela? They could interview St. Augustine, talk about how it felt to be a god with Amenhotep, and settle the world's religious arguments once and for all. They could interview Richard III. ("And what did you think of how Shakespeare portrayed you?") They could talk with Columbus on the way to the New World, and get the native reaction as the galleys appeared on the horizon. He loved the possibilities.

The moderator on *Heavy Hitters* was trying to get one of the experts to quiet down long enough for someone else to say something.

The show that would really draw the ratings would be the talk show from the future. *Tomorrow's News Today.* Imagine how many people would tune in to watch that. Shel pictured himself as host.

He checked his watch. It was 8:47.

A car pulled up outside. Doors opened and closed. Laughter. Then the car pulled away.

"Love in Bloom" sounded. He picked up. "Hi, Dad," he said. "You're early."

"Shel?" A woman's voice.

"Yes. Who is it, please?"

"Charlotte." His cousin. *"Have you heard anything new about your father?"*

"Nothing yet, Charlotte. Listen, let me get back to you. Just a few minutes. I'm expecting a call."

"But you haven't heard anything? I wondered because you answered sort of funny."

"No. I think I got confused, Charlotte. Listen. I'll call you right back." He disconnected and put the phone down on the coffee table. Beside the connector. The calibrator. Whatever the damned thing was called. And he started thinking how he'd explain it to Charlotte. And Jerry. And everybody else.

Maybe it wasn't just his father's problem at that.

HEAVY *Hitters* was running commercials. Take this to increase your sexual prowess. Take that to get rid of arthritic knees. The moderator returned, posed against the standard background of the Capitol dome, inviting everyone to be with him tomorrow when his special guest would be Elizabeth Staple, who was head of the House Judiciary Committee. Then he was gone, and the nine o'clock show, *The News Room*, started, with its discordant theme that suggested the world was going mad. Host Bob Ostermaier appeared behind his desk with a handful of papers. "Tonight," he said, "Washington has a brand-new sex scandal involving a senator who's spent most of his career running on family values."

Shel turned it off.

He sat in the sudden stillness. He could hear music somewhere.

It was two minutes after nine.

He picked up the phone, put it in his pocket, and went out

to the garage. Fifteen minutes later, he pulled into his dad's driveway. Under the basket. The house was dark, save for the security lights.

HE waited an hour. He sat in the car with the converter on the seat beside him and the cell phone in his pocket, and he realized he'd done the wrong thing. Shouldn't have caved in. Should have insisted he be allowed to go along. But of course he'd *always* caved in to his father.

He took out the cell phone and punched in Dave's number. It was late, but that was what friends were for.

Dave was in a restaurant somewhere. *"Hello, Shel,"* he said. He took a minute to speak to someone else. Then he was back. *"Anything wrong?"*

"Yeah. You teach Greek and Latin."

"More or less."

"How's your Italian?"

"It's okay. Maybe a little shaky. Why? You headed for Rome?"

"Dave, are you doing anything Saturday morning?"

"I'll be on the run. What's wrong?"

"I've got a problem."

"What do you need, Shel?"

"I want to show you something."

CHAPTER 7

Americans generally do the right thing, after first exhausting all the available alternatives.

—WINSTON CHURCHILL

DAVE was at one of those stages in his life where nothing special was happening. He'd gotten bored with classroom work. He spent most of his evenings grading papers, preparing seminars, and watching old movies on TV. There were a few women drifting around the fringes. But none for whom he could work up any passion.

Except Helen. His heart fluttered every time he saw her. Every time he thought about her.

She'd been the reason he'd hesitated when Shel asked about Saturday morning. She usually ate a late Saturday breakfast at the Serendip on Cleaver Street. He'd seen her there occasionally and had planned to run into her. Accidentally, of course. Why, Helen, nice to see you. He'd liked her for a long time, but her reaction to him had always been not exactly cool, but indifferent. He'd asked her out a few times, but she'd always found a reason why she couldn't manage it. Next time maybe, she'd told him. But the message was clear enough: Take the hint, Dave. He was accustomed, though, to pretty much getting his way with women. If he stayed with it, he was sure he could win her over.

Discovering that Shel was on her track had come as something of a shock. He should have informed Shel that first night, at the show, of his interest. But ultimately that would have required him to admit his lack of success with her. Couldn't let that happen. No way.

He'd known Adrian Shelborne all his life. They'd gone to the same schools, hung out together, even been in Scouts together. Once, they'd chased the same girl. She'd eventually run off with one of the male cheerleaders, embarrassing them both. Short of combat, nothing can bond males like being dumped by the same young woman.

Shel's father had money, and prestige, and had helped Shel get to Princeton. Dave had gone to Temple, a local school that his family could afford. But he'd done well, discovered a facility for languages, and learned Greek so he could read Homer in the original. *Ho phylos esten allos autos.* A friend is a second self. He'd gone on to master Latin.

There was something majestic in the classical tongues, a sense of dignity and power that, somehow, didn't surface in English. Maybe it was simply a matter of too much familiarity. Whatever it was, he eventually found himself immersed in Hellenic and Roman culture, acquired French and Spanish along the way, and was now in the process of learning Italian. Two years earlier, he'd published *Speaking in Tongues*, a treatise on the development of language and its connection to social mores.

Shel had always been a wild type, a guy who'd been everywhere, who had pictures of himself standing in front of the Vatican, riding a camel around a pyramid, standing on a rope bridge in Turkestan. He'd once played a guitar with the Popinjays in Dallas, and had apparently fit right in. How could Dave, whose folks thought hanging out in the Poconos was a big deal, keep up with that?

Nevertheless, they'd remained close friends over the years. Despite his advantages, Shel was a solid guy. No pretense. No illusions about self-importance. And the last person who was likely to suffer a blackout and wake up two hundred miles away. That business Wednesday had sent chills through Dave and left him with a sense that reality was coming undone. It was like an experience he'd had when he was about ten. His folks had taken him to see a magician perform at the Walnut. The guy had made basketballs float through the air, put a woman into a cabinet and taken the cabinet apart and she wasn't there anymore. They'd put chains around the magician, put him inside a narrow box, and hung the box from the overhead, so there was no way he could have gotten out of it without being seen, and when they lowered the box and opened it, he was gone, and in his place was the woman who'd disappeared from the cabinet.

It was the night in which Dave came to believe in magic. To conclude that anything could happen, that there were no rules. No boundaries. Wednesday had felt like that, too. The bewildered look in Shel's eyes, the way he'd sat slumped in the car on the road back from western Pennsylvania, the way his voice shook when he tried to explain what had happened and discovered he had no idea what had happened.

Sometimes it was just magic.

Then the phone call: Something had happened again. Shel hadn't admitted it, but it was in his voice. The guy was scared.

SO Dave passed on Helen and the Serendip, and was dutifully waiting when Shel pulled up outside a little before nine. It was raining, one of those steady, bleak October drizzles. "What's wrong?" Dave asked.

"It's hard to explain." Shel was carrying a computer bag. He dropped the bag on the floor, took off his jacket, and fell into a chair. "Dave," he said, "I know what happened to my father."

The room grew still.

"Is he okay?"

"No. I don't think so." The weather rattled the windows. "I also know what happened Wednesday."

Dave sat down on the sofa opposite him. "What happened?"

"Okay, what I have to show you is off-the-wall stuff. I mean *seriously* off the wall. But before I say any more, I want you to promise it'll go no further."

"Okay."

Shel's eyes narrowed. "You promise?"

"Yes."

"Say it."

"Come on, Shel. I promise."

He picked up the computer bag, unzipped it, stopped, thought about it. He looked at Dave as if he were a stranger. And opened the bag. He removed a Q-pod from it. Or maybe one of those new game-playing devices that were always coming on the market. Dave had lost track of the technology years ago.

Shel held it out as if it had special significance. "What is it?" Dave asked.

"I'm not quite sure what to call it. My father called it a converter." He handed it to Dave.

Dave took it, turned it over, and shrugged. "So what's it do?"

"Lift the lid."

Dave complied and watched the converter light up. A lot of numbers appeared on-screen. "Okay. What do you want me to do with it?"

"I'll show you. You'll need a jacket, though."

"We're going outside?"

He smiled. But it was a dark smile. A smile that signaled *way outside*. "More or less."

Usually, Shel was straightforward. This kind of juking around was utterly unlike him. Dave felt his hair beginning to rise. The way it had Wednesday when he'd picked him up at the Chevron station. "Whatever that means," Dave said. He got up and went over to the closet. Took out a lined plastic jacket and pulled it around his shoulders. Then he walked to the door.

Shel shook his head. "Not that way, Dave."

"Shel—"

He reached into the bag and produced a second Q-pod.

"I don't know how these things work. They're above my pay grade. But just trust me for a minute, okay?"

Dave frowned at the two units. What in hell was Shel talking about?

"Hook it onto your belt. There's a clip on the back." He waited until Dave complied. Then he did the same.

"What's the thing do? We going to listen to a concert?"

"You see the big black button?"

"Yes."

"On a count of three, push it. Okay?"

"Okay. But—"

"Just be patient." Shel checked his watch. "One." He zipped his jacket. "Two." Dave slid his thumb onto the unit and found the large black button.

"What's—"

"Three."

DAVE, utterly puzzled as to what he was—as he thought—going to hear, pushed the button. The room began to fade. To grow darker. Momentarily, he thought he was passing out. But he didn't grow weak. Simply became mystified. And scared. Then the lights came back, and he got knocked aside.

A guy in a scruffy brown overcoat bounced away from him. Where the hell'd he come from? And the living room was gone. The walls had vanished, and he was looking at a street scene. At night. Horns blaring, music playing somewhere, lots of old-fashioned cars. The guy who'd collided with him looked back with a snarl. "Watch where you're going, will you, buddy?"

The world was full of moving traffic, streetlights, theater marquees. People crowded around him, moving in both directions. Some were trying to get across the street, waiting for a break in traffic.

And it was *cold*.

"You okay, Dave?" Shel was at his right hand. Just a foot or two away.

"Where are we?" His voice squeaked. "What happened? How the hell did we get here?" His knees buckled, and he'd have fallen had not Shel grabbed him and prevented him from going down.

Shel pointed at his Q-pod. "It's a time machine."

"For God's sake, Shel, where are we?"

"David, we aren't in Philly anymore."

"I can see that." He was breathless. So much so it was hard to get the words out. The cars were *all* vintage models. Tall boxes with bumpers. An old-fashioned trolley was unloading passengers, guys with fedoras, women with their hair piled on top of their heads. A horse and wagon.

"Don't worry. We can get back home anytime we want. Just don't lose the converter."

"I won't." He looked down at it. Grabbed hold of it. "Time machine? It's not possible, Shel. It can't be done."

"Look around you."

"My God." Dave was having trouble breathing. "What happened to my house?"

"We left it. It's back in 2018."

They were in a theater district. But not the one along Chestnut and Walnut in Philadelphia. They were standing in front of the Erlanger Theater, which was showing *Naughty Marietta*. Across the street, the Imperial was running *Laugh Parade*, and the Shubert had *Everybody's Welcome*.

The women wore jazz-age clothes, and a lot of them were wrapped in furs. Skirts were long.

Shel's hands were in his pockets. He stood quietly, gazing around, taking everything in, making no real effort to conceal how pleased he was. Behaving as if he did this every day. "Dave," he said, "we're in New York. On West Forty-fourth Street."

Dave's voice had deserted him. He needed a minute to get it back. "Not possible," he said.

"It's 1931."

"Come on, Shel." Dave leaned against a doorframe.

"December thirteenth."

He wanted a place to sit down. But there were no benches. They were standing outside a music store.

"There was no way to warn you about this," said Shel. "Or prepare you for it."

"Time travel—" Dave shook his head. "They only do that in the movies."

"You want to ask a cop?" Shel nodded toward a police officer strolling in their direction.

The policeman took a quick look at them as he passed. And apparently decided they didn't constitute a threat. Snippets of conversation caught Dave's attention:

"—I heard it on WEAF—"

"—Hoover's going to figure it out—"

"—the Roadster. We're *all* going."

Dave's hand gripped the black device attached to his belt. "It really *is*, isn't it? A time machine?"

"Yes. And it's how I got out into western Pennsylvania."

"And you didn't *know*?"

"The thing didn't come with instructions, Dave. How could I have known?"

"My God, Shel. Where'd you get it?" And suddenly he understood. "Your father."

"Yes."

"It's how he disappeared out of his house."

"That's right."

"So where'd he go?"

"I don't know exactly. He said maybe he was going to talk to Galileo. Maybe Ben Franklin. Maybe Albert Einstein. Hell, who knows?"

Dave burst out laughing. "Galileo."

"It's why I need you."

"He's dead. They're all dead."

"Come on, Dave. Stay with me."

"You're going after him."

"Yes. I'm going to try Galileo first."

"And you need somebody who speaks Italian."

"Right again."

"Let me understand what we're talking about here. You want to go back to the—what is it?—the seventeenth century to look for your father?"

"You always were quick, Dave."

"Shel, I don't know how to break this to you, but the Italian they spoke several hundred years ago isn't going to be the Italian they speak today."

"Dave, you're my best shot. Please—"

"Do you know *when*?"

"What do you mean?"

"Do you know precisely when and where in the seventeenth century he was planning to go?" He frowned. "Listen to me. I sound like a nut."

Shel managed a pained smile. "No," he said. "Only that he would go to see Galileo."

"Well, you have a time machine. Why don't you go back and ask your father before he leaves?"

"I've already done that. I don't think I can do it again." They were standing with a crowd at an intersection, waiting for the light to change. It did, and the crowd started across. A car making a turn tried to push its way through. There was some yelling.

"Why can't you?" asked Dave.

"It's complicated. But he says if I create a paradox, bad things will happen."

"What kind of bad things?"

"Heart attacks, maybe."

"What?"

"He lost a partner during an experiment. The event's over. I can't go back and change it."

"Shel, I can't believe you're willing to buy that story."

"After what I've seen these last couple of days, I'm inclined to be cautious."

DAVE would remember that moment the rest of his life. Crossing the street, the traffic, the people, Shel talking about heart attacks. "You know," he said, "it sounds as if your father's one of those mad scientists."

"I guess you could say that."

"Who else knows?"

"Nobody. He wanted it kept quiet." They were still walking. Toward the Imperial and *Laugh Parade*. He noticed a familiar name among the cast members. Ed Wynn.

Incredible.

They walked, and stopped, and looked around. And walked again. They stopped at another traffic light. "Just installed," Shel said.

"What is?"

"The lights. They were just starting to use them."

"Hard to imagine New York without traffic signals."

"They've also just finished the Empire State Building." Somebody blew a horn and, as if on cue, the light changed. They started across and turned right onto Third Avenue. "Will you do it?" Shel asked. "Will you help me?"

How could he not? "After we bring him back," Dave said, "is that going to be the end?"

"*If* we bring him back—" Shel shook his head. "If he didn't come back on his own—"

"—It doesn't mean something happened to *him*. The device, the converter, might have broken down."

"That's what I'm hoping."

"I mean, if the Inquisition or somebody had grabbed him, he can get out just by punching a button, right?"

"Yes."

"Okay. So it has to be the converter. I don't think you have anything to worry about."

"I hope so." They were moving again, passing an Italian restaurant. Dave wondered how many of the businesses on that block would still be around in 2018. In *his* time. "Shel," he said, "I still can't believe this is happening."

Shel stopped a couple of women and asked if they had the correct time. It was, one of them said, consulting a watch she took from her purse, a quarter after ten.

Shel adjusted his own watch and flagged down a passing cab.

"Do we have an appointment?" asked David.

"Yes, we do." The driver pulled over and they got in. "Seventy-sixth Street and Fifth Avenue, driver," he said.

"Why? What's going on there?"

"We're going to meet someone."

"We *know* somebody here?"

"We will, shortly."

They got out across the street from Central Park. Shel gave the driver a dollar. "Keep the change," he said.

The driver thanked him and pulled away.

Dave shook his head. "Where'd you get the money?"

"Always come prepared."

"But how'd you do it?"

"I came back last night with a few old coins. Played the races. Won a long shot."

"You won a long shot?"

He grinned. "It's pretty easy when you have a time machine. And it gave me plenty of spending money."

Dave grinned. "So who are we going to see? Noel Coward? George M. Cohan? Ethel Merman? Al Jolson?"

"Just be patient."

It was cold. "I should have worn a heavier coat."

"Next time we— Wait a minute. This might be him now."

"Who? Where?"

A taxi was slowing down across the street. It pulled alongside the curb and stopped. A man wearing a topcoat and bowler got out. He paid the driver and began looking for a chance to cross.

He was overweight, in his late forties or early fifties, and he looked lost. There was something familiar about him, but Dave couldn't place him. He'd probably turn out to be a character actor in movies of the period. Of which Dave had seen very few.

The cab pulled away.

"Do you recognize him?" asked Shel.

"I've no clue. Who is he?"

"Watch. But no matter what happens, do not intervene."
He placed a restraining hand on Dave's shoulder.

The man waited for his chance to cross. Traffic was
two-way along the avenue. But he was looking to his right.
The wrong way. Dave watched with horror as the man shifted
his weight and prepared to step into the street.

Shel's grip tightened. "Habit," he said. "And he doesn't
look like the most patient guy in town."

He lurched out directly in front of an oncoming sedan. The
driver plowed into him, *then* hit the brakes. People screamed
and brakes screeched. The car dragged him about twenty feet.
It left him crumpled and moaning near the curb.

Somebody ran into the street waving at the traffic to stop.
A couple of people hurried to the victim's aid.

"Who is it?" Dave was out of patience.

Shel sighed. "Winston Churchill."

THEIR view was blocked by the crowd. Horns blared. The
driver got out and ran back, bleating that he didn't mean it, he
was sorry. "Are you all right?" he demanded of the victim.
His voice rose over the crowd in a wail. Within minutes they
heard sirens, and a police car arrived. One officer got out and
ran to a call box. His partner took charge of traffic, allowing
only one lane to move at a time.

A second police car pulled up. One of the officers hurried
toward the victim while the other tried to push the crowd back.
And, finally, an ambulance. Medical people, ambulance attendants, whatever they called them in 1931. They jumped out,
examined the fallen Churchill, and after a few minutes they lifted
him carefully onto a stretcher. They spoke briefly with one of the
officers, then put Churchill into the ambulance. Two of the attendants got in with him and, escorted by a police cruiser, it left.

"You knew it was going to happen," Dave said.

"Sure."

"Why didn't we stop it?"

"That's what my father was concerned about. That somebody would meddle somewhere and create a problem."

"Like how? Churchill survived. What could we have changed?"

"Probably nothing. But we don't really know. Anyway, no harm was done."

"No harm? He looked as if he'd broken something."

"Two cracked ribs and a scalp wound. I think he develops pleurisy later because of this. But he was lucky. In any case, we know the accident happened. If we'd tried to prevent it—"

"—We get heart attacks—"

Shel shrugged. "I don't know."

They stood quietly watching the remaining policemen interviewing the driver and a bystander. "So we just watch," said Dave. "We can go back to Dealey Plaza, but we can't do anything. Shel, I don't think I'm going to care much for this line of work."

"Dave, I thought you'd react that way. So let's do something."

"What? What can we possibly do now?"

They walked back to 76th Street, looking for a cab. It took a few minutes, but one finally pulled over. "Driver," Shel said, "Lenox Hill Hospital, please."

"What are we going to do? Get him some flowers?"

"You're a hard man, David."

Dave closed his eyes and sank back in the seat. "Why are we going to the hospital? That *is* the one they're taking him to, right?"

"Yes." He fished some bills out of his pocket. "We're going to do a good deed."

THE taxi let them off in front of the emergency room. They went inside, where the injured Churchill sat in a clunky-looking wheelchair at a reception counter. A middle-aged woman was doing paperwork for another patient. Seven or eight other people were in the waiting room.

"We're not going to tell him who we are, are we?" asked Dave.

"No. No, that wouldn't be a good idea."

Churchill was obviously in pain. A male attendant stood beside him.

The receptionist completed some paperwork and, finally, it was his turn. She took a piece of paper out of a stack and turned in his direction. "Name, please."

"Winston Churchill," he said in a barely discernible voice.

"Address?"

"I'm a British statesman."

She looked up from the form. "I see. Do you have an address in the United States, Mr., um, Churchill?"

"Use the British consulate."

Patiently: "What is *their* address, please?"

"I really do not know, madam." Churchill tried to get more comfortable, but twisted something and cried out.

"Be careful, sir," she said. "Try not to move around too much."

He cleared his throat. "Madam, I was injured out there this evening. I'm in considerable pain. Would it be possible to administer something to alleviate my situation? Perhaps some chloroform?"

"We'll try to help you, Mr. Churchill. How do you wish to pay?"

"Can't we settle that later?"

"I'm sorry, sir. But we require payment in advance."

With his teeth clenched, Churchill fumbled in his pockets. Came out with a few dollars. "How much did you want?"

The receptionist glanced at the money. "Mr. Churchill, this is insufficient."

"All right," he said. "Call the Waldorf. My wife is there. She'll bring some money over."

Shel turned to Dave and handed him a wad of bills. "You do it," he said.

Marvelous. He took the money, whispered thanks to Shel, and strode to the counter. "Mr. Churchill," he said, "I'd like to help, if I may." He held the bills up for the receptionist to see. "Please get some assistance for this gentleman. Quickly."

Churchill's eyes looked up at him. And for the first time, Dave *saw* the future prime minister. "Why, thank you, sir," he said. The voice was a shadow of the one Dave remembered from the World War II audios. The one that challenged Hitler and spoke to the world in its darkest moment. "I am in your debt, sir."

"I think we are in yours, Mr. Churchill."

CHAPTER 8

It cannot be maintained that dressing has in this or any country risen to the dignity of an art. At present men make shift to wear what they can get. Like shipwrecked sailors, they put on what they can find on the beach, and at a little distance, whether of space or time, laugh at each other's masquerade.

—HENRY DAVID THOREAU, *WALDEN*

THE converter brought them back to David's house, six seconds after departure. It was still just before nine Saturday morning.

"Thanks, Dave," said Shel. "I appreciate your coming."

Dave was still having a problem grasping what had happened. "My God," he said, "are you serious? I still don't believe it."

"I know. I doubt we'll ever get used to it." He held out his hand for the converter, which was still attached to Dave's belt.

"You don't want me to hold on to it?"

"It wouldn't be a good idea, Dave."

"I wouldn't lose it."

"Dave."

"Or misuse it."

"Not a good idea. Not that I don't trust you, but—"

"Okay." He unclipped it and handed it over. "When are you going after your father?"

"I want to give it a little time. No point in my going back there if I can't speak Italian."

"Maybe you should try Ben Franklin first."

"I think Galileo's our best bet."

"Okay. You'll have to take some language lessons."

"That's the plan."

"Good. Now, when you've done that, and you're ready to go—"

"Yes?"

"I'm invited, right?"

"Of course. It's why I came. You *will* come—"

"Sure."

"Okay. I'll call you when I'm ready." He started for the door.

"Shel, one more question. What happens if we materialize in midair? Does the thing always set you on the ground?"

"It wasn't something I thought to ask. We can put it to him when we find him." He opened the door. Paused. "Dave, thanks."

"Sure."

"And don't forget: Tell nobody, right?"

"Absolutely."

"It won't be easy. I want to talk about this to everybody I know."

"I hear you. That was once in a lifetime out there tonight."

SHEL was dead right. Dave wanted to call everybody. Old friends, his folks, his occasional girlfriend Katie Gibson, the guys on his bowling team, his department chairman at the university. Listen, Professor, you won't believe this, but guess where I was earlier today. Or no, that wasn't quite correct. Guess where I was one night in 1931, well before you were born. And who I talked to.

He should have brought something back. And remembered that he had. He reached into his pants pocket and retrieved it: a receipt from Lenox Hill Hospital for an amount that would barely pay a decent restaurant tab today. Dated December 13, 1931.

Looking as if it had been issued within the last hour.

Tomorrow he'd buy a frame. That baby was going to hang over his desk.

He should have tried to get Churchill to initial it. Should have taken some pictures.

Had he recalled Helen, he'd have realized he still had plenty of time to try for his accidental meeting with her at the Serendip. But she never entered his mind.

IT was almost impossible to get through his Monday classes. Latin 311 was reading Plutarch, the lives of Demosthenes and Cicero, and Dave couldn't resist himself. "Try to imagine what it would be like," he told his thirteen students, "if we could go back to classical Greece for an afternoon and join the crowd listening to Demosthenes. We'd hear a great orator persuading the Athenians to make war on Alexander. They lost, of course. And what's the lesson, Jim?"

Jim laughed. "Just because somebody is articulate doesn't mean he makes sense."

That was as close as he got to telling them the truth, but it was a near thing. He wanted desperately to let them know that it really *was* possible to travel in time. No: more than that. That *he* had walked across to another century. That he had *done* it. Gone to another time. And he, by God, had the receipt from the Lenox Hill Hospital to prove it.

Hardest for him was sitting in the department meeting two days later, listening to Larry Stevens, unctuous, self-important, always going on about his latest linguistic conclusions. The evolution of the German verb *arbeiten*, whose earlier forms, it seemed, had appeared further back than anyone had realized. "Think what that means."

Nobody ever ate lunch with Larry.

And Dave would have loved to point out that, if it really mattered, he could take Larry into a second-century Bavarian forest, where they could settle the business about the German verb once and for all.

The department chair was staring at him.

Later someone told him he'd been giggling.

* * *

KATIE had come into a small inheritance. She celebrated by taking him to dinner and a movie. "What did you want to see?" he asked her.

Thurgood. The film was, of course, a biopic of Thurgood Marshall. "Is that okay with you?"

Not really. But he didn't conceal his lack of interest very effectively. "Sure," he said.

"What's wrong? It's gotten good reviews."

"Nothing's wrong. Let's go see it."

"Dave . . . ?"

"No. It's fine." Dave had developed a resistance to any kind of drama written around racial conflict. He'd never been able to bring himself to read *To Kill a Mockingbird.* Or to see *A Raisin in the Sun.* His folks had given him a copy of *The Souls of Black Folk,* which included some of DuBois's essays and letters. It was painful reading, and Dave didn't like pain. He refused to watch movies about terminal illness or marital breakups. He wanted his entertainment *light.* Entertainment, he insisted, should *entertain.* Life can be hard enough.

"What do *you* want to see?"

There was a baseball romance, *Rounding Third,* that he'd have liked. "No. Let's go see *Thurgood.* That's fine."

"You're sure?"

"Absolutely."

FOR Shel, discretion was even more difficult. Helen had swept him off his feet. On that first date, soon after he'd taken Dave to 1931, they'd gone to dinner at Fayette's, his favorite luxury nightspot. There they ate by candlelight, while a pianist played "It Had to Be You." They talked about trivia. She was commenting on how enticing the atmosphere was, and he said something about work or maybe about a movie he'd seen recently. Like Dave, he was aching to talk about how he'd been walking the streets of Depression-era New

York, that he could take her there *now*. That he could take her anywhere. To any *time*. She liked George Bernard Shaw, and he could take her back to London at the beginning of the twentieth century to watch the opening of *Man and Superman*. *You want the date of a lifetime, sweetheart?*

"So what exactly *do* you do, Shel?" she asked. And managed to look interested.

What did he do? "I do public relations for Carbolite. Basically, we sell engineering systems. To individuals or to manufacturers. Anybody who wants to build a better house, we can show him how."

Yawn.

"Really?" she said. "How does that work?"

Well, the truth is, love, I travel in time. The other night I rescued Winston Churchill. Tomorrow, I'm going to pop by and say hello to Cicero. He explained about making presentations to engineers and how people had better washing machines because of Carbolite technology. It took only a few minutes before her eyes began to glaze.

"But enough about me," he said. "How's life in medicine these days?"

She was too smart to take the bait. She asked whether he really enjoyed the theater or actually used the Disciples as a way of meeting women. What did he do when he wasn't selling better washing machines? (She didn't phrase it that way, but he understood what she meant.) Where did he want to be ten years down the road?

That one stopped him cold. Where indeed? He had no ambitions, really, beyond the moment. A decade from now, he'd like to be making a substantial amount of money. And he'd like to be happily married, maybe with one or two kids. But suddenly that all sounded mundane. And it occurred to him he could take his time device and go look. Find out what he'd be doing. Find out what they'd *both* be doing.

And he wondered, while he talked in a circle about ambitions he really didn't have, how it would affect them if he *did* take her forward so they could find out.

Let's go look.

"I'd like to be with a larger corporation," he said, finally. "One of the blue chips, maybe GE, running *their* PR office."

"Well." She sipped her rum and Coke, and looked at him across the rim of her glass with those spectacular blue-green eyes. "Good luck with it, Shel." She almost sounded as if it all had some significance.

There was a time when he had seriously believed in the transformative power of public relations. Image is everything. If you believe it's a better world, it *is* a better world. But somehow selling a more efficient computer system to the *Wall Street Journal* no longer galvanized his sense of worth. The existence he had imagined for himself, creative, appreciated, a guy who walked into the room and everybody automatically got quiet—it had happened. But he couldn't see that it mattered.

He wondered if Helen would be interested in talking baseball.

GALILEO had been born in February 1564, in Pisa. It was a time when Aristotelian astronomy was held in high regard, when the assumption that the sun and planets rotated around the Earth was dogma, and when any who disagreed risked more than their reputations. (Although it *was* possible to venture an opposing opinion, so long as you did so, as Copernicus had, in Latin. And were careful not to be too loud about it.)

"He first heard about the telescope in 1609," said Shel.

"When did he die?" asked Dave.

"In 1642."

"So, if we assume that your dad would want the meeting to take place after Galileo started using the telescope—"

"We can't assume that."

"We can't?"

"There's a good chance he'd have wanted to see the Pisa experiment."

"Dropping cannonballs off the Tower?"

"Yes."

"When did that happen?"

"Sometime between 1589 and 1592."

"That leaves us half a century to search."

"Actually, it's possible the Pisa thing didn't happen at all. Some people think the experiment is just a legend."

"All right." They were in the den at Shel's town house. "I guess our more immediate problem is the language. *Parla italiano?*"

Shel smiled. *"Devo andare adesso."*

"You said, 'I have to go now.' "

"It's a joke. *Parlo italiano* like a bandit."

"I see we're in for a long trip."

"I'm not especially competent, Dave. But I've been working at it. We went to Rome a couple of times, and once to Venice. I was in high school then, but I picked up some of the language, so I wasn't really starting from nothing."

"So now you want to practice?"

"If you have the patience."

"I'm at your disposal, Shel."

"Okay. No more English for the rest of the night."

IF there was anyone David could have confided in, it was Katie Gibson. Katie was a lifeguard at the local YWCA. They hadn't exactly been doing a lot of dating, but he and Katie were friends. Both were waiting for the One and Only to show up. Meanwhile, they were marking time with each other. Had even slept together a couple of times. But the chemistry wasn't really there. Dave had even let Katie know about his interest in Helen, whom she'd never met. She was horrified when he told her about introducing Helen to Shel. She'd wished him luck and advised him to be more aggressive. "Get out front with her," she'd said. "Hire a brass band to follow her around if you have to."

"That would put her off," Dave had said.

"Not if there's anything there. If she likes you, you need to take some action. Sweep her off her feet. If she's really not interested, nothing you can do will change that."

"You're saying I've nothing to lose."

"Exactly."

Still, he hadn't hired the brass band, though they'd have been a magnificent sight, standing outside her office down at the medical plaza.

Nor, of course, did he tell Katie about the time travel. As he had elsewhere, he came close. He was on the phone with her, and they were talking about upcoming movies, when she commented that the Churchill biopic, *Her Finest Hour*, would be opening in a couple of weeks. She was anxious to see it. One of the things he especially liked about her was that she was not much inclined toward chick flicks. Katie enjoyed conflict. Especially the ones featuring an ordinary guy, or woman, who simply decides he's had enough and takes on whatever constitutes the evil empire, the local mob, corrupt politicians, or maybe just the bully across the street. *"It looks like fun,"* she said.

And he imagined himself telling her: *Katie, I've talked to Churchill. In 1931. Really.*

"You're laughing," she said. *"If you don't want to—"*

So then I said to Winston— "No, no," he interrupted. "That's good. Let's do it."

"What was so funny?"

"Umm. No, I was thinking about something else." A new Superman film was opening. Dave had never thought about it before, but it must have been hideously difficult for Clark Kent to keep his secret. Especially in the face of Lois's superior attitude.

DAVE sent Shel some Italian films, with the suggestion he watch each of them until he could actually follow the dialogue. Meanwhile, he refreshed his own skills by reading editions of seventeenth-century Italian classics in the original. He settled in each evening with Machiavelli and the poet Giambattista Marino. He read *La Reina de Scotia*, a drama about the trial of Mary, Queen of Scots, by Federico della Valle. He struggled through Dante, and for the first time read the entire work, and not simply *The Inferno*. When he was finished, he understood why people still read *The Inferno* and ignored the other two books. He suggested that they watch some operas together. "I've no taste for opera," Shel said. But they downloaded *L'Orfeo*, *Pagliacci*, and *Lucrezia Borgia*, and, for opening night, *Don Giovanni*. They got some pizza in, invited Helen and Katie, and turned it into a party. But Shel and Katie both suffered visibly through the opera, and it did nothing for Shel's Italian.

Two nights later, they did *Pagliacci*, this time without the women. Shel spent much of the evening glaring at the screen. "Give it a chance," said Dave. "Relax and enjoy the show."

Shel tried. "But," he complained, "I never know what's going on."

"That's the whole point of the exercise. Your Italian's a bit weak."

"They could be singing in English, and I don't think I could follow it. There's got to be an easier way." He held up one of the software packages his father had been using: Speak Italian Like a Native.

"Good," said Dave. "How about the movies I sent over? Have you watched any of those?"

"*Amici Miei*."

"Okay. And...?"

"*Il Ciclone*."

"Good comedies."

Shel looked doubtful. "Absolutely."

"Can you understand them?"

"Some."

"Okay. Hang in."

WHEN, several weeks later, Shel had finally gotten a handle on the language, they decided it was time to go find his father. "First, though," he said, "we'll need a wardrobe. And it probably wouldn't be a bad idea to grow a beard." He'd already started one.

"You're kidding."

He frowned at Dave's jaw. "I think you'll look out of place like that."

They drove into Center City and visited Emilio's Costume and Wardrobe Shop on Walnut Street. The walls were covered with photos of people dressed as sheiks, Roman soldiers, princesses, and Zorro. Some high-school kids, with a teacher, were wandering among the racks, apparently selecting costumes for a play.

Dave was measured for two doublets, both with a calico design. He also got a soft blue huke, which was a kind of cloak, lined in white squirrel fur. When he tried it on, it hung to his thighs. "We'll have to take this one in a bit," said the clerk. "And let this one out." He made notes, then put the garments aside.

Hats were next. They tried several types but wound up with pillboxes. "What is it for?" asked the clerk. "A festival? Or are you in a show?" He was middle-aged, sporting a brown beard with streaks of gray, with gray eyes, full cheeks, and an attitude that Dave could think of only as theatrical pretense. This was a guy who, if he weren't working at Emilio's, wanted you to think he'd be directing on Broadway.

"It's a show," said Shel.

"Which show?"

Shel glanced toward Dave.

Dave smiled. "*Two Gentlemen of Verona.*"

"That's interesting," said the clerk. "I don't think we've ever had anyone do that locally." He adjusted the pillbox on Dave's head, looked satisfied, and announced it was perfect. "Which theater are you gentlemen with?"

"Delaware Township," said Shel.

The clerk let them see he'd never heard of them, but he said nothing.

Eventually they came to the footwear. Dave found a pair of soft round-toed green sandals that he liked. "These should complete the costume nicely," said the clerk, handing him a pair of stockings almost as long as his legs. They were also green, but of a darker shade. And they were complete with leather soles. Dave went back into a dressing room, got out of his slacks, pulled the stockings on, and slipped his feet into the shoes. They were surprisingly comfortable. He came back out and submitted to inspections by both the clerk and Shel. The clerk pronounced himself pleased, and Shel said he looked the very picture of a Renaissance scholar.

When they'd finished, Shel insisted on paying. The clerk promised to have everything ready within two days, and arrangements were made to ship overnight.

They came out onto Walnut Street and turned west toward the parking lot. "Time travel," said Dave, "isn't the way I would have expected it to be."

"I'M not sure how to go about this," said Shel, "but I think we might start by trying to reach Galileo in his later years. When he was in Arcetri. I think that's when my dad would have been most interested in talking with him."

Arcetri was located in northern Italy, on the southern edge of Florence. Shel had prepared a chart of the area, which he'd spread across his kitchen table. The chart showed roads thought to be in existence during the early years of the seventeenth century. "We want to arrive as close to Arcetri as we can," he said. "Preferably without showing up in the central square."

"You got us onto Forty-fourth Street in New York."

"I'd made the jump before, so I could get readings on the location. Once I've been somewhere, I can lock it in." He pointed at an area close to several roads. "This is what I'm aiming for. If I've got it right, we'll arrive within a few miles, just after dawn, during the early spring of 1640." He handed Dave his converter. "It's ready to go. Once we get there, it'll automatically reset to return you here. If there's any kind of problem, anything at all, just punch the button, and it'll bring you back. Okay?"

Shel put a photo of his father into an envelope and slipped it into his pocket. They were dressed in the gear they'd bought at Emilio's. And both now sported beards. "You look good," said Dave.

"Ah, yes." Shel took out the second converter. "The latest styles for the interdimensional traveler."

CHAPTER 9

I do not feel obliged to believe that the same God who has endowed us with sense, reason, and intellect has intended us to forgo their use.

—GALILEO

IT was raining. Pouring. They were in a glade, lined by a few small trees. "I don't guess you thought to bring umbrellas?" asked Dave.

The sky was dark, and a strong wind blew through the branches. Shel looked for shelter. "That hillside." He pointed. "Might be a grotto."

They started trudging toward it, but Dave stopped. "I have a better idea."

"Make it fast, okay?"

"Sure. The storm should be over in an hour or so."

Shel pulled his huke tightly around him. Stroked his beard. (Helen did not approve of it.) "What are you talking about?"

It was six in the morning. Dave was resetting for eight. "We've got *time* machines. We don't have to wait for storms to pass."

"Of course. Yeah. I wasn't using my head."

Shel locked his unit on eight o'clock and they went. The gray light dimmed, the storm went away, and they were standing in wet grass. The sky was still pallid, but it was brighter than it had been. "You know," Dave said, "these things really have possibilities."

Shel pulled out a map and compass, studied both for a minute, and then pointed toward some distant hills. "That way," he said. "North."

"How do you know where we are?"

"I'm assuming we landed more or less where we expected to."

Thunder rumbled somewhere. "Shel, what's your father going to say when he sees *me*?"

"I think he'll be too relieved at being rescued to worry about it. Though if I know him, we'll both get lectured."

"Do you think he'll still want to disassemble the converters? When we get home?"

"Probably. But let's do this one step at a time and find him first."

EVENTUALLY, they came across a road. "Which way?" asked Dave.

Shel consulted the map again. "To your right."

It was showing signs of becoming a pleasant morning. The ground was drying. Birds sang, insects hummed, and squirrels scampered up the sides of trees. They passed a vineyard and, minutes later, were overtaken by a donkey cart driven by two teenage boys. In his best Italian, Dave asked whether they were on the road to Arcetri.

"Left at the fork," came the response. "We're going that way. You want a ride?"

"Please." The cart was loaded with planks. They climbed in.

Shel tried his own Italian: "You boys ever hear of *Il Giojello*?"

They were about fifteen. They appeared healthier than Shel had expected, although one of them could have used some dental work. They looked at each other and both shook their heads.

"What's *Il Giojello*?" Dave asked in English.

"It's Galileo's villa. But we shouldn't have a problem finding it. It's on the map."

IT was uphill most of the way, on a winding road. A tower stood near the summit. Shel asked the boys whether it was the *Torre del Gallo.*

"Yes," the driver said. "That's it."

Shel used his cell phone to take a picture of it. "It dates from the Middle Ages," he said.

"It strikes me," said Dave, "that we're pretty much *in* the Middle Ages."

"I won't argue the point."

"Is that where he lived? Galileo?"

"No. Not really."

"How do you mean, *not really?*"

"The legend is that he used the tower as an observatory. It was the place where he was able to separate himself from the Inquisition. Get away from them."

"But it's a legend? That he came here?"

"Yes. It probably never happened. They kept him bottled up in his villa. The guy had trouble getting out to see his doctor."

Houses were becoming numerous. The cart stopped at a connecting road. "We're going *this* way," the driver said, pointing. "Arcetri's straight ahead. About a mile."

They thanked the boys, and Shel gave them a couple of coins. The kids lit up. There were cries of *"Ringraziato, signore."*

"My pleasure," said Shel in English.

They climbed down, and the boys kept showing each other the coins and shaking their heads in disbelief. "What did you give them?" asked Dave. "Gold?"

"They're *carlinos.*"

"Carlinos?"

"They're silver. And they *are* worth a bit."

"You came prepared."

"Of course." He shielded his eyes from the sun and looked uphill. "Looks as if we walk from here."

Dave was still admiring the tower.

"In our time," Shel said, "it's been overhauled and refurbished. It's now a museum and library dedicated to Galileo's memory."

"He's near the end of his life?" asked Dave. "Here, I mean."

Shel was moving briskly toward the cluster of houses at the summit. "He has two years to live. And he's almost totally blind."

IL *Giojello* stood on a small street near a piazza of modest proportions. Several people were gathered in a park, playing a game that might have been bocce ball. "Did they have bocce ball this far back?" asked Dave.

Shel shrugged. "Don't know."

Two riders on horseback entered the street from the opposite end, moving casually, and raised their hands to say hello to Shel and Dave as they passed.

Shel pointed toward a large villa on the far side of the piazza. "There's another famous place," he said.

"What's that?" asked Dave.

"Some historians claim it's the birthplace of comedy."

"That sounds mildly subjective. What *is* it?"

"If I'm reading my directions right, it's *Il Teatro*."

"The Theater."

"During the Middle Ages, comedians are supposed to have performed there." Shel was looking at his map again. "On *this* side," he said, pointing at a villa on their left, "is *Il Giojello*."

The house straddled three sides of a courtyard. It was two stories high, surrounded by spiked bushes. Vines climbed walls constructed of smooth gray stucco. The courtyard was of modest dimensions, and there was some open ground beyond it. Olive orchards and vineyards were clustered on either side.

"How do we get in?" asked Dave. "Is the Inquisition watching?"

"No. They left Galileo's son Vincenzo in charge. To see that he didn't violate the rules."

"His son?"

"Vincenzo was supposedly a good Catholic. The Inquisitors believed they could trust him."

"Could they?"

"Apparently."

"So how do we get past him?"

They'd stopped a few paces from the house. "The restrictions during Galileo's later years became less stringent. They knew he had only a short time to live. And he couldn't get around very well. He got visitors periodically. In fact, John Milton will be here next year to see him."

"Milton?"

"Yes."

"My God, Shel, that's when we should have come."

"You want to talk to Milton?"

"I'd love to."

"Maybe we can arrange it. Meanwhile, though, let's do one thing at a time. Let's get my father back first." He extracted a rolled document from his jacket. "If Vincenzo is at all reluctant to let us in, we give him this."

Dave frowned at it. "What is it?"

"A letter from Cardinal Picollomini instructing him to grant us entry."

"Where'd you get it?"

"Same place I got the carlinos. What did you think I'd been doing these last few weeks?"

Dave was impressed. "Very good," he said.

THE door was opened by a cautious-looking elderly servant. "Yes?" he said. "May I help you?"

"I hope so." Dave took the lead. "This gentleman is Adrian Shelborne, and I'm David Dryden. We're admirers of *Professore* Galilei. We'd like very much to speak with him about his discoveries, if we may."

"I'm sorry, gentlemen, but the professor does not presently receive visitors."

"We have authorization."

Dave was about to present the Cardinal's letter when he heard a male voice inside: "Who is it, Geppo?"

"Sir, there are two persons who identify themselves as admirers of the professor. They would like to see him."

A new face appeared at the door. A small man, probably in his thirties, literally dwarfed by Dave. "I'm sorry," he said. "But he's quite busy."

"Are you Vincenzo?" asked Shel. Judging from Dave's expression, he must have butchered the pronunciation.

The man looked annoyed.

"He's German," Dave explained. "His Italian still needs work. But we are speaking to . . . ?"

"Vincenzo. Yes, I caught my name." He made no effort to hide his contempt, either for his visitors or for Germans.

"We've heard much about you," said Dave.

"That you are very like your father," added Shel.

Vincenzo didn't quite know how to receive that. His father, after all, was generally perceived as a heretic and a disturber of the peace.

Dave decided to cut the conversation short before Shel got in over his head. He signaled Shel to produce the letter, which he handed to Vincenzo. "We applied to Cardinal Picollomini," he explained. "He said he wishes us to be admitted to the professor's presence. We are experts in planetary motions."

"I see." Vincenzo squinted at the letter, moving his lips while he read. Then he signaled Geppo, and they both stood aside. "He isn't well, and it would be most advisable if you make your visit brief."

"Of course."

The interior wasn't particularly congenial. The furniture looked stiff and uncomfortable. The floor was brick, and the ceilings were vaulted. "Have a seat, please," he said. "Geppo, advise the master."

"Yes, sir." The servant disappeared into a passageway. Dave heard a brief conversation in back. Then Geppo returned. "Sir, your father says he will be out in a moment."

"Very good." Vincenzo turned to the visitors, who were still on their feet. "Please make yourselves comfortable, gentlemen."

They both sat down. The place desperately needed air-conditioning.

Shel remarked what a lovely town Arcetri was.

Vincenzo agreed. "Sometimes, when you live here, you forget how very pleasing it can be." He crossed one leg over the other. "Would you like some refreshment?"

Dave had a brief flash of what might happen to him and Shel if they had a bit too much to drink. Maybe they'd make for Cardinal Picollomini and tell him flat out what they thought of the Inquisition.

"But of course," said Shel.

Geppo produced a flask and filled three glasses. Dave tried it cautiously, not sure about homemade wine. But it was quite good.

They heard more movement in the back of the house. Then a door closed. Geppo showed no inclination to go to his master's assistance, which suggested Galileo did not want help.

The great man's breathing became audible, and they heard the thunk of a cane or crutch. Vincenzo glanced at his visitors and shook his head. He was obviously not impressed by his father. Finally, a large man with shriveled skin limped into the room. He was virtually blind, and on crutches. But he found his way directly to an armchair that must have been reserved for him and collapsed into it. His hair had retreated, leaving a domed skull, and his beard showed streaks of white. "Father," said Vincenzo, "Mr. Shelborne and Mr. Dryden are here to see you. They have approval from the Cardinal."

Galileo took a deep, rasping breath. "I am told you are interested in the motions of the planets." He wasn't sure precisely where his guests were seated, so he raised his head and spoke to the room at large. "I'm glad someone in this dark country has some curiosity left about the world."

"You're quite right," said Dave. "Actually, however, we had a different reason for seeking you out, sir."

"Really? And what might that be?"

"Adrian here is looking for his father, Michael. Michael has always been interested in your work, and we believe he came to Arcetri expressly to see you. Unfortunately, he has gone missing. We hoped you might be able to help us find him."

"And his last name?"

"Shelborne," said Shel. "Professor Michael Shelborne. Do you know him?"

Galileo considered it, and shook his head no. "Unfortunately not. I don't think I ever met him. You say he's a scholar?"

"Yes."

"Many scholars come here. Now that the priests have decided I'm too old to be a threat to them. When would he have come?"

"We're not sure," said Dave, taking the photo from Shel. "We have a picture of him here. May we show it to your son and your servant? Maybe one of them would remember."

Galileo seemed not to have heard. A small table stood on one side of the armchair. Geppo placed a glass of wine on it and guided his master's hand to its stem. He explored it with his fingers before lifting it. At last he raised it to the level of those blind eyes. "To all of us who are lost," he said. "But you say you have a picture of him? You mean an oil painting?"

"Something like that," said Dave.

"Well, of course you may."

Vincenzo's eyebrows rose when he looked. "What *is* this?" he asked.

"It's a portrait. As I said."

Vincenzo held it close to an oil lamp. "I've never seen anything like it."

"It *is* quite sharp, isn't it?"

He sat admiring the photo. Then he shook his head. "No," he said. "I've never seen this person." He handed it to Geppo, who was equally mystified.

"Maybe," said Shel, "he hasn't gotten here yet."

"It's possible," said Dave in English. "But if he waits much longer, his subject won't be breathing when he does show up."

"I'm sorry we can't help you," Galileo said. "If he comes, we will tell him you were here."

CHAPTER 10

The grandfather paradox is simply a way of pointing to the fact that if the familiar laws of classical relativistic physics are supposed to hold true in a chronology-violating space-time, then consistency constraints emerge.

—JOHN EARMAN, *BANGS, CRUNCHES, WHIMPERS, AND SHRIEKS*

MICHAEL Shelborne had apparently changed his mind about Galileo. He'd gone somewhere else. But where? Shel suspected he might find him among the witnesses at the signing of the Magna Carta, say. Or watching Washington's troops come ashore on the road to Trenton. Or any of several thousand other possibilities.

Unfortunately, Michael had not left a notebook or a journal. He admired Tom Paine, and it seemed probable he'd go back at some point to meet him. Like Shel, he was a Jack Benny fan, and it was possible Benny would get to say hello to an unusual visitor. But there was no practical way to pinpoint the time of any such meeting.

It was Friday night, almost a week since they'd made the Italian trip. Shel was sitting, drinking coffee, running over possibilities, scratching ideas onto a legal pad. He kept coming back to one reality. There was no need to go into the historical past to find his father. He didn't know with any precision where he'd been before he came back to Philadelphia.

But he knew with absolute certainty where he'd been on the evening of Monday, October 15: He'd been home, talking with Shel, first on the cell phone, then inside the house. After Shel had left, he'd made up his mind where he wanted to go, and took off. All that was necessary was to repeat the visit. Wait until the earlier Shel was out of the house, and then go in and talk sense to him.

No paradox there. And it should be easy.

Do it now.

He got into his car, drove to his father's house, and parked in the driveway. Then he set the converter to take him back to 10:55 P.M., October 15, climbed out of the automobile, listened for a few seconds to the chirping of crickets, and pressed the button. The concrete, the trees, the side of the house, and the crickets faded out and came back. The car was gone. And lights were on inside the house.

Okay. He walked to the end of the driveway, and turned toward Parvin Street, which intersected with Moorland about two hundred feet away. He crossed over, turned into Parvin, and took station behind a hedge. A police car came up behind him, paused at the stop sign, and went left. He put his hands in his pockets and tried to look casual. Just out for a stroll.

At eleven sharp a brief glow appeared on his father's lawn, and he watched himself step out of it, look around, and start for the front door. His heart picked up. Never going to get used to this. The other Shel knocked, the door opened, and Dad appeared. Even from this distance, Shel could see the dismay on his father's face. Somehow, he'd missed that the first time around.

They spoke for a few seconds, the other Shel went inside, and the door closed.

More lights came on.

Shel waited.

A dark blue Saber came slowly down the street. Al Peterson and his wife, Anna. They pulled into their driveway and stopped. The car doors opened. They'd always been good to him when he was a kid. They bought chances and contributed to the candy drives. The problem was that they quarreled a lot. Loud quarrels, screams you could hear in the next block. Their daughter Ilyssa had been Shel's first girlfriend.

They got out of the car and went inside. They weren't actively fighting now, but he couldn't help noticing that Mr. Peterson simply walked away from his wife, behaving as if she weren't there. He opened the front door and went inside, leaving it ajar.

Somewhere, music played. The obnoxious modern stuff. And it was loud.

More traffic came through.

Jay Tucker brought out his trash. Collection day tomorrow.

Down at the far end of Moorland, a couple of people were sitting on a front porch. It was probably the source of the music.

He checked his watch. It was a quarter after. He didn't think the conversation with his father had lasted more than a few minutes.

Another car, filled with teens, drifted past. A door slammed. In the distance, a siren began to wail.

He was trying to remember how those last moments with his father had gone. Shel had suggested he accompany his father on the trip. His father had declined. "Let's talk about it another time." A little joke there.

He'd said okay or something like that. Have to go. Good to see you again, Dad. Then he was on his way out the door.

That was right, wasn't it? At the end he was functioning on automatic. He might have simply used the converter inside the house. No. He hadn't done it that way. Absolutely had not.

While Shel tried to settle the matter in his mind, the door opened, and the other Shel reappeared. He watched them say good night. Watched himself stride down the front walk. The door closed behind him. *Then* he touched the device attached to his belt and vanished.

All right. Give him a minute or two.

Shel rehearsed his lines, checked his watch, told himself to take a stand this time. When he was ready, he came out from behind the bush and started for the house.

Lights appeared behind him. A car.

The *police* car.

It pulled to the curb beside him. There was only one officer. He got out. "Good evening, sir," he said. He was tall, half a foot taller than Shel. With just a touch of a British accent. And suspicious eyes.

"Good evening, Officer."

At his father's house, the downstairs lights were going out.

"May I see some identification, please?"

"Umm. Is something wrong?"

"ID please, sir."

Shel fished out his driver's license. The cop took an unconscionably long time to look at it. He scanned it, said something inaudible into a cell phone. Then he turned back to Shel. "What are you doing out here, sir?"

"I was just taking a walk."

"Mr. Shelborne, you've been standing here at least twenty minutes."

"I was getting some air, Officer."

"Are you waiting for someone?"

"No. My father lives over there—" He pointed.

"The house you've been watching?"

"I—I wasn't really watching—"

The policeman had more questions. Did his father know he was here? What was that thing he was wearing on his belt?

A call came in. Apparently the results from the scan. The cop listened, nodded, listened some more. Said okay.

He looked at Shel. "Why don't we go over and say hello?"

"Okay. That would be fine."

But they'd gone only a couple of steps when the upstairs lights went out.

THEY eventually let him go. They asked more questions about the converter but seemed satisfied with his story that it was experimental electronic gear that he was developing for Carbolite. He was advised not to indulge in "undue loitering." And with that it was over.

But his father was gone, and he had to start over.

Well, to hell with the paradox issue. He'd go back and try again, but this time he wouldn't wait around. When Shel arrived, the other Shel, he'd walk right up to him, and when his father opened the door, they'd *both* be standing there. Hi, Dad. *You didn't come back the second time either.*

HE set the converter for 10:59 P.M. He glanced over at the hedge on Parvin Street, which, when he arrived, would be shielding a third Adrian Shelborne. He took a deep breath and pressed the black button.

The trees and the driveway began to fade. In a moment, he knew, they would come back and only the time would have changed. But the vaguely churning mix of concrete and vegetation hung on. The driveway hung on. Faded out. Came back. Then everything went dark.

He was having trouble breathing.

He tried to step out, get clear, but there was nothing solid underfoot. He sucked in water. Began choking.

The world filled with water.

Panic seized him. He kicked and headed up.

His lungs screamed for air.

Then he broke out into the night, gasping and coughing. It was dark, no moon, no stars, nothing. He rode up the side of a wave and down the other. Water flowed over him, and he went under again.

He got to the surface and saw ocean. Fighting panic, he felt desperately at his pockets. Yes! The converter was still there. He dragged it out and hit the black button. If nothing else, it should put him back in his own town house.

More water washed over him.

The converter was dark. No response. No power. Damned thing. It had gotten wet. He tried to jam it back into a pocket and missed. It slipped away.

Not that it mattered.

He rode up the side of a wave and back down. Ahead, a light moved slowly from right to left. But it looked a thousand miles away. He turned, looked back, and almost screamed with pleasure: An endless band of lights cast their glow into the sky. A shoreline.

Thank God.

He got out of his shoes, salvaged the wallet from his jacket, and let the jacket float away. Forty-five minutes later, the current carried him in. He stumbled half-frozen onto a beach.

Piers extended into the ocean on either side. An illuminated boardwalk ran along the edge of the shore. He staggered through the sand, found some wooden steps, stumbled up them, and collapsed.

THE doctors pronounced him okay, except for a touch of hypothermia. He looked around and saw two of them, and a couple of cops, both women. He was in a hospital room. The police wanted to know what he'd been doing in the ocean. "My boat sank," he said.

"We didn't have any emergency calls tonight. Didn't you have a radio?" The cop couldn't believe anybody could be so dumb. She was a young woman, not especially attractive, but okay. Brown hair cut military style. If she could have smiled, she'd have looked a lot better.

"It wasn't working."

She closed her eyes and shook her head. Happens all the time. "Is anybody else out there? Were you alone?"

"I was alone."

She was examining his driver's license. "Where are you staying?"

"I beg your pardon?"

"Where are you staying? You are staying in Atlantic City, right?"

"Um. One of the hotels."

"Which one?"

"I forget."

She turned back to the doctor. "You going to keep him here tonight?"

"We thought it would be a good idea. Until we're sure he's okay."

She took the doctor aside and spoke quietly to him. He nodded a couple of times. If he gives you any trouble, Doc, let us know, okay? Then they both walked out.

IN the morning, he called Dave. "I could use some help."

"Sure. What's the problem, Shel?"

"I seem to have had another one of those incidents."

"Are you okay?"

"More or less."

"What happened? Where are you now?"

"Atlantic City."

"You going to tell me you don't know how you got there?"

"Pretty much."

"It was the converter, right?"

"I'll tell you about it later. Can you pick me up?"

"Sure." He didn't sound happy.

"I wound up in the ocean this time."

"Really? How'd you manage that?"

"I don't know."

SHEL was still in a state of near shock when his ride arrived at the hospital.

Dave tried to turn it into a joke, and they both laughed. But Shel's heart wasn't in it. They got into the car. "So how'd it happen?" Dave asked.

Shel told him.

"Where's the converter?"

"In the ocean."

"Probably the best place for it." It was a cloudy, cold morning. "Am I taking you home? Or to your father's place?"

"I don't know." He sighed. "My father's place, I guess. That's where the car is."

Dave pulled out of his parking place and eased onto Pacific Street.

But Shel was searching his pockets.

"What's wrong, Shel?"

"I think the key was still in my jacket when I got rid of it."

"What key?"

"The key to my dad's house. I'm going to have to break the window again." He grunted. "Looks like *my* keys went, too."

They drove in silence for a while. Finally, Dave sighed. "How many converters do you have?"

"Now? I've two left."

"Do you have any way of checking them? To make sure they don't malfunction, too? I mean, suppose the thing had dumped you out in the middle of the Atlantic instead of close to shore?"

"I don't think it was a malfunction."

"What do you mean?"

"I think it was the cardiac principle."

Dave took a long time to answer: "It's hard to believe."

"I can take a hint."

"So what are you going to do about your father?"

SINCE Shel had no keys, Dave delivered him instead to the town house. It was shortly after noon when they arrived. By then, Shel had been grumbling for an hour. "Going to have to figure out where he went. Find him *after* he left." He got out of the car, glanced toward the front door, and led the way around back.

"You don't have a spare key stashed anywhere, do you?" asked Dave. "Maybe in a flowerpot, or something?"

"No. My other set of keys is inside." Shel picked up a rock and was about to break a windowpane when Dave raised a hand to stop him. "Hold on," he said.

"Why?"

"I have an idea."

"We could use one."

Dave grinned. "You didn't try the front door."

"I always lock the front door."

"Try it anyhow."

"Okay," he said. "Whatever you say."

The front door was mostly chiseled glass with an angled

frame. Shel turned the knob. And the door opened. "I'll be damned." He stared at Dave. "This is the second time this was supposed to be locked."

"How about that?" said Dave.

"Good day to play the horses."

"Shel, I need you to get me one of the converters. Preferably the one I had in New York and Italy, that I know works okay."

"Why?"

"Just do it for me, please. And I'll show you something."

They went into Shel's den. He retrieved a key from a cup that had the Phillies logo and used it to unlock his desk. Then he opened the bottom drawer and removed a converter. "What are you going to do?"

"Will you set it for me?"

"Okay."

"You don't think it'll drop me in the ocean?"

"We'll have to see."

Dave looked at his watch. "It's a quarter after twelve. I want to go back fifteen minutes."

"Where? Here?" And a light went on for Shel. "My God. And it actually worked?"

"Apparently."

"Brilliant, Dave."

"Thank you."

"I'll take it from here."

"Okay."

Shel opened the lid, set the device for default, and pressed the button. Dave and the den faded. The den came back, without Dave. Shel shook his head, amazed at the possibilities of the device. He came out of the aura, walked into the entryway, and unlocked the glass door. Then he went back to the den and returned to his base time.

"Very good," said Dave.

"How did you know?"

"I didn't. But I made up my mind that when we got inside, we'd use one of the converters to go back and unlock the door."

"No more broken windows."

"*Nessuno.*"

* * *

"SO where," asked Dave, "do we begin to look for him?"

"He brought a book home with him."

"What book was that?"

"I'm trying to think. Something about the wind. It was by John Lewis." He walked over and googled Lewis's name. *Walking with the Wind.*

"The civil rights era," said Dave. "Seems like odd reading for a physicist."

"My dad was a lot more than a physicist."

"He was *that*. He's starting to sound like the ultimate Renaissance man."

"Yes. But I don't know that it helps us."

"Shel, it might be where he went."

"Where's that?"

"John Lewis was the leader of the Selma march."

"Selma—"

"It was the turning point in the civil rights era."

Shel knew there'd been a demonstration of some sort in Selma. But he didn't remember any details.

"Bloody Sunday," said Dave. "The marchers got attacked by police. Without provocation."

They exchanged glances. "You may be right," said Shel.

CHAPTER 11

I've seen the promised land. I may not get there with you, but I want you to know tonight that we as a people will get to the promised land.

—MARTIN LUTHER KING JR., APRIL 3, 1968,
THE NIGHT BEFORE HIS ASSASSINATION

THEY arrived on the side of a highway as a tractor-trailer thundered past. Dave landed upright, but the sudden blast of air knocked Shel off his feet. He went down, rolled over, and came up sitting in the grass. "Eventually," he said, "I should be able to get the hang of this."

It was 10:00 A.M., Sunday, March 7, 1965. Shel got up and watched a car race by in the opposite direction. Tractor-trailers haven't changed much over a half century, he thought, but cars have. It was an oversized green convertible.

He took out a compass. "Northeast is *that* way." He indicated the direction the truck had taken. "This is probably Route 22, which goes directly through Selma, then turns north."

The air was cool. Windy. A few clouds were scattered across the sky.

"The day that started the revolution," said Dave. At that moment, hundreds of people, tired of discrimination, tired of not being able to vote, tired of being pushed aside because their skin was the wrong color, were gathering at the Brown Chapel in Selma.

Shel nodded. "Maybe we should march with them." He intended it as a joke, but Dave didn't laugh. They'd watched the video record, had seen the troopers attack. That was enough. "Best for us," he continued, "is to just hang around the church for a bit. Meet some of them. Feel what it's like. And then get out of the way."

"I guess." Dave looked uncomfortable. But why not? They were on the cusp of one of the pivotal moments in American history, but a price was going to be paid.

"This is our chance to meet Rosa Parks," said Shel. "And Hosea Williams." They started walking. Uphill along the side of the road.

Dave had his hands in his pockets. "You know," he said, "we talked about going to the Colosseum to watch the gladiators. This is worse. These people don't get to defend themselves."

Another car was approaching. One of those late-fifties models with four headlights and a set of tailfins. They held out their thumbs, hoping for a ride. But the car swept past.

A few minutes later, a pickup stopped. A couple of kids. "We're going into town," the driver said. "You can ride in back if you like. It's about five miles." He raised a Coke bottle and took a gulp. "Where you headed?" He looked barely old enough to have a license.

"Selma," said Shel. "That *is* it up ahead, right?"

"Oh, yeah. Where in Selma you goin'?"

"The Brown Chapel. It's just a few blocks off Broad Street."

The driver made a face. "That's not a white church, you know."

"I know."

"You guys part of *that* crowd? Maybe you ought to get down and walk."

Shel flashed a ten. "We'd appreciate the transportation."

The kid thought about it. Took the money. "Okay. Climb on."

They pulled away with a jerk. Mostly they drove past cotton fields and farms. After a few minutes, they saw occasional houses and gas stations. Street signs identified Highway 22 as West Dallas Avenue. A large well-kept golf course appeared, the Selma Country Club. And finally they were at the city limits.

Selma looked typically Southern, long streets shaded by maple trees, pleasant homes with manicured lawns, signboards urging passersby to get right with the Lord. On this day, Confederate flags flew everywhere.

The center of town was home mostly to stores and warehouses. People on the sidewalk turned and watched as they passed. A few waved to the kids in front.

Traffic got heavy, and the pickup pulled over to the curb. The kids looked at them and shook their heads. "This is as close as I want to get," said the driver. "The church is over that way." He pointed northwest.

They got down. The passenger made a sucking sound. "If I were you guys," he said, "I'd stay out of it." They pulled away, made a left at the next intersection, and disappeared.

"Appreciate the ride," said Dave.

They walked a couple of blocks to Broad Street, which was the commercial heart of Selma, such as it was. There was a bank, the El Ranchero Café, a drugstore, and a movie theater. On this day, police were everywhere. East on Broad, the city extended a few more blocks, then opened out into a highway. That would be US 80, which the demonstrators planned to follow on their march to Montgomery, the state capital.

Shel and Dave crossed Broad Street and entered the black section, located on the north side. Streets were unpaved, houses lay in a general state of disintegration, and trash was scattered everywhere. They walked three or four blocks north, then turned west. A few minutes later, they were at the Brown Chapel.

It was an attractive Romanesque church with twin towers. Several hundred people, mostly black but with some whites, had gathered outside. They'd spilled onto a ball field and some basketball courts. A few angry-looking whites stood across the street, watching. They made obscene gestures at Shel and Dave as they passed. Shel thought he heard a rifle bolt slide forward.

"Don't look at them," Dave said. "Just keep walking."

In the church grounds, a few people were showing others how to protect themselves if attacked. Cover vitals. Head down. No violence.

"I don't see him," said Shel.

There were a lot of kids with the demonstrators. Young ones. Seven, eight, nine years old. The news footage of the police assault had concentrated mainly on the leaders of the march, mostly adult males. Shel had seen a few women attacked, as well. And he'd known there'd been children. But somehow they hadn't been the focus.

An older black man in clerical garb shook their hands. "Welcome, brothers," he said. And a young woman smiled at them. She was watching two boys, about eight or nine, tossing a ball back and forth.

Shel leaned close to Dave. "Who'd bring kids to something like this?"

A white guy, standing a few feet away beside a post, looked in their direction. He might have been about twenty years old. "Maybe because it means so much," he said. "Everything's on the table here."

"Worth a kid's life?"

"As things are, these kids don't have lives." He moved their way. He was about Shel's size, compact, with an inner energy that suggested you could trust him. "Anyhow, we're glad to see you. We need all the help we can get."

Shel nodded. "My name's Shelborne. This is Dave Dryden."

"Josh Myers," said the stranger. "Good luck. Keep your head down out there."

"Josh Myers?" Shel examined his features. Hard to tell. "You from Tucson, by any chance?"

The guy's eyes went wide. "Yes. How'd you know?"

Shel tried to think of an explanation. "Somebody back

there"—he gestured toward the chapel—"mentioned you were from there." He changed the subject: "They're not serious about marching all the way to Montgomery, are they? It's sixty miles."

"No. I think they expect to get arrested before they get very far out of town. If these nitwits don't shoot us first." He looked over at a guy across the street who was pointing a rifle in their direction, taking pretend target practice.

Shel tried to look unmoved. "I guess it's especially dangerous for white people," he said.

Myers shook his head. "Not really. When it's over, if we're still standing, we get to go home. Everybody else has to go on living with it."

After they'd moved on, Shel asked Dave if he'd recognized Myers. "Sure," he said. He was the guy who, almost a half century later, would write the definitive history of the second Iraq war, *They Never Threw the Roses.*

SHEL had been glad to see whites among the demonstrators. They included a handful of nuns. A couple of ambulances pulled onto the church parking lot. There were already two in front of the building. Medics climbed out. "Where are they from?" Shel asked a man standing next to him.

"They're volunteers," he said. "They came in from New York yesterday. They're setting up inside the parsonage. Just in case."

"My name's Shelborne." Shel put out his hand. "You're with the marchers?"

"Yes."

"Good luck." And, after an awkward moment: "This is Dave."

"Glad to meet you, Mr. Shelborne." He shook the hand. Shook Dave's. "I'm Harry. Thanks for standing with us."

Shel felt a charge at that. *"Thanks for standing with us."* Well, in a way they were. They represented history's judgment.

"Like hell," said Dave. "We're just hanging out. Pretending to be part of this."

"Hey, why are you getting annoyed with *me*?"

"I'm not a hero; I just play one on TV."

"C'mon, Dave, relax. At least we're here." They introduced themselves to Ralph Abernathy, and when he asked where they were from, Shel wanted to say, "The next millennium. When things will be better."

And *there* was Rosa Parks, talking to a group of young girls, barely teens.

And Andrew Young. Surrounded by reporters, white and black.

"They all seem upbeat," said Shel.

"It's because they don't know what's waiting for them."

"You think it would change anything if they did?"

"Don't know. I can tell you it would stop me."

"Me, too," said Shel.

They wandered among the crowd for the better part of an hour, shaking hands and wishing everyone luck. The demonstrators responded in kind, and Shel felt good. Warm. Respected.

"We're fakes," Dave insisted.

"Come on, champ. Loosen up."

"Look," Dave said, "there's Amelia Boynton."

"Who's Amelia Boynton?" Shel had never heard the name.

"In a lot of ways, Shel, she was the heart and soul of the movement. She was the lady who wouldn't let go. Who kept pushing."

When Shel went over to talk with her, Dave stayed where he was.

Amelia smiled. Thanked him for being there. "I know it's not easy," she said.

Shel nodded. Wished her luck. Dave's face was unreadable. Shel was getting a bad feeling.

A guy with a microphone announced they were ready to start. People began forming a line, two abreast. John Lewis issued a brief statement to the reporters. Then they knelt, and Andrew Young led them in prayer.

Two of the nuns passed close. Smiled at Shel. "God bless you," one of them said.

Somebody else shook Dave's hand. "Appreciate your being here."

The line began to move. Dave looked at them, looked at Shel. "I don't like standing aside."

"I know. Maybe it was a mistake, coming here. Maybe you were right, and we ought to just stay away from this kind of stuff."

Lewis was up front. In a light trench coat. Hosea Williams walked beside him.

THE ambulances, four of them, pulled in behind the marchers, keeping pace. They walked quietly. A few people, watching as they passed, cheered, and some sang. *"People get ready; there's a train a-comin'."* But they were joined by only a few isolated voices among the marchers.

They moved along Water Street, out of the black area. Now there were whites waving Confederate flags. And sometimes wielding guns. The few voices went silent.

They turned right at Alabama Street and marched along the river. Shel and Dave followed. Shel wanted to warn them what was coming.

Dave hesitated. Closed his eyes.

"What?" said Shel.

"I can't deal with this."

"Okay. Let's go back."

Dave showed no indication he'd heard. "I can't stand here and not do something."

"There's nothing we can do."

"Yeah, there is."

"Dave—"

He lurched out into the street. Toward the moving line.

Shel hurried after him, grabbed hold of his arm, tried to talk sense to him. But Dave shook him off.

Several marchers looked in their direction.

"I can't walk away from this."

In the line, two elderly women watched them approach. "Dave, don't be a nitwit. You can't change anything."

"Maybe that's the point." He crossed the last few feet and got in behind the two women.

Shel backed off and watched him go. Somewhere, a voice said, *"You don't need no baggage; you just get on board."*

Dave was one of the tallest people in the crowd. He'd make an easy target.

At Broad Street, they turned left onto US 80 and started toward the Edmund Pettis Bridge.

SHEL pushed ahead, trying to angle himself so he could keep an eye on Dave. But it was hard to get through the crowd lining the street. Then he became aware of movement behind him. Two men were following him. One was the guy who'd been pretending to pick off people with his rifle. The weapon now was nowhere to be seen. But the other wore a large floppy hat and carried a shotgun.

When their eyes met, the one with the shotgun grinned. "You left your momma back there, didn't you?"

Shel kept walking.

"Hey," said his partner, "we asked you a question."

Shel fingered the converter.

"You *did* ask him a question, didn't you, Alvin?"

"I don't think the son of a bitch is friendly, Will."

"Why don't we ask him?"

It was enough for Shel. He disconnected the converter from his belt. Hoped they wouldn't think he was pulling a gun. Set it for the same location, ten minutes earlier.

"You know, you son of a bitch, you come here and make trouble for—"

Shel pressed the button.

WITH the extra ten minutes in hand, he had no trouble beating the marchers onto US 80. He was watching when they came out of Alabama Street in a long file and turned toward the bridge. The crowd waved the Stars and Bars and screamed, but the police kept them at a distance.

Dave was about a third of the way back. He kept his eyes straight forward. They all did.

It was a beautiful day, maybe a bit chilly. The sky was clear, and the Alabama River sparkled in the sunlight.

When you walked onto the Pettis Bridge, from either end, you went uphill until you hit the center. So the marchers couldn't see what lay at the far end of the bridge until they topped the rise in the middle.

Shel told himself Dave was in no real danger. All he had to do was use the converter when things got rough. He could get out of there anytime he wanted. Just as Shel had.

Lewis was still in the lead. And Hosea Williams.

He watched them move onto the bridge. It was a long line of maybe five hundred people in all. They moved in absolute silence, two or three abreast.

Shel tried to follow them, but police stopped him.

The bridge carried four lanes of vehicular traffic and a pair of walkways. Lewis and his people stayed on the north side, on the walkway. Shel knew, though he could not see them, that police cars and state troopers and a mob of deputized citizens were gathered, along with a host of TV cameras, at the eastern end of the bridge. He watched the marchers walking steadily up the incline. Eventually, the head of the line reached the top, where they could see what awaited them. But they never paused.

The line continued forward. Shel focused on Dave and the two women, as they climbed the slope, reached the top, and started down. After a minute or two, they were out of sight.

CHAPTER 12

I know no method to secure the repeal of bad or obnoxious
laws so effective as their stringent execution.

—U. S. GRANT

DAVE had never thought of himself as particularly coura-
geous. He didn't much like heights, always played it safe, and
avoided confrontations whenever possible. Now he was walking with the heroes of Bloody Sunday.

A kid, about eighteen, bounced along beside him. Probably
false bravado, but he seemed unfazed by the threats and guns.
"Don't worry about it, man," he said. "They'll just throw us in
jail for a day or so. It's what they always do."

"What's your name, son?"

"Lennie."

"Lennie, you've done this before?"

"Marched? Sure. And hey, they'll put *you* in the white jail.
You'll have a lot more room tonight than I will."

Dave was thinking he'd maybe been a bit hasty. He wondered what his chances would be of slipping back into the
crowd. But how could he do that in front of Lennie? How
could he do that and face Shel, who was still watching him
from the safety of the sidelines?

More important, how could he justify it to himself? Well, maybe there was an easy answer to that one: This wasn't *his* fight.

Screams of rage and obscene gestures followed them through the streets. It didn't seem to matter that there were children among both the marchers and the bystanders.

They'd watched George Wallace, the Alabama governor, in the video record. He'd made his feelings clear enough about the demonstration. It was a public-safety issue, he'd claimed, and he would not allow it. The impetus for the event had probably been the murder of twenty-seven-year-old Jimmie Lee Jackson during a civil rights demonstration in Marion three weeks earlier. But the anger and frustration on both sides had been building for a long time.

The people lining Broad Street strained against the police lines.

THE Alabama River was beautiful in the late-morning sunlight. Dave was thinking how he'd like to drop in on Wallace and show him how history would record his name.

They stayed on the pavement as the walkway angled up. Ahead, the front of the line had ascended to the midpoint of the bridge and started down. Dave knew that Lewis and Williams were now able to see the waiting troopers.

Despite what Lennie assumed, there'd be no jail for these people. Broken bones lay ahead. Concussions and tear gas and a lot of blood. Some of the marchers would carry the marks of this day for the rest of their lives.

"I thought they'd stop us before we got out of town," Lennie said. "I didn't think we'd get this far."

They reached the top of the incline, and the troopers became visible. There were three lines of them, maybe a hundred altogether, backed up by local cops on horses. And people behind the cops who were not in uniform. They were Sheriff Jim Clark's deputies. Drafted thugs.

The troopers carried billy clubs; the deputies had clubs and whips. A state police commander, his bars glittering in the sunlight, stepped forward and held up a hand. His name was John Cloud.

Television crews on the far side pointed their cameras. A couple of reporters were talking into microphones.

"HOLD it," Cloud said. His voice was thin.

Lewis raised a hand, and the people immediately behind him slowed and stopped. Gradually, the entire line came to a halt. "We don't want any trouble here," said Cloud. "You have two minutes to break this up and go back."

Lewis replied. Dave was too far away to make out his words, but he knew what he was saying: "We'd like a moment to pray."

The commander stared at Lewis. And waited.

Seconds ticked by. Then, apparently forgetting the two-minute grace period he'd promised, Cloud gave a hand signal and moved back. The troopers and the deputies strode into the marchers, swinging clubs and whips. Tear-gas canisters exploded like gunshots.

Screams erupted, and the onlookers cheered and laughed. The demonstrators scrambled for safety. But there was no-where to go. More police and deputies moved in from the flank and rear to cut them off. Blows rained down, and people fell into the roadway, their hands over their heads. Some were dragged to their feet and clubbed again.

Police on horses rode into them. Drove the marchers to their knees. Trampled them. Kids screamed and cried. Lennie covered his head and was hammered by a three-hundred-pounder with a nightstick.

When they came for Dave, he tried to back away. They kept coming, two cops with smoldering eyes and batons. He did the only thing he could think of: He held up his hands to show he had no weapon and would not resist. He was accustomed to reasonable police officers and, despite what was going on around him, was shocked when one of them hit him in the mouth.

His reflexes kicked in. The cop, who expected Dave to take

his beating submissively, made no effort to protect himself. Dave nailed him in the jaw and hit him again as he went down.

Somebody screamed at him from behind. He started to turn when the lights went out.

HE wasn't sure what had happened or why he was standing in front of a counter with a uniformed officer behind it. "Name?" said the officer.

Every time he moved, a stab of pain ripped through his ribs. One eye was swollen shut. "Dryden."

Someone was going through his jacket. Pulling out his wallet, car keys, a couple of pens, a cell phone. And they had the converter.

"First name?"

He hesitated, still not certain what was happening. "David."

"You're sure?"

"Yes." He touched his eye. It hurt. He began to remember the march. Remembered walking on the bridge. "Am I being charged with something?"

"Assaulting an officer." He looked at Dave with contempt. "Where are you from, Mr. Dryden?"

"Philadelphia."

"What were you doing out there?"

He was trying to remember when the cop holding his wallet extracted his driver's license. He held it up to the light, made a face, and handed it to the booking officer. There was some whispering. Then the booking officer stared suspiciously at him. "What's this?" he asked.

"It's my license."

He rubbed it, frowned. Showed it to a fat, bald-headed guy with sergeant's stripes. "Look at this, Jay."

Jay took it, tapped the edge of it on the counter, and turned back to David. "Pennsylvania's doing *plastic* licenses now?"

Plastic licenses? Sure. Oh, wait. It was 1965. "Yes," he said. "Started this year."

Jay's frown deepened. "Mr. Dryden," he said, "I see you're a joker."

"I don't know what you mean." Most of it came back to him with the query about the license. Selma, the Brown Chapel, and the march. He couldn't remember anything, though, after walking up the incline on the bridge. Never got to the top.

Jay put the license back on the counter where the booking officer could see it, and pointed at it. The booking officer broke into a large smile. Shook his head. Jay turned back to David. "Tell me your name again."

"Dryden."

"Your *real* name?"

"Dryden's my real name."

"Look, sonny. You have any idea what can happen to you for falsifying state documents?"

"I didn't falsify anything."

"This thing says it was issued in 2016."

"Um...Oh."

"That all you got to say?"

"I..." Dave could think of no way to explain it.

"All right." Jay shook his head. "Get him printed and put him in back. Let me know if he decides to tell us who he is." Jay led him to a desk occupied by a woman. A plate identified her as the property officer. One of the other cops put his personal belongings, including the converter, down in front of her. She took a form from her top drawer and started an inventory.

"Mr. Dryden," she said, examining his cell phone, "what's this?"

Jay was still hanging around. She handed the instrument to him. He looked at it. Looked at Dave. Turned it over and opened it. "I think the officer asked you a question," he said.

The cell phone wasn't going to work in 1965. "It's a tabulator."

"What's that?" she asked.

"It counts things."

"It counts things?"

"It's an adding machine."

Jay sneered at it and put it down. Then he scooped up the converter. "How about this?"

Dave was tempted to tell him to lift the plastic cover and press the black button. "It's a game box."

"A *what*?"

"You can play games with it."

"Sure you can. Like you're doing now." Dave held his breath, fearing that Jay might do something to it. But he only shook his head before putting it back on the table.

The property officer bagged everything and passed the inventory sheet to him. "Please sign both copies," she said. She'd dutifully logged a game box and an adding machine, putting both items in quotation marks. Dave signed, she initialed, and she put the papers into a pile at her right hand. Then she dropped the bag into a metal basket.

They fingerprinted him and took him back to the cellblock. Several others, three or four, he couldn't be sure, were locked away. All white males. "Here's one of the sons of bitches now," said the guard, to nobody in particular.

He was guiding Dave toward a cell that held a prisoner who must have weighed four hundred pounds. "Yeah, Charlie," said the prisoner, "put him in here."

Charlie smiled at Dave. "What do you think, Dryden? Want to stay with Arky here? No?"

Arky delivered some comments about Dave's racial preferences, reached through the bars, and laughed when Dave kept his distance.

Charlie shook his head. "You *do* have a way of gettin' people riled," he said. "Better put you in a cell by yourself."

The cell had two cots. He sank onto one, hoping he hadn't broken a rib.

HE'D been in the cell about five minutes when Charlie and another officer returned. "You're sure?" asked the new cop.

"Absolutely, Al. You can look for yourself."

Al took a quick look around. "Makes no sense."

"I don't know nothin' about it."

"Okay. I guess you're right. But where the hell'd he go?"

"You check the break room?"

"Yeah. It's the first place I looked. Harvey said he thought he was coming back here."

"If so, he never got here."

They left. Fifteen minutes later, they were both back looking at Dave. "This the one?" said Al.

"That's him."

Charlie began unlocking the door. "Get up, Dryden," said Al.

"What do you want?"

"Just do what I tell you. Get up."

They opened the cell door and held it for him. Dave climbed painfully to his feet and limped out. His knee had begun hurting, too. Al took him back to the booking area, and he was shown into a side office, where the woman who'd done the inventory waited, along with a guy wearing bars. The sheriff.

"Mr. Dryden." The sheriff had a permanent scowl. He looked worn-out, tired of putting up with troublemakers. The bag with Dave's belongings lay on the desk in front of him, as well as a copy of the inventory. "You had something with you that you described as a 'game box.' "

"Yes, I did. Nothing's happened to it, has it?"

The sheriff ignored the question. "What exactly is it?"

"What do you mean?"

"Let me put it this way. Is it valuable?"

"Yes."

"Why? What was the damned thing?"

Dave shivered at his use of the past tense. "It's an experimental device I was working on," he said.

"What kind of experimental device?"

"It helps people learn languages."

The sheriff's eyes grew hard. "Who exactly are you, Mr. Dryden?"

"My name's David Dryden."

"What do you do for a living?"

"I'm a language teacher."

"Mr. Dryden, I'd like not to waste either your time or

mine. I wonder if you'd explain why you're carrying fake documents?"

"My driver's license?"

"Yeah."

"That's hard to explain."

"Try."

"It's a bogus license."

"I can figure that out for myself. Did you lose your license?"

"Yes."

"Why?

"Drunk-driving offenses."

"It figures. But if you're going to buy a bogus license, how in hell can you be so dumb about the birth date?" He looked at it and shook his head—1989.

"That was the way they did it. I didn't notice it until I got home. The guy who made the thing got in trouble and took off, so I never got it fixed."

"What's your real name?"

"Dryden *is* my real name."

"Are you a communist, by any chance?"

"No, sir."

"You say that game box is valuable."

"Yes, it is."

"*How* valuable?"

"A lot. It's hard to put a price on it."

"You know, Dryden, things are going to go a lot easier for you if you tell us the truth now. About whatever's going on."

"There's nothing going on."

"Okay. Have it your way."

He signaled for one of the cops to open the door. "Take him back inside."

As David was leaving, the sheriff turned to the inventory officer and lowered his voice. "Any sign yet of Jay?"

"Nothin', Sheriff. I'll let you know as soon as he shows up."

CHAPTER 13

Do not say things. What you are stands over you the while, and thunders so that I cannot hear what you say to the contrary.
—RALPH WALDO EMERSON, *LETTERS AND SOCIAL AIMS*

SHEL lost track of Dave. The victims, still choking on tear gas, lay broken and bleeding in the roadway. The crowd began to disperse. There were scattered voices, people saying they deserved it, maybe next time they'll know better, got no choice. They wandered back into Selma. The police, after a delay, allowed the medics in.

They put the more seriously injured on stretchers and loaded them into the ambulances. Others staggered away, back toward the Brown Chapel.

Shel got a whiff of the tear gas, and his eyes began to water.

"Look out," said a guy behind him. "Wind's coming this way."

The man stood a few feet away, shaking his head silently.

"Where are the victims going?" asked Shel.

"Probably Good Samaritan," he said. "It's the only hospital that'll take them."

* * *

HE went back to the Brown Chapel. The demonstrators stumbled in amid sobs and screams. Two of the ambulances were unloading. Volunteers helped victims into the parsonage and tried to calm hysterical children. As he watched, a victim was carried out of the building on a stretcher and placed in a waiting hearse. Moments later a second hearse joined the first. A man got into the driver's seat. One of the stretcher carriers climbed in back and pulled the doors shut. A woman hurried around to talk to the driver. "Wait, James," she said.

"What's wrong?"

"They're filling up at Samaritan. Take them to Burwell. You know where that is?"

"Sure."

"Go."

Shel intercepted her on the way back inside. "How bad is it?"

"Bad," she said. "They're all maniacs." She took a moment to control her voice. "Broken bones mostly. But the tear gas was the worst. They can't get it out of their lungs." Her eyes were ice-cold. "Those homemade clubs. They used garden hoses with nails. The sons of—" She started to cry, shook it off, and hurried back inside.

Shel followed her in and did what he could. He helped carry stretchers, took fresh bandages to the doctors, got water for people whose legs had been broken. After a while it became more than he could take, and he went outside. He sucked in air, tried to block off what he was seeing, watched a child carried screaming from the building. Then he went back in.

FINALLY, the worst of it seemed done. The more seriously injured patients had been hurried away. The others had returned to their homes or to whatever temporary shelters had been arranged. The Burwell Infirmary turned out to be a nursing home operated for forty years by Minnie B. Anderson. Prior to the day's events, it had been jammed to overflowing, but they'd made room.

Shel had had enough. This was a day that would change him forever. He had not believed human nature, on a mass scale, capable of such depravity. Not that he wasn't aware that it had happened. But reading about things like this, and experiencing them—living through it— It had been a long time since he'd cried.

There was no sign of Dave. Probably, when things got bad, he'd hit the trigger and jumped out of there. Gone home. He hoped so. He walked back toward Broad Street, looking for a place that was more or less empty. But there were people everywhere. Eventually, he decided the hell with it, turned onto Broad, saw two deputies approaching, walked into the entry of a clothing store—which was, since it was Sunday, closed— and hit the button. He didn't think anyone had noticed.

Didn't really care anymore.

HIS den had never looked, felt, safer.

He had just begun to relax when a nimbus formed. Thank God. Dave was okay. He drew a deep breath, but then held it. The figure inside was *not* Dave.

The light grew brighter, started to fade, and a puzzled, overweight little guy in a police sergeant's uniform staggered out, grabbed hold of a chair arm, and looked around in a state of shock. He was holding the converter in his right hand. His eyes locked on Shel while his jaw dropped. "What the goddam hell happened?" he demanded. "Where am I?"

"It's okay, Sergeant," Shel said.

The cop was terrified. Where is this? What happened to the goddam jail? Then he took a second look at Shel. "I know you."

"I don't think so. We've never met."

"You were out at the bridge. A little while ago."

"Yes. But I didn't see you."

"Hell, you didn't. You were staring at me."

"Take it easy, Sarge. I think you had a blackout."

"What are you talking about? I don't have goddam blackouts. Where is this place? How'd I get here?"

"This is what did it," said Shel, pointing at the converter. He reached for it, tried to take it. But the sergeant snatched it back.

"Tell me what's happening, damn it."

"The converter. In your hand. It packs a wallop. An electrical charge."

"What?"

"Electricity. I think it shocked you. Better put it down." He flipped it like a hot rock. "What's your name, Sergeant?"

"Jay. Jay Taylor."

"Okay, Jay. My name's Shel. Everything's under control."

"So where the goddam hell are we?"

"Listen." Shel picked up the converter, pretending to handle it with great care. "Let me fix this. Then we can go out and get in the car, and I'll take you back to the station."

"I still don't—"

"Just hang on a second while I make sure this thing can't do any more damage." He matched its setting to his own unit. When he was satisfied, he held it out to the sergeant.

"No, thanks," Taylor said.

"It's okay. I turned it off."

The guy was staring across the room at his computer. "What's that?" he asked.

"My TV."

"That's not a TV."

"Listen, you want to get back, don't you?"

"Yeah."

"Okay." He opened the cover and held out the converter again. "Hold this while I get my car keys."

He took it. Reluctantly. Shel pressed the black button, and immediately did the same with his own unit.

THEY were back on Broad Street. In the entry to the clothing store. The sergeant staggered, and Shel grabbed for the converter. But the policeman tried to hold on to it. "Malfunction, Jay!" Shel said. "Let go of it. Quick."

He did. Shel grabbed it. They drew the attention of a deputy about sixty feet away. He came running. "What the hell, Jay?" he said. "You okay?"

"He's not feeling well," said Shel. "Jay, I think you had another blackout." He turned to the deputy. "I'm glad to see you."

The deputy tried to take hold of the sergeant, but he shook free. Backed against a wall and faced Shel. "Goddam it," he said. "Who are you, anyway? What's goin' on?"

"I don't know," said Shel. "I was just trying to help." And, to the deputy: "I think he needs medical help, Officer."

"Stay clear," growled Jay. "I don't need any help."

Shel backed away. "He's had a hard day," he told the deputy.

Jay was enraged. He charged. Grabbed Shel by his jacket. "*You're* going to have a hard day, you little son of a bitch, if you don't start answering questions."

At that, the deputy also tried to get hold of Shel, who, being able to take a hint, pushed the button.

BACK in his town house again, Shel took a minute to sit down. The fact that Jay had come into possession of the converter suggested Dave was in jail rather than a hospital. That was good news. The bad news was that it would be easier to get him out of a hospital room than a cell.

Shel was getting better at manipulating the converter. He'd been able to lock in the precise location of the west side of the Pettis Bridge, and from that was able to calculate a decent estimate to get to the eastern side. If he could accomplish that, he'd be able to see precisely what *did* happen. And he needed to get there while the attack was still going on. Damn. The prospect of having to watch it all again did nothing for his state of mind.

First, he needed to shower and change. It had been a long day. Literally. (He allowed himself a smile at that.) And he hoped that Dave hadn't been hurt.

He hurried through his shower. Haste made no difference, of course. He could take his time, but he couldn't get past a sense of urgency. When he'd gotten into some fresh clothes, he did his calculations and reset the converter. There was a risk: His father claimed he could count on landing on a solid surface. (Shel knew the hard way that idea didn't hold water.) Okay. He'd be arriving near the Alabama River. So he decided to take no chances and put his converter in a waterproof bag. He didn't want to take a chance getting stuck in 1965.

Rescuing David would be easy, of course, if the cops would allow him to carry two converters into the jail and hand one to their prisoner. But that wasn't going to happen.

He put David's unit into a box, padded it with newspapers, closed the box, and taped it shut. Then he wrote the following instruction on the front:

To: Adrian Shelborne
U.S. Post Office
Selma, Alabama
To Be Kept Until Called For

He clipped the other converter to his belt, put on a light jacket, and picked up the box.

SHEL arrived immediately behind the state police just as the front of the line was passing the midway point of the bridge. Some of the troopers were on horses. They were backed up by a swarm of men not in uniform but clearly looking for a fight.

The marchers kept coming. A deadly silence settled over the scene. Then John Cloud stepped forward and held up a hand. He looked like an ordinary guy. Shel wondered if he had a family. And that was what rendered this so chilling. Would Cloud order the unprovoked assault on the marchers, then go home and have dinner with his wife and kids?

Lewis and Williams were, of course, in front. Cloud moved directly into their path. The marchers slowed. And stopped. He spotted Dave, just coming over the rise.

"We don't want any trouble here," Cloud said. "You have two minutes to break this up and go back."

Jay and another sergeant were standing with the city cops.

Jay was looking around, making sure his men were doing their duty, and he caught Shel looking at him. He stared back for a moment, then turned away.

What had Jay said?

"You were out at the bridge. You were staring at me."

The cops and their allies tightened their lines. Brandished weapons. He saw a few with tear-gas canisters. There must have been a signal, but Shel didn't see it. Nevertheless, they moved forward as one and went after the front of the march, swinging nightsticks. The air filled with the sound of batons striking flesh and bone. The marchers broke before the onslaught, and the screaming started. Less than a minute had gone by since Cloud had issued his warning. By then more police had moved in, and the entire line of demonstrators was under attack.

Shel backed away. The TV people shouted directions. Someone was talking into a microphone.

SHEL lost sight of Dave during the attack, but when it was over, he was lying in the roadway. He watched as two policemen hauled him to his feet and dragged him toward a waiting van. Shel tried to go to his aid, but again he was pushed back. "He's hurt," Shel told one of the officers. "He's a friend of mine."

"We'll take care of him, sir," the policeman said, with a warning stare.

When the roadway was clear, ambulances began to arrive. They recovered the more seriously injured and pulled away.

Shel set his converter to take him back two days. It deposited him again just outside the clothing store. On Friday. Twenty minutes later, he was at the post office. He gave them the package containing David's converter, got a receipt, and returned to Sunday on the far side of the bridge.

When he was sure he wasn't being watched, he strode off US 80 and into the trees that lined the river. He found a patch in a remote location, removed his converter, put it into the plastic bag, and hid it in a thick cluster of bushes. He marked the spot with a couple of rocks to ensure he could find it again.

He'd divided the units because if something went wrong and they disappeared, he and Dave would be stuck. This way, if either went missing, he could use the other to track it down and, he hoped, recover it.

Caution was the watchword.

HE flagged down a taxi. "The jail, please."

The driver, a beefy red-faced guy who smelled of beer, laughed. "They're pretty busy down there today."

"Yeah. So I hear."

"You get a chance to whack any of 'em?"

"No," said Shel.

They pulled away from the curb. "I wish I'd been there. But I had to work today."

"Pity. You know, I'd always thought that when everything else went to hell, we'd still have taxi drivers."

The driver turned sideways. "What do you mean?"

"It's okay," he said. "Forget it."

DESPITE the driver's assertion, the police station was quiet. You would not have believed there was anything unusual going on in Selma. Shel looked around and was relieved that Jay wasn't there.

He needed somebody who was relatively unoccupied and settled on an officer with congenial eyes and a large bristly mustache. "Pardon me," Shel told him, "my name's Shelborne. I think you've arrested a friend of mine. I was wondering if I could see him?"

The officer frowned. Studied him closely. "You're not one of *them*, are you?"

"No, no," Shel said, reassuringly.

"Okay. Look, in case you haven't noticed, we're a little tied up. Why don't you come back in the morning?"

Shel couldn't see that anything much was going on. A couple of guys doing paperwork. That looked like about it. "Officer, I only need five minutes with him. I'll make it worth your while if you can arrange something." He showed him a fifty.

The cop looked at the bill. Then at Shel. "Empty your pockets, please."

Shel complied. There wasn't much. His wallet, a comb, and a handkerchief.

The cop did a quick patdown to make sure he wasn't carrying any weapons. Then he shrugged and took the fifty. "Okay, Mr. Shelborne, who did you want to see?"

"David Dryden."

"White guy?"

"Yes."

"Arrested today?"

"Yes."

"At the bridge."

"Yes."

He looked disgusted, but didn't comment. "Over here, please." He picked up a form and got Shel's name, address, and phone number. Then he led him into a side room, divided down the middle by a screen. "Wait here." He left, closing the door behind him.

Within moments he was back. "He'll be here in a minute," he said, taking a position off to one side.

"Thanks."

The opposite wall had a door. It opened, and Dave came in. He smiled sheepishly when he saw Shel.

"You look terrible," said Shel.

"Yeah. I guess I kind of screwed things up, didn't I?"

"Yes, you did. You okay?"

"I think so. My ribs hurt."

"And you've got a black eye."

"It's that noticeable, huh?"

They were both conscious of the police officer, who showed no sign of going anywhere. "You look as if you need a doctor," Shel said.

"They've been telling me they'll take care of it when they can."

Shel mouthed the words *Arrange it.*

"How?"

"You know," he said, "every time you do something dumb like this, I get palpitations."

"They think I'm a communist, Shel. I'm going to be under guard for a while."

"They call in the FBI yet?"

"That's probably next."

Shel pressed his index finger against his jaw and used it to signal *one*. Without saying anything aloud, he formed the words *One hour*.

Dave nodded. "I'd appreciate any help you can give."

The cop gave them another minute or two. Then he broke in: "We're done, guys. Dryden, you can go back now."

THEY led Dave back to his cell. There was no clock anywhere, and they'd taken his watch, so he had no easy way to determine the passage of time. He eased himself back onto the cot, while the other prisoners laughed at him and told him what they'd do if they ever found him outside. It was a new experience. He'd never before attracted open hatred.

He closed his eyes, and after a while the threats stopped. They began talking *about* him, rather than *to* him. And gradually the conversation shifted in other directions, notably the quality and performance of the ladies at a local service organization.

He could hear occasional sounds from the booking area. Laughter. People talking. Doors banging. More laughter. They were in a good mood out there.

He tried counting but got bored with that when he hit about two hundred. Time travel had its downside. Not going to do this again, he thought. If I get back home, I'm going to stay there.

Nineteen sixty-five. The Vietnam War would be heating up. Lyndon Johnson was in the White House. John Wayne was still making movies. Neil Armstrong and the first moon landing were four years away. Computers were large pieces of hardware and came with punch cards.

His ribs ached. Hurt every time he inhaled. Something was probably broken.

After a while, the jailer brought meals. Coffee, chicken, potatoes, and a vegetable, but God knew what the vegetable was, and the rest of it tasted like mush. He ate a little.

When the guard came back and approached the cell, Dave bent his head, looked directly at the officer, and swallowed hard. "I need a doctor," he said.

The guard looked annoyed. "Sorry to hear it."

Dave clamped his teeth, pressed one hand to his chest, started to roll over, and screamed as if in sudden pain. "Bad heart."

"Yeah? You sure?" The guard retrieved the dish and cup.

"Please." Dave didn't have to try hard to look as if he was seriously hurting. "I'm having a heart attack." He was gasping for breath.

The jailer delivered a string of epithets. "I'll be back in a minute, Dryden," he said. He went out and returned with the sheriff.

The sheriff looked annoyed. Better things to do. "What's the matter, Dryden?" he asked. "Something bothering you?"

"Heart," Dave said, clamping down on the word as if saying it was sheer agony. "Stroke. Last year."

The sheriff's features softened. "Okay. Hang on a minute. We'll get you some help."

CHAPTER 14

At times, history and fate meet at a single time in a single place to shape a turning point in man's unending search for freedom. So it was at Lexington and Concord. So it was a century ago at Appomattox. So it was last week in Selma....

—LYNDON B. JOHNSON

SHEL came out of the jail onto the street and approached the first policeman he saw. "Pardon me, Officer," he said, "but my uncle Bob was picked up drunk last night. They tell me he got sick and they took him to the hospital. Which hospital would that have been?"

Armed with the information, he flagged down a taxi, rode across the Pettis Bridge, asked the driver to wait, and retrieved his converter from the bushes along the Alabama. The cab then took him to the Selma post office.

He used the converter to return to Saturday morning, and walked inside the building. "My name's Shelborne," he told the clerk. "You have a package for me."

With both units now in his possession, he returned to Sunday afternoon and caught another taxi to the hospital. He still had at least a half hour before Dave was likely to arrive.

Time travelers wait for nobody. He thought about moving forward, say two minutes at a time, rather than hang around. But he wasn't sure how many jumps the power pack would support before the red warning lamp came on. So he simply went inside to wait. The reception area was crowded. Not, apparently, by victims of the attack on the marchers, though. Everybody was white, and no one seemed to be bleeding. Shel went back out and began strolling around the hospital sidewalks.

An ambulance showed up, but they were carrying a woman. And, a few minutes later, another one, with what appeared to be an injured child.

Then, finally, Dave.

Two ambulance attendants hauled him out of the rear of the vehicle on a stretcher and transferred him to a gurney. A cop climbed out afterward, and they all went inside.

Shel followed.

They wheeled Dave into the reception area and through a pair of swinging doors into a side room. The cop took station beside the swinging doors. Shel sat down where he had some vision into the side room and picked up a battered copy of *Sports Illustrated*. After about twenty minutes, one of the doors opened, and a doctor spoke to the cop. The cop nodded and followed him back into the room. The door swung shut.

Still holding the magazine, Shel got up, strolled over, and pushed the door ajar. They were taking Dave out another exit. He was connected to a monitoring device and he looked unconscious. A nurse noticed him and frowned. He smiled back, trying to appear casual, and retreated. When she turned away, he hurried through the swinging doors, crossed the room, and went out the other side.

Dave was still on his gurney. Two attendants were moving him down a passageway, while the cop trailed.

They turned off into a connecting corridor, walked past the cafeteria, and stopped in front of a bank of elevators. The attendant pressed the UP button.

The police officer looked his way while they waited. Shel slowed his pace but kept walking. He got there just as the elevator did. When the doors opened, the cop made it clear he wanted no company. Shel kept his eyes averted and walked past. Dave lay supine on the gurney. His breathing seemed shallow.

He heard them get into the elevator. Heard the doors close. He hurried back and pushed the UP button.

Dave's elevator stopped at the fourth floor. And again at the fifth.

Three women were walking toward him. His elevator arrived, and the women picked up their pace. He got in. One of them called for him to wait for them. He ignored the request and pushed the fourth-floor button, then closed the doors. They shut just before the women arrived.

The elevator went to the second floor. And stopped. The doors opened. A doctor, bald, annoyed, shaking his head, stood just outside talking with an efficient-looking well-dressed brunette. "No, Suze," he said, "I wish you wouldn't get us into stuff like that."

"I'm sorry, Jim, but he asked for you specifically." Her hand reached in to prevent the door from closing.

"You know what pinochle's like over there."

"Jim, I didn't have much choice. I didn't want to insult them."

It went on like that for a full minute before Jim sighed and agreed to go, told Suze she owed him, and came into the elevator. She released her hold, and he pushed the button for the third floor.

The doctor got off there, the doors closed, the elevator went up another level and stopped. Shel stuck his head out and looked both ways. No sign of Dave and his attendants. Two nurses sat at desks in a glass enclosure. He got out and walked toward them.

He needed a few moments to get their attention. "Nurse," he said, when one finally turned his way, "did somebody just get off here with a man on a gurney?"

The nearer one looked up from a clipboard. "I don't think so," she said. "Why? Is something wrong?"

Yes. There were several more floors and they could be anywhere. "They dropped a pen," he said.

She smiled tolerantly. "I wouldn't worry about it."

Too time-consuming. He went back to the elevator. It was passing the second floor on the way down. He pushed the button again. Then went back to the nurse. "Miss, is there a stairway?"

She pointed. "At the end of the corridor. Go left. You can't miss it."

It was too far. He returned to the elevator, and rode it up to the fifth floor. But the corridor was empty. And this time there was no one to ask.

Damn.

He stood frustrated, wondering what to do.

Then he recalled the converter. He set it to take him back five minutes, and was standing well off to one side when the elevator arrived, and Dave and his escort got off.

They walked about halfway down one of the corridors and turned left. By the time Shel reached the intersection, they were at the far end of the passageway, entering a room. The eighth one on the right. The policeman hauled a chair outside the door, set it against the wall, and sat down. Minutes later, the gurney and the attendants reappeared and started back in Shel's direction. Almost immediately, a doctor arrived, nodded to the cop, and went past him into the room.

Shel pulled back out of sight. Next task was to get past the guard.

He set the converter for ten minutes earlier and pushed the black button.

TWO people who'd apparently gotten lost were in the corridor. They looked startled when he appeared, seemingly out of nowhere. Shel walked past them while they stared, said hello, asked how they were doing, and kept going. He counted to the eighth room on his right and let himself in. A male patient lay in one of the two beds. An older man, with white hair. Every vein in his arms and neck was visible. He looked languidly at Shel.

"Oops," said Shel. "Wrong room. Sorry."

The man saw him but didn't react.

It was a standard hospital room, with several wooden chairs, a tray table, and a window overlooking a parking lot. It also had, of course, a washroom. The washroom was just inside the entrance, with the door facing away from the patients. Shel slipped into it, hoping the patient hadn't noticed.

He closed the door as quietly as he could and waited.

A few minutes later, Dave arrived. Shel heard the gurney, and a woman's voice. "You'll be fine, Mr. Dryden. Just need to rest a bit. Dr. Hollis will be in to see you shortly."

There was no response.

"Okay, Mack," she said. "On three."

The voice did the count, and he heard somebody grunt as they lifted Dave into bed. Then a male voice: "I'll be right back." Footsteps came toward the washroom. Shel backed up so he'd be behind the door if it opened, and set the converter forward thirty minutes. The knob turned, and he pressed the button. The door swung in as the washroom faded from view.

THE hospital room outside was silent. Shel opened the door.

Both patients were breathing quietly. But the guy with the veins was lying staring at the ceiling, and he spotted Shel as soon as he came out of the washroom. "You again."

Shel tried to shush him. "It's okay," he said.

"What are you doing in here?" The guy was trying to sit up straight, but he looked close to a stroke.

Dave's eyes opened, then opened wider. "Shel. How'd you get in?"

"You're not supposed to be here," said the patient. Then he yelled for the guard.

The door pushed open and the cop strode into the room. "Where the hell'd *you* come from, mister?"

Shel lobbed the second converter to Dave, who was trying to disconnect himself from the monitoring device. "Just hit the button," he said. "You're ready to go."

He turned back toward the officer and smiled disarmingly. "Who are you?" the guard demanded. "How'd you get in here?"

The aura began to build around Dave. The cop's eyes swung

past Shel and fastened on what was happening in the bed. The guy with the veins stared. "Mother of God."

Shel hit the button, wondering what the police report would look like.

WHEN they got to the town house, Dave asked whether Shel had seen any sign of his father.

"I was a little busy," he said. "But no, I didn't see him any-where." He got some ice for Dave to put on his eye. "Did you want to go back and try again?"

Dave needed assistance getting to the sofa. "I can see you're a bit miffed with me," he said.

"You dumb son of a bitch." Now that they were safe, the anger erupted. "You could have gotten us both killed."

"I know. I'm sorry."

"You're sorry."

"What else do you want me to say?"

"I mean, it didn't even make any sense. You knew how that was going to end back there."

"I knew."

"And you did it anyhow."

"I guess."

"Son of a bitch. You remember the agreement we had? We *watch*. We do not get involved."

David tried to stretch out. And winced.

"What's wrong with your side?"

"Cracked rib."

"Great."

"They wrapped it in the hospital."

"Anything else I should know about?"

He closed his eyes. Opened them again. "Look, Shel. I couldn't just walk away from those people."

"I noticed."

David tried again to adjust his position. The sofa was too small for him. "Maybe you *do* need a hospital."

"I've already done that. They told me not to move around any more than I have to. Said I'd be okay in a couple of weeks."

"All right. I guess we were lucky. You should probably get it checked anyhow."

"I don't think you need to worry."

"What were they monitoring?"

"My heart, I guess. I had a coronary."

"That must have shaken them up. At the police station."

"I don't think they believed me."

"How'd you fool the doctors?"

"Just told them I could feel a weight in my chest. Told them I'd had problems before. I don't think it occurred to them somebody would lie about something like that." He sighed.

"What's wrong?"

"School Monday." Two days away.

"Uh-oh."

"I can't very well go like this."

"Not exactly. You'll have to take some time off."

He grumbled something Shel couldn't make out. "A day or two wouldn't be a problem. But two *weeks*? What's my story? That I got hurt on Bloody Sunday?"

"You might tell them you fell down the stairs. Or maybe you were in a car accident." Shel took a deep breath. "None of this would have—"

"I know, Shel. Let it go."

"Okay."

"And let's not do any more of this living history, all right?"

"It wasn't supposed to be like that." He was thinking about Monday. "You know, you don't need to take time off from school if you don't want to."

"I can't go in like this."

"How about if I take you home? You stay there until you're okay. Keep away from the school. Take two or three weeks. Whatever you need."

Dave laughed. "Yeah. Right."

"You'd better keep your converter."

"That sounds good. Yeah. I'll be careful with it."

Shel nodded. "I know you will." He cleared his throat. "Your family has a cabin in the Poconos, right?"

"Yes."

"Would anybody be there right now?"

"At this time of year? No. Not a chance."

"You could recuperate there."

"But who's going to cover my classes?"

"You will, partner. Just leave it to me."

PART TWO

FOOTPRINTS ON THE SANDS

CHAPTER 15

For I dipt into the future, far as human eye could see,
Saw the Vision of the world, and all the wonder that would be;
Saw the heavens fill with commerce, argosies of magic sails,
Pilots of the purple twilight, dropping down with costly
    bales. . . .

—ALFRED, LORD TENNYSON, *LOCKSLEY HALL*

IT was a two-hour drive to the cabin. The last eight miles took him up a single-lane dirt road with a series of hairpin turns. Dave's father, in his most unflinching style, had picked the highest place in the area for the family cabin. The woods were thick, and the cabin had a magnificent view of Starlight Lake. But the stars were hidden by thick clouds when he arrived. Even the lights along the lakefront were little more than distant smudges.

There were supposed to be bears in the area, but he'd never seen one. All the same, his folks had kept him close when they'd come here during his childhood summers. They'd expected he would love the place, but the problem had been a lack of other kids. The only people close by were the Bakers and the Hertzogs, both of whom were retired couples.

He was near the top of the road when he saw headlights around the curve. He edged cautiously forward, found a space off to one side, and pulled over to make room for the other vehicle. It blinked its lights as it passed.

The cabin was a triple-decker, with living room, kitchen, and veranda at midlevel. His folks still came here every summer, and he usually spent a week or so with them.

He slipped into the driveway, the security lights came on, and he got out. The place had always been too remote for him. But at the moment it was ideal.

He'd brought a few books. And he'd stopped and picked up some groceries and painkillers. He needed two difficult trips up the outside staircase to get everything indoors. It was mid-December, and the cabin was cold. He turned on the lights, and adjusted the thermostat.

He plugged in the refrigerator and put everything away. Then he made a sandwich and topped it off with a rum and Coke. Unsure how the painkillers would interact with the drink, he left them aside, eased himself into an armchair, and put on the TV. One of the cable news shows.

They were still getting fallout from the failure of the Syrian-Iraqi peace effort, but he didn't care much about politics at the moment. He just wanted voices in the room. Shel had made him promise he'd call when he arrived. So he did, using the landline since he'd left the cell phone, along with his driver's license, with the Selma police.

Shel asked what he planned to do while he was there.

"I'm just going to hang around here and sleep and read."

"Good. No hiking, huh?"

"I think I'll pass on that."

"Okay. I've got an interesting piece of news for you."

"What's that?"

"Your sub is here. He came in early this evening, about two hours after you'd left."

"Okay. That's good to hear."

"Yeah. It's weird. But I thought you'd want to know. As long as everything's okay, I'm going to head for bed. Been a long couple days. I'll talk to you later, Dave."

AFTER he'd gotten past childhood, life at the cabin had been pleasant. It held good memories for him. He'd brought women here from time to time. But it was a long trip, so there had been only a few. Those he'd really liked. One in particular. Erin Stackpole. An odd name for so beautiful a woman. And Katie had been there once.

Erin was the only woman who'd ever really hurt him. They were never formally engaged, but he'd assumed an altar lay in their future. Then one night, with no warning, at least none that he'd picked up, she'd simply told him it was over. That she wouldn't be able to see him anymore. She'd offered no explanation, no mention of someone else having come into her life. Just the announcement: "I've enjoyed it, Dave. But it's time for both of us to move on."

Both of us.

He hadn't questioned her. Too much pride for that. "Okay," he'd said. "You're sure?"

She said she was. And Dave had shrugged and walked away.

Looking back now, he suspected he could have held on to her. But he'd never actively pursued her. Never let her know, never *told* her, how he'd felt. He'd thought she could see what he felt. That it was enough. His feelings were out there, visible to the world.

So she'd said good-bye, and he had simply acquiesced. He'd never called her again. Do that, he'd thought, and she won't realize what she'd lost. No, it was better to wait for her to signal that she wanted him back. Dumb. But he'd waited for a call. Or a chance meeting that wasn't really a chance meeting. Or a Christmas card.

Something.

But, of course, it never happened. And he never saw her again. A year later he'd heard she was getting married.

The conversation on the TV drifted in and out. Scandal in high places. Charges of corruption. A deranged preacher claiming a recent volcanic eruption in Alaska had been a divine reaction to something or other. The lunacy never stopped.

The pain in his ribs drifted in and out, as well. And his legs had stiffened during the long drive. Funny how little of the attack on the bridge he actually remembered. He still didn't recall precisely what had happened to *him*. But the doctors had told him that was not unusual. Gradually, they said, it would come back.

THE sofa was too small for him. So he limped upstairs, climbed into bed, shut off the lights, and allowed the darkness to swallow him. The cabin, with its locked doors, and its mountaintop isolation, provided a barricade against the outside world that, at the moment, he needed.

He'd always thought of the present in Henry Thoreau's terms, as a narrow dividing line between two infinities, the past and the future. But that had changed. If he could go back and *visit* Galileo, living on the cusp of the Renaissance, then it meant that nothing ever *ended*. In another place, at this moment, they were still fighting the English Civil War. But no, that was the wrong terminology. Not at this *moment*. Rather, in some hidden compartment along the timeline, the violence was always there, the killing still going on. Selma was never really over. There was another compartment where Russians were trying to hold on against Napoleon. And still another in which the Inquisition was burning Giordano Bruno.

Sure, you could argue there was a positive side. Socrates could still be found in the dimensions, discussing faith, beauty, and the good life with his friends. There was still a place where Dave was happily in bed with Erin. But what were the pleasures of ordinary people when measured against the Holocaust? Or the butcheries of a Stalin? Or the African genocides still being carried out in an age that pretended to be enlightened?

Sleep came late, though it *came*. It stole up the stairs and wrapped him in its dark folds, and he slipped finally into oblivion.

SUNDAY was unseasonably warm. Branches swayed in a mild breeze, and a pair of blue jays had landed on the veranda railing. Far below, a few sailboats were out on the lake.

He made bacon and eggs, added orange juice and coffee, and realized how much he missed the morning paper. There'd be no mail either, of course. The post office, remarkably, *did* deliveries up here, but there was a hold on for the cabin.

Big Al, the ranking morning cable news show, had nothing but a celebrity divorce story, predictions about a sales surge during the holiday season, and stories about the secretary of state who had been caught by a live mike saying that the world would never have peace as long as it had religion. His office had just issued a "clarification," probably making things worse, by specifying which religion he was talking about. And a battle had erupted over battery-powered garments that permitted telephone sex.

He shut off the TV and picked up one of the books he'd brought along. It was Michael Corbett's *Winter of Discontent*, which had urged the introduction of lie detectors to presidential debates and IQ tests for candidates. There was no attempt to set a minimum standard, but Corbett's plan would require that results be placed on the record. Candidates, of course, could decline, but only at their peril. However, no one really knew what the effect might be. Recent studies had shown that a majority of voters would be put off by a candidate with a high IQ.

Winter of Discontent was essentially a manual on how to make government more responsive. And more rational. He liked some of the suggestions, but they all required an electorate that paid attention. Maybe the problem, he thought, was the way history was taught. The classes he'd attended in high school and college had consisted mostly of committing factual information to memory. Dates of battles, names of politicians and generals, and descriptions of events that changed society, like the Reformation and the Napoleonic Wars.

Why not give students a hypothetical time-travel device? "You can go back and talk to one person in an effort to change an outcome. Say, to head off the Civil War. Who do you talk to? And what short-range outcome are you looking for?"

He read for a while, but it took an effort with one eye swollen half-shut. Eventually, he gave up and drifted off to sleep.

* * *

IN the middle of the week, Shel called again. *"How are you doing?"*

"Okay."

"Good. In a few more days, you'll be fine."

"How's my replacement?"

"He seems to be enjoying himself. I think he might want the job permanently."

"I doubt it."

"Helen and I are going to dinner with him tonight."

Dave laughed. "Who's with him? Anybody I know?"

"Katie."

"The guy has good taste."

"I always thought so. By the way, I've been reading the Selma book Dad had. The one by John Lewis."

"And what have you concluded?"

"I'm beginning to realize how sheltered I've been."

HE started feeling sorry for himself, cooped up in the cabin. It was almost Christmas, and he didn't even have a light to hang on the door. So, as the aches in his ribs and legs diminished, and the swelling around his eye receded, he decided it was time to get out. On Saturday the twenty-second, he drove down to Clifton, the closest town of any size, bought a cell phone to replace the one he'd lost, and treated himself to a turkey dinner at a family-owned restaurant. Then he selected a ringtone. He'd had a few chords from Chopin's Prelude in E Minor on the old one. That used to get people staring. Maybe it was time for something a bit less majestic. He decided, eventually, on a simple bell chime.

When he'd finished, he went to a movie, the latest installment of the Batman films. Then he wandered into Mac's Bar, which had loud music and a lot of women.

He danced away the night and drank too much. Not a good idea when he had to negotiate a mountain road going home. He spent much of his time in Mac's with a young woman whose name was Marie Dupré, and he wondered whether he could persuade her to drive him back to the cabin.

She smiled politely when he issued the invitation. "I think you made a mistake, Dave," she said. "I don't do that."

"That's not what I meant."

"Good."

"Sorry."

It was just as well. He didn't need any complications. But the alcohol, and maybe Marie, had made him nostalgic. While talking with her, he'd been thinking about Erin.

Still, he wasn't sure how he was going to get home. Dave wasn't much of a drinker to start with. And he couldn't very well sit in Mac's Bar and slug down Cokes. He wondered whether the town had a taxi.

But if he did that, he'd have to get back down the mountain in the morning to retrieve the car. Larry's Cut-Rate Full Service Motel, HBO included, was three blocks away. He started the engine and twisted his head around to back out. But the world began spinning.

That was enough. He left the car where it was, got out, and locked it. He staggered the three blocks and checked himself into the motel.

IN the morning, he had breakfast in town, picked up an *Inquirer*, and drove back to the cabin. It was just after ten when he arrived. He spent the rest of the morning with the paper. The Eagles were playing the Giants, and that would give him something to do during the afternoon.

It would have been nice to have Katie with him. Or Erin.

The first time he'd brought Erin to the cabin had been a Saturday evening in March three years before. He remembered everything about that evening. How they'd stood on the veranda looking out at the stars, how they'd stayed out there and danced to Jerome Kern's music, how they'd broken open a bottle of champagne to celebrate a promotion Erin had just gotten. (She designed AI systems.)

Until that night, there'd been an unspoken agreement

between them, limiting what was proper. Part of the under-
standing grew out of the fact that she did not travel to the
mountain cabin. Whenever he'd suggested it, she had found
a reason not to go. Somebody wasn't feeling well. It was a
long ride.

Something.

But on this occasion, *she* had suggested it. They'd been
having dinner at Michaelson's and, completely out of left
field, she'd asked whether the cabin was still in the family.
That had been the exact phrasing.

And he'd said, "Sure. Would you like to see it?"

"Yes," she'd said. "It's a beautiful night. Perfect for a view
of the lake."

So he'd known from that moment.

Her name now was Erin Olshefska. He ran a search across
Pennsylvania for her phone number. Found two women with
that name, but neither was the right age.

He ached to see her again.

And he had the converter.

He got it out of the side table and looked at it. Checked the
universal calendar on the computer. It had been late in the
month, either the twenty-second or the twenty-ninth. They'd
arrived at the cabin an hour or so before midnight.

He shouldn't do this. But resistance, as they'd said in one
of the old SF classics, was futile. He set the time and date for
the earlier night, grabbed his sweater, and against a ton of better judgment, made his jump.

THE cabin was dark again. He remembered a strange detail
from that night: As they'd come up the mountain road, he'd
seen a light on in the living room. His first thought had been
that his parents had come up, unexpectedly, and would be waiting inside when he walked in with Erin. *Hi, Mom and Dad.*

Erin had noticed it, too. And she'd asked about the possibilities.

"No," he'd assured her. "They don't come here until summer,
or on a holiday weekend. And they always let me know when

they're coming." That had been telling her more than he should have. She'd laughed, but it had left him feeling like an idiot.

They'd pulled into the driveway while he'd formulated what to do if his parents *were* there. *Just stopped by for a drink. And to take in the view.*

He didn't remember which light had been on, only that it had been in the living room. But it probably didn't matter. He leaned over and switched on one of the table lamps.

The cabin was cold. But he'd have to leave that for the happy couple. He draped his sweater over the back of the sofa and sat down in an armchair that afforded a view of the road. You could see headlights coming for the better part of a mile, so he'd have plenty of warning. Then there was nothing left to do. Except feel his heart begin to race as it had years before whenever Erin had settled into his arms.

When they hadn't arrived by eleven thirty, he decided he had the wrong Saturday and was about to try the later date. At that moment, the headlights showed up. They were swinging round one of the turns, still several minutes from the house. As he watched, they disappeared. He put on his sweater, looked around to make sure he hadn't left anything that shouldn't be there, and slipped outside.

He locked the door behind him, and was horrified when the security lights came on. He crossed the driveway quickly and hurried into a stand of trees.

There was a delay factor built in, and they did not go off.

He was sure they hadn't been on when he'd come with Erin. "Come on," he told them. "Shut down."

He could see the doorway, the veranda, half a dozen windows, the outside stairs that went up to the second level, and the carport. The living-room lamp was barely noticeable against the lights.

He still couldn't see the car, of course, but he could hear the engine as it struggled up the steep incline preceding the last turn.

And, finally, they went off.

He got well back, moving with caution so the motion detectors didn't pick him up and switch the system on again.

The headlights reappeared, and the car started up the final sixty yards or so.

He felt uncomfortable. A little bit like a voyeur. Or a stalker. But if there'd ever been a special occasion, this had been it.

The car turned into the driveway. And yes, it was his white Regal, only a few weeks old then. The interior was dark. But he could make out the driver and the passenger. Then the lights were on again. And there she was.

Erin.

The driver killed the engine, and the two people in the car sat for a moment. Talking about the light that was on in the house. Reassuring themselves that everything was okay because there was no other car in the driveway. Then they opened their doors. And he wasn't sure which jolted him more, seeing himself climb out of the driver's side or watching Erin, trim and elegant and endlessly lovely, get out on the other.

She walked around the car and crossed in front of the headlamps. Then they climbed the stairs, and David watched himself insert the key. He pushed open the door, and switched on the interior lights. She paused momentarily, looking out over the valley, over Starlight Lake. She turned, while he waited beside her, said something to him, and went inside. He followed her and closed the door.

More lights came on. He heard his own voice, though he could not make out what he said. Erin wandered past one of the windows. The outside lights went off. He wondered what would happen if he showed himself, walked up the stairs, and said hello. *"Hi. My name's Dave, too."*

"Why, Dave, you never told me you had a twin."

It had delicious possibilities.

They were out of sight now. But he remembered the details. He was showing her around. First the dining room. Then the kitchen. Then downstairs.

That night had been his chance. *Tell her, you idiot. She's come this far. Commit to her and tell her you want her forever and always.*

More lights came on around the cabin.

There'll never be a better time.

In a few minutes, they'd be drinking whatever had been handy that night, and Jerome Kern would make his appearance.

He stood in the trees and his heart ached. He knew who was inside with her, but it didn't matter. He hated the guy.

WHEN next he called Shel, he didn't mention what he'd done. "I'll be going back tomorrow," he said.

"Okay. Happy New Year, by the way."

"Thanks. You, too."

"See you tomorrow, Dave. I'm inclined to say it'll be good to have you back, but the truth is, it doesn't seem as if you've been gone."

THERE was one more thing he was wondering about. Well, actually there were several things. But for the moment, what was the range of the converter? How far back could he go?

He pressed a white stud that moved the numbers. Decades and centuries rippled past. Millennia.

Ten thousand.

Twenty.

Finally, it came to rest at 31,118 years. An odd number. Maybe it was a reflection of the energy level.

Could he actually go back that far?

He pulled his sweater on again and went outside. The moon was just a blur in a cloudy sky, but there were lots of lights in the valley.

Maybe he should go *forward.* Downstream. Thirty-one thousand years into the future. What would the world be like then?

My God.

Would there still be people? He and Shel had not really discussed going forward. It was too scary. And they'd been thinking in terms of next week, or next year.

But where would humanity be in the far future?

What the hell. He reset the converter to its limit. Took a deep breath. Got on his feet. And pushed the button.

THE stars vanished. Came back. He stumbled forward but did not fall. The flat floor mutated into a grassy slope. The air was cool and clean and smelled of mint. Crickets chirped, and a full moon drifted through the night.

The trees were different. Bigger. There was no sign of his cabin. He looked down at a valley full of light. It came from buildings scattered around the shoreline. But it seemed softer, had less glare, than the sort of artificial illumination he was used to. Other lights were airborne, moving through the sky, coming and going between a site on the lakeshore and a mountaintop, where they were settling back to earth.

He didn't recognize any of the constellations. That was, of course, not significant since he didn't know any back home either, except the Dipper and the Belt of Orion.

The lake was somehow closer. Bigger.

What did people look like in this era? He'd read all the predictions, the notions that humans would plug themselves directly into computers, would shed their skin for titanium shells. That they would achieve virtual immortality.

Should have thought to bring the binoculars. He could still go back and get them, but for the moment he simply stayed and watched.

He wondered about the world outside the Poconos. Philadelphia now would be far older than the pyramids had been in his time. New York and the United States were probably distant memories. If that.

A swirl of light was approaching. He backed against a tree. Keep out of sight. No way to know how friendly these people might be.

It *was* an aircraft. Flying silently, not more than a few hundred feet high.

Who was in it?

It headed out over the lake. Then he heard the unmistakable

sound of a horn. Something like an oboe. And some stringed instruments.

The music was coming from the mountaintop. Where all the lights were.

A voice rose above the trees. He couldn't make out what it was saying. Then it went quiet, and with a clash of drums and cymbals, a concert began.

Dave sat down, back against a tree, to listen. Despite the fact it was a summer evening, no mosquitoes bothered him.

The music filled the night.

And, most enthralling, each time it stopped, he heard applause.

CHAPTER 16

Here are two points miraculously co-uniting...two stories
with double Time; separate, and harmonising.

—CHARLES LAMB, *THE ESSAYS OF ELIA*

IT was time to go home. Dave packed up and locked the
cabin. His rib cage delivered only an occasional twinge now,
and his eye had long since gotten back to normal. He went
down to Starlight Lake and, anxious to get started, settled for
coffee and toast. He felt on top of the world. The human race
was not only going to survive; it was going to do pretty well
for itself.

He told a rather ordinary-looking waitress that she was
probably the loveliest woman in the state, left her a fifty-dollar
tip, and started for Philadelphia.

He tried driving with the windows halfway down because
he loved the air and the smell of the woods, but it was January, and even though it was a relatively nice day, the heater
couldn't begin to compete, so after a few minutes he rolled
them back up. He stayed off the expressways and turned onto
every two-lane road he could find, requiring only that it be
headed in the right general direction. He passed farmhouses
and barns. He cruised through small towns and waved at

anybody who looked his way. Some waved back; some might have thought he was a nut. On this third day of the new year, he didn't care.

Eventually he encountered a series of signs for a place called Shel's Diner. BEST FOOD NORTH OF THE MASON-DIXON LINE. It sounded like fate calling, so he pulled into the parking area, went inside, and ordered a double cheeseburger. He was way off his diet, but it just didn't matter. Not today.

He got lost a couple of times, and the people he asked for directions kept trying to tell him how to get to the interstate. Life's not an interstate, he thought. At least, not if you're smart. The interstate's all about getting someplace. Yeah. Life is roads with curves, and maybe somebody broken-down up ahead, and stopping for glazed donuts. And homes in the middle of nowhere. And attractive women in convenience stores.

A guy in a pickup beeped at him. They had a double line, and the guy couldn't pass. So sometimes, he thought, you have to hit the gas. He did. They went around a curve, the road opened up, and the pickup roared past. The driver gave him the finger.

It didn't matter. Nothing could wipe away the goofy grin that afternoon.

THERE was never any doubt that he'd tell Shel about the concert. Had to. And if Shel decided to confiscate the converter, never let him near it again, so what?

He pulled up in front of the town house during the late afternoon. Shel appeared at the door before he could ring the bell. "You look good," he said.

"I feel good."

They went inside and sat down in the den. While Shel got a round of drinks, Dave threw his feet up on a hassock. King of the world.

Shel took two glasses down out of the cabinet, put ice cubes in them, and turned around. "What's going on?" he asked.

"Did you ever check the range?"

"Of the converter? Yes."

"And?"

"It's somewhere around thirty-six thousand years."

"That's a bit more than mine has. Probably depends on the power pack, right?"

"How do you know, Dave? You haven't done that, have you? Gone back with the savages?"

"No. But I've gone downstream."

"Forward."

"Into the future, yes. And I'm happy to report everything turns out okay."

"How do you mean?"

"No ice age. People are still there. I think. Doing okay."

"Really?" Shel's features darkened. "Dave, I wish you'd stop the nonsense. That's irresponsible."

"Who says? What's the risk at that range?"

"I don't know." Shel bristled. "That's what makes it dangerous."

"Come on, Shel. Make sense."

"Okay, then. You gave your word. And you broke it. You promised you wouldn't do anything like that."

Dave couldn't remember making any such promise, but he let it go.

When Shel got no response, he went back to mixing the drinks. "So what did you see?"

Dave described the thick forest at the mountaintop. The lights. And the music.

"That's it?"

"Shel, we've survived. Despite all the talk about climate change and runaway technology and loose nukes, we're still here."

"Well, that's good. You didn't happen to go over there, did you? To the concert?"

"No. I thought I'd just sit back and listen."

"So all you know is that you heard music."

"Yes."

"Okay."

"Why? What's the matter?"

"Nothing. I just *hope* it's us."

"I doubt it was Martians."

"Yeah. I'm sure you're right, Dave."

Damn. The mood had become a bit intense. "I probably better get going."

"You didn't get your drink yet."

"Let it go."

"Look, Dave, I'm sorry, but—"

"Let it go, Shel. I understand." He stood up and unclipped the converter. Set it for the next jump. It would take him back almost three weeks to Saturday, December 15, the evening they'd come back from Selma.

"Set it for ten o'clock," said Shel. "In the evening."

That was a couple of hours after he'd left for the cabin.

NOTHING changed in the town-house den except that a magazine appeared on the coffee table, and the television was on in the living room. The big wall clock said 10:00 P.M. precisely.

Shel was parked in front of the television, but he was asleep. Dave sat down in one of the chairs, watched the show for a minute—it was a sitcom—let his head drift back, and closed his eyes.

"Dave." Shel's voice. "How long have you been here?"

"Just came in. I didn't want to wake you."

"Everything healed?"

"Far as I can tell."

"Good. How about something to eat?"

"I'm not really hungry, Shel. I think I'll just head home and get some sleep."

"Okay. It's good to have you back." He got up, went over to the desk, and took out a key. "There's a rental car waiting in the driveway."

It was a black Bangalore. A torpedo. Dave got in and drove to his home on Carmichael Drive. It was good to be back.

* * *

HE knew how the Eagles game had turned out Sunday, so he spent much of the day at the gym and the pool. On Monday, two days after the Selma experience, he was back in class. It was an odd feeling to sit up there on the edge of his desk, as he often did, knowing that at that very moment he was at the cabin waiting for his wounds to heal.

His first period was Greek. Twelve kids who claimed to be interested, more or less, in Homer and the classical dramatists. "Aristophanes invented comedy," he told them. "He was the first guy we know of to go for laughs. And Sophocles"—he took a moment to look out at the sky—"gave us better theater than Shakespeare."

They were shocked. No one had ever said anything like that to them before. Shakespeare was, of course, the name before which all heads bowed. But he could see they agreed. Not that Sophocles was so good, probably, but that Shakespeare was overrated.

Suzy Klein, a wide-eyed African-American, flashed a smile. Knew it all the time. But she asked why he would say that.

"He has all the power of the Bard," said Dave. "But it's concentrated on a smaller stage. Remember Aristotle?"

"Sure," said Suzy, while the other kids leaned forward.

"What did he say about unity?"

"Ummm." She looked uncertain.

A hand went up in back. Roger Gelbart. "What did he say, Rog?"

"Use the minimum number of characters necessary to carry the action. In Sophocles, the conflict involves, at most, a handful. In a Shakespearean play, you need a scorecard."

"What about time?"

Another hand. "The action should take place over the shortest possible time span. Preferably the length of the play itself."

"Good." He'd begun to think how it would be to go back to classical Athens, circa 420 B.C. And see *Antigone* performed under the stars.

He could actually *do* it. Although it was hard to imagine Shel consenting. Maybe if they were able to locate his father and bring him back, get rid of the urgency, maybe then he could be persuaded.

SHEL laughed when he mentioned it indirectly, talking about how much fun it would be to take his students on a field trip to Athens in the fifth century B.C., to watch a performance, say, of *Medea*.

"Your students understand Greek?" Shel asked.

"More or less."

"*Do* they?"

"Not very well, actually."

"That's what I figured." He grinned. "A trip like that, though, would seriously shake up the academic community."

"And, I suspect, a few parents."

"Dave," Shel said, "I found something that might help us find my father."

"What's that?"

"I did a search of his computer. He's like you, always had a taste for the classical age. When we used to travel in Greece and Syria, I don't remember how many times he'd show me a site where there was nothing but rubble and explain how it had been a temple to Juno or somebody. It upset him that the Christians, when they took over the empire, destroyed so much of its architecture. And its literature."

"So where are you going with this?"

"He'd been collecting notes for a long time on Aristarchus."

"Who is...?"

"He was the head librarian at Alexandria in its heyday."

"Your father was—is—a physicist."

"My dad is a Renaissance guy."

"Okay. That's interesting. Aristarchus was at one time the keeper of the world's knowledge. So, what—"

"There's a better than fair chance that when my father found himself with a time-travel capability, Aristarchus is the guy he'd have gone to have lunch with. Even more than Galileo."

"How long was he there? At the Library?"

"About six years. From 153 B.C. to about 147. Anyhow, I'm going to go back and ask. I'm going to try to learn a little Greek. So it'll be a while." He hesitated. "Will you come?"

"Sure, I wouldn't miss it. But I have a condition."

"Okay."

"Most of the work by the Greek playwrights has been lost. Do you know, for example, how many of Sophocles' plays survived?"

Shel had no idea.

"Seven."

"That doesn't sound bad."

"Out of more than a hundred."

"Oh." Shel sat back. "Well, why don't we plan on spending an afternoon at the Library and take some pictures?"

"It would be criminal not to."

"Okay. Then it's settled."

"When do we leave?"

"Let's give it a couple of weeks. I need time for my crash course."

"We might have a problem, though."

"What's that?"

"You don't want to tell anybody about the converters."

"Yeah. I've thought about that. If we can recover some of this stuff, how do we explain where we got it?"

"Bingo."

"We'll cross that bridge when we get there, Dave. Look, we can send whatever we get anonymously to, I don't know, Penn. Or LaSalle. Or maybe Temple. Maybe spread it around. Give everybody some of it. It'll drive them crazy trying to figure out where they're coming from."

"They'll think they're forgeries."

"Sure they will. But I bet my foot that when the experts have a chance to look, they'll figure out they're legitimate." He poured another round of drinks. "What do you think?"

"I say we try it. And I know exactly the person we should send the stuff to."

"Who's that?"

"Her name's Aspasia. I knew her in graduate school."

"A Greek?"

"Seems right to me."

THEY met for dinner the following evening. Helen accompanied Shel. Dave took Madeleine Carascu, a member of the Penn English Department. Like Dave, she had red hair and green eyes. She was also armed with a dazzling smile, a quick wit, and a ton of energy. The kind of woman who has so much going for her that she scares most men off. But she didn't scare Dave, who spent most of the evening hoping that Helen would get jealous.

They went to the Chart House on Delaware Avenue, a place with its own interior waterfall, and got a table overlooking the river. And the women didn't need long to figure out that he and Dave were celebrating something. "What's going on?" asked Helen.

"Breakthrough in transdimensional warp theory," Shel said.

"What's that?"

Madeleine looked at Dave. "Are you following this?"

"He talks like that a lot."

Helen plunged straight ahead. "Why are we so happy?"

Shel grinned. "Dave and I are having dinner with the two most beautiful women in Center City, and you wonder why we're enjoying ourselves?"

Her steady gaze shifted to Dave. "What can I tell you?" he said. "When the guy's right, he's right."

Shel turned the conversation in a new direction. They talked about *Morgan*, that season's hot new antiterrorist TV drama. And wondered whether the new Josh Baxter film, *Nightlight*, could really be as good as the critics were claiming. Madeleine asked Shel whether he thought the effort to establish solar collectors in orbit and beam the power down to groundside stations would ever get off the ground. "Pardon the pun."

"Eventually," he said. "The problem is funding. There's no money for the research." They finished and went over to Larry's for a nightcap. Then they were breaking up and going home. Madeleine lived in an apartment at 22nd and Spruce.

She was quiet on the way, and Dave knew she wasn't satisfied with the evening. She hadn't said anything, but there was a coolness in her manner that was hard to miss. It had been their first date, and he knew there would not be a second. He suspected she'd picked up his interest in Helen. Or maybe she saw him as a poor second to Shel. So he took her to her door, said good night when she opened up, and kissed her lightly.

"I enjoyed the evening, Dave," she said. "Thank you." Lights went on. She smiled at him and slipped inside. And he thought that this was an evening he would one day come to regret.

DAVE celebrated Christmas with his family in Scranton, much better than the Christmas he'd spent alone in the cabin a couple of weeks ago, subjective time. A week later he took Katie to a New Year's Eve party, where she asked how the hunt for Helen was progressing.

"I think she's in love with Shel," he said.

"I'm sorry."

"How's it going with Harry?" Harry Begley was her current target.

"I've written him off," she said.

"Oh. I didn't know."

"You must have noticed it's New Year's Eve. And I'm not out with him."

"Yeah. I noticed." They were in each other's arms, and Dave must have been staring at her.

"Something wrong?" she said.

"You're gorgeous."

FINALLY, there was the January 3 call from Shel. *"You just left the cabin,"* he said. *"You—the other you—should be*

*here late this afternoon. I'll call you when it's okay to come
pick up the car.*"

"Thanks, Shel." The world was going back to normal.
Being in two places at one time was unsettling.

CHAPTER 17

Time is but the stream I go a-fishing in.
—HENRY DAVID THOREAU, *WALDEN*

SHEL had stayed away from the future. He wasn't sure why. Maybe it was that, unlike the historical past, it was unknown territory. And he didn't want to find out what lay ahead. Much of the pleasure that comes from being alive is day-to-day discovery. Will SETI succeed during my lifetime? Have we got it right about multiple universes? What will the next ten years of my life look like? Will it include Helen? Kids? Does anything positive come out of the converters?

If he went thirty or forty years downstream, he'd be even more tempted to stray from the general to the specific, to find out what his life had been like, and he wouldn't want to discover that he'd ended up bored, that his career had gone nowhere (which was precisely what he suspected would happen), possibly even that he would come down with Boltmeyer's Disease and at some future date spend most of his time mumbling at a TV, or whatever would pass for a TV in another few decades. The bottom line: He didn't want to see a summary of his life. And in general did not want to see the future.

Still, knowing which way the markets might trend would be helpful. And whether hydrogen vehicles would finally come on line to replace electric and gas-powered cars. And where real-estate prices were going. He could even set up shop as a prognosticator. And, after he'd proven deadly accurate a few times, people would start to pay attention. He could provide warnings weeks ahead about an oncoming hurricane. Or where an earthquake would strike. Don't get on that plane, lady; it's going down.

It was an interesting possibility. He could eventually become a major ecumenical figure. Maybe even found a religion. But, to get serious for a moment, would he be violating any of the temporal conditions if he warned someone, for example, that a nutcase with a gun was planning to attack a mall? Was the future as fixed as the past seemed to be?

He had no idea. Thinking about it made his head hurt. When Dave had told him about traveling thousands of years downstream, he'd been alarmed. But maybe as long as they kept it long-range, there was no risk. The reality, though, was that he didn't care that much about the next millennium. He was interested in next week. In whether he had a future with Helen. In the next political campaign. In the religious crazies who thought it was okay to lob bombs at infidels.

Both converters were now safely locked in his desk. He'd been uncomfortable asking Dave to return his. He hadn't told him in so many words that he didn't trust him. But the implication had been clear enough.

HE was never sure what actually prompted him to go forward. It may have been curiosity; it may have been simply that he was tired of trying to learn Greek. In any case, on Saturday, January 19, he came home from eating lunch at Spanky's, picked up one of the converters, and drove into Center City. He parked the car in a one-hour zone, put the converter in his pocket, and walked over to Rittenhouse Square, where he picked an empty bench and sat down. He waited until no one seemed to be looking his way and pulled out the converter.

Why not?

He set it to keep him in his present geographical location, roughly two months later, in mid-March. Then, when no one seemed to be watching, he stood and pushed the button. The park came and went, and the bench on which he'd been sitting was covered with snow.

He pushed his hands into his pockets and tried to stay warm. The park was empty save for a few people hurrying through. He walked quickly, shivering, crossed Walnut Street, and turned east.

Center City didn't look any different. He stopped in front of a variety shop and peered through the plate-glass window at a stack of *Inquirer*s. Should he buy one? The headline said something about Saudi Arabia.

But it was dangerous. Best let it go. He moved on. Decided he should get serious. Visit the future, or don't. What would Philadelphia look like in sixty years? A few minutes later, he decided what the hell, walked into a clothing store, found a place in back where he couldn't be seen, set the converter for spring, 2079, and pressed the button again.

HE arrived inside a hotel lobby. Several people were staring at him. He tried to smile back. Do this all the time. A tall, awkward-looking guy shook his head at a woman. "You're crazy, Laura," he said.

Shel hurried out through an automatic door. Walnut Street was gone, replaced by moving walkways and broad lawns. Rittenhouse Square was still there, now somehow the center of a lush garden. Birds sang, and the central fountain in the park still worked, sending a bright cascade into the air. Kids fed the squirrels, and pigeons perched atop a sculpture of arms, legs, eyes, and flashes of light, a work right out of Dalí.

The area was as crowded as ever. The shops had retreated into malls. Clothes were lighter, brighter, more formfitting than in his time. Men and women both wore hats. Hairstyles for women were more formal. Among the men, he saw only one or two beards.

Two new skyscrapers had been added, giant towers dwarfing the old skyline. The ground shook briefly, signaling the passing of an underground train.

He rode one of the walkways, enjoying the warm air, his coat folded over one arm, and wandered into another hotel, the Shamrock. He stopped by the convenience store but saw no magazines or books. He would have liked to buy a chocolate bar, which were on plentiful display, but nobody seemed to be using paper money.

He wondered about himself. He'd be ninety-one now. There was a lot of talk about life extension during the first two decades of the century, but as of 2019 nothing much had happened. It was possible he was still charging around out there, playing tennis, living the good life. If that were true, the Shelborne of 2079 would remember that his younger self had visited Rittenhouse Square on this day. And he'd be here, somewhere, to say hello. Wouldn't be able to resist that.

It was 11:03 A.M., May 12. A Friday. Okay. He made a mental note. I'll be here.

He stopped walking. Waited. Looked around.

Nobody.

Of course, the area was crowded. The walkways were filled with people. Some shoppers. Some with kids. Many apparently on business. He'd be hard to find.

One thing he couldn't help noticing: The downtown area was home to as many beautiful young women as ever. It looked as if civilization was moving along nicely.

Dave had it right.

HE got onto a northbound walkway, discovering in the process that they were referred to as "tracks." What had once been Market Street was now a long canal, with tracks on either side. He stayed northbound and crossed on a bridge, headed for the old Parkway.

It was still there, although, aside from an electric train, there were no vehicles of any kind. It was strictly grass, trees, fountains, and benches. To the southeast, the original City Hall remained, and William Penn still stood guard over the city. At the opposite end, the Art Museum appeared unchanged. He wondered if the statue of Rocky was still there.

The Philadelphia Library, which had, in his time, been located on the north side of the Parkway, was now a museum. A larger, more imposing library had been constructed behind it. He got off the track and walked inside.

The bookshelves were gone. Well, he shouldn't have been surprised at that. Even in his own time, books and magazines were disappearing. Booths equipped with display screens were everywhere. Most were occupied. He found an empty one and sat down.

The screen lit up. A message appeared: PLEASE PUT ON EARPHONES.

He complied. A voice said, *"Hello."*

"Hello," he said.

"How may I help you?"

"Scientific advances of the past sixty years, please."

The screen gave him a series of categories: ARCHAEOLOGY, ASTRONOMY, BIOLOGY, ELECTRONICS, GEOLOGY, MATHEMATICS, MEDICINE, PHYSICS, ZOOLOGY. *"Please choose one."*

He stared at the screen. What would happen if he did a general search and entered his own name? What would he read about himself?

God, he was tempted.

"Sir, would you prefer alternative choices? Perhaps delineated more specifically?"

What had been happening in the world over these last sixty years? Was the nation at peace? Had we succeeded in getting rid of nuclear weapons? Had the religious fanatics gone away?

Did we still have elections?

"Sir?"

Most of all, he wondered what his own life had been like. He turned away from the screen and looked behind him, half-expecting to see an older version of himself coming toward him. Smiling at him. Reassuring him.

CHAPTER 18

There is nothing done by human hands that ultimately time does not bring down.

—CICERO, *PRO MARCELLO*

SHEL and Dave arrived in Alexandria during the late fall of 149 B.C., more than a century, according to Plutarch, before Julius Caesar invaded the area in his war against Ptolemy XIII and accidentally burned the Library down. "That's probably not the way it happened, though," said Shel, who'd read everything he could find on the subject. "It might have been the Christians who did it. Which would have been a few hundred years later."

"Persecuting pagans."

"That's correct. They were demolishing everything associated with the old gods. Temples, statuary, manuscripts, anything they got hold of was burned or wrecked. The guy behind it here was, umm—"

"Theophilus," said Dave. "He didn't approve of pagans. But nobody's really sure who was responsible. The Library might have survived as late as the seventh century."

Shel checked a paper notebook. "Caliph Omar," he said.

"Right. The story is that he thought the books would either

contradict the Koran, in which case they should be destroyed, or they would agree, which would make them superfluous."

"Never a shortage of idiots."

The celebrated Alexandria Lighthouse commanded the mouth of the harbor. It was situated on the island of Pharos and connected to the mainland by a walkway. It would in time be declared one of the seven wonders of the ancient world. Like the Library, it would eventually vanish.

"Did Alexander really found this place?" Shel asked. "I couldn't find anything definite."

"That's the legend. I don't think anybody really knows."

The anchor of the Library complex was the Museum, named for the Muses. It was a majestic structure, wide as a football field, and could easily have served as a temple. It was two stories high at the center, rising to five along its periphery. A silver dome rose over the roof.

It was built of white marble and polished stone. The surrounding grounds were filled with statuary and fountains and greenery. A pair of colonnades connected it to three buildings of comparable grandeur though of more modest dimensions. "This is my father's kind of place," said Shel.

They wore togas and sported beards again. Two of Dave's female friends had complained about the beard, suggesting he was getting pretentious. Helen had simply raised her eyebrows and asked Shel whether he and Dave had a bet going. They strolled quietly through the complex, marveling that the ancients were capable of such magnificent architecture. Seeing artists' representations, and seeing the real thing, constituted vastly different experiences.

The grounds were filled with visitors. Some appeared to be scholars. Children played variations of tag and threw balls around while their mothers watched. As Shel and Dave approached the Museum, a group of teenagers made their exit, descending the marble steps. There was an older woman with them. A teacher, possibly. They looked relieved, happy to be outside again. And Shel thought how some things never change.

Two statues, each about twenty feet high, flanked the approach: a winged female and a bearded deity who must have been Jupiter. Shel paused to admire them, trying not to gape. "Wish we could get one of them home," he said.

"We could try transporting one," said Dave. "See if the converter would take it."

"Are you serious?"

"No. Not really. They belong here."

At the front entrance of the Museum, the steps mounted to a portico. Massive columns supported the roof.

There were more carved gods in the portico. Shel recognized Apollo. And Mercury, with his winged heels. And two females. One had a bow slung over her shoulder. That would be Diana. Her companion was older. Probably Hera.

The front doors were massive, maybe three times Shel's height. They were adorned with more deities, as well as warriors, triremes, chariots, vines, and trees. Two of the doors were ajar.

They passed inside.

THERE was a cluster of large rooms. Halls, really. Lush carpets covered the floors. The walls were dark marble, decorated with oil paintings of warships and scholars poring over scrolls and beautiful women watching the moon rise and couples making love. Narrow columns screened walkways around the perimeters of the rooms. Tables and chairs were everywhere. Men and women sat reading in some areas and carried on meetings in others. Wide windows in walls and ceilings admitted sunlight. A librarian was stationed behind a long, curved counter.

Shel felt self-conscious in his toga. It was a bit too long, and too wide. He decided he'd have it taken in when they got back to Philadelphia. "You have any idea where we go from here?" asked Dave.

"I'd say the information counter. Let's go check out your Greek."

The librarian was a young man, barely twenty, extremely thin, with brown hair and brown eyes. He smiled and said something.

"Hérete," said Dave. *"En érgon tou Sophocléous zitoúmen."*

"Poíon akrivós, kírie?"

"Éhete katálogon ton iparxónton?"

Shel understood some of it. Dave had told him they were looking for one of the Sophoclean plays. Which one? And Dave had asked whether there was a list.

"There are catalogs over there." The librarian pointed toward a table. "If you know what you're looking for, I believe we have every play extant." A woman approached and placed a scroll on the counter. She glanced up at Dave and smiled.

The outside of the scroll was marked. If Shel's spoken Greek was shaky, his ability to read text was nonexistent. "Dave, can you tell what it is?"

Dave tried to look without seeming unduly curious. "It's number eleven of *The Journals of Themistocles.*"

"Themistocles? He was . . . ?"

"The guy who saved Greek civilization during the Persian Wars. But I don't think there's any record of a journal."

The librarian picked up the scroll, made a note in a ledger, and looked at Dave, who had not moved. "Is there anything else, sir?"

"Yes," said Dave. "Do you know if Aristarchus is available? We'd like very much to speak with him."

"And your name, sir?"

"Davidius. We're visiting scholars."

"Very good. Do you have an appointment?"

"No, we don't."

"All right. Let me see if he's available." He signaled a teenage girl and sent her to make the query. "It'll take a few minutes. Where will you be?"

"Looking at the catalogs."

The catalogs were in scroll form, works listed by title and by author. Dave zeroed in on Sophocles, and Shel took out his notebook.

"Incredible," Dave said.

"What?"

"He was right. They must have *all* his plays. There are more than a hundred of them listed here."

Shel couldn't make anything out of the Greek characters.

"Here's the *Achilles*." David ran his finger down the list. "*Theseus. Odysseus in Ithaca*." He gave a silent cheer and raised a fist in triumph.

"Good." It was a pleasure watching Dave get excited. Shel thought he was going to explode.

"The *Troilus*."

"Dave, is it possible the other ones got lost because nobody really cared?"

Dave paid no attention. "*The Last Labor*," he said. "Probably Hercules."

"What else is there?"

"*The Hawks. Parnassus.* Hey, here's an interesting one."

"What's that?"

"*Circe*. And one I'm not sure how to translate."

"Try."

"*Hours in Flight*. No. *Time Passing*. Maybe *Last Days*. And *Andromache at the Gate*." He couldn't take his eyes off the list. "And *Leonidas*."

Shel was fingering his gooseberry, which they'd use to get the pictures. "Which ones do we want to start with?"

A middle-aged man in orange robes joined them and addressed Dave: "I understand you are Davidius? Do I have that right?" He was too young to be Aristarchus, who would have been in his sixties.

"That's correct. This is my associate, Shel Shelborne."

"Pleased to meet you. I'm Clovian. One of the librarians." He looked at Shel. "An unusual name, sir. May I ask where you are from?"

"Philadelphia," said Shel.

"I never heard of it."

Dave could see Shel struggling, so he broke in: "It's a long way from here."

"Britain?"

"Farther than that."

"Really? How long will you be staying in Alexandria?"

"Only a few days."

"I see. Do you have a book with you? If you do, we'd like very much to see it. And possibly, with your permission, make a copy."

"No. I'm sorry. We didn't bring one along."

"Pity. But all right. It's not a problem. Had you planned to look at any of our books?"

"Yes, we did."

"Of course. But before we can allow you to do so, you'll have to join the Library."

"We'd be pleased to do that."

"There's no charge." He handed each of them a sheet of paper. "Please print your name, your profession, and tell us where you can be reached. And date and sign."

Clovian wandered off while they filled in the requested information. Shel signed his and frowned.

"What?" asked Dave.

"What's the date?"

"Let's find out." They got up and went to the desk, where the young librarian was leafing through the ledger. He looked up. "Sorry about the wait," he said. "We haven't heard anything yet. It will take a while."

"Okay. Can you tell me today's date?"

He took a moment to think. "Hathyr seventeen."

The form also needed a year. Shel could see Dave consider the matter. There was no way to ask. Finally, he scribbled a date and handed the paper back. Shel did likewise.

The librarian squinted at the forms, looked as if he had a question. But then he shrugged, opened a drawer, and dropped the documents inside. "Thank you, friends. By the way, I've heard of the University of Pennsylvania."

"It's well-known."

"Yes. Well, it's an honor to have you here. Which book did you wish to see?"

Shel looked at Dave. *You* call it. "*Achilles*," said Dave.

The librarian nodded and went into the back room.

"Do we have any idea what year it is?" asked Shel.

"Thirtysomething year in the reign of Ptolemy VI."

The librarian returned with a scroll. "You understand you may not take it out of the building."

"Yes. Of course."

"I'll notify you when we hear from the director."

THEY took the scroll into a side room, sat down at a table, and unrolled it. Shel looked at the Greek characters, and his level of frustration rose. "I'm never going to be able to read this," he said. "What's it about? When he kills Hector?"

"Give me a few minutes. Let me look at it."

They were alone in the room. Shel got up, circled the table a few times, and went back out into the main library area. He stood admiring the art, observing the visitors, and trying not to look out of place. Sixty or so people were scattered around the tables and visible in the side rooms. A couple of elderly men near a rear entrance argued quietly about something. Two gray-haired women and a girl who was about sixteen were seated in modern-looking armchairs, all absorbed in their reading. (It was an odd thing: Shel had always thought of the ancient world the way Hollywood portrayed it: a place inhabited by warriors, elderly philosophers, and maidens who need rescuing. Somehow, older women had been missing, and he'd never visualized teens in armchairs.)

A middle-aged man carried a scroll to the desk. The librarian made a note, they spoke briefly, and the man turned and left. The librarian carried the scroll into the back room.

Eventually, Shel went back and sat beside Dave. "I'm working on it," Dave said, without looking up. "It's Achilles trying to make peace at Troy."

"Okay."

"After Hector's death."

Shel cleared his throat.

"What?" said Dave.

"Why don't we read the rest of it at home?"

"Oh. Sure. Okay."

Shel handed him the gooseberry, which combined an imager, a telephone, a flashlight, a game player, and a recording and storage device. Dave went back to the beginning of the scroll.

"Here," said Shel, "let me hold it flat."

Dave raised the lid of the device, the red power lamp blinked on, and the screen brightened. A half dozen icons flashed across the screen, and finally the words, *Ready to go, big guy.* He activated the imager and started to record.

They took three pictures of each section, just to be safe. Explanations might be awkward, so they both kept an eye on the doorway in case someone came in. When they'd finished, they took *Achilles* back to the desk and returned it to the librarian.

"That was quick," he said.

Dave nodded. "We were just doing some research."

"I see. Do you teach literature?"

"Theater."

"Excellent. It's good to know there are still dedicated people out there. Kids today need all the help they can get. Nobody asked me, but I think the world is going downhill." He shook his head sadly. "How do you like our library?"

"Asyngrito," said Shel, showing off his skills. *Unequaled. Without parallel.* "You'd never guess how much," he said in English.

The librarian smiled. Said something Shel didn't catch. Looked amused.

Dave checked his notes. "Might we see *Odysseus in Ithaca*?"

"Yes. Of course."

"Why don't we try to move it along," said Shel in English.

Dave nodded. "There are also two *Tyro* plays, *Tyro Shorn* and *Tyro Rediscovered.* Could you get them for us, too?"

The librarian gave them a pained expression. "You want *three* books at the same time?"

"Yes. If that's feasible."

"I'm sorry, but it's against the rules. Unless you are a member of the Benefactors' Society. I'm not aware that either of you is a member."

"No. Unfortunately not."

"Then I'm sorry, but you're limited to two."

Shel decided it was as much a security measure as a means to collect contributions. The scrolls were all copied by hand and must have been immensely valuable. And the situation would not have been helped by the fact that everybody wore togas.

"Okay," Dave said. "We'll take the *Odysseus* and the first *Tyro.*"

"Certainly. One minute, please."

When he'd retreated in back, Shel asked why the librarian had seemed amused when he'd described the library as matchless.

"You used the wrong ending for the adjective. *Asyngrito* is modern Greek. The classic version would have put an 's' at the end."

"Oh. So what did he say?"

" 'Not bad for a barbarian.' "

"What?" Shel looked toward the door behind the counter. "That little nitwit."

"Actually, it was a compliment, Shel."

ODYSSEUS in *Ithaca* was set after the Trojan War, when the hero had returned home. He is an old man by then. One night, while walking on the beach, he meets a stranger. It is his son, Telemachus, come to find his celebrated father. But they do not recognize each other. And because both possess an inclination to deceive for amusement, or out of habit, they quickly find themselves at odds after a misunderstanding. Ultimately, challenges are issued. Combat ensues. Telemachus finds the spine of a sea beast that has washed ashore and uses it to kill his father. Then he discovers the identity of the victim.

"Sophocles wasn't strong on comedy, was he?" said Shel.

"No. He's not exactly light reading."

They recorded both plays and returned them to the desk. Next, they checked out *Theseus* and *Circe*. Then *Parnassus* and *The Hawks*. They were getting ready to return *Troilus* and

Eurydice when the librarian came into the room. "The director is free now. If you'll follow me, I'll—"

"No need, Ajax," said a second voice. It belonged to a tall man who appeared outside the door. "Sorry to keep you waiting, gentlemen. What can I do for you?"

"You are Aristarchus?" asked Dave.

He was. Dave introduced Shel, said how honored they were to meet him, how they'd heard of him in their homeland, which was very distant. "You have a marvelous collection," he added.

The director tried to wave it off. "I'm just the librarian," he said. "But you're very kind." He had a sharp nose and narrow features, but he looked congenial, and Shel got the impression he'd have been right at home in Philadelphia.

"We've come a long way to find Shel's father," Dave said. "We know that he was an admirer of yours and of the Library. He was a world traveler, but he's disappeared."

At a signal, Ajax collected the two plays and withdrew, closing the door behind him.

"I'm sorry to hear it," said Aristarchus. "I hope no harm has come to him."

"As do we. In any case, there's a possibility he would have come to the Library to speak with you."

"What was his name, Davidius?"

"Shelborne. Michael Shelborne."

"Interesting name. It would be difficult to forget. But I'm sorry to say, I have no recollection of such a person."

"May I show you his image?"

Aristarchus frowned. "You have brought his portrait with you?"

"Yes." Shel produced four photos of his father. Two in business suits, one casual, one in a lab coat. The director's eyes widened. "What *are* these?" he asked.

"Photos, sir. It's a new technology. I don't think Alexandria has it yet."

"No. I should say not. But yes, I *have* met this man."

"Can you tell us when?"

Aristarchus cleared his throat. Tried to remember. "He

was only here briefly. And I wouldn't remember him, I don't think, except for his strange accent. Like yours."

"I see."

"Yes. He was very interested in the Library." He smiled at the memory. "Of course, everyone is. But Michael insisted on taking us out to celebrate. Me and half the staff."

"To celebrate what?"

"I never really understood that part of it. The completion of a journey, I believe. It was something like that."

"Can you give us a general idea when he was here?"

"Oh, it's been two or three years. At least. I'm not sure."

"Do you think any of your colleagues might remember?"

"Come upstairs with me, and we'll ask."

NOBODY knew definitely. Two years ago last summer, I think, said one of the staff. No, another insisted, it was shortly after my brother died, four years ago this fall. In the end, they could not narrow it down enough to be of any use.

Aristarchus expressed his regrets. Then asked a question of his own. "Ajax did not understand why you had checked out several books, returned them promptly, and apparently planned to check out the entire works of Sophocles. During the course of the afternoon."

"We were doing research," said Dave.

"So I understand. Nevertheless, in perhaps an excess of caution, he notified his supervisor. The supervisor saw something odd. And he notified me."

"Odd? In what way?"

Shel thought he already knew.

"Gentlemen, I saw something I cannot explain. Rather like your, uh, photos."

Dave played it straight. "And what might that be, sir?"

"You have a metal object of some sort."

"I beg your pardon?"

"It produces light. I wonder if you would be so kind as to show it to me."

Dave translated for Shel. Shel nodded. "Show him."

Dave produced the gooseberry. "You probably saw a reflection," he said.

"Perhaps. May I ask what it is? And what you and your associate were doing with our books?"

The tone did not sound threatening. Merely curious. "We've done no harm," said Dave.

"I did not mean to suggest you had. I would simply like to know who you are. And what has been happening."

"My name is Davidius. This is Shelborne. We are visiting scholars."

"I know what you have said. There is no need to repeat it." He held out his hand for the gooseberry. "May I see it, please?"

Dave gave it to him. "Be careful with it," he said.

Aristarchus examined it. Ran his fingers along the sides. "It's very smooth. Is this actually metal?"

"Plastic." Dave used the English word. He didn't know a Greek equivalent.

"What is 'plastic'?"

"It's—" He cleared his throat. "It's hard to explain. It's like metal. But more pliable."

"I see." He found the lid. Opened it. The screen lit up, and the red power lamp came on. Aristarchus almost dropped it. But he hung on. Icons appeared, one by one. Then the voice, volume turned to a whisper, in English: *"Ready to go, big guy."*

It might as well have been a cannon blast.

Aristarchus flipped the gooseberry into the air. Dave, who was ready, caught it on the fly.

"It speaks," said Aristarchus. His voice had gone up an octave.

"There's an explanation," said Dave.

Aristarchus stared at it. "I'm sure there is."

Dave looked to Shel, and Shel studied the ceiling.

"The supervisor," said Aristarchus, "thinks you are messengers from the gods. I am almost persuaded he is correct. What language is it speaking?"

"It's English."

"I'm not familiar with it. But I suppose that is of no consequence. *How* does it speak? Who lives within?"

"I can explain."

"Please do."

"No one is inside. It is advanced technology."

"Really? You can produce light in a piece of metal? Plastic? Whatever you call it?"

"Yes."

"And this thing *speaks*?"

"Yes."

"What did it say?"

"It said it was ready to operate."

"And when it operates, precisely what does it do?"

Dave turned to Shel. "I can't see any harm in showing him."

"Go ahead," said Shel.

He brought up the *Achilles* and held it so Aristarchus could see. The sun was shining through a skylight. The director shielded his eyes and watched the pages flicker past. "The entire play is contained in this thing?"

"All of the plays we looked at today."

"Incredible. It produces a better product than an army of scribes."

"Yes."

"Where did you get it?"

"It was built. At home."

"Clovian tells me that is a place called Philadelphia?"

"Yes."

"I would very much like to visit this *Philadelphia*."

"It is very far, sir."

"I'm sure. Though I have never heard of it, it is clearly the capital of the world." Aristarchus held out his hand for the gooseberry.

Dave hesitated. Then, once again, gave him the device.

He examined it. Turned it over. Held it up to a window. Raised the lid again and watched the lights come on. "I would like to buy it." He closed the lid and laid the gooseberry on the table. "Will you sell it?"

"I'm sorry. We cannot."

"We would offer a very generous price. Perhaps you could even get more of these?"

"I wish we could, Aristarchus. But it is impossible."

"May I ask why?"

"Distance," he said. "It is very hard to reach Philadelphia from here."

"I see." His lips tightened. "Davidius, I cannot in good conscience allow you to leave with this instrument. I don't know yet what use we would make of it, but it is a matter we would wish to explore." He leaned forward, and those intense eyes swung to Shel. He understood who would make the decision. "I prefer," he said quietly, "to let reason prevail."

While Shel considered his answer, the director got up, walked to the door, and opened it. One man came into the room. Another took station directly in the doorway. "Perhaps," he continued, "you would be willing to let us retain this for a time. So that we may unravel the technology. Perhaps manufacture some of our own. Again, we would pay generously for the privilege."

"I would not wish to insult you, Aristarchus, but please believe me that your best technical people would not be able to duplicate this."

"I fear I must insist." The librarian picked up the gooseberry. And inserted it into his robe.

The guards moved closer.

Dave went back to English: "Time to go home," he said.

"Good idea," said Shel. "Do it, but don't make any sudden moves."

Dave nodded. Reached casually into his toga. One of the guards, who was almost as tall as Dave, and considerably beefier, frowned and came a step closer.

Dave pulled out the converter. All eyes locked on it. He looked at Shel, who hadn't moved. "We going to do this on a count of three?"

"You go."

"Me? What are you—?"

"A demonstration. I'll be there when you get there."

"English again?" asked Aristarchus.

"Yes," said Dave. He turned back to Shel. "And if you're not there?"

"Don't come back."

"Shel—?"

"Just go."

"You can't even speak the language."

"I've got enough to get by."

Dave shook his head and lifted the lid. "This is crazy, Shel," he said. Then he pushed the black button, shimmered briefly, and was gone. The guards whooped and fell back, while the director tightened his hold on a chair but otherwise remained firm.

"Who are you?" he asked. His voice was barely audible.

Shel spoke slowly. He had to, picking his words from a limited vocabulary: "A traveler. I mean no harm."

"I am glad to hear it. Why are you here?"

"It would be helpful if you dismissed your aides."

But he didn't understand what Shel was saying. "My Greek is not good," Shel said. He repeated his request, speaking slowly, enunciating carefully.

"Oh. Yes," said Aristarchus. He directed the guards to go. They surprised him by refusing to abandon him to what must have seemed a demon.

"I must insist," said Shel. "What I have to say is for you only."

Aristarchus repeated his directive. Reluctantly, the guards left. When they were gone, Shel produced his converter and showed it to Aristarchus. "If we had wanted to create a problem," he said, "surely you realize no one here could have stopped us."

Aristarchus repeated his question: "Who are you?"

"A friend of the Library."

"Why are you here?"

"As we told you, to find my father."

"You *are* human."

"Yes." He paused. Took a deep breath. "When we said we were travelers from a distant place, we were telling you the literal truth."

Aristarchus gathered his robe around him. "The world is wide," he said. "I suspect it is about to get wider."

Shel nodded. "We travel in both space *and* time."

"Explain, please."

"We come from another *era*. We come from an age when the glory of Hellas and Rome are still admired. But they have been gone a long time."

"You come from a time that has not yet happened? Is that what you're saying?"

"Yes."

"After what I've seen today, Shelborne, I am prepared to believe almost anything."

"Then know that, in my time, the Library, *your* library, is also gone."

His eyes closed briefly. "What happened to it?"

"No one is sure. But it persisted a long time."

"What about the books?"

"A majority of them will be lost also."

"Diana help us."

"We will not even have a good accounting of what was here. Only that it was the pride of the ancient world."

His head sagged.

"Aristarchus, your name will survive."

"That's not much consolation." His eyes lost their focus. For a long time neither spoke. Shel became aware of the rumble of the sea. "That is the *real* reason you have come."

"It is one reason. I had hoped to find my father."

"And to reclaim what is here."

"We reclaimed a little of it today."

"Is this the first time you've been here?"

"It is."

He allowed himself a pained smile and reached into his toga for the gooseberry. He put it on the table in front of Shel. "You looked at nine books today."

"Yes."

"Nine books," he said again. "We have half a million."

"Fortunately, some books survived. From other sources. Others, perhaps, have lost their utility."

"You were planning to come again?"

The answer to that, a few minutes ago, would have been *no*. But something had changed. "Yes."

"I will alert my staff. When you return—"

"No. Don't tell them about me."

"Why not?"

"I ask it as a favor. I'm probably in violation of my father's code even now. By telling you as much as I have."

"All right. I suppose I can understand that. But when you come again, let us know, let *me* know, and I will see that you get everything you need." He stood. "Shelborne, I am more indebted to you than I can say. We *all* are."

Shel was missing some of what he said. But the general thrust was obvious enough. "Then we help each other."

"Yes." He paused. "I am almost afraid to ask my next question."

Shel waited.

"How far have you come?"

"More than two thousand years."

"At least the disaster is not imminent." His eyes narrowed. "It *isn't* imminent, is it?"

"No. The Library has a long life ahead of it."

"Good. Thank you." He lowered himself into a chair. "What is your world like?"

"How do you mean?"

"Do people live in harmony?"

"Some do."

"Have you maintained the rule of law?"

"Yes."

He saw something in Shel's face and frowned. "Maybe I should stop while I still like your answers."

CHAPTER 19

I have drunken deep of joy,
And I will taste no other wine tonight.
                    —PERCY BYSSHE SHELLEY, *THE CENCI*

IT was, Aspasia knew, another manuscript. But this one came in a plain manila envelope with no return address. The date stamp indicated it had been mailed in Levittown, Pennsylvania. First class.

Since she'd won the Athena Andreadis Award for scholarship in classical literature, she'd been awash in manuscripts by people who thought she could help them get published somewhere. Usually, they were Greek family histories of no interest to anyone, but there had been two or three academic gambits of interest. The manuscripts arrived regularly. Sometimes they were book-length, with the writer unable to understand why the Oxford University Press had not gobbled it up. Others were commentaries intended for *Classical Heritage* or *Hellenic* or *Greek Life*.

They usually came online. But not always. And there was a tendency among those who used the post office to neglect sending self-addressed stamped envelopes. With the current cost of postage, sending them back was expensive. But

Aspasia had never been able to bring herself simply to dump the manuscripts.

She put this one aside, with a couple of bills, and opened the more interesting mail first. A note had arrived from Kingsley Black informing her that his classical literature class had profited from *Showtime at Rhodes*, her analysis of the reasons for the decline of classical drama. *"Excellent book,"* he concluded. *"Best I've seen on the subject."* Well, of course, he *would* say that, but she *had* broken new ground. *Showtime at Rhodes* had been the principal reason she'd won the Andreadis.

Two or three letters took issue with her conclusions, and one quibbled with the dates of two of Aeschylus's plays. As if it mattered.

Penguin Group wanted a blurb for a Margaret Seaborn book on Archimedes. That would be an easy assignment: Seaborn was always reliable. And the University of Kansas wanted her to speak at their graduation next year.

Eventually, she worked her way back to the manila envelope, which was sealed with tape. It wasn't *too* heavy. Not book-length, at least. She couldn't find her letter opener—Aspasia was not good at putting things back where they belonged—and eventually she had to get a knife from the kitchen.

The envelope did indeed contain a manuscript, but it was in *Greek*. Classical Greek. And the title startled her: *Achilles*. By Sophocles.

Someone's idea of a joke.

There was an accompanying note. Hand-printed.

Jan 26, 2019

Dear Dr. Kephalas:

We have other ancient manuscripts as well. If you'd like to see more, post an English translation of this one at your Web site. If there's no response within thirty days, we'll take what we have elsewhere.

No signature.

There was nothing else.

It was, of course, a hoax. And what a pity. Tempting her with one of the lost plays. If only—

She looked at the list of characters. There were five: Achilles, the priest Trainor, Polyxena, Paris, and Apollo. And, naturally, a chorus.

She dropped the note and the manuscript into the trash.

ASPASIA had an afternoon class. It would require some preparation, and she also had to meet with one of her graduate students. A stack of essays waited in a bookcase.

She sighed, retrieved them, and started on the first one. It was an analysis of *The Odyssey*. The student was trying to show it had been created by a woman. And, in any case, by someone other than the author of *The Iliad*. Nothing new there.

The second was a commentary on the development of the epic. Its Bronze Age beginnings. Its popularity in the preliterate world. A third essay listed the author's suggestions for six additional epics to complete the Trojan cycle. Paris makes off with Helen. Agamemnon rallies the troops but has to sacrifice his daughter. And so on.

She wondered if the lost epics had been as powerful as the two that had survived. Most experts thought not. If they'd been lost, the reasoning went, it was because they deserved to be lost.

Nonsense.

How nice it would be to find one of the other works in the cycle. Perhaps stashed in a trunk in an attic in Athens. Or maybe it would come in the mail.

Like Sophocles.

The trash can stood beside the computer table. She looked at it. Allowed her irritation free rein. That someone would play this kind of joke.

She fished the manuscript out.

By Sophocles.

Scene one was set in the chapel of Apollo.

The chapel would have been located outside the walls of Troy so that soldiers from both sides could worship there. One version of the story maintained that Achilles had violated the chapel by killing the young Troilus within its walls.

In the play, it is early evening, and Achilles stands with the Greek priest Trainor just outside the chapel door, reluctant to enter because of his crime, wishing there were a way to appease the god, when he sees the beautiful Polyxena. "Who is she?" he asks Trainor.

"The daughter of Priam," he replies. "She comes here every evening now. To pray for an end to the conflict."

Achilles remarks that those prayers are probably in vain. But, in the manner of classical drama, he is hopelessly in love with Polyxena from the first moment. When he approaches her, however, she asks, "Are you not Achilles, destroyer of my people?"

It's not a good start for a romance. But the hero is smitten with her. And of course no one could accuse Achilles of being shy. In a moving scene on the edge of the Trojan plain, he wins her love.

Polyxena sees an opportunity to use her influence with him to stop the war. But she blunders by taking her brother Paris into her confidence. And Paris sees an opportunity to take Achilles out of play. "I must talk with him," says Paris. "Can you have him meet me in the chapel?"

Polyxena assures him she can manage it. When she exits, Paris looks out at the audience. "I would not betray my sister. Nor strike from the dark, which is a coward's way. Yet it is the only way to bring him down. The Acheans without Achilles would be hawks without talons. They would still bite, but they would draw no blood." It is a heartbreaking decision.

Aspasia's heart was picking up. It might not be Sophocles, but it was surprisingly good.

Achilles is also weary of the unending war. But he does not trust Paris. "It is the will of the gods," says Trainor, who shares the general impatience with the fighting. "They have provided a path whereby you might win back the favor of Apollo."

Ultimately, Achilles accedes to the rendezvous and enters the chapel. Paris is waiting in the shadows with his bow. And Apollo guides the arrow. Polyxena collapses over the dying Achilles, rages against her brother's betrayal, and brandishes a dagger. She cradles her lover's now-lifeless body and raises the weapon. "Let us go together from this dark place," she tells him.

Paris, seeing what she is about to do, pleads with her, but she cannot be appeased. She plunges the dagger into her breast and, within moments, Paris follows her lead.

The narrative, and the staging of the action, is very much in Sophocles' mode. And the language is classical Greek. Aspasia doubted there were three or four people in the United States who could have gotten the details right. Someone had gone to a lot of trouble.

SHE called Miles Greenberg, who taught programming. He was an easygoing guy, recently divorced, lonely, but glad to be out of a marriage that had never worked. "Got a problem, Miles."

"What do you need, Aspasia?"

"I have a copy of a play that someone claims was written by Sophocles. Is there some software that can do an analysis?"

"Of Sophocles?"

"Yes."

"Who's making the claim?"

"Don't know. It's anonymous."

"And you want to do what? Determine whether it might be authentic?"

"Yes."

"You can't tell by reading it?"

"No. It's not an obvious forgery."

"Aspasia, it has to be a fake, doesn't it?"

"Probably."

"So it's in Greek, right?"

"Of course."

"A number of years ago, when they were trying to decide who really wrote Shakespeare, somebody developed a package."

"For Shakespeare."

"Yes. I don't know what it looked like. But it would have ana-
lyzed the way he used various word combinations. And it would
have looked at sentence lengths. And probably the way he punc-
tuated. And other kinds of patterns. Like how many clauses did
he use? And under what circumstances? I could track down the
package, probably. But then we'd have to adapt it for Greek.
Then let it do an analysis of how Sophocles writes."

"Okay."

"How many of his plays do we have?"

"Seven."

"All right. Maybe it'll be enough. I'll get back to you."

She was due at school and reluctantly decided to put the
issue aside until evening. It is, she told herself, a fake. Don't
get your hopes up. If it weren't, why on earth would they have
sent it anonymously?

At the end of the day, she got tied up in a faculty meeting.
Consequently, it was almost dark before she got home. She
came in the door, the place lit up, and she dropped her bag
on the nearest chair. She had a message waiting from Miles:
"Aspasia, I have the software. Call me when you can."

IT was Miles's busy season, so it was almost a week before
they could get together. For Aspasia, it was a difficult time.
She read and reread the *Achilles*. And yes, it *did* have the
power of Sophoclean drama, the classic confrontation in
which the moral course is unclear, and any decision might
easily prove lethal.

She wanted this to be what it pretended to be. If she actually held in her hands one of the lost plays, it would give her
life a level of meaning for which she could never have hoped.
And because she so desperately wanted it to be true, she knew
she could not manage an objective judgment.

The reality was that she could probably have produced a
play of this calibre herself. All that was needed was a command of the language and a familiarity with classical dra-
matic technique. One could not read a work of literature and

safely assign greatness to it. That was something that came only with time. With the approbation of generations. All she knew at this point was that the play *touched* her, that it struck her sensibilities as *Antigone* had, and *Oedipus at Colonus*.

She told herself to relax and tried to forget the manuscript. She made no effort to do an English translation. That would mean she was taking it seriously, and only an idiot would do that.

Still, emotionally, she moved into that nondescript chapel outside the Trojan wall. She saw it as it would have been, had it existed at all: a modest stone structure with a statue of Apollo near the altar, the whole illuminated by a series of flickering candles or oil lamps. A handful of worshippers would be kneeling before the god, heads bent, praying that they might return from the endless conflict to their families. And in back, hidden among the shadows, would be Paris, waiting with that notched arrow.

Finally, Miles showed up with the software. It was called Reading the Syntax. It wasn't the original Shakespearean program, but something more recent that was being used in classrooms in an effort to help students become creative writers. It analyzed *their* work. "But," he said, "I can't see that it won't be just as effective. And we can adjust it for classical Greek."

Miles was in his thirties, with dark hair and good features. His eyebrows were always raised, giving him a permanently surprised look. He was endlessly enthusiastic about computers and, given the least encouragement, would talk endlessly about the latest technological achievement.

Aspasia had already scanned the seven extant plays into the computer. Miles sat down and loaded the software. Then he asked some questions about Greek verbs and sentence structure and relative pronouns and so on. He entered her responses, directed it to compare the *Achilles* to the other seven, and to establish a degree of likelihood that all eight came from the same author. He looked up at her, said "Good luck," and clicked on START. "Shouldn't take long," he said.

The system hummed and beeped for a minute or so. Then it provided a few bars of Rachmaninoff, signifying that the process was complete.

PROBABILITY ONE AUTHOR: 87%

"There you go," said Miles.

Oh God, let it be so. "But, if I were trying to imitate Sophocles, I bet I could produce a strong similarity, too."

"Maybe," said Miles. "I don't know. Not my area of expertise."

Yeah. How do you measure genius?

She looked again at the letter that had accompanied the manuscript: *If you'd like to see more…*

What else did they have?

After Miles left, she began translating *Achilles* into English.

FOUR days after she'd posted the translation, another package arrived. Again, with no return address. This one mailed from Cherry Hill, New Jersey. She had the letter opener ready this time.

LEONIDAS
by
Sophocles

Again, it was accompanied by an unsigned note:

February 11

Dear Dr. Kephalas:

Are you convinced?

She turned the manuscript over to Reading the Syntax, which produced almost the same result. PROBABILITY ONE AUTHOR: 86%.

She went to her Web site. Up front, page one: Leonidas *received. Who are you?*

She sat over the computer until well into the evening. She skipped dinner, read the play, which was not about the battle of Thermopylae, but about the Spartan negligence and delay that had preceded it. That had made it necessary to sacrifice three hundred Spartans and their Thespian and Theban allies.

Sparta had known for a long time that Persia constituted a major threat. But their rulers had not taken it seriously. They'd ignored all evidence that disagreed with their conviction that Xerxes was a coward. That he would not dare attack. Leonidas, despite his exalted position, was unable to move the bureaucrats who effectively ran the country. Even when the threat finally materialized, when the Athenians brought their warnings that the Persians were marching, a religious festival was going on, and they could not react. Dared not offend the gods. Ultimately, the decision was made to send the small force to hold the pass at Thermopylae. Just hold on until the celebration is over.

The climax depicts an outraged Leonidas buckling on his sword and inviting his colleagues to share in the bloodletting their indolence was about to cause. Nobody makes a move.

SEVERAL hours after she'd posted her question at the Web site, an answer of sorts was returned:

> *We have seven more Sophoclean plays.*
> Who are you?
> *If we gave you access to the plays, what would you do with them?*
> Give them to the world, of course. Make them available to any who want them.
> *Do you want them?*
> Of course. Do you really have seven more?
> *Yes.*
> Where did you get them?
> *That's of no consequence.*
> How can you say that? It's essential information.
> *It's of no consequence.*
> What's in it for you?

*You ask a lot of questions. We'll start by sending you two
more. After we see what happens, we'll decide what to
do next.*

THE Homeric Society, consisting of approximately four hundred classical scholars, was concentrated across the Western
world. But it had a scattering of members in Japan and China,
in Africa, and in the Middle East. Two days after Aspasia's
conversation with her mysterious benefactors, each member
received, as an e-mail attachment, copies of the *Achilles* and
the *Leonidas.*

A claim has been advanced for the validity of these plays,
Aspasia's note read. *I am interested in your opinion.*

Dave was among the scholars receiving the documents. He
showed the package to Shel, who glanced over it approvingly.
"I guess you were right about her," he said.

"I've known Aspasia a long time, Shel. She's cautious, but
she's very good."

CHAPTER 20

Do not think of life as a matter of consequence. Rather, look at the vast voids of the years to come and the years that are past, and recall that your hours are few.

—MARCUS AURELIUS, *MEDITATIONS*

"SO he went to Alexandria," said Shel.

"Who knows," said Dave, "how many places he might have gone to that night?" He was trying to be encouraging. Maybe, somewhere, they could still find him.

Shel could think of other sites, events, people that would have interested his father. The elder Shelborne had read Carl Sandburg's biography of Lincoln while Shel was in high school, and had left the volume in conspicuous places around the house to encourage his son to pick it up. Shel had, and he'd read pieces of it, but Lincoln was too far away, and it was too much for him at a time when his primary interests were girls and baseball.

But it suggested a strategy. It was, in any case, all he had. He and Dave subsequently began showing up at the Lincoln-Douglas debates. They attended the first one, in Ottawa, Illinois, on August 21, 1858, and each of the other six, which concluded in Alton, October 15, of that same year. Douglas pleaded for an America that would be "the north star that shall guide the friends of freedom," and that it would do this by maintaining slavery within its borders.

"I'd love to ask the son of a bitch a few questions," said Dave.

"I'm sure you would," Shel said. "But I thought Mr. Lincoln managed a reasonable response."

In the end, of course, the voters elected Douglas. And if Shel's father showed up, they never saw him.

AFTER Lincoln-Douglas, they needed something light, something that came with a party. Consequently, they went to New York on August 15, 1945, V-J Day, where they joined the end-of-war celebration. (Shel had suggested they don military uniforms for the event, but Dave refused. "No. That's more or less what we did at Selma." Shel was offended, but he gave in.)

Unsure how to continue the search, they drifted. They went to concerts by the Kingston Trio. They attended festivals in classical Athens, enthusiastically celebrating the rites of spring, watching the annual petition to Athena, and attending performances of plays not seen in two thousand years.

They were giddy times.

And there were more serious moments. On January 10, 49 B.C., when Caesar and his army crossed the Rubicon, Shel and Dave sat in a boat, apparently fishing in the middle of the river. "He never came," said Dave, as the army ferried itself across.

"Who never came? Dad?"

"According to the story, Caesar wasn't sure he wanted to go through with this, so he hesitated at the river's edge until a god showed up and directed him to cross."

"You didn't actually think it would happen that way?"

"No. But I was tempted to play the role of the deity." He grinned at Shel's shocked reaction. "Just kidding."

They joined the crowd on the mall for the "I Have a Dream" speech. In August 1944, they were in Paris when the Allies arrived.

* * *

MICHAEL Shelborne had liked Charles Lamb. So they went to London in the spring of 1820, planning to meet the celebrated essayist. But they arrived outside the city and were almost immediately accosted by highwaymen. It was broad daylight, but it didn't seem to matter. The bandits laughed while inviting them to empty their pockets. Dave and Shel shrugged, said good-bye, and returned to the town house.

They tried again, after resetting the converters to get closer to London. They arrived during early evening, having allowed time for Lamb to get home from his job clerking for India House. They got lucky this time, and stepped out into Covent Garden, only a few blocks from his home on Russell Street. They picked up a bottle of wine en route, and presented themselves at the front door as admirers of Lamb's work. At that point, though Lamb was in his forties, the great essayist had written little of note.

"We're reviving the *London Magazine* next year, Mr. Lamb," Shel told him. "We'd like very much to have some of your time, if you don't mind."

"Of course, gentlemen," he said. "Please come in." Lamb was thin, about average height, with an easy smile. He led them back to a sitting room, where a middle-aged woman was reading.

They did a round of introductions. The woman was Mary Lamb, who had murdered her mother twenty years earlier in one of her occasional bouts of insanity. Fortunately, at the moment she seemed fine. She was not unattractive, although there was a stolidity in her features that suggested she wasn't especially flexible.

The sitting room looked out onto Russell Street, where several children were playing with a ball. Framed pictures of people Shel couldn't identify hung on the walls. Bulging bookcases stood on opposite sides of the room. A newspaper was spread out across a coffee table in front of a sofa where Lamb had apparently been seated.

"The first issue," said Shel, "will be out in July. We'd like very much to have an essay from you, if you'd be so kind."

"An essay? Mr. Shelborne, I don't want to disappoint you, but I haven't written anything for twelve or thirteen years. Why would you come to me?"

"Trust me, Charles. May I call you *Charles*?"

"Of course."

"All right, Charles." Shel glanced over at David as he said it. He'd toyed with the idea of trying *Charlie*. "Perhaps you know my father, Michael? He has always been quite enthusiastic about your work."

"Michael Shelborne?" Lamb considered it. Shook his head. "I don't know the gentleman."

"Let me show you a picture." Shel produced the usual photo.

Lamb reacted much as Aristarchus had. But no, he had no recollection of the man.

"In any case," said Shel, trying not to show his frustration, "we've looked at your *Tales of Shakespeare*. And at the *Works of Charles Lamb*."

"And you liked them?"

"Of course. We'd like you to write essays for us. On a regular basis."

"Are you serious, sir?"

"Of course I am."

"If I may ask, I'm not familiar with your name. Will you be the editor?"

"I'm financing the project. Behind the scenes, you understand. My name won't appear anywhere." Shel told him who the editor would be.

"I see." Lamb grew thoughtful. A suspicious look passed between him and Mary.

"Listen," said Shel. "I'd be doubtful, too. But what have you to lose? All I ask is that you send us an essay. Find out whether I'm serious."

Everybody's mood lightened. Shel asked whether he and David might take the Lambs out for dinner. "To celebrate."

"I'd like to, very much," he said. "But we have friends coming this evening."

Mary looked at Shel. "Perhaps," she said, "if it's convenient, Mr. Shelborne and his associate might like to join us next week."

"We'd be delighted," said Dave.

Lamb smiled. "Sam will be here Wednesday. He would enjoy meeting you."

SAM turned out to be Charles's longtime friend Samuel Taylor Coleridge. He was something of a comedian, a quality Shel would never have guessed from his written work. Not that he'd read much of it. He had a hearty laugh, and he commented that Shel's interest in Charles demonstrated his impeccable taste. "The truth is," he said, "I've been trying for years to persuade him to move in my direction, to switch over to poetry, where the big money is."

That brought a hearty laugh. And Lamb corrected him: "*Romantic* poetry." Even Mary thought that was funny.

"With Byron and Shelley running loose out there," said Coleridge, "God knows we need all the help we can get. By the way, has anyone here read *Frankenstein*?"

"I have," said Mary.

"What did you think?"

"I saw some resemblances to 'The Ancient Mariner.' In fact, I'm not sure it wasn't an homage to you."

"Really?"

"Do you *know* Mary Shelley?" asked Dave.

"Oh, yes." Coleridge lit up. "She's a talented young woman." He glanced at Lamb for confirmation.

"Haven't read it," he said. "But yes, she is."

Coleridge admitted the book was occasionally slow going. "She could have picked up the pacing a bit, though I'm sure she'll figure that out for herself. But I liked the notion of an artificial man with a taste for Milton. Mary has an exquisite sense of humor."

* * *

MICHAEL had been a baseball fan. On a hunch, they showed up at Wrigley Field on August 25, 1922, to watch the Cubs beat the Phillies 26–23, in the highest-scoring major-league game ever. And they went to Berlin for Jack Kennedy's celebrated "*Ich bin ein Berliner*" address. Finding anyone in either of those crowds was, of course, out of the question. But Shel was enjoying himself. There was an especially moving aspect to sitting in on an event armed with a historical perspective. As to finding his father, he was close to giving up.

"You know what's really painful?" he said, moments after they'd returned from Berlin.

"That your father probably didn't have time to do much of what we've been doing?"

"It goes deeper than that, Dave. Truth is, I don't know how many places he visited. But what strikes me is, we're getting a kind of godlike view of the world."

Dave nodded.

"We stood out there today, listening to Kennedy, and we know what's coming. We know the Cold War will end, that everything will turn out okay in Europe. And we know that in five months, Kennedy will be dead."

"Yeah."

"The whole time we were listening to him, that was what kept running through my head. That he was going to be taken out by that nutcase in Dallas, and nobody would ever even know why."

"I know. I thought about that, too."

"When we were watching Lincoln, it was the same thing. And King. I don't like knowing what's coming."

Dave unclipped the converter and sat down.

Shel's eyes lost their focus. "I hate that part of this."

"I saw a movie once."

"Yeah?"

"It was called *TimeQuest*. A time traveler goes back and does what you're talking about: He warns JFK."

"How does it turn out?"

"A lot better. We stay out of Vietnam. We get Moonbase. King survives and becomes the first black president. Kennedy dies peacefully fifty years later in his bed at Hyannisport."

"I wish we could arrange something like that."

"So do I. But we're talking about the ultimate hubris now. I suggest we keep our hands off."

DAVE'S classes at Penn had become impossible. Getting through the days talking about Greek pronouns and Latin verbs was overwhelming him. He wanted to tell his classes that he'd been to the Library at Alexandria. And to Selma. Tell them he was planning to go to classical Athens that weekend to see *Prometheus Bound*.

He ached to go down to the next English Department meeting and describe his conversations with Lamb and Coleridge. That maybe, if he was in the mood, he'd wander over to Oxford this evening and have tea with A. E. Housman.

"Life has become better than I'd ever dreamed possible," he told Shel one evening at the Wan Ho Chinese Restaurant. "The only downside is that we haven't been able to find your father. And that we can't tell anybody about what we're doing."

"I know, Dave."

"We should write a book."

"I've been doing something like that."

"What?"

"I've been keeping a journal. Everything's in there, pictures, recordings, my reactions. Everything."

"Really?"

"Yes."

"What are you going to do with it?"

"Probably nothing. It's for *me*." And, after a moment: "It seemed as if there should be *some* kind of record."

THEY went back to the Library, took Aristarchus to lunch, and recorded some more plays, mostly Sophocles and Euripides, and a substantial section of the Periclean journal. Aristarchus asked whether they'd found Michael. "It's hard to believe," he said, "that men with such godlike capabilities can't locate him."

They sent the Periclean material, and two more plays, *Troilus* and *The Hawks*, to Aspasia. She reacted by posting a message at her Web site, pleading with them to contact her.

That night Shel and Dave met in a restaurant in King of Prussia. Both were eating cheesesteaks when Shel said, quietly, "There's one more possibility we haven't tried."

"What's that?"

"Thomas Paine. My father has his collected works at home. Always thought he was really the guy who drove the Revolution."

He'd caught Dave in the perfect mood. "Tom Paine? Yes. Of all those guys at the beginning, *he's* the one I'd most like to meet."

"We could go down to Emilio's Saturday. Get some clothes."

PAINE had spent much of his time on the road, traveling with the army, and had been a frequent visitor at their camps. "We have a couple of dates when he was present at Valley Forge," said Shel. "That would be the right setting. The place to find him."

Dave frowned. "Bring a good jacket."

"Not a problem."

"Also not a good idea."

"You think they'd take us for British spies?"

"I think they'd take us for guys who don't belong in the camp. We'd be questioned and probably jailed. If we were lucky."

"What do you suggest?"

"Arrange the encounter to happen *after* the war."

"That takes all the passion out of it. Anyway, I think my father would have wanted to see him at the height of the action."

"Okay." Dave googled Paine. Flipped through the entries.

"Here's one," he said. "He was in Philadelphia in 1777. In September. Arranging for publication of *The American Crisis*. The Brits closed in, and he cleared out."

"Where'd he go?"

"He had a friend in Bordentown, New Jersey. Joseph Kirkbride. He went up there and stayed with him through the winter."

BORDENTOWN lay on the Delaware River, northeast of Philadelphia. Its population was small, but it was a hotbed of anti-British sentiment. Consequently, the British sent their Hessian mercenaries to seize the town in 1776.

Shel and Dave had no interest in landing in the middle of the fighting. Late 1777 seemed relatively safe. The British Army, by then, was still in the general neighborhood, but there was no record of action in the immediate area.

They arrived Saturday, September 21, at 10:30 A.M.

In someone's backyard. Dave found himself staring at a startled woman in a bridal gown. Her eyes had gone wide, and hysterical people were backing away. A guy who might have been a groom screamed. An older man in ceremonial garb seized a cross from a small table and thrust it in his face. A deep voice behind him growled that "It's exactly what happened over at Robbie's last week." Dave would have laughed had circumstances been a bit different. Absolutely, he thought, apparitions everywhere.

The cleric stepped forward, shielding the bride from whatever intentions Shel and Dave might have, and made the sign of the cross in the air. "Begone, Satan," he said. "In the name of the Lord, I command you, begone. Leave this place."

Footsteps were rushing up behind them. And Shel's voice: "Clear out, Dave."

"I say, *Leave, Spawn of the Devil.*"

Dave hit the button, and moments later he was collapsing in laughter on the sofa in the town house, waving at Shel, who was coming in across the room. In near hysteria.

When they'd calmed down, he said, "Think of the stories they'll have to tell their grandkids."

"Placement was perfect," said Dave, when he got a semblance of control over his voice. "We were right up front. I bet you couldn't do that again in a thousand years."

"He'd probably just asked whether anyone had a reason why this couple should not be joined in holy wedlock."

"Well, I've been called a lot of things—"

"All right. Shall we try again?"

"Sure. But let's move a little to the north. The other side of town."

Shel sat down with the converters. "I'll set them to arrive a week earlier this time. Just so we don't run into anybody who recognizes us." He handed Dave's unit back to him. "Ready?"

THEY were in a field. The ground was flat, with lots of grass. There were a silo and a barn, some trees, and a grazing horse. And, just past the barn, a farmhouse. In the distance they could see a river. That would be the Delaware.

A man carrying what looked like a hoe came out of the barn, saw them, and stopped to stare. "Bordentown should be south," said Shel, consulting his compass.

Before Dave could respond, a howl came from the direction of the barn. Two hounds raced out of the open doorway and charged. The guy with the hoe threw the implement aside, ran back into the barn, and emerged with a shotgun.

"Go," said Shel. "Clear out."

Dave pressed the button, watched the dogs fade into spectral light, and was glad to see the walls of Shel's den materialize. He waited for Shel.

And waited.

Shel should have appeared over by the armchair near the fireplace.

But he didn't.

CHAPTER 21

When I contemplate the natural dignity of man; when I feel (for Nature has not been kind enough to me to blunt my feelings) for the honour and happiness of its character, I become irritated at the attempt to govern mankind by force and fraud, as if they were all knaves and fools....

—THOMAS PAINE, *RIGHTS OF MAN*

IT'S hard to stay cool when two drooling hounds are coming after you. Shel should have simply stayed still and used the converter to leave. But he hadn't attached the instrument to his belt, still had it in his hands, which, ironically, was what he'd started doing after the incident with the highwaymen. If he were holding it, he'd reasoned, he could press the button in an eyeblink. Get out of there at a moment's notice. It had even been his advice to Dave.

The problem with having it in his hands was that it also made the device hostage to involuntary physical reactions. When the hounds showed up, Shel shrieked and flipped the device into the air.

He almost dived after it, but reflexes took over, and he froze. The dogs growled and snarled and dripped saliva and showed their teeth, but they didn't attack. The farmer, though, had seen Dave vanish, and he now stood watching Shel with a shotgun pointed at him but held in trembling hands.

"Don't shoot," said Shel, trying to look friendly.

He was in his twenties. A kid. Yellow hair, the beginnings of a beard, sallow skin, thin lips. He just stared, with his mouth hanging open.

"Sorry," Shel said. "I guess we—"

"What are you?" the kid asked.

"I'm just—"

"Where'd the other one go?"

Then Dave reappeared. First the aura, a silver glow—it was silver by daylight, gold in the dark—then a human form taking shape, growing solid. The kid swung the gun toward it while he stumbled backward. The radiance went away, and Dave stood there, Dave in all his glory, gawking at the weapon, carrying two pork chops from Shel's refrigerator.

The dogs went after him. Dave tossed them the meat, but they paid no attention. One sank its teeth into Dave's leg. He yelled and went down. And vanished again.

If the kid had been scared a moment before, his mental state now went to pieces. He screamed and fired a blast at a tree. "Look," said Shel. "I know this looks strange—"

"Keep your hands up." It was part screech. The weapon was a single-shot, and the kid was making no effort to reload, but the dogs were still there.

"Okay." Shel raised them as high as he could.

The kid kept raising the barrel of the shotgun, signaling *higher, higher.* At the same time, he begged Shel not to hurt him.

"I won't. I wouldn't hurt anyone. Look, my name's Shel—"

"Don't tell me your name." He was still backing away, eyes terrified. My God, at best, he was going to leave Shel with the hounds.

The converter was lying at the base of a tree. Too far away. He couldn't get to it before the dogs got to *him.*

The kid switched the weapon to his left hand and began crossing himself. He seemed unaware that the chamber was empty. The hounds kept making false lunges at Shel and licking their lips. The kid stumbled into a hole and juggled the weapon and finally went down.

Then he was on his knees, the weapon still aimed at Shel. "Hey," said Shel. "The dogs. Take the dogs with you."

"Yeah," said the kid. "Okay." Absolutely. Anything you want. "But you go away, right?"

"Yes. Sure. Absolutely. Won't come back."

"Oscar," he said. "Roamer. Come over here."

The dogs turned to look at him. Then turned their attention back to Shel.

"Over here," the kid said, as sternly as he could manage. Then somebody else came running. Out of the farmhouse. "Jake, what's going on?" He was a big guy, probably would have been as tall as Dave had he stood straight, but he hunched over. His face was full of wrinkles and whiskers.

"Dad, we got some kind of devil."

Dad was coming as fast as he could. "Just relax, Jake. Don't shoot him."

One of the hounds was sniffing at the converter.

Shel started to drop his arms, but the father told him to keep them in the air. "What's he doin' here?"

"Dad, there were two of them."

"Two? Where's the other one?"

"Don't know. He just went away. Disappeared."

The father surveyed the area. It was wide-open, except for a few scattered trees. "What are you talking about?"

"They come and go," Jake said. "The other one came back." His weapon was still trembling.

"You better give me that," said the father. He checked the weapon, reloaded it, but pointed it at Shel's feet. One of the hounds went over and began rubbing Dad's leg. "Who are you, mister? And what are you doing here?"

"I'm a researcher," Shel said. "Conducting an experiment. But I got lost."

"Is there somebody else?"

"Another man?"

"Yes. What did you *think* I meant?"

"I don't know," said Shel. "I came alone."

Jake snarled. "You're a *liar*. There *was* another one, Dad. I'm telling you—"

"If there was, where is he?"

"I don't know."

"Sir," said Shel, "I dropped that over there." He nodded at the converter. "I'd like to get it back, if it's okay."

"What is it?"

"It, um, measures light. We're trying to make better lamps."

Dad walked over and picked it up. He looked at it and put it in his pocket. "You know what I think?" he said. "I think you're a spy for the goddam redcoats. Why don't you just come with me?"

"Okay. But could I have my inclinator?"

"Is that what you call it?"

"Yes."

"Why? What's it do again? Measures light?"

"It measures the *inclination* of the light."

Dad laughed. "Whatever that means." He checked to be sure Shel had no weapons, and found the gooseberry. "What's this?"

"It's part of the light-testing system."

Dad laughed again and appropriated that, too.

Jake grabbed his father's shoulder. "Dad, I'm telling you, there were *two* of them. One just came and went. He's some kind of devil."

"And he went where?"

"I don't know. Just faded out when the dogs got after him."

"Shut up, Jake. You're imagining things. You ever hear of a devil that's scared of dogs?"

Jake threw up his hands. "I don't care. They—"

"*Shut up.*" He pointed toward a clutch of trees about a hundred yards off. Away from the river. "You can go, mister. Property line's a quarter mile *that* way. It's marked. If I see you out here again, I'm going to put a ball in you. You understand that?"

"Yes."

"Okay. Good-bye."

"Can I have my property back?"

Dad took out the converter and the gooseberry. Started fingering them.

Please don't turn anything on.

He tossed them in Shel's direction, but Shel let them hit

the ground. Make no sudden moves when a gun is pointed at you. After a minute, Shel picked them up. He thought about using the converter, but he wasn't sure what would happen if the weapon fired right after he pushed the button. Best to just walk away.

He put the gooseberry in a pocket and kept the converter in his hand. The shotgun was still aimed at his feet. The hounds started toward him, but Dad stopped them with a word.

Shel turned his back and started walking. Behind him, father and son were arguing. Jake was still trying to convince his father that Shel was not human.

WHEN he reached the property line, he looked back and saw that they were gone. As were the dogs. Good. Time to go home.

Poor Dave. He'd looked scared to death when he'd seen the shotgun.

He pushed the button and the daylight started to fade. Then it came back.

He tried again. This time nothing at all happened.

CHAPTER 22

Older men declare war. But it is youth that must fight and die.
And it is youth who must inherit the tribulation, the sorrow,
and the triumphs that are the aftermath of war.

—HERBERT HOOVER, JUNE 27, 1944

DAVE had had enough surprises. From now on, when he
was traveling, he'd keep a finger on the button and be prepared to move out at a moment's notice.

He was bleeding, and he was going to need shots. His
inclination was to go right back after Shel. But there was no
reason he couldn't go for repairs first.

Twenty minutes later, he limped into an emergency room.
They gave him tetanus and antibiotics and whatever else he
needed, and stitched him. On the way back to the town house,
he bought a pair of binoculars.

He reset the converter to take him back to the farm five
seconds after he'd left it. And to position him a hundred yards
west of the confrontation.

A gun might have been a good idea, too, in case he had to
deal with the animals again. But he didn't want to shoot the
dogs, and in fact had handled a firearm only once, at a range.
And that had been at least ten years ago.

* * *

HE made the transit lying down, so he emerged flat on the ground. Shel still had his hands up. The dogs seemed to be under control, and the kid was still holding the shotgun. Then he saw someone else coming, an older guy from the direction of the farmhouse. When he arrived, he took over the conversation and the gun.

Once or twice, one or the other of the farmers glanced in his direction, but he was reasonably sure he couldn't be seen at this distance. And he was upwind, so the dogs would not be likely to pick up his presence.

They talked for a few minutes. The guy with the shotgun did most of the talking. He picked something off the ground. The converter. He talked some more. Took something else from his captive. Probably the gooseberry. Eventually, he tossed both units toward Shel, who let them drop.

And they apparently told him he could go. Shel picked up the equipment, turned, and began walking away. The two farmers watched for a minute or two before taking the dogs and starting back toward the farmhouse.

Dave stayed down until they were safely inside. The dogs peeled off into the barn. Then he reset the converter, instructing it to take him forward five minutes. And deposit him, if he had his distances worked out correctly, about fifty yards in front of Shel.

"WE'VE got to work out a better way of doing this," said Shel. "How's your leg?"

"Okay. I've been to the hospital." He kept an eye on the barn. No sign of the animals.

There was a dirt road directly ahead. And a marker, a gray rock, painted with the words PRIVATE PROPERTY.

Somebody was approaching on horseback. Guys laughing and talking. Three horsemen came around a curve.

The lead rider had a tangled beard. He must have been

eighty, a guy who was all elbows and knees. When he saw Dave and Shel, he reined in beside them. "You fellas okay?"

"Yes," said Shel. "Thanks. We're fine."

"You look lost." The other two, one white, one black, nodded to each other. Sure do. Out in the middle of nowhere, no means of transportation, problem here somewhere. "Where you boys headed?"

"Bordentown."

"Well, you're there. But it's a long walk into town. You want a ride?"

Dave wasn't sure he knew how to climb onto the back of a horse. "Sure," said Shel.

Shel, Dave knew, had ridden camels in Egypt while traveling with his father. If you could climb onto a camel, he thought, you could climb onto a horse easily enough. But Dave had never been on one in his life. One of the riders saw his discomfort, smiled, and offered a hand.

Shel prudently waited until Dave was safely on board before climbing up himself. Twenty minutes later, they dismounted in front of a pleasant green-and-white house on the edge of town. They knocked but got no answer.

"Let's go forward a few hours," said Shel. "Give them time to get home."

"They might be in the next county," said Dave. "Two weeks would be better."

Dave left, and Shel pressed the button. Nothing happened. He tried again. This time it worked.

A woman answered the door. "We'd heard," said Shel, "that Thomas Paine is staying here. Is that by any chance correct?"

She frowned. "Who are you, please?"

A young man appeared behind her. "I heard my name. Were you looking for me?"

"Mr. Paine," said Shel. "We're headed for Pennsylvania to join General Washington's army."

Dave winced. He wished Shel would calm down a bit.

"We heard you were here as we were passing through," Shel continued, "and we hoped you wouldn't find it an imposition if we stopped to express our appreciation. For what you've done. For the cause."

Dave hadn't been aware that Shel was planning to concoct the story, but he was getting used to his fabrications. It was Selma again.

They were standing on the porch of Joseph Kirkbride's home, in the early evening of Thursday, October 9. Paine looked embarrassed by the adulation, but Shel was enjoying himself. "I suspect the day will come," he continued, "when you will be remembered as the voice of the Revolution."

Paine was lean, informal, relaxed. Dave, expecting a firebrand, was surprised. "Thank you, gentlemen," he said. "I appreciate your going out of your way to come here. And I need not say how pleased I am that you're going to join General Washington's force. They need good men."

A larger, heavier man appeared in the doorway behind him. He bestowed a disapproving look on Paine but kept his voice level: "Maybe your friends would like to come in, and join us for a drink."

"Of course," said Shel. "We'd love to, wouldn't we, Dave?"

Dave had a bad feeling. But the door swung wide. Paine and Shel went inside, into a parlor. When Dave hesitated, he found himself looking at a musket. "Really," said the big man, "I insist."

Shel glanced back, and the weapon swung in a short arc to include him, too. His jaw dropped.

Paine also seemed surprised. "You think they're spies, Joe?" he asked.

"I don't know." He waved Dave into the parlor. It was a pleasant room, paneled with oak. Three thick linen-covered armchairs and a couch were arranged around the walls. A table, complete with three cups, stood in front of the couch. The woman who had answered the door had backed well out of the line of fire. "It's all right, love," Joe said. "These gentlemen are friends. Aren't you?"

"You bet," said Dave.

Shel tried to look indignant. "What would spies want with Bordentown?"

It might have been the wrong thing to say. "Bordentown isn't very popular with the redcoats," Joe said. "Or with the traitors who support them. Especially when Mr. Paine is in town." He signaled them to sit down. On the sofa. He looked at Paine. "Tom, who knew you were coming here?"

"Nobody, Joe."

He swung back to Shel. "Why don't you tell us how you found out he was here?"

Shel couldn't very well say he'd googled it. "It's common knowledge."

"I don't think so." Joe stayed on his feet. "I assume you know what happens to spies?"

"We're not spies," said Shel.

"Good. Tell us who you are."

"My name's Adrian Shelborne. This is David Dryden. We're both from Philadelphia. We made the trip here specifically to see Mr. Paine."

"Why?"

"Because we wanted to meet him. Because he's made a major contribution to the Revolution. That's the truth."

"Okay," said Paine. "I'd like to accept your story. But it *is* a little hard to believe. So why don't you tell me how you knew where to find me?"

Shel was straining for an answer.

Dave kept his hand close to the converter so he could clear out on short notice. "Let me, Shel," he said. "All right, we promised we wouldn't say anything. We had a hard time persuading him to tell us, and he was afraid we'd show up here and take a lot of your time."

Joe's eyes got hard. "Who?"

"John Kearsley."

"Dr. Kearsley?" said Paine. "You know *him*?"

"We're old friends."

"How did *he* know where I was?"

"He didn't say. Probably through Dr. Franklin. I was

talking with him, telling him how much I admired your work, and he let it slip that you were going to be here."

Paine thought it over. "It's possible." He looked over at Joe. "When I was coming in from England, three years ago, I came down with typhus. On the ship." His eyes looked momentarily far away. "I don't think we'll need the musket, Joe."

"Who's Dr. Kearsley?" asked the woman.

"A friend of Ben's. When I was sick, he took care of me. Took me into his home for several weeks."

"Is that generally known?" asked Joe.

"I don't think so. Ben knew." Paine shrugged. "Anyhow, I don't think we need be concerned. These men don't look dangerous to me."

Joe lowered the weapon, placed it inside a cabinet, and closed the door. Then he sat down, and Paine introduced his hosts, Melissa and Joseph Kirkbride. Melissa was an attractive woman, with light brown hair wrapped in a bun, and expressive blue eyes. Whenever they turned toward Paine, they shone with pride.

Joe never did quite warm up to Shel and Dave. He watched them carefully and looked ready to challenge them at a moment's notice.

But Shel paid no attention. And a conversation that Dave thought would last four or five minutes stretched out for an hour. Mrs. Kirkbride produced blueberry muffins and tea, and they discussed the condition of the Continental Army, and the difficulties facing the British in putting down a rebellion that was becoming more widespread every day. Paine, however, admitted that he did not have high hopes for the success of the Revolution.

"Why not?" asked Shel.

"Resources. We have no money to speak of. Our major advantage is the weakness of British leadership. They don't know what they're doing, but in the long run, it might not matter."

"By the way." Shel went into his casual mode as he fished several photographs of his father from his pocket. "You might be interested in these."

Paine looked at the pictures. Handed them to Melissa and Joe. "What are these?"

"Photographs. It's a new science. Still at an experimental stage."

"Brilliant," Paine said. "I've never seen anything like them."

"Do you by any chance recognize the man?"

He shook his head. "No. I don't think I've ever seen him before. Why? Should I know him?"

"He's one of the researchers. He said he met you once in London. But it's of no concern."

The conversation wandered back to Franklin. Shel pretended to be acquainted with him, "slightly." He held up his hands in a self-deprecating manner. "I don't really see him often."

"No," said Paine. "I rather think he's busy these days."

"By the way," Shel said, "I enjoyed the most recent of the *Crisis* essays."

Paine tried to look modest. "Well," he said, "it's encouraging to think it might be having an effect."

"I especially liked your comment to General Howe at the end." He looked at Kirkbride. "I assume you've read it, sir."

"Of course."

"Pointing out that Howe is nothing more than a tool of a—how did you put it?—a miserable tyrant, and that he has an obligation to stand up for the truth. And, for that matter, for his troops, who are being killed off daily because the king's an idiot. Brilliant, sir."

"I didn't say that last part, Shel."

"You implied it, Tom. You don't mind if I call you *Tom*."

"No, of course not."

"It's all there. People in power need to speak up when authority gets abused. Unfortunately, even in democracies, sometimes they sit back and let the idiots run things."

Paine was enjoying one of Mrs. Kirkbride's biscuits. "I'm sure it would get abused. If there *were* any democracies."

"We have one here, sir."

"Not yet."

Dave couldn't resist jumping in: "Dr. Franklin was wondering whether you've been making any progress with your history of the Revolution?"

"At the moment, I'm preoccupied, sir. But I'm keeping a journal. It'll happen eventually."

"Good."

Dave knew, of course, that it would not. Paine would be preoccupied for a lifetime.

"I'm also thinking about writing a treatise on religion."

"Really? That would be interesting."

"I hope not to offend either of you gentlemen, but unbridled faith creates enormous problems. And generates stupidities that leave me breathless." He shook his head. "It's on my mind because we had two incidents here during the past few weeks."

"Really? And what might they have been?"

"Two demons allegedly showed up at a wedding."

"You're not serious, Tom."

By now, even Kirkbride was loosening up. "There were a dozen people," he said, "who swore they simply popped in out of nowhere, then vanished again. Before everyone's eyes. Frightful-looking creatures, they said."

"A week or so before that," Paine added, "the son of one of our local farmers claimed to have seen something similar. A devil who floated down out of the sky."

Shel laughed. "It just amazes me what people will believe."

Paine finished his third muffin and expressed his compliments to Mrs. Kirkbride. Then to Shel and Dave: "We get indoctrinated when we're young. Some of our people are as bad as those New England idiots. They hear about witches and devils, and they start seeing them."

"What did they look like?" asked Dave.

"The ones at the wedding had horns," said Kirkbride. "Eyes on fire, claws, the usual. I don't recall hearing anything about tails. Did these creatures have tails, Melissa? Do you know?"

"Not that I heard, but I wouldn't be surprised."

"The world," said Dave, "needs a book about common sense."

"I've already done that."

"I mean, common sense about other things. Not just politics."

Melissa took offense at that. "Tom's book was not simply about politics," she said.

"You know," said Paine, "the world really does need such a book. Something that will make a stand for reason rather than the ravings of lunatics." He cleared his throat. "It *would* need a provocative title, though."

Shel thought about it. Smiled. "How about *The Age of Reason*?"

CHAPTER 23

My stern chase after time is, to borrow a simile from Tom
Paine, like the race of a man with a wooden leg after a horse.
—JOHN QUINCY ADAMS

THEY left Joseph Kirkbride's home and walked away from
the town into the woods. To a place where they couldn't be
seen. "Somebody sees us come out of there," said Dave, "and
vanish, it would create some problems for them."

"You mean where Paine gets picked up for witchcraft and
never completes *The American Crisis*? He hasn't finished it
yet, has he?"

"I don't think so. He's published the first four parts. I don't
know what else has actually been written."

"So the rest of it goes by the board, and the Revolution
fails. We go back to a country run by the U.K. That's the way
these things usually work on television."

"That's the way."

"I don't think," said Shel, "we'd need to worry about a
witchcraft trial. This is south Jersey, not New England."

"You saw those people at the wedding. I wouldn't be too
sure."

They seemed safely lost among the trees. "Ready to go?" asked Shel.

Dave's converter was clipped to his belt. He lifted the lid. "All set."

"See you at home."

Dave pressed the button and watched the trees and sky begin to fade, watched the familiar walls of Shel's den take shape. The leaves and twigs underfoot were replaced by soft carpet.

He looked for Shel.

And waited.

Come on, Adrian.

HE set the converter to return to the point of origin, and went back to the forest. Shel was standing there, holding the unit in his hand, and impatiently stabbing at it with his index finger. "It doesn't want to work," he said. "I had a problem with it earlier, too."

"What's wrong?"

"How the hell would I know?" He sat down on the trunk of a fallen tree and removed the power pack. "It got dropped a couple of times while we were dealing with those farmers. Something's probably loose. But let me try a test." He handed the power pack to Dave. "See if you can make yours work with that."

Dave exchanged the power packs, hit the button, and went back to the town house. Moments later he'd returned to the forest. "It's okay," he said.

Shel scratched one ear and looked at his own unit. "Okay. So now it's official. It's broken."

"I've got room for a hitchhiker."

"I don't think it's a good idea."

"What do you suggest?"

"I don't know."

"You're sure there isn't another converter at home somewhere?"

"None that I know of."

Dave put a hand on his unit. "So we try it with this one and find out what happens."

Shel ran his fingers through his hair. "Okay," he said finally.

Dave moved next to him and grabbed hold of his belt. "Ready?"

"Okay."

Dave hit the key. The road and the countryside faded. And came back.

"Try again," said Shel.

Dave tried again. It left them still standing in the woods.

"Well." Shel looked distinctly unhappy. "What now?"

"I don't know."

Shel sat back down on the log. He closed his eyes for a few moments, then brightened. "I have an idea."

DAVE returned once more to the town house. He took the converter off his belt, tied it to a cushion, set it to return to the woods, and sent it on its way.

Except that it didn't move. It and the cushion remained solid and immobile on the floor. He tried it a second time, with the same result.

Damn.

He went back to the forest, looked at Shel, and shook his head.

"What happened?" asked Shel.

"Nothing. Apparently it doesn't like to transport pillows."

Shel lifted his hands at the sky. "Why me, Lord?"

"I guess," said Dave, "it won't work unless somebody's connected to it."

"It's a fail-safe, Dave."

"How do you mean?"

"They've built something in to prevent its activating accidentally. Like if you drop it."

"How would you do that?"

"Damned if I know. But that's what they've done."

"This is turning into a donkey drill."

"I know. Maybe it's time I started looking for a hotel."

"Not yet." A large yellow butterfly drifted past. "Can I get into your computer?"

"Password is *spiffy*."

"*Spiffy?*"

"Don't ask."

DAVE returned to the town house. They needed Shel's father. Maybe there was a better way than all the historical guesswork.

He googled *Michael Shelborne*. And got hundreds of hits. Michael Shelborne at the Smithsonian. At the University of Maryland. Shelborne's paper on temporal anomalies. His paper on slotted-line measurement. Shelborne gets Tindle Award. Kraus Award. Invited to annual Vatican symposium.

There were several other Michael Shelbornes: a mystery writer, a former senator from Idaho, a noted chess player, a serial killer, and a pioneer in the development of stage lines in central Italy during the mid-seventeenth century.

But he could find no clue revealing where *the* Michael Shelborne might have gone. Then, suddenly, he wondered how many people in seventeenth-century Italy had owned a name like *Shelborne*.

He went back and looked at the biography. There wasn't much. Shelborne's birth date, 1570, was given as an approximation, as was his date of death, 1650. He'd lived in Caréo, near Florence, during the middle of the seventeenth century, where he'd been deeply involved in connecting Rome, Florence, and Naples via stagecoaches.

He looked at a map: Caréo was only a short distance from Arcetri, Galileo's home.

DAVE was on his way out to his car, intending to drive home and change into robes, when he realized he didn't need to go back to the Renaissance looking for Michael Shelborne. There was a much easier way to rescue Shel.

He used the converter to put him back inside the town house at two o'clock the previous Friday, when Shel was at the office. Once there, he retrieved the key to the desk from the Phillies cup. He opened the bottom desk drawer. It held both converters. One was the same one he had clipped to his belt; the other would break down later in Bordentown. He knew of no way to distinguish them. Not that it mattered. He took one, closed the drawer, and locked it.

He set his own converter to take him back to Bordentown, and was relieved when he emerged only a few feet from Shel, whose eyes bulged when he saw the second unit. "Where'd you get that?"

Dave explained. Shel laughed and shook his head. "Good idea."

"Let's go home."

Shel nodded. And this time, both appeared more or less simultaneously in the town-house den.

DAVE'S first act was to go back an additional two days and return the converter he'd borrowed to Shel's desk. "Can't be too careful," he said, when the task was finished.

"You know," said Shel, "it looks as if we have as many converters as we could possibly want."

"You mean by going back and retrieving them."

"Yes."

"That might be Cardiac City."

"That's begun to seem a little silly now. Anyhow, you're okay, aren't you?"

"I'm okay. I'm not sure whether that would hold true if we didn't put the converter back." Dave was taking off his jacket. "Shel, remember the Atlantic."

"I know." Shel sank into a chair. "We're down to one converter now. So we're not going to be able to do this anymore, the way we have been."

"Maybe."

"What do you mean, *maybe*?"

"Shel, I'm not sure, but I think I've found your father."

CHAPTER 24

Galileo was obliged to retract by those mitred marionettes
who are today tyrants and the shame of Italy.

—VOLTAIRE, *NOTEBOOKS*

"WE put the extra converter away too soon," said Shel.

"I guess," said Dave. "Let's hope this is the last time."

Shel used the working converter to go back to the early
morning and retrieve both units, for a total of three. That provided an additional one for his father, should they find him.
He assured the Powers That Be that he'd replace them literally
within seconds after their return from Italy.

Now they were ready to go after Michael Shelborne again.
By then, both were convinced that the man in Florence would
indeed turn out to be Shel's father. "We're going to find out,"
Shel predicted, "that he dropped the converter. And got stuck.
Just the way I did."

They arrived in open country, in a field, on a cool morning
in May 1640. Two young men, probably teens, were working
in the field, about a mile away, and the first thing Shel did was
look for dogs. The kids saw them. One waved. Shel and Dave
waved back and started in their direction.

They were on their knees, doing something to the soil,

spreading fertilizer, perhaps. One got up as they approached. "Hello," he said. "Are you lost?"

"Yes," said Dave. "We're looking for Caréo."

"You have to get back on the road." He pointed in the direction from which they'd come. "Go left. It's about a twenty-minute walk."

DAVE stopped an elderly couple traveling in a cart and asked if they knew of a Michael Shelborne, who lived in Caréo.

"Well, he *used* to live here," said the woman.

"Has he moved?"

"Oh, no, sir. He's *dead*."

Mòrto.

Shel didn't have to wait for the translation.

"Are you sure?" asked Dave.

"Oh, yes. It was three or four years ago, wasn't it, Poppa?"

"Yes," Poppa replied. "He was a good man. Did you know him?"

Shel showed the photo.

"Oh, no," Poppa said. "Michael was much older than this man."

The woman studied it. "It could be him. When he was young."

A young woman confirmed it. "That's him," she said. "He's buried at Santo Pietro."

"A churchyard?" asked Shel, in English.

Dave translated.

"Sì."

"He wasn't much of a churchgoer," Shel objected. "It must be somebody else."

"Can you show us?" Dave asked.

The woman's name was Carlotta. She was attractive, with dark, luminous eyes and a quiet smile. She said it was only a short distance, and they fell in behind her. Shel walked almost in a daze. He wasn't sure what he'd expected to find in

Galileo's Italy, but certainly nothing like this. For one thing, his father was immortal. Whatever else might change, he would be there, always ready to laugh, to demonstrate what living really meant. *Carpe diem.* Make the most of your time because you will not forever enjoy the daylight. And that very attitude had somehow imbued him with a cloak of invulnerability.

Carts clattered past. People worked in the fields. Farm animals nibbled on grass. Occasionally, someone rode by on a horse.

Carlotta knew everyone by name, greeted every person they passed, answered questions about her mother's well-being by saying she was all right. Coming along. *Bene.* When Dave asked, she explained that her mother had recently delivered another child but had had a difficult time for a while.

When she learned that Shel was Michael's son, she offered condolences. "You look like him," she added. The remark induced another chill.

They moved at a steady pace, around a curve out of a cluster of trees, and a town came into view. It was a small town, maybe a hundred houses. Carlotta pointed out an attractive villa with a broad deck and bright green shutters, atop a hill. "That is where he lived," she said.

"Michael Shelborne?"

"Yes."

They passed a winery and more houses. And finally they approached an old stone church. It was small and looked abandoned. Shel doubted they could have gotten fifty people into it.

"No," said Carlotta. "Santo Pietro's still has an active congregation. But they have no money."

Its lonely steeple thrust up through the trees. "It doesn't look safe," said Dave.

Carlotta smiled. "I can't imagine anyplace safer."

An angel with spread wings dominated the churchyard, standing guard over three graves. "Priests," their guide said. "Father Patrizio, Father Agostino, and Father Cristiano. They were good men. Father Agostino baptized me."

"Carlotta," said Dave, translating for Shel, "do you know what Shelborne's connection was with this church?"

"Only that he was a member."

"Of *Santo Pietro's*?" said Shel. "That's not possible."

"I think he must have been. He left his estate to the parish."

"You mean, to the *church*?"

"Not directly. As I understand it, it was left to the *par-ròchia*. Had he left it to the church, it would have simply gone to Rome. This way, Father Valentini was able to use it to help the poorer families in the district."

"You think well of him," said Dave. "Father Valentini."

"Of course."

"You do not sound as if you care much for Rome, however."

"It is like everything else. The priests have no real power. They do what they can to make life easier for us. Without them, I'm not sure what hope we would have."

THEY went behind the church, where there was another statue, probably of Mary, looking heavenward. She held a tablet, inscribed with the words RIPOSI IN PACE. And maybe two hundred headstones. They looked through the markers, and it was Carlotta who found it. She pointed and stood aside.

It was a plain headstone with an engraved cross.

MICHAEL SHELBORNE
M. 1637

"Date of death?" asked Shel.

Dave nodded. "Yes." The graveyard was very still. "Three years ago."

"That can't be right. The Internet entry said he died in 1650."

"It was a guess."

"He's only been gone a few months," said Shel.

"It's different here. It looks as if he's been here for years."

"He wasn't a believer."

While they stood looking at the marker, a door opened in

the church, and a priest appeared. He raised a hand in greeting, seemed about to go back inside, when Shel signaled, asking him to wait.

It was Father Valentini. Carlotta introduced them, then explained she had work to do. Shel gave her some *carlinos*. She tried to decline, but he insisted.

When she was gone, the priest invited them inside. "How may I help you?" he asked.

"Adrian," said Dave, "thinks that Michael Shelborne may have been his father."

"There *is* a resemblance," said the priest.

"Father," said Shel, "can you tell me if there was a connection between Michael and Galileo?"

The priest's features brightened. He was about sixty, his hair almost gone. His beard was white, and he had sharp amber eyes. "Galileo? Yes. Michael Shelborne knew him, but it was a long time ago."

"Galileo denied all knowledge."

"Ah, you've been to see him. I'm surprised you got past the Inquisition."

"Is there any reason he would have lied?"

"I don't think that's what happened. Your father was, as far as I know, only a casual acquaintance, and that was a long time ago."

"Can you tell me when?"

"I believe it was at the time of the nova."

"The nova?"

"The new star. Professor Galilei was teaching mathematics at the University of Padua when it happened. It was visible for a year and a half, I believe, and was for a time the brightest object in the sky. Except the sun and moon, of course." He shook his head. "It was so bright, we could see it in the twilight. But you're too young to remember. We never did figure out what it was. A sign of some sort, perhaps."

"When was that?"

"I believe 1604. It was one of the things that got the professor in trouble with the Church."

"Why?"

"Because the new star did not move through the sky like the moon. So he said it was farther away than the moon."

"And...?"

"It was like the stars. It remained in a single place, and moved across the sky with them. He declared it *was* a star. A *new* one."

"Why would that have created a problem?" asked Dave.

"Aristotle does not allow for an ongoing creation. You cannot *have* new stars. It is not supposed to happen."

"And Michael Shelborne was here then?"

"He was in Padua also. It was, I believe, where they first met."

Dave looked at Shel. "What do you think?"

"That sounds like the way he would do things. Why pop by Arcetri when you can be in town for a supernova?" He looked out the window at the statue of Mary. And the tablet: RIPOSI IN PACE. "Father, of what did he die? Do you know?"

"I assume it was of old age, *signore*."

"Old age?"

"He was not young."

"How old would you say he was?"

"He must have been in his eighties."

THEY stopped at a *caffé* for a drink and some dinner. And to get out of the sun. The menu was posted on the wall. It was midafternoon, and the place was almost empty. Shel commented there were no sandwiches on the menu.

"I don't think they've been invented yet," said Dave. The waitress brought two cups of cool wine. "We could go back and watch the supernova," he continued. "Catch your father when he first arrived."

"And do what?"

"Take him home."

"If it really was him, he died here."

Dave hesitated. "I don't know how I'm supposed to answer that."

"Maybe it doesn't matter," said Shel. "I don't know. I just don't know the rules."

Dave took a long pull on his wine. "I hate to point this out, *compagno*, but he's already changed a few things. By his presence here, how could he *not*?"

Their waitress was back. She looked good. Black hair, brown eyes, big smile. They decided to try the eggplant, baked with mozzarella cheese. And to refill the cups.

When she'd gone, Dave leaned across the table. "You didn't answer my question."

"How can I?"

"That's my point. There's already been a disruption. The time stream, whatever that *is*, has already been thrown off course. Hell, for all we know, you might have a couple of siblings here. Maybe even that young lady who just took the order."

"I'm my own grandpa."

"It's possible."

"Look, Dave, I'm not a physicist. I don't know. My father didn't know. Maybe we'll go back home and discover Italy's ruling the world. But I'm not excited about going to see him in Padua, a day or two after he'd arrived, and telling him what we know."

"Maybe he already knows."

"How do you mean?"

"Look, this is wild stuff. But maybe the Michael Shelborne in 1604 had already visited this time. Hell, he might have seen the marker himself. Or maybe he googled himself before he came."

"That's goofy, Dave."

"You think time travel isn't goofy? Anything goes."

The waitress returned with more dark wine and utensils.

"This whole thing scares me," Shel said.

"I think we should just go home and forget it."

"No," he said. "What did you say at Selma? I can't just walk away from it."

CHAPTER 25

I now believe that television itself, the medium of sitting in front of a magic box that pulses images at us endlessly, the act of watching TV, per se, is mindcrushing. It is soul-deadening, dehumanizing, soporific in a poisonous way, ultimately brutalizing. It is, simply put so you cannot mistake my meaning, a bad thing.

—HARLAN ELLISON, *STRANGE WINE*

THEY returned to the villa with the green shutters, set the converters to keep them in the same location, but to take them back seven years. They arrived on a sunny morning in the spring of 1633. Birds sang while five or six children ran in circles through a field. A light breeze was coming out of the west. The house looked much the same, except that the east wing was missing. A later addition, apparently. A middle-aged man was clipping a fern. He saw them approaching, wiped his hands on a cloth, and came forward. "Ah, *signori*, may I help you?"

"Hello," said Dave. "We understand this is the home of *Signore* Shelborne?"

"Why, yes," he said. "It is. Did you wish to see him?"

"If you will."

"Does he know you're coming?"

Dave looked toward Shel. "*This* is Adrian Shelborne," he said. "He is Professor Shelborne's son."

Shel felt something closing over him. Please let us be wrong—

"Ah, *Signore* Shelborne." He bowed. Tasted the name. "*Eccelénte*. I am Albertino. And I do believe the master will be delighted to see you." He led the way to the front door. "He has spoken of you many times."

God. But Shel kept his smile in place. "How is he? How is his health?"

"He's quite well, sir, thank you." He opened the door for them and stood aside. Albertino was short, with a full face and black curly hair. Probably in his fifties which, in this age, was well along. "Please go in, gentlemen."

They followed him into a spacious, comfortable living room with several armchairs and a sofa and a pleasant view of the town. A full bookcase stood near the door. Oil paintings adorned the walls: a landscape, two portraits of young women, and one of a passenger vehicle drawn by a team of horses. Potted plants stood on a shelf and on a small side table. The servant addressed Dave: "May I ask *your* name, sir?"

"David Dryden."

"Thank you. I'll tell Dr. Shelborne you're here."

He left the room, headed toward the back of the house through a pair of double doors. Shel could barely restrain himself from following. Especially when he heard voices in the rear and, a moment later, hesitant footsteps. He was on his feet when his father, supported by a cane, entered the room.

The world fell away.

He was an old man.

Shel had to look closely to be sure it was his father. His hair had turned white, and his skin was pale and creased. He wore a beard now.

Michael limped forward, gait uncertain, and put his arms around his son. "Adrian," he said, "is it really *you*?"

"Dad— What happened?"

"I had an accident. Adrian, it's so good to see you."

"Good to see *you*, Dad." They embraced again, then pushed apart to look at each other.

"My God," said the old man, "I never expected to see you again."

They clung to each other. Albertino came in but stood off to one side, pretending that nothing unusual was happening.

Then Michael turned irritable. "You shouldn't be here."

"Neither should you. Do you have any idea what we've been through? Everybody thinks you're dead."

"I'm sorry about that." Michael eased himself into a chair. Then glanced at Dave. In Italian, he asked, "Do I know you?"

Dave replied in English: "I'm Dave Dryden, Professor."

"Oh, yes." He turned a withering eye on Shel. "So much for keeping things quiet."

"I won't say anything," said Dave.

Michael nodded without taking his eyes off his son. "Let's hope not." He signaled for Albertino to leave them. "Do you realize what you've done, Adrian?"

"No, Dad. As a matter of fact, I *don't* know what I've done. Maybe you should explain it to me."

"Sit," he said. "It took you a long time. Coming after me."

"I didn't know where to look. All you told me was 'Galileo.' "

"Oh." He smiled. "Did I do that?"

"Yes." It was almost a shriek. "You've been here—what?— thirty years?"

The question hung in the air.

"And you were in Alexandria."

His lips curved into a wistful smile. "I went there first, right after you left the house." He stopped. Had to think. "Or maybe it was Cicero first."

"Cicero?"

"During the period when they were trying to stop Caesar." He shook his head. "No, I went to the Library first. I made several trips that night before I came here."

"Dad, I wish we'd known where you were. We could have—"

Let it go. "It hasn't been a bad life."

"I'm sure." Shel cast a contemptuous look around the interior. No power. No phone. No TV.

"Look, I'm glad to see you, son. You know that. And I'm sorry if I seem ungrateful."

"What happened?" asked Shel. "Why didn't you come back?"

"I'd have gone back had I been able. My God, it feels strange to have you here."

"Dad—"

"You and Dave can stay awhile, right? Spend some time with me. There's a lot to see. But when you go home—"

"Yes...?"

Michael hesitated. "When you go home, I want you to take the instruments apart. Get rid of them."

"You're going back with me, Dad."

"Adrian, no. I'm happy here."

"What?"

"I've been here a long time. This is my home. I've a good life here. Much better than I ever had working at Swifton."

"Dad, that's crazy. This place is primitive."

"Not really. You're right, in a way. Civilization's just getting started. But this is where it's happening."

"Come on, Dad. You're talking like a crazy man. The truth is, we've just come from your grave site."

It was an accusation. A heavy silence settled on the room. Michael sighed. "I'm sorry to hear it. It's one of the temptations with the converter, isn't it? You can always move forward and find out what happens tomorrow. That's not necessarily a good thing."

"Dad—"

"Don't give me any details. Please."

"Dad, I want to get you out of here."

"It feels so strange to be speaking your kind of English again."

"Why did you do it? Why'd you stay here? You promised you'd come back. And call me. You remember that?"

"I remember."

"So what happened?"

"There was an accident."

"How? Did the converter break? Power pack run down? What?"

He looked tired. Looked as if thinking about it wore on him. "Adrian, it's designed to find a solid surface, reasonably horizontal, so you don't materialize, say, thirty feet off the ground."

"And...?

"When I came here, it was December—"

"You came for the supernova."

"You know about that?"

"Yes."

"Very good. Anyway, I came out on a frozen pond. On the surface. I found myself standing on ice."

"And...?"

"This is Italy, son. Ice tends to be thin. I fell through into the water. Could have drowned. Anyhow, the converter got wet. The power pack died. And I've been here since."

Shel was getting annoyed. And scared. "All right. But it's over now. I can't believe you'd really want to stay here."

"But I do." His words carried conviction. "How's everything back home? How's Jerry?"

"Jerry's fine. Nothing's changed. What would you expect? It's only been a few months since you left."

"Ah, that's right. It's not easy to keep track of the details."

"To say the least, Dad."

"Does Jerry know?"

"No."

"Okay. Leave things as they are."

"That's hard on him, Dad."

"I know. But I don't see an alternative." He cleared his throat. "We were never that close anyway. He won't miss me."

The house looked okay. The walls appeared to be walnut; the bookcase was carved and polished, the furniture comfortable. "You seem to have done reasonably well for yourself."

"Life is good. I could have used a dentist a couple of times. But other than that, yes, I've been content here."

"Dad—"

"Adrian, I'm on the edge of the Enlightenment. And I know who the players are."

"But people *always* know who the players are."

"No, they don't. It usually takes a couple of generations to figure that out. Contemporaries only know the authority figures and the loudmouths. And the people born into power. But it takes perspective to know who's carrying the load. Nobody here has a clue who Johannes Kepler is. All they know about Galileo is that he's a teacher who got in trouble with the Inquisition. I doubt anyone's heard of Francis Bacon. Even in Britain, nobody really knows him. He's just a guy with a funny name."

"How've you managed to live?" asked Shel.

"In the beginning, I became a field hand. I worked in shops. Been a waiter. When I came here, Santo Pietro took me in. Eventually, I founded a company that promoted the use of table utensils."

"You're kidding."

"Twenty years ago, they didn't have them. People ate with knives and their fingers." He smiled. "Ah, the good old days."

"And," said Shel, "you got into the transportation business."

"You know about that, too? Good, you've done your homework."

"Dave found it."

"I see. There's a lesson to be learned, Adrian."

"Which is?"

"Time is flexible. Or did we talk about this before?"

"We did."

"Okay. Stay away from paradoxes. Otherwise, it appears you can influence history. Become part of it."

"How do you define a paradox?"

He considered the question. "Where you make an event known to have occurred impossible." He laughed. It was a hearty, good-humored reaction. The guy was seriously happy. "What you do becomes part of history. Your part in it, in a sense, was always there. I've always been a factor in this era. And yes, I made my money in the development of stage lines among central Italian cities. What you must do is avoid shooting your ten-year-old grandfather." Shel and Dave smiled. "I mean it," he said. "Avoid the irreparable act."

Michael commented that his visitors must be hungry. But

nobody was, so he simply had Albertino bring out some wine. "I can't resist asking," he said finally. "Where else have you been?"

THEY stayed through the night. The beds were soft, and Shel was surprised to discover indoor plumbing, including a flush toilet and a shower. "They're in common use," said Michael, in the morning.

"You could use some air-conditioning."

Michael glanced over at Dave, who was busily looking elsewhere. "You're spoiled," he said.

"I know." Shel sat back. They'd just had a superb breakfast of bacon and eggs and the largest pieces of toast he'd ever seen. "Dad," he said, "seriously, I'd like not to hear any more talk about happy times in the Renaissance. The cavalry's here. I want you to come home with us."

"I can't do that, son."

"You talked about a dentist. You could probably use a physical. In any case, you can't stay here."

"Why not?"

"Because this isn't where you belong."

"You said you saw my grave ahead somewhere."

"It's one more reason we want to get you out of here."

"If I go back with you—"

"Yes?"

"Who's in the grave?"

"I don't know. Does it matter?"

"You want to talk about paradoxes. I'm not sure what would happen if you tried to take me back." He refilled his glass. "Anyhow, I don't *want* to go."

"Dad—"

"I mean it. I like it here. You might find it hard to believe, but it's a much more social climate than you have at home."

"Dad, this is getting off track."

"No, it isn't. People here spend time together. They visit. They talk to one another. There's always a party somewhere.

Back in Philly, they all watch TV. Or sit at a computer. I don't want to go back to that."

"You're kidding."

"Do I look as if I'm kidding? Adrian, listen to me." It seemed as if Dave were no longer in the room. "No matter what I do now, I'm near the end of my life. I've been here thirty years, give or take. Look at me. You can barely recognize me. How do we explain that to the people at the lab? To my customers? My neighbors?" He took a deep breath. "I don't need all that. Let it go."

"Dad, I can't just walk away from you."

"You're going to have to."

"No, I don't." He looked down at the converter. "I can go back to the year of the supernova. What was it? 1605?"

"Close. It was 1604."

"Okay. And I'll pick you up *there*. After the converter got wet. I suspect you'd welcome a rescue."

"Yes, I would have. I'll admit that was a bad time. But please do not do it. Don't even think about it."

"Why not?"

"Haven't you been listening?"

"Hell with it. We do what we have to."

"And if you do, you go back there and pick me up on the ice, assuming you're able to do it at all, which I doubt, what do you think happens to *me*?"

"What do you mean?"

"*Me*, Adrian. The Michael Shelborne who's spent a lifetime in Italy, who's living the good life right now near Florence. What happens to *me*?"

"I don't know."

"You're proposing a scenario in which I never existed. You take me back in 1604, and *I'm* gone. My years here don't exist anymore. Do me a favor. Just leave it alone.

"And stop feeling sorry for me. Listen, Adrian, I have talked politics with Ben Jonson and Connie Huygens. Played chess with Tom Hobbes. Gone horseback riding with Descartes. I showed up at a party one night, and Claudio Monteverdi was playing the viol. I knew John Milton when he was a teenager. I've talked about the human condition with John Donne. I was in the Globe for the opening performance of *King Lear*. And I should add that Florence has some of the loveliest and most talented young women I've ever seen. And you want to take me away from them?"

"Okay, Dad. I get the point."

"Good. And as long as you won't take my advice and stay away from the damned things—" He got up, left the room, and came back with something wrapped in cloth. "You might as well have this, too." It was *his* converter. "In case you need an extra."

Shel took it reluctantly. "I'd rather leave it with you."

"I've no use for it."

"All right."

"As far as I know, all it needs is a power source. But run a test. Make sure."

Albertino brought wine to the table, and Dave offered a toast to Michael Shelborne, the world's first time traveler.

They touched glasses and drank. "And never forget," Michael said, "time travelers never die. No matter what you saw up ahead, about me, I'll always be here."

CHAPTER 26

There is some awe mixed with the joy of our surprise, when this poet, who lived in some past world, two or three hundred years ago, says that which lies close to my own soul, that which I also had wellnigh thought and said.

—RALPH WALDO EMERSON, "THE AMERICAN SCHOLAR"

IT would be an overstatement to say that Aspasia and her plays were getting substantial attention from the mass media. Sophocles was not exactly a subject to boost ratings, but the mystery surrounding the appearance of plays thought lost for two thousand years did interest a couple of the cable news show hosts. Michelle Keller on *Perspective* observed that it sounded as if a real-life Indiana Jones was charging around out there somewhere, and Brett Coleman, a guest on *Down the Line*, commented that the world had been greatly enriched by the discovery, although he seemed to think that Achilles was a *Trojan* hero.

But if the world at large took little notice, the academic community became embroiled almost overnight in debates over the validity of the texts. Some argued that the style could not have been duplicated so effectively by someone perpetrating a hoax, while their opponents maintained that computer analysis was insufficient for the task of measuring genius. Most scholars came down in the middle: They would not weigh in until the source had been revealed and explanations offered.

Reputations, of course, were at stake. No one ever ruined his career by remaining skeptical, but anybody who buys into a new idea that turns out to be silly has a hard time walking away from it.

Shel and Dave made a few more visits to Alexandria, during which the third converter tested out. They collected more plays from Aristarchus, who always treated them as VIPs, and sent them to Aspasia. Dave was especially impressed when he watched her, during an interview with Keller, divert all credit *"to the person or persons who made the work available."*

"She's just trying to protect her rear end," said Shel. "In case it doesn't turn out well."

"Is there any real doubt in your mind?" asked Keller.

"Of course there is."

"But everyone seems to agree that the work is at the level and in the style of the classical playwrights."

"That proves nothing, Michelle. We just don't know what we have."

"But a hoax of this magnitude—who could do it?"

"We'll have to wait on that one."

"You really don't think they're legitimate, do you?"

"Michelle, I'd love to know where these plays have been for two thousand years. If whoever sent them is out there now, watching this show, I wish he would step forward and answer some questions. It would help the process immensely."

"Have you asked them to do that?"

"Yes."

"And they've refused."

"I haven't heard a word."

"Nothing at all?"

"No. And to be honest, Michelle, I can't imagine a good reason why that would be. If the plays are what they claim."

"NO." Shel was adamant. "We don't do anything like that. Let them sort it out themselves."

Dave was frustrated. "Look: We've been saying all along that eventually we'll destroy the converters. Okay, we can admit our part in this and do a demonstration. Then throw them into the Atlantic."

"No."

"Why not? The stuff we brought back is priceless." They now had more than forty plays, histories, speculations, philosophical documents. They were piling up. "But what good are they if nobody accepts them?"

"I'll tell you why not. Right now, everybody thinks time travel's a fantasy. So we prove them wrong, and every physicist on the planet's going to try to figure out how it's done. No. If they decide to declare everything a hoax, then so be it."

"But what's wrong with it? If they figure it out, and a few of them try to abuse it and end up in the ocean, so what?"

"That's nickel-and-dime stuff, Dave. Whether there's really a cardiac principle, I don't know. It certainly seems as if there is. And if so, and hundreds of converters show up, it might be subject to overload."

"You're talking black magic, Shel."

"Am I? Okay: We're also talking about a world in which people can travel into the future and bring home the news. Tomorrow's news, today. What happens when people find out in advance when they'll die? What their lives are going to amount to? What happens to science if we can just ride into the future and bring back all the answers? What happens to the Phillies when we know in advance what the pennant races will look like for the rest of the century?

"No. We leave it alone."

They were in the town house, and Shel was seated on his sofa with a collection of classical architectural drawings in his lap. It was a copy of the original plan for the Temple of Zeus at Olympia. The document, later stored at Alexandria, had been signed by Libon, the architect. The plans marked off the space reserved for the majestic statue of Zeus, which would be done by Pheidias.

"So what do we do now?"

"Send the lady some more work. Why not one each from

Aeschylus, Euripides, and Aristophanes? And we might include one or two of Herodotus's commentaries. Nobody's ever seen those before."

"I'll tell you," said Dave, "what'll blow their minds: The memoirs of Thales of Miletus."

"The scientist?"

"More than that, Shel. He was the guy who *invented* science. Not much is known about him except that he wanted people to look for rational explanations for everything. But nobody realizes he left behind a series of journals. They might be the most valuable thing we have."

"Okay," he said. "Let's send them to her. And you know, there's someplace else I'd like to visit."

"What did you have in mind?"

Outside, there was a squeal of brakes and angry voices. Somebody yelled something about kids in the street.

Shel paid no attention. He was still looking down at the schematic for Zeus at Olympia.

THAT weekend, they went back to Alexandria and spent a couple of hours talking with Aristarchus. They expressed their appreciation for his assistance and told him how grateful the future world was to recover so much of Alexandria's treasures. Ultimately he asked the question that must have been on his mind since the beginning: "Do you visit other times and places, as well?"

"Yes," Shel said.

"Ancient Egypt?"

It seemed odd to be sitting in Alexandria in 149 B.C. listening to someone bring up *ancient Egypt* as if it were a remote time. But of course, he was thinking one or two thousand years before his own era. "If we wished, we could go there."

"Where else *do* you go?"

"This is the earliest time we've visited," said Shel, whose Greek had improved considerably.

"I see. But you *could* go back earlier?"

"Oh, yes."

"And, if I may—"

"Yes, Aristarchus?"

"I must confess I'd like very much to visit *your* world. Is that possible?"

"Let me think about it," said Shel. "It would require some preparation."

"I would be extremely grateful."

"Of course," said Shel. "We'll try to arrange it."

"I wonder, also, whether any of our dramas have been staged yet? In your time?"

"Not yet," said Shel. "Unfortunately, we're having a problem getting people to accept the authenticity of the documents."

"How could that happen? Surely they know where you got them."

"No, they don't." Shel tried to explain, but it was too complicated for his Greek, and Dave took over. When he'd finished, Aristarchus sat quietly stirring the herbal drink he'd ordered.

"So the future is not quite as welcoming as you said."

"No," said Shel. "I may have exaggerated."

Aristarchus laughed. "Take me there, and I will vouch for their authenticity."

Dave broke into a broad grin. "You'd be the hit of the season on *Down the Line*."

"And what is that?"

"A forum."

"I can see that the action is not practical."

"Probably not."

"I could give you a signed statement." This time all three laughed. "So what will they do with the books?"

Dave was reluctant to answer. "Ignore them, probably," he said. "For the time being."

Aristarchus sighed. "It's almost as if the Library will be destroyed a second time."

"No." Shel's eyes blazed. "The books will survive. One way or another, they will. You have my word."

The director looked out his office window at the sky. It was night, and the Lighthouse cast its beam out to sea. "Before you came, it is what I thought, too."

CHAPTER 27

Rejoice! We've won!
—PHEIDIPPIDES, BRINGING THE NEWS FROM MARATHON

ATLANTIC *Online* carried a story by a prominent Greek scholar stating that the Kephalas Papers, as the plays had become known, were clearly a fraud. *"It is impossible to imagine that anyone,"* it read, *"could confuse these pathetic impostures with classical drama. (Dr. Kephalas), no doubt, has allowed her enthusiasm to cloud her judgment. One can only hope that she will soon step back and allow reason to prevail."*

Others were similar in tone. The *New York Times* thought the plays had no merit, and one *"had to be an idiot"* to think seriously that the hand of Sophocles had produced *"such mundane nonsense."*

The *Washington Post* agreed, calling the plays imbecilic. The *Inquirer* said they were simply *"sad impersonations."*

Aspasia was roundly criticized for promoting the hoax. *"It boggles the mind,"* said the *Wall Street Journal*, *"that a scholar of Ms. Kephalas's reputation could be so completely taken in."* That Aspasia had been skeptical from the start was not mentioned.

She had left English translations of the *Achilles* and the *Leonidas* up at her Web site, along with a plea for the person or persons who had provided the plays to come forward. *"If these are genuine, you owe it to the world to establish that fact."*

THE commotion had died down somewhat when Shel called Dave with another project in mind. *"I want to take a look at the Temple of Zeus. At Olympia. Can I talk you into coming along?"* Dave had known the invitation was imminent.

"When?"

"How about tomorrow?" It was a Friday afternoon.

"Sure," he said. "What time?"

"About nine. We'll leave from my place."

"I'll be there."

He had a date that night with Marie Rendell, a dark-eyed beauty that he'd met in a bookstore. He took her to a high-school concert, at which one of Marie's cousins, a twelve-year-old whose name was also Marie, played the piano competently. David went to the event expecting the worst and was surprised at the abilities of the kids.

Afterward, they had a drink, and she charmed him with an electric smile. "What do you do in your spare time, Dave?" she said. "When you're not teaching?"

"I read a lot. And I enjoy live theater."

She looked at him curiously. "You're laughing, Dave."

"No, I'm not."

"What is it, really? Are you a hit man? Do you work for the CIA? What?"

"No. I lead a quiet life." *Though tomorrow I'm going to drop by a Greek temple.*

DAVE stored his costumes upstairs in a walk-in closet. He went up, picked out one of the robes that he thought had a

Hellenic flavor, brought it downstairs, and shook the wrinkles out. When he was finished, he carried it out to the car, folded it carefully, put it in the backseat, and started for Shel's.

THE temple was located on a modest rise of land. Shel and Dave stood beneath a cluster of olive trees, watching a small group of people mounting three steps onto the portico, where they passed between columns and disappeared inside.

A series of sculpted figures stood in the gallery.

"Pelops and Oenomaos," said Shel, indicating two males apparently confronting each other. "And that's Zeus in the center."

"Who are Pelops and Oenomaos?"

"Pelops wanted to marry Oenomaos's daughter. Her father didn't like the idea, so they agreed to race. Winner would get the prize."

"Why didn't Oenomaos simply say no?"

"Don't know. Maybe it wasn't culturally correct. Anyhow, one version of the story is that Pelops bribed one of the father's people to sabotage the chariot. In any case, it fell apart during the race, Oenomaos was killed—"

"—And the couple lived happily ever after."

"Some of the Greek tales are a bit strange."

They climbed onto the portico, walked from end to end, admiring the statuary. And finally, they went inside.

Dave caught his breath. The statue of Zeus, still famous in the third millennium even though long gone, dominated the interior. It was magnificent, painted predominantly in silver and blue, and it stood about four stories high.

"The temple will be here for a thousand years," said Shel. "Then it'll be hit by an earthquake. And what's left will sink into floodwaters. It'll get lost, and will be forgotten until it's rediscovered in the eighteenth century."

The people who'd preceded them inside stood quietly, their heads bowed. There were others, two women in a dark corner, a man in military garb holding a helmet under his arm, and a group of teens gazing up at Zeus.

Oil lamps provided an amber luminescence. Other sculpted figures occupied niches in the walls. Dave couldn't make out everything in the uncertain light, but he saw grapes and swords and wings.

IN a sense, the genie was out of the box. After visiting the Library and the Alexandria Lighthouse and the Temple of Zeus, seeing them at their zenith, there was no way they could avoid dropping by to see the Colossus of Rhodes.

They arrived next day, just after sunrise. The Colossus was another majestic giant, this one dominating the harbor in the manner of the Statue of Liberty.

Dave couldn't take his eyes from it. "Apollo?" he asked.

Shel shook his head. "Helios. The sun god."

Ships were tied up around the port, and a frigate was just entering the harbor. At least Dave thought it was a frigate. He saw what looked like weapon racks on deck.

They found a café with a view of the waterfront and went inside. Dave had problems reading the menu, and they never did figure out what they'd ordered. There was scorched meat, and eggs—but not from chickens—and a reddish vegetable. It was served with a hot drink that had a lime taste. In all, not something to get excited about, but it didn't matter. They were in an extravagant mood by then, and anything would have tasted good.

DURING the next month, they visited the Great Pyramid at Giza, the Hanging Gardens, and returned to Rhodes for the Temple of Artemis. They were in the cheering crowds at Athens when Pheidippides arrived after a twenty-four-mile run, with news that the Athenians had beaten the Persians at Marathon, and driven them into the sea.

They couldn't hear what Pheidippides said to those who'd hurried out to greet him, to catch him as he collapsed. But they knew the content. The danger was not over. The army was returning, but the city should prepare against the possibility of a new attack.

Pheidippides was carried away. If he in fact died, as the histories all say, he must have done it later. Because he was still breathing, and still talking, as he and his rescuers disappeared into the crowds.

On October 31, 1517, they were outside the castle church at Wittenberg, waiting for Martin Luther to show up and nail *The Ninety-Five Theses* to the door. They were there more than two fruitless hours before Dave suggested they travel through to the morning to determine whether he'd actually performed the deed. They did, and he hadn't.

"The date was never certain," said Shel. "Should have thought of that earlier." They tried the next day, though this time they checked the morning results first. Again, there was nothing.

It happened on the evening of November 3, at a little past nine o'clock in the evening. Dave and Shel were sheltered by a group of trees about fifty feet away from the church door when Luther arrived, a coat pulled around him to protect against the cold. They took pictures and resisted the inclination to shake his hand. "I like rebels," said Dave.

THEY spent two hours with Aristotle, pretending to be scholars from Rhodes (Shel's idea of a joke), asking questions about the movement of the stars and listening sadly while he talked of the ether and stars and planets orbiting the Earth in a complex system of fifty-five spheres, which, remarkably, usually gave the right answers regarding what would be in the sky at any given time. And he knew the Earth was round. Although he thought it was permanent and unchanging.

Afterward, Shel shook his head: "I've never seen anyone so obviously brilliant who has everything so wrong."

"It's a time without science," Dave said. "Nobody knows anything. I felt sorry for him. Trying to make sense of orbital mechanics with no telescope. That was what, 330 B.C.?"

"331."

"I think we should cut him a break."

"Yeah. I was dying to tell him the sun is a star. That he's thinking small."

"That might be one more reason we shouldn't be doing this. But you're right. I was sitting there the whole time with one of the most famous guys in history. And I kept thinking, You don't have a clue what you're talking about."

WHERE else would they like to go? Some of the more interesting events, Custer's last stand, Pearl Harbor, Actium, Hastings, Waterloo, the Teutoburg Forest, all involved a degree of personal risk that neither was anxious to assume. "In any case," said Shel, "you can't really show up and watch the battle. Even if you didn't have to spend all your time hiding behind a tree, you'd still not be able to see anything except a small segment of what was going on."

Dave agreed. "How about the assassination of the archduke?"

They looked at each other. Ferdinand's death in Sarajevo on June 28, 1914, was unquestionably one of the pivotal events in world history. "But," said Shel, "I'm not excited about watching somebody get killed."

"Okay. Yeah, that's a point. I'll tell you what I'd like to do."

"What's that?"

"How about we go see *Hamlet*?"

Shel laughed. "See it on—"

"Opening day. Your father talked about seeing the first performance of *Lear*. We could go him one better."

"When was that?"

They were at David's place. He got up, walked over to the computer, and tapped the keys. "Somewhere around 1600 or 1601."

"That's the best we can do?"

"Nobody knows for sure. But *here's* something interesting. Shakespeare never published his plays."

"How do you mean?"

"They were performed. Not published. The plays we have

today were apparently more or less copied. I guess by people at the Globe."

"You know what?" said Shel. "We could go back and get the originals. Grab one of the scripts. It shouldn't be that hard. He's got to give them out to the actors."

"And then do what with them? Send them to a Shakespearean scholar and ruin her reputation? Let's just go watch the show."

"Okay."

"If we can find out when it was performed."

THEY needed several trips to get the exact date, April 11, 1601.

The Globe was an open-air amphitheater. Seats were arranged in sheltered compartments at three levels. They were expensive. Cheaper admission could be had into "the pit," where the general audience had to stand, or sit, as conditions permitted.

The stage was about five feet off the ground. It projected out over the pit. Its rear was protected by a roof, which was supported by columns. The back wall had several doors and curtains, allowing the cast members to move onstage and offstage. It was a cool afternoon, and a substantial portion of the audience, especially in the pit, had brought food and alcohol along. "I wonder," said Dave, "when the candy counter was invented?"

Several of the actors were handing out copies of the printed program. *HAMLET,* it said, *by William Shakespeare.* Dave looked at the cast. All were unfamiliar names, of course. Except one: The ghost was played by the author.

He folded it carefully and slipped it into a pocket.

Shel absentmindedly checked the time, and a young man sitting next to him gazed uncertainly at the watch. "What's that?" he asked.

No point lying. "It tells time."

"It's a *clock*," he said. "It's really possible to make a clock you can strap to your wrist?"

Shel showed it to him. "It's something new. Picked it up yesterday."

"Where?" asked the young man. He looked to be in his midtwenties.

"Marboro Street, I think." Shel turned to David. "It *was* Marboro, wasn't it, Dave?"

Dave had no idea whether London even *had* a Marboro Street. "I think so," he said.

"Excellent," said the young man. "I have to get myself one of those. May I inquire your name, sir?"

"Adrian Shelborne." He went on to introduce Dave.

"I'm pleased to meet you, gentlemen," he said. "My name's Ben Jonson."

Dave almost fell out of his chair. When he recovered, he extended his hand. "The author of *Every Man in His Humour*?"

Jonson smiled. "The same."

"Excellent. It's a pleasure to meet you."

"Thank you very much."

"Your work is exquisite."

"That's very kind of you, Mr. Dryden."

"My friends call me Dave."

Somewhere a horn sounded, followed by the mournful wail of a flute. Onstage, a military guard appeared and began walking his post. The flute died away. Something creaked.

The guard turned in the direction of the sound. "Who's there?"

THE production ran more than four hours. Dave tried to imagine a twenty-first-century audience, many with no chairs, enduring a performance of that length.

When he'd first looked at conditions in the theater, and saw the crowd bringing in beer and food, he'd expected a noisy, raucous evening. But once the show started, the audience became surprisingly attentive, and when necessary, they policed themselves.

It was hard to get a good look at the playwright. The ghost

wore a long dark robe, and his features were hidden within the folds of a black hood.

There were no breaks between the acts. The show simply rolled on. But the audience was involved from the start. They watched breathlessly when the ghost appeared, and waited in expectant silence while Hamlet contemplated killing Claudius at the altar. They seemed relieved when he backed off. They roared with laughter at the idiotic Polonius, who gave everyone endless advice on how to behave. One of the loudest reactions of the night was provoked by his long-winded observation that brevity was the soul of wit.

They cheered when Hamlet stabbed him through the curtains, and groaned when Ophelia turned up dead.

They sat riveted during the mass bloodletting at the finale, and were silent during the closing moments as Horatio expressed his hope that they could learn from the debacle, and Fortinbras paid a final tribute to Hamlet. The bodies were carried off to a dirge. And somewhere a cannon fired.

The actors took their bows to wild, and moderately inebriated, applause. Shakespeare, while onstage, remained hidden within the ghost's raiment. And finally the crowd began filing out.

STAFF people, or somebody, showed up with brew and food for the cast, and they celebrated backstage. Dave and Shel said good-bye to Ben Jonson and headed for the party. But there were stagehands posted at all approaches. "Nobody allowed back here except the cast," one of them said. He wasn't quite as big as Dave, but he looked considerably more willing to do what was necessary.

"We're friends of Mr. Shakespeare's," said Shel.

"Are y' now?" he said in a Scottish brogue. "And what's your name?"

"Ben Jonson," said Shel.

The stagehand laughed. "Yer no more Ben Jonson than I am. Go on, now; y' must have better things to do than hang around here."

Shel and Dave backed off but stayed close enough to watch for actors leaving the theater. "I'm a little nervous about this one," Dave said.

There were several who resembled what Shakespeare was supposed to have looked like. They had two misfires before striking gold. "Yes," he said. "I'm Will Shakespeare. Hope you enjoyed the show."

Then he was carried off by his friends. Shel called after him: "It was good, Will. Really good."

They watched him disappear.

"Well," said Dave, "that was certainly worth the wait."

Shel smiled. "At least we got to see him."

"You know," Dave said, "I assume eventually we'll get to see Einstein."

"Maybe."

"When we do, are we going to call him 'Al'?"

"Hey," said Shel, "it was the way he introduced himself."

"I know." Dave smiled. "We could tell him that relativity is good."

"Okay," said Shel. "Let it go."

"*Really* good, Al."

CHAPTER 28

Awake, my heart, and sing!

—PAUL GERHARDT (HYMN)

ASPASIA routinely turned her phone off during social events. She arrived home from a party, and had just gotten drinks for herself and her date, when she saw a missed call from Harvey Barnard. She and Harvey had gotten their doctorates together and had remained friends. He was currently on the faculty of the classics department at Wesleyan.

It was after midnight, so she let it go until morning. By then she'd forgotten about it. He called again while she was walking out to get into the car.

"I've a question for you, Aspasia. Yesterday Rob Cutler got in touch with me. I think you met him when you were here last year."

"I might have. Don't recall, Harv."

"Okay. It doesn't matter. He runs the Riverside Theater in Princeton. I'd shown him the plays you sent. He wants to know whether they can do the Achilles. *I checked to see whether anybody holds a copyright. Just in case."*

Aspasia had already looked into the possibility.

"Anyhow, they want to put it on the fall schedule. I think it's a great idea, but I thought I'd better run it by you."

"I do, too, Harv. But let me look into it, and I'll try to get back to you in a couple of days. Okay?"

SHE put the request on her Web site: AMATEUR THEATER GROUP WANTS TO PERFORM *ACHILLES*. DO YOU HAVE OBJECTION? PLEASE REPLY FROM LAST POST OFFICE.

That had been the main post office in Philadelphia, and, since she didn't know whom she was dealing with, it would serve as confirmation.

The response came by overnight mail.

Dear Dr. Kephalas:

We see no problem. The plays can be considered in the public domain.

The letter, like the earlier correspondence, had no return address. And, of course, with no signature, wasn't worth much. "But I'd be willing to bet," she told Harvey later that day, "that whoever's doing this will show up at one of the performances."

"You have any way of recognizing him?" said Harv.

"Zip. Maybe, though, he, or she, will do something that would give him away."

"You really think so?"

"Not a chance."

"Okay. Anyhow, I'll keep you apprised."

DAVE'S cabin in the Poconos had been in the family as long as he could remember. He loved the view, loved the mountains, loved the isolation.

He would have given a lot to be independently wealthy, so he could live in a place like that without having to worry about finances. For him, the ideal outcome would be to live up there with Helen and simply while away his life watching TV, reading, hiking, and hanging out on the deck in the moonlight. But the money part of it was never going to happen. He'd tried investing shortly after he'd begun his teaching career, hoping to ride some small company into big money. But he knew now that, no matter how the market went, twenty shares in a small electronics company wasn't going to take him to glory.

He hadn't entirely given up on Helen. There was a good chance that Shel would walk away from her, and if that happened, he might be able to turn the situation to his advantage. But his odds would be much better if he had something to offer.

Helen had admitted she was tired of her career track. The world, she'd told him several times, was full of hypochondriacs, people who craved attention and could find no way to get it other than by either pretending to be sick, or convincing themselves that they *were* sick. She'd begun talking about going into teaching. Get herself a position at a medical school. The odd thing about such pronouncements was that she always made them when Shel was out of earshot.

Dave had told her on occasion about his dream of moving into the cabin, and she'd encouraged him. Told him it sounded like a good way to live. That didn't mean she'd necessarily find it appealing, but there was a chance.

He never ceased regretting that he hadn't challenged Shel for her from the beginning. He could have been more persistent with her. Moved on her like a Marine landing party, the way Katie had suggested. But he'd let it go, constantly put it off, hoping that, in some idiotic way, his chances would improve if he remained aloof.

Aloof.

He'd paid a price for that.

Talking with Tom Paine, and Galileo, and Aristarchus, had shown him how shallow and dreary his own life was. Not the time-travel part, of course. But his *real* life. He and Shel had visited Rome in the glory days of the Republic, and he'd come home to bored students who had no appreciation for, nor interest in, the power of living languages. Or the instability of democratic forms of government.

Maybe it was time to stop playing by Shel's rules.

ON the impulse, without waiting to think it out, knowing that if he did, he'd back away, he set the converter for the same location, his living room, at 10:00 A.M. five days later, and punched the button.

The living room faded and came back. The only thing that had changed was that the books and a newspaper on the coffee table had moved around. It was Monday, April 28, and the future Dave Dryden was, of course, at school. He didn't want to start appearing in the house when he was already there. That was too much of a mind bender.

He listened to the faint whir of an air vent. Why did his own house feel so strange? "You're not here anywhere, are you, Dave?"

Nothing.

Good. He sat down at the computer and checked out the weekend race results.

CHAPTER 29

Being ignorant is not so much a shame, as being unwilling to learn.

—BENJAMIN FRANKLIN, *POOR RICHARD'S ALMANACK*

FOR Shel and Dave, life had become a lark. Though neither spoke the language, they navigated through a Russian week, visiting Moscow in 1913 to attend a concert performance of Sergei Rachmaninoff's *The Bells*. The next evening, they traveled to St. Petersburg, December 23, 1888, to listen to Rimsky-Korsakov's *Scheherazade*. They took two nights off so Dave could grade some papers, then returned to the Bolshoi, March 5, 1877, for Tchaikovsky's *Swan Lake*.

They sat down one evening at Lenny Pound's and put together a to-do list: Dave thought they should find a way to spend an evening with Marcus Aurelius. Shel didn't know who he was, but when Dave explained, he said okay.

Shel wanted to meet Michelangelo. "Preferably, we should catch him early, before he becomes famous. Maybe get to him at about the time he arrives in Rome."

Check.

What else?

Dave inspected his beer. "I'd like to ride downriver on Mark Twain's steamboat."

"Okay," said Shel. He was making notes. "I'd like to see the comet of 1811."

"Big one, was it?"

"Enormous. Double tail."

"Put it down."

"I'll tell you what else I'd like to do."

"What's that, Shel?"

"Socrates. I'd like to be there for the last dialogue."

"You mean when he drank the hemlock?"

"Yes."

"I thought we wanted to avoid killings and stuff."

"This is different. He talked about life and death during those last hours. It would be painful, and my Greek is still not that good, but—"

"Okay."

Shel made the entry and looked up. "What else?"

Dave took a healthy swig of his beer. "Ride with Kit Carson."

"You? I've seen you on a horse."

"I'll learn."

"Okay." He wrote it down.

Shel thought he'd enjoy spending an evening with Charles Darwin.

Dave wanted to meet Lord Byron.

"Speaking of meeting people," said Shel, "I'll tell you the guy I'd particularly like to meet."

"Who's that?"

"Leonidas. I'd like to run into him on the way to Thermopylae."

And so it went. They recorded ideas and wrote down names, and eventually they got to Ben Franklin.

Dave pushed his empty glass aside. "Yes," he said. "I'd enjoy that. But how do we get in to see him?"

"Shouldn't be hard. How'd we get to see Tom Paine? Make something up."

* * *

THE first step was to travel to London in October 1726 to pick up a copy of *Gulliver's Travels*, then just published. They stopped at Carleton's Book Store, off Regent's Park. The sales-clerk, who was also apparently the owner, told them they'd been lucky, that he couldn't keep the book in stock. "Only got one left," he said. "I'll confess, I don't understand the thing myself. But it's getting a lot of attention." He was about sixty, congenial, with enormous eyebrows.

Except it wasn't there, on the center shelf of the fiction section, where he'd expected. He had to change glasses to go looking for it. Shel helped out, and they hunted through the romance shelves. "I was sure," the clerk said, "I put it here."

It was prominently displayed, in two volumes, in the front of the store. He changed glasses, took them down from the shelf, and handed them to Shel.

"Needs bifocals," said Dave.

"Pardon?" asked the clerk.

"Nothing important," said Dave.

Franklin, of course, was only at the beginning of his career. But help was on the way.

The volumes were bound in velvet. The book had been published anonymously.

"What don't you understand about it?" Dave asked the dealer.

"What all the fuss is about. It's got tiny people. Giants. Horses that talk. It's a book for children." He went back to his original spectacles. "No wonder the author's keeping his name quiet. I would, too."

IN 1727, Franklin had founded the Junto, a group of twelve friends who met in Philadelphia at the Indian King Tavern on Friday evenings to discuss philosophy, politics, ethics, and whatever other subject seemed worthwhile. The meetings, as far as Shel could determine, were closed to nonmembers. But they took place in a bar. How difficult could it be?

They arrived down the street from the tavern on Friday evening, January 19, 1728, at a quarter to seven. Shel carried the copy of *Gulliver's Travels*, wrapped in a paper bag.

It was cold. They could *hear* the tavern before they saw it. There was music from a stringed instrument, and raucous laughter, and a strong aroma of hops. Candles glittered happily in the windows. It occurred to Shel as they approached the place that he'd almost become accustomed to a world without electricity. And that the guy who was going to change that world forever would be here tonight.

Two young men were coming from the opposite direction. They'd started their drinking early, and they had to help each other into the tavern.

Shel and Dave followed them inside. The interior was filled with tobacco smoke. The clientele was all male, and most seemed reasonably well-to-do. Some were seated at tables, eating dinner. Others had collected at a bar. The music was being provided by a middle-aged guy with a guitar.

They ordered a couple of beers and were just starting on them when four more men came in, passed directly through the room, and mounted a set of stairs in back. "That should be them," said Shel.

"I don't see anybody who looks like Franklin."

"He might be up there already."

Dave eased out of his chair. "Shall we go?"

"Let's wait till seven. We don't want to get there before *he* does."

The beer was good. More visitors entered and headed for the second floor. "How long do these meetings last?" asked Dave.

"About an hour. Hold on."

One of the newcomers, a young man, stopped at a table to talk and exchange handshakes. Shel had no idea what Franklin had looked like at twenty-one. But this might be him. He was a little taller than average, with brown hair and alert eyes. He finished the conversation and started for the stairs.

Shel waited until he was gone. Then he wandered over to the table. The two men were in their early twenties, one white, one Hispanic. Both looked prosperous. "Pardon me," he said, "but I'm trying to find a Mr. Franklin—"

"Ben?" asked the Hispanic.

"Yes."

"That was him a minute ago. He just went upstairs."

LAUGHTER drifted down from the second floor. And applause. They went up the staircase and into a corridor. A door was open, and a noisy group of men was gathered inside a meeting room. Most were young, in their twenties. Shel and Dave stopped at the entrance, where an open ledger had been set up on a small table.

Franklin had just signed in and was deeply engaged in conversation with a portly gentleman who was puffing on a large cigar.

A man with spectacles spotted Shel and Dave. He shook his head no, but when Shel entered anyway, he got up and came over. "Gentlemen," he said through a regretful smile, "I'm sorry. This is a private meeting."

"I know," said Shel. "Forgive me, but this *is* the Junto, is it not?"

"Yes, it is, sir."

Shel fixed his eyes on Franklin. "We'll only take a moment of your time. We wondered if we might speak briefly with Silence Dogood." He raised his voice sufficiently to be heard inside the room.

Franklin turned to look at them. "Really?" An amused glimmer appeared in his eyes. "And what do you know of Silence Dogood?"

"We lived in Boston for several years," said Shel. "If you are the man, I must tell you how much I enjoyed your work."

He came over. "I have it, Hugh," he told the individual who was trying to get them to leave.

"We were subscribers to the *New-England Courant*," Shel continued. "You were the best thing in the paper."

"That's very kind of you, sir." They had everyone's attention now. Franklin smiled and shrugged his shoulders, enjoying the moment. "How did you know *I* wrote the features? Only a few were aware of that."

"I've heard it from several sources, Mr. Franklin. You *are* Mr. Franklin?"

"Yes, I am."

"I'm sorry if we interrupted at an inopportune time, sir. I hope you're not offended. But when we heard you were going to be here—" He stopped midsentence. "My name is Adrian Shelborne. This is David Dryden. When we heard you were going to be here, we just couldn't resist coming by to wish you a happy birthday."

"You don't sound like a New Englander, Mr. Shelborne."

"I was born and grew up in Philadelphia, sir."

"I see. Well, I thank you for the good wishes."

The two men from the table downstairs arrived at precisely that moment. "I see they found you, Ben," said the Hispanic.

Shel smiled and held out the package. "Mr. Franklin, we brought you a gift."

Franklin looked curiously at it, but made no move to accept it.

"It's a book," said Shel.

He took it, finally. He opened the bag and withdrew one of the volumes. "Interesting," he said. He held it up so everyone in the room could see it. "*Gulliver's Travels.*" He glanced at the second volume and turned back to Shel and Dave. "That's a substantial gift for someone you do not know."

"It's small enough return for one who has given us so much pleasure."

A man with shaggy red hair laughed. "The Brits say whoever wrote it is a troublemaker."

"Good," roared another. "Troublemakers always make the best reading." He smiled up at Franklin. "Don't they, Ben?"

No one else seemed to have known it was Franklin's birthday. They thanked the newcomers, passed a motion that Franklin not be permitted to pay for his drinks, and, after some discussion, passed another suspending the rule barring nonmembers from participating in meetings. Shel and Dave were shown a copy of the bylaws, which informed them, while on the premises, they must keep open minds, that no unprovable assertion would be considered sacrosanct, that strong opinions would not be tolerated, and that speakers were not to monopolize the time.

"We are not a debating club," Franklin said. "Our goal is to get at the truth, where that is possible."

THE topic for the evening was the willingness of human beings to be influenced by the social milieu in which they live. Tribalism. The damage that unthinking groups, following what would eventually be called memes, inflict on each other. The discussion rapidly veered off into whether rebels are as dangerous to a peaceful society as those who are unthinkingly obedient and respect authority.

It went back and forth. Without authoritarian controls, chaos would ensue. But people acting in the name of authority, or of a group, will commit atrocities they would never perpetrate on their own.

Take the New England witch trials, for example.

Shel found himself thinking of the Holocaust. He wondered how many in that room would believe that such an event was even possible in a supposedly civilized nation. If it could happen in Germany, could it happen anywhere?

The man who'd taken them into the hall, Hugh Meredith, wondered if it wasn't possible to establish strict controls on authority. "Give ultimate power to the people," he suggested.

"I agree," said John Jones, Jr., a shoemaker. "Surely there is a place between authoritarian rule and chaos."

"Perhaps," said Franklin, "we should resurrect Rome. Cicero's Rome."

"Divide the power." Voices were joining in from all over the room.

"Two consuls."

"A senate."

"And vote them all out every couple of years."

* * *

AT the end of the evening, as the members were leaving, Franklin took Shel and Dave aside. "I think you will be receiving an invitation to join our group," he said. "I will hope to see you again."

"Ah," said Shel, "we appreciate the compliment. Unfortunately, we do not live close enough that a membership would be practical."

"That's a pity. Where *are* you living currently?"

"Baltimore."

"Yes." He sighed. "Well, we were glad to have had you with us for the evening." He gazed down at *Gulliver's Travels*. "And thank you for this. I've heard interesting things about it."

"I think you'll enjoy it, Ben." (They were by then on first-name terms.)

"By the way," said Dave, "I wonder whether we didn't see an example of tribalism here tonight?"

"By *us*?" asked Franklin. "How do you mean?"

"The club," Dave said. "There were no women present."

CHAPTER 30

I have often thought that if there had been a good rap group around in those days, I might have chosen a career in music instead of politics.

—RICHARD NIXON, AUDIO, THE NIXON PRESIDENTIAL LIBRARY

THE lack of women participants at the Junto led Dave and Shel to Sojourner Truth. They were among the very few males present when she delivered her "Ain't I a Woman?" speech in 1851 at the Ohio Women's Rights Convention in Akron.

They spent an evening with Alexander von Humboldt in eighteenth-century Berlin discussing celestial mechanics and politics.

They hung out in a Milan bar several evenings with Ernest Hemingway, while he was recovering from wounds incurred driving an ambulance during World War I.

A few nights later they were in eastern France, at the Chateau de Cirey, talking with Voltaire and his lover, the Marquise du Châtelet. Actually, Dave did most of the talking, because Shel's French was nonexistent. But they hit it off. Voltaire, whose name was actually François-Marie Arouet, was simultaneously the funniest and the most passionate man Shel had ever encountered. And this despite the fact that everything had to be translated.

The evening went well, and they were invited back. Shel worked on his French, and the next time they went, he was better able to participate.

Voltaire loved parties. They met Ibrahim Muteferrika at one and Alexander Pope at another. Jonathan Swift was to have traveled with Pope, but he failed to arrive. "I think," Pope said, "he has no taste for traveling long distances."

On October 1, 1932, they were in the stands at Wrigley Field when Babe Ruth called his shot against Charlie Root. (And yes, there was no question in Shel's mind what Ruth intended when, on a 2–2 count, he stepped out of the box and pointed his bat toward the right center field bleachers.)

At Fort Bridger, in 1868 Wyoming, Dave bought a round of drinks for Calamity Jane. In France after the Great War, they arranged to meet the Unsinkable Molly Brown while posing as reconstruction volunteers. (And, in fact, she successfully coerced them into doing some work.) Years later, her time, they partied with her on the Hannibal, Missouri, social circuit.

But the big catch was to be George Washington. Claiming to be journalists, they attended the award ceremony for Mary Hays McCauly. Mary, the general explained, had accompanied her husband to the battlefield, and "on a blazing hot day, paid no mind to incoming artillery shells, and carried pitchers of water to thirsty soldiers. When her husband was wounded, she took his place at the gun." He presented her with her warrant. "Henceforth, Mrs. McCauly will be known as Sergeant Molly."

In fact, of course, history knows her as Molly Pitcher.

After the ceremony, in their anxiety to talk with Molly, they let Washington slip away.

THE converters were hopelessly addictive. Shel and Dave were traveling constantly, visiting Caesar's Rome, wandering through Florence at the height of the Enlightenment, offering advice to Van Dyck and El Greco. On August 3, 1492, they stood at the mouth of the harbor in Palos, Spain, watching Columbus's three ships depart westward, ostensibly for India.

They visited Henry Thoreau, jailed in Concord for refusing to pay taxes during the Mexican War; and Harlan Ellison, jailed in southeastern Louisiana for participating in civil rights protests.

They spent an afternoon in Dayton, Tennessee, at the Scopes Monkey Trial, and rode on Mark Twain's riverboat. They were on a crowded rooftop in the Battery at Charleston, with several dozen others, when, at 4:30 A.M., April 12, 1861, the Confederates opened fire on Fort Sumter.

It was during this period that they moved the base of the operation from the town house to Dave's modest home on Carmichael Drive. By then there were too many costumes to manage equitably, and Dave had the ideal walk-in closet.

They made a second try for George Washington. During the Revolution, it was impossible to get close to him. They compromised, and spent a few minutes with a younger version of the man in an Alexandria tavern in 1759. He was twenty-seven at the time, but already a veteran of the French and Indian War. Shel and Dave pretended to be journalists, as they had so often. But Shel's impression was that, while he was courteous, Washington wasn't particularly receptive. He was unwilling to submit to what he perceived as an interview and took the first opportunity to excuse himself from their company.

But the evening began a tradition of meeting presidents well before they'd become political forces.

A twenty-year-old Andrew Jackson actually unnerved Shel. They were in Salisbury, North Carolina, in 1787. Jackson had recently been admitted to the bar. Shel and Dave, pretending to have just learned about his accomplishment, were helping him celebrate when a couple of oversized roughnecks made lascivious comments to a passing woman. Jackson directed them to leave.

When they challenged him, he took off his jacket and invited either, or both, to try their luck. He glanced at Shel, and smiled. Shel realized, with horror, he was being invited into the fight. Fortunately, it wasn't necessary: Both thugs backed off.

They located Herbert Hoover at twenty-six in China during the Boxer Rebellion. He introduced himself as "Herb," and said he was glad to see some fellow Americans. Shel was in the middle of explaining why they were there, how they were on a round-the-world tour, when gunfire and explosions interrupted the conversation. Several nearby houses exploded. Others erupted in flames. Hoover charged into one of them and began carrying out wounded kids. Shel and Dave hesitated briefly, then followed his lead.

They interviewed Woodrow Wilson in Atlanta, in January 1883, allegedly for an article to appear in *Georgia Law*. During the interview, Wilson discussed his political ambitions. "Of course I'd like to be president," he said. "The country needs to change its direction."

"In what way, Mr. Wilson?"

"The government, as it is presently constituted, invites corruption. We need to rewrite the Constitution. Bring it into the modern age."

"You think the Constitution is obsolete?"

"It's hopelessly eighteenth-century, sir. Hopelessly."

THEY stopped by the Grant & Perkins leather shop in Galena, Illinois, on the brink of the Civil War, to talk with Ulysses Grant about saddles and incidentally his feelings on the tension with the Southern states. "Eventually," he said, "it's going to come to a shoot-out." He shook his head. "Far as I'm concerned, we might as well get it over with."

They tried on hats at the Truman & Jacobson haberdashery in Kansas City in the summer of 1920. In 1833, they left clothing to be repaired at Andrew Johnson's tailor shop in Greenville, Tennessee.

Expecting to get away from politics for a time, they traveled to the Lamplight, a restaurant in 1937 Durham, N.C., to encounter, accidentally, Aldous Huxley, who would be there that evening with friends. While they waited, the piano player took a break, and a young dark-haired guy, who was one of a group of students seated in back, came forward at their urging and sat down on the bench. He rippled through the keys, and it became immediately evident that he was quite good. While his friends cheered, he played "These Foolish Things." Huxley came in during the rendition, and Shel got up, started across the room, and stopped abruptly, pretending shock at recognizing, as he put it, the writer he admired most in the world. "You *are* Aldous Huxley, aren't you?"

Huxley smiled uncomfortably. Nodded. "Yes, I am." And: "Hello."

"I love your work," Shel said.

Dave, meantime, recognized something familiar about the piano player.

"*Brave New World* is brilliant," Shel continued. "I wish I had my copy with me so I could have you sign it. Would it be all right if I took a picture?"

"Well—" Huxley hesitated. Looked at his three companions. "Sure."

"Dave? We need the camera."

The pianist finished and started another number. "In the Moonlight in the Chapel."

Dave took out his gooseberry and waved Shel closer to Huxley so he could get them both in the shot.

"Say," said Huxley, "what kind of camera is *that*?"

"Newest model," said Shel.

Dave took the picture. And two more.

"May I see it?"

Dave handed it to the author, with the first picture on-screen. "That's the photo," said Shel.

Huxley was impressed. "Magnificent," he said. "Where can I get one of these?"

Dave handed the gooseberry to Shel and walked over to the pianist. "You have a nice touch," he said.

The young man smiled. "Thanks." He was in his early twenties.

"You're a student?"

"Duke Law."

"Very good. That should give you a running start."

The smile widened. "I hope so."

One of his friends, a young woman, pushed into the conversation. "Dick," she said, "how about 'Taking a Chance on Love'?"

Dick winked at her.

"I'm talking about the piano."

"Oh," he said. "Sure." He gave Dave a thumbs-up and started playing.

Dave went back to their table. Shel by then had returned. "You recognize that guy?" Dave asked.

"Who?"

"The guy at the piano."

Shel looked. Shook his head. "No."

"You're sure?"

"Who do you think he is?"

"Think 'Checkers.' "

" 'Checkers'? Who plays checkers?"

"Not the board game. The dog."

Shel stared. He shook his head. "Not a chance," he said.

CHAPTER 31

On life's vast ocean diversely we sail,
Reason the card, but passion is the gale.
—ALEXANDER POPE, *ESSAY ON MAN*

THAT remarkable evening was made even more memorable because it was the night Dave met Sandy Meyers. Sandy was one of two women enjoying an animated conversation on the other side of the restaurant. She had deep brown eyes and rich chestnut hair swept up in the style of the time. And a laugh that shook Dave's world. Shel had not bought Dave's theory regarding the young man who'd sat down at the piano. He was back with his friends now, and the house pianist had returned. But Shel had wandered over to speak with him, while Dave kept an eye on the woman with the electric smile. Dick nodded a couple of times. Then Shel caught his breath and started taking pictures, and Dave knew he'd been right. But something more important was taking over his life at the moment.

Twice, the woman caught him looking at her. The first time, her gaze moved past as if he were invisible. A few minutes later, it happened again, and that smile flickered briefly. It lasted no longer than an eyeblink, but it was there.

Her companion was a blonde, and they were exchanging

war stories. Each had a briefcase tucked beside her. There were no businesswomen during this era. And no female lawyers. So he concluded they were teachers.

He wanted to get up, go over, and say hello. Usually he had no problem walking up to strange women and introducing himself. But this time an odd reluctance overtook him. And he watched forlornly as they finished their meal, called for the check, put a couple of bills on the table, and got up to go.

She's walking out of my life.

What kind of approach did he have available? All the usual lines seemed dumb. *Pardon me, but I think we've met before.*

Maybe he could fake another heart attack.

Then he caught a break. She'd picked up her briefcase, but she was leaving a hat behind. It was, he decided, an invitation. He gave her time to get to the door, then spotted a waiter zeroing in on the hat. David literally leaped from his chair, moved quickly to block off the waiter, scooped up the hat, and started after her.

They were at the curb and appeared to be looking for a taxi. "Pardon me," he said, showing them the hat, "but I think one of you ladies left this behind."

Her eyes touched his, and his heart picked up a beat. "Thank you," she said.

"My pleasure." He paused. "It's a lovely hat."

THAT was how it began. She and the other woman were going for a drink at Halo's. Would he care to join them?

"I have a friend inside," Dave said.

"He's welcome to come along."

But Shel was still in a state of shock at his double score in the Lamplight. "See you at home," said Dave.

He went back to Sandy and her friend, and they were on their way. Twenty minutes later, they commandeered a table at Halo's and eventually drank and sang the balance of the evening.

"What does she do for a living?" Shel asked, when they were back in the town house.

"She's a math instructor at Duke."

"Good. So where do you go from here?"

Dave had no idea. But it had been a long time since he'd been so enthralled, so quickly, by a woman. Not even Helen had hit him that hard.

WITHOUT saying anything to Shel, he returned to Durham two days later and called Sandy from a drugstore. They made a date for a Saturday evening concert. He told her he'd look forward to the evening, hung up, and used the converter to move forward to Saturday night, grabbed a cab, and arrived outside her apartment fifteen minutes later.

She looked even better than he remembered. He'd already told her what he did for a living. "Where do you teach?" she asked.

He should have been prepared. He needed a local school, but his brain froze, and he told her he was at Penn.

"I'm surprised," she said, "you can get away during the semester. How'd you manage that?"

And that's what happens when you start telling the truth. He made up a story about a sick relative and got the distinct impression she knew he was lying. But she let it go, and minutes later they were inside the theater listening to Sergei Rachmaninoff, who was on tour, play several of his own compositions.

IT was a dazzling night, and a week later, for her—though the next night for him—he took her to see a British film, *Gangway*, with Jessie Matthews and Alastair Sim. This time he'd had to claim he'd driven in from Philadelphia to see how his sick cousin was doing. (But after the show he couldn't remember the specifics of what he had told her. Sick cousin? Or had it been his mother?)

"It's not easy," she said, "getting information from you."

He tried to laugh it off. "There's probably not much to get. Except that beautiful women seem to enjoy my company."

They returned to the Lamplight the following evening, ostensibly the day before he was to go back to Philadelphia. She liked him, smiled at all the right times, and let him know in a hundred different ways that he *mattered*. Even though she'd known him only a couple of weeks, she wanted to keep him around.

But there were problems. "Where's your car?" she'd asked. "Why are we using a taxi?"

He should have told her he'd taken the train, but it hadn't occurred to him. "I left it with Sarah. In case she needs it."

"She must be doing much better."

"Oh, yes," he said. "She's much improved."

After he'd dropped out of sight, which was an inevitable outcome, she might make phone calls and find out he'd lied to her. No David Dryden at Penn. Maybe no David Dryden even in the Philadelphia phone book. At least none who was likely to be teaching languages anywhere.

And that hurt. Losing her would be bad enough. But to send her off knowing he'd been a fraud?

The Lamplight, he decided, reluctantly, would be their last evening together. The longer he delayed, the harder it would be on both of them. He wanted to do it, get it over with, put it all behind him, but he couldn't bring himself to say the words.

She gave him the perfect opening when she read his face and asked what was wrong. But he just wasn't ready. Maybe it would be best to think it through anyhow. He decided he'd talk to her during the week and tell her there was someone else in his life. That he was going to ask this other woman to marry him. He'd apologize, and say how much he'd enjoyed being with her and he understood if she was angry. But that, however things played out, she'd always have a friend.

They were seated at the table Huxley had occupied. The pianist was doing "It's a Sin to Tell a Lie."

"Nothing," he said. "Life couldn't be better."

She looked at him closely, and apparently decided to go along with the game. "Our special place," she said.

He squeezed her wrist. "Forever."

But it must not have been in his voice. "That's easy to say, Dave." Her eyes glittered. "You want to call it a night?"

"No," he said. No. He didn't want to call it a night. Didn't want to say good-bye. He could imagine himself coming back to this evening, watching from across the street as they left the Lamplight, as he had watched himself and Erin at the cabin, regretting he had let her go. And yet what other choice did he have?

"You feel like dancing?" she said.

She knew a good spot, so they went across town. It was his first attempt at doing the Charleston, and she seemed mildly surprised that he was less than accomplished. From there they went to the Flamingo for a nightcap. And then it was over and the taxi was pulling up in front of her apartment house, and she was inviting him in.

But he passed. "Wiped out," he said. He asked the taxi to wait while he walked her to the door. He kept thinking *never again*. Thinking how he would miss her. When he drew her into his arms, all the suppleness was gone.

She *knew*.

"I'll be in touch," he said.

HE had an option: He could tell her the truth and bring her forward to 2019. When he got home, he googled her, hoping there'd be no record of her, or at least nothing beyond the time when they'd met. *Sandra Myers, a beloved math teacher at Duke who, on a summer night in 1937, vanished utterly. No trace of her was ever found....*

Unfortunately, he saw that she'd married in 1939, two years after Durham, to a David Collins.

Another David.

They'd had a son. When World War II broke out, Collins went into the Navy. He apparently spent most of the war in the Pacific, was at Midway and Guadalcanal, won a Purple Heart in the Philippine Sea during the Great Marianas Turkey Shoot, and had been at Leyte Gulf. He'd been decorated, and returned a hero. Eventually, he and Sandy had had another son and a daughter.

After the war, they'd settled in Durham. Sandy stayed on at Duke, and made a reputation as a theorist. She'd written two books on math, *Biomath* and *Universal Mathematics*, and eventually made a name for herself as a popular scientific essayist. There were some pictures of her from those early years, including one as a bride.

She'd died in 1993 at the age of 81.

HE went back to Durham one more time after that, took her to dinner again, and told her the story about getting engaged. (He hadn't been able to bring himself to do it over the phone.) "I'm going to ask her next weekend," he said. "I wanted you to know."

She took it well. Better than he'd liked. But she nodded, bit off a piece of steak, and chewed it for a long time. "I'm glad you told me," she said.

"I'm sorry."

"I guess it wasn't easy for you." She managed a smile, a weak one, and pushed the mostly uneaten dinner away. "Good luck with it."

"Thank you."

Then she was gone. He wanted to tell her that "These Foolish Things" would always be *their* song. But he didn't dare.

PART THREE

TIME OUT OF JOINT

CHAPTER 32

If the first woman God ever made was strong enough to turn
the world upside down all alone, these women together ought
to be able to turn it back, and get it right side up again.

— SOJOURNER TRUTH (ISABELLA VAN WAGENER)

THE forays into the historical past continued unabated. In
what they'd hoped would be a highlight of their adventures,
Shel and Dave introduced themselves to Archimedes, but the
conversation never really went anywhere. Archimedes simply
had better things to do than entertain two barbarians.

They had no more luck with Solon. The great lawgiver
explained that he'd enjoy talking with them, but he was busy
at the moment.

Still, those were the exceptions. In the Yukon, in 1911,
they spent a week whooping it up in every saloon along the
Klondike with Bob Service. Looking for comedy, they took in
the A.D. 67 Olympics, which had been hijacked by Nero. The
Emperor turned it partially into a musical contest, in which
he won every event he entered. And he also won the chariot
race, despite falling out of the vehicle during one of the turns.

They visited Alice Paul in a Virginia prison in 1917, and
assured her that her cause would triumph. Women would get
everything they were asking. "And soon," said Dave.

"I'd like to believe you," she said. "We'll see what happens."

Shel ached to tell her what he knew, to take her out of there and show her what the future held. But he simply asked her to keep the faith.

After the visit, they moved several weeks upstream and watched the demonstration outside the White House that had provoked the arrests. A mob of angry men screaming insults at women carrying signs demanding the right to vote. Calling them pigs and traitors.

Shel just stared as one oversized guy had to be restrained by police from physically attacking Alice.

ARTHUR'S Camelot had an element of danger. But they decided to take a chance on it anyhow. They made several efforts but never found it. Nobody had ever established a precise geographical location for it, nor was there any certainty about the dates of its existence. For that matter, there was serious doubt whether it had existed at all. "If we could take a decent means of transportation back with us," said Shel, "maybe we could nail it down. But trying to walk all over England isn't a very efficient way to do this."

It was while they were wandering around the British forests that Dave surprised him. "It's good to be away from my classes. It's one of the advantages of the converters. I can wander off for weeks and not even think about the next essay exam."

"You don't like your new classes?" It was September, both at home and here in Britain.

"It's not the kids. They don't change from year to year. And I shouldn't expect them to arrive with unbridled enthusiasm. Instilling that is my job. It's just—"

"What?"

"When you've been looking for Lancelot and Guinevere, declensions get pretty dull." He stopped for a minute to listen to a scuffle in the branches. "This is going to be my last semester."

"You're going to quit?"

"I think so. The time has come."

"What are you going to do?"

"I've made some money at the track."

"The horses? You've been playing the horses?"

"Yes."

"You've been downstream, reading the race results."

"Once or twice."

Dave looked as if he didn't want to say any more. But he shrugged and plowed ahead. "Shel, I have an original oil, a hawk in flight, by N. C. Wyeth. It took everything I had to buy it, back in the twenties. But it's priceless now. I have bids for it that are out of the world. I'm going to take some of what it sells for, go back, and pick up an abstract desert landscape by Georgia O'Keeffe. I'm going to become an art dealer."

Shel didn't like it. But he couldn't see any harm. "Good luck," he said, reluctantly.

Dave grinned, pleased that Shel had taken it so well. "There's room for both of us," he said.

"Thanks." Shel didn't really need the money.

They gave up on Camelot, and made the final stop on their grand tour, though neither knew it at the time, on the beach at Cape Kennedy, July 16, 1969, where they relaxed and watched the launch of Apollo 11.

And the subject came up again. "You know," said Shel, when it was over and the applause had died down, "I like the idea of collecting art."

"What did you have in mind?"

"Michelangelo."

"That's a good place to start."

"I mean, why bother with some relatively minor-league stuff when we could go get a portrait or something by *him*?"

"I'm with you."

"He was only twenty-one when he first went to Rome."

"And—?"

"Nobody knew yet what he could do. We could pay a visit. Give him a commission. Let him do a sculpture for us. It wouldn't cost much, and it would encourage him." He paused and looked out to sea. A freighter was passing. "What do you think?"

"A sculpture of what?"

"I don't know. Athena would be nice. Maybe we could have him do an Aphrodite, too. One for each of us."

SHEL, in fact, had been spending time in Philadelphia, circa 2100. It was lovely, delicate, strong, beautiful. All the dire predictions of his own era had proven wrong. Yes, there were still problems, overpopulation primary among them. But world leaders had apparently long since gotten serious, and steps either had been, or were being, taken. Global warming was being brought under control, and the world's nukes were gone. Famine still existed in spots but was not as widespread as people at the beginning of the century had feared. At home, the American dollar, eventually grown worthless after years of irresponsible fiscal policies, had been replaced, twenty to one, by "capital dollars."

He was tempted to go farther afield, to find out what life would be like in the twenty-third century. Or in the fourth millennium. But in the end he decided to let it go.

A new skyscraper, the Claremont, would soon be going up. It was in Center City, with a magnificent view of the new city hall and the Parkway. They weren't taking reservations yet for condos, of course. But that was not a problem for Shel. He simply moved downstream a year and a half and secured a penthouse, which became his base. He furnished it lavishly, installed the best computer he could find, and bought a giant 3-V projection system. He spent more time there than he did in the town house.

He debated showing it to Dave. But that would mean explaining why he'd violated his assurances about traveling into the future. He knew Dave would say it was okay, forget it. But he'd conclude that Shel couldn't be trusted. The future, for Dave, and maybe for both of them, was still a scary place.

Shel's career with Carbolite had come to seem impossibly mundane. Dave's decision to leave Penn inspired him to pull the plug. The morning after they'd returned from watching the moon shot, Shel gave Linda his resignation. Effective in thirty days.

She was shocked. "I thought you were happy here, Shel. I had no idea you were contemplating anything like this."

"I've *been* happy," he said. "It's not that. But I came into some money, and the truth is that I'd just like to take it easy for a while."

"Okay." Linda sighed. "Shel, you understand I won't be able to hold the job open for you."

"Of course."

He was tired. Traveling took a lot out of him. He never quite knew what time it was. Or what day of the week. After he'd talked with her, he went back to his office to work on a sales brochure for the new solar-energy system they were preparing to market.

STORM clouds gathered through the day, and it was raining when he left. It was a Thursday afternoon. He and Dave were planning to go out again Saturday, back for another party with Voltaire, which had rapidly become Shel's favorite pastime. His French had improved immeasurably. He wasn't fluent, certainly, but he could not remember a time in his life when he had so much enjoyed himself.

The storm was breaking up and drifting east toward Jersey when he got home. He put aside the work he'd brought along and crashed for an hour. Then, on a whim, he called Helen. "If you don't have anything planned," he said, "I'm looking for a beautiful young woman to take to dinner."

"I'll see if I can locate one," she said.

"Ah, mademoiselle, surely you josh with me."

"Surely. How's Voltaire coming?"

The response jolted him. Then he remembered that he'd mentioned during an evening out last weekend that he was reading the French philosopher. "Okay," he said.

"Good. All right, Shel, if you don't mind, I'm in the mood for some pizza."

"You're going to give me a cheap date."

"You know me."

* * *

"YOU seem down tonight, Shel." She nibbled at her salad.

"No, I'm good."

"What happened?" She lifted her Coke, looked at him, and put it back down.

The scent of candles mixed with the warm aroma of oregano. The candles were inside globes mounted on the walls. "I quit my job today."

"You left Carbolite?"

"Yes."

"Why?"

"I was bored."

"Okay. That's a good reason." She smiled at him, inviting him to explain where he was going next.

"I thought I'd just take some time off and decide on a new career path."

That must have sounded foolish, but she didn't react, other than to show she sympathized. "You going to be all right?" she asked.

"You mean for money?"

She said yes with her eyes.

"Yeah. I'm fine. Money's not a problem."

The pizza came, and he thought about inviting her to join him for an evening with Voltaire.

"There's something else on your mind."

Maybe there was. "Helen, I miss you when we're not together."

She was dividing the slices. "Ah, Shel, that's a bit over the top. But the truth is, I miss you, too."

"Really?"

"Well, up to a point."

He leaned across the table. "Helen, this doesn't feel like the right time to ask, but—" The world squeezed down to the tabletop, the Cokes, the candles, and the pizza. And those large, lustrous eyes. "I'm in love with you." He lowered his voice. "I'd like you to share my pizza forever."

She laid a piece on his plate. "Is that a proposal?"

"Yeah. I'm sorry. I know this isn't exactly a romantic spot."
She laughed.

"And I don't have a ring with me. I didn't expect to do this
tonight—"

"When *did* you expect to do it?"

"I don't know. But anyhow—"

"Yes," she said.

HE dropped her at home. "I'd invite you in, Shel," she said,
"but tomorrow's my day at the hospital. Starts at dawn."

"I know."

"It's not exactly the way to launch our engagement, but I
have to be awake."

"I know. Call you tomorrow night."

"I hope so."

He walked her to the door. She delivered a deep kiss,
and held on to him for a long minute. Then she laughed and
pushed him away. "I better go."

She put her key in the lock, looked back briefly, with glow-
ing eyes and a happy smile. Then the door opened, and she let
herself in just as a bolt of lightning brightened the street. Seconds later, thunder boomed, and rain began to fall. "Appropriate staging," he said.

She laughed. "Good night, Shel."

He drove home through a downpour. Life with Helen was
actually going to happen. And yes, this weekend he'd take her
to meet Voltaire.

HE didn't like his living room anymore. The twenty-second-
century penthouse was better. It was, in fact, spectacularly
better. He could sit up there and look down at the city lights.
Helen would love the place. And he'd take her there, too. Maybe
take her there first, so she could get used to the jumps. Come
to think of it, Voltaire might not be a good idea. He had no
clue whether she could speak French.

He'd call Dave in the morning and tell him.

But now there would be three travelers. It was getting crowded. He could imagine his father's reaction.

He made a drink and listened to the rain pounding on the roof. The storm had become torrential. Lightning lit up the curtains, and thunder shook the place.

He was wide awake, so there was no point going to bed. Couldn't put on the TV or the computer during the storm. But, of course, he had options.

He got a converter out of the bottom drawer in his desk, set it for the penthouse, and traveled out.

HE arrived on a clear, cool summer evening. There was a concert getting ready to start down on the Parkway, and lights were just coming on at the Art Museum. He'd brought his drink along, and he went outside onto the balcony to finish it.

He was still excited, too ramped up over Helen to sleep. He thought about going down and joining the crowd. But he'd need her along. In the end, he simply made himself another drink.

He listened for a while. The band was mostly strings, and they were playing pop music. Some of it was familiar, tunes that had been around in his own time.

Eventually, he went back inside, sat down in front of his computer, and turned it on. He checked the news on *Wide World*. A price-fixing scandal had erupted among food distributors. Somebody had filmed a celebrity orgy, and it was playing all over the Internet. Congressmen had been caught taking money from China to influence U.S. policy. Crime rates were dropping again. The National Football League had gone back to salary caps. And a prominent physicist was saying that antigravity was close.

Then, without giving himself time to think about it, he did what he'd been wanting to do ever since the converters became available. He ran a search.

On himself.

CHAPTER 33

Time is like a river. As soon as a thing is seen, it is carried away and another takes its place, and then that other is carried away also.

—MARCUS AURELIUS, *MEDITATIONS*

DAVE was out with Katie when the storm arrived. She'd just unloaded a guy who, a few weeks earlier, had looked like the one she'd spend her life with. But he'd proven to be too wrapped up in himself. Good-looking, kind to animals, bright future. Still, his conversation was limited to his own interests, to *himself*, and she'd given up. So they'd sat in Lenny Pound's, and Dave had listened, assuring her everything would be okay, and she was lucky to have found out before she'd become emotionally involved (which, of course, was not at all the reality). The thunder had rumbled through the night, and eventually he'd taken her to her apartment. He saw that she didn't want him to stay, so he'd suggested dinner the following evening, gone home, and turned on the late news. But a few minutes later, a lightning bolt knocked out the power.

He switched on a battery-powered lamp, picked up the *Inquirer*, and was still on the front page when the lights came back on.

Life was good, and getting better. The stacks of essays

that lined the walls of his room would, by January, be gone. He would no longer have to worry about getting up in the morning. He would have no boss. And he saw no reason why he wouldn't become wealthy. Overnight. He'd begun looking around for a new home. Something a bit more plush. He'd lost interest in the cabin-on-a-mountaintop plan. Maybe because his options were opening up. Maybe because he no longer felt an inclination to hide from the world. However that might be, he sat with the paper folded in his lap, thinking about Katie, wondering how he'd explain his new financial status to his family, and feeling fortunate. Everything—almost everything—was breaking his way.

The storm dwindled to a light sprinkle and an occasional rumble. He went out to the kitchen, got a piece of chocolate cake, and switched on the computer. A news roundup was reporting a six-car pileup on I-95. In Connecticut, a young man officially designated as retarded would be competing for the state chess championship, and another bank robbery had happened in South Philadelphia.

Then it was on to sports and weather. The Eagles' new all-pro tight end had fallen down a flight of stairs and broken an ankle. A front was moving in from somewhere. Another storm.

Last time he'd had chocolate cake, he'd been sitting across the table from Sandy.

She would linger, he knew, a long time.

Against his better judgment, he tapped her name into the computer.

Her doctoral thesis was available. And some commentaries. He looked at them, but they were written for mathematicians, not for a love-struck time traveler.

Her three kids had also been successful. One had become a professional baseball player, though he'd never made it to the big leagues. Dave found a picture of him in a college uniform. Looks like me, he decided. Ah, that it could have been so.

Her husband had been a graduate of Wesleyan University. That would have been around 1928. On a whim, he called up the list of graduates for that year, but found no David Collins.

There was also none in 1927 or 1929.

Odd. He found himself hoping that maybe there was something not quite legitimate about Collins. Something that would cause Sandy to wish, somehow, she had been able to hold on to *him*. It was a selfish reaction, and pointed to a weakness in his character. But there it was.

In fact, he stayed with the search and discovered that Collins had graduated several years later. At the age of twenty-six. He'd started school late because he liked sailing. He owned a boat, and had made a part-time career taking tourists out to sea near his home on St. Simons Island, Georgia. For a time, he said, he was content with sailing and thought about passing on college altogether. Ultimately, after the war, David Collins had become a dentist.

Dave sighed and shut the system down.

He always read for a while before going to sleep. Back in the old days, before Shel had shown up with his converters, it had been mostly novels, and maybe a few political books. But now he found himself reading Voltaire and Lamb and biographies of Galileo and Molly Pitcher. It felt both strange and exhilarating to know he had heard their voices, had known the sound of their laughter.

The book that night was *Shoot-Out: The Life and Times of Calamity Jane*, by Michael Hevner. He turned on the bedside lamp, settled into the sheets, and began to read. Calamity was out in the Rockies someplace, functioning as a scout for the cavalry. And yes, he could literally *see* it. See *her*. He remembered her touch. Remembered the way she'd smiled when he bought her a whiskey.

He was, he decided, the luckiest man on the planet.

HE slept peacefully through the night. Once or twice he woke to the rumble of distant thunder. But the rain had stopped altogether. He wondered if maybe one day a time traveler from the distant future would come back to meet *him*.

By morning, the storm had passed though the sky was still gray. Dave showered and dressed, went downstairs, and started a couple of hard-boiled eggs while the TV pundits switched over to the deteriorating relations between India and China over food and energy. The president had offered the services of the United States to assist with negotiations.

He made two pieces of toast, collected his eggs, and put them in a cup. He decided to go with grape jelly for a change on the toast and poured a glass of orange juice.

The new Star Trek film was being released tonight, and everybody expected it to top the charts. Susan Holvik and Gary Park, a pair of Hollywood superstars married amid considerable hoopla eighteen months earlier, were splitting. And Evin Cowper was rumored to be taking over the James Bond role.

Same old stuff. Dave turned off the TV, and ate his breakfast with the current *Newsweek* propped up in front of him. When he'd finished, he picked up his briefcase. Later today he would go back to 1936 Britain to buy an early bronze from Lynn Chadwick, then in his early twenties. The bronze was part man, part eagle, with wings spread, and a distinctly threatening aspect. Dave didn't know much about sculpture, but he liked the piece, and he knew its value would multiply substantially over the price he'd negotiated.

He was getting his converter out of the sock drawer when the phone rang. It was Jerry Shelborne.

"Dave," he said, *"have you heard the news?"* His voice was hollow.

Dave's first thought was that there'd been a terrorist attack. "No. What's wrong, Jerry?"

"Shel's dead."

"What?"

"It happened this morning. Lightning hit his place. It burned to the ground."

"He didn't get out?"

"No."

DAVE got it up on the computer. The lightning had struck the town house at about four thirty in the morning. The fire department had responded within minutes, but they were unable to rescue Shel, who was apparently asleep in his bed-room when it happened. The body had been burned beyond recognition.

Dave read the report through, then simply sat, empty of all feeling. He knew, absolutely *knew*, it wasn't possible. Shel couldn't be gone.

The phone rang again. *"Dave, I just heard."* It was Katie. *"I'm sorry, Dave. He was a good guy."*

"Yeah."

"Are you okay?" She paused. *"I guess that's a dumb question."*

"I'm okay," he said.

HE was still in a state of shock when he got into his car and headed for the town house. It was going to turn out to be a terrible mistake. Had to be.

When he arrived, the place was a smoking ruin. The walls and roof had collapsed. At the side of the house, the garage was blackened but still standing. Shel's Toyota was appar-ently okay. The music store that flanked him on one side was moderately damaged. The pharmacy, on the other side, had escaped the conflagration. A police car and a black vehicle marked CITY OF PHILADELPHIA were parked at the curb. Yel-low tape sealed the property off. Two people from the fire department were standing to one side. He could make out a corner of the sofa, which was half-buried under blackened rubble. And what remained of the coffee table. And the frame of Shel's desk. Where he kept the converters. No way they could have survived.

Several people watched from across the street.

He stopped and got out. A police officer came toward him. "Have to move on, sir," she said.

"I'm a friend."

"I'm sorry for your loss. But there's nothing here, and you're blocking traffic."

"The newspapers say that Dr. Shelborne was found in his bed."

"I believe that's correct."

"Are they sure it was him?"

She was a tall woman. About thirty. Kept looking from him to his car. "The body was pretty badly burned. I don't think they've been able to do a formal identification yet. But as far as I know, there doesn't seem to be much question. May I ask your name, please?"

She wrote it down, added contact information and relationship, and suggested he call the next day for more details.

He drove away, went several blocks, and pulled over. He hesitated, then took out his cell phone and punched in Helen's number.

A young woman answered. *"Dr. Suchenko's office. May I help you?"*

"Ma'am, this is David Dryden. Is Dr. Suchenko available?"

"I'm sorry, Mr. Dryden. She's with a patient at the moment."

"Tell her I called, please? It's important. I'd appreciate it if she could get back to me as soon as possible."

"Mr. Dryden, is this a medical emergency?"

"No, ma'am."

"Okay. I'll see that she gets the message."

HE was back in his living room when Helen called. *"What's wrong, Dave?"*

"Are you sitting down?"

"Dave, I'm awfully busy."

"Shel's dead."

"What?"

"Lightning hit the house last night. It burned down."

"No. That's not—"

"He was in bed. They don't have a positive ID yet. But—"

"Where are you now, Dave?"

"At home. I've been over there. There's nothing left of the place."

"My God."

"I'm sorry."

No response.

"You okay?"

"Yeah. I'm all right." Her voice was tight.

"Helen, if there's anything I can do—"

"I know, Dave. Thanks."

HE put on the TV and let it play. A game show. He never watched game shows, never really watched much of anything except news. And of course the Phillies and Eagles.

But at the moment he needed voices in the house.

What were the odds against a lightning strike?

He closed his eyes and tried to wish it away. Tried to make it a day like every other day, in which Shel might call at any moment, in which the only real concern was where they would go this week.

Where they would go.

So much for Voltaire.

He wondered whether he should go back to Italy and inform Professor Shelborne. Maybe that would be an unnecessarily cruel act. But if he didn't, he would go on from day to day, waiting for his son to show up again.

The converter was in his bedroom. It was on a side table, where he'd left it when he hurried out of the house an hour earlier. The last unit.

And a sudden possibility froze him. If you can travel in time, there are no limits to what you can do. He still tended to think of yesterday as a place that existed only in memory.

But Shel was alive back there. As surely as his father. As surely as Nero was still, somehow, some*when*, falling out of his chariot.

Everything is forever.

He could go back and warn him.

The local news came on. More bad weather coming. A woman had been assaulted by two masked kids in Brandywine. A bus driver had suffered a heart attack and plowed into an outdoor food market. There was confirmation about the victim killed last night in the lightning strike. Dental records showed it *was* Adrian Shelborne, thirty-two, the son of the eminent Philadelphia physicist who'd disappeared mysteriously almost a year ago.

HE drove back to the town house and parked down the street. The tape was still up, but the investigators and police had gone. He picked up the converter and attached it to his belt. A couple of people were standing near the tape, but they weren't paying any attention to him.

He set the instrument for 11:00 P.M. the previous night. He took a deep breath and, with more reluctance than he'd ever felt before, pushed the button.

Torrential rain poured down on him. The sky was full of lightning. But lights were on in the town house. Downstairs.

He moved beneath the overhang of a storefront, which provided some shelter from the storm.

A van cruised past and turned right at the intersection.

The curtains were drawn in the town house. The garage was open, as it had been when he'd arrived to see the results of the fire.

He stood watching, trying to make up his mind. He could save Shel, but he knew that hadn't happened. Knew he hadn't gone in and told him what was coming. But did that really mean he couldn't do it?

If he brought Shel back, how would they explain it? He was officially dead now. Hopelessly, definitely dead. Identified by his dental records.

The experiments had scared him. Plan on taking the book out of the briefcase, and bad things happen.

The overhang wasn't providing much protection. Another car rolled past. At one of the houses across the street, a door opened, and he heard voices.

"Good-bye, Babe."

"See you tomorrow, Lenny."

It took another minute or two before a guy with an umbrella appeared. He came in Dave's direction, stopped, and got into a car. The headlights came on, he backed into the street, turned the wheel, and splashed away.

Dave stared at the downstairs lights. There was no hurry. He didn't need to make up his mind at that moment. There was no reason he couldn't wait and think things out. He could come back whenever he chose.

HE bought a couple of books on the subject of time, Edgar Mathews's *Time in a Bottle*, and Rice Bakar's *All the Time in the World*. He couldn't make much sense out of either. What he needed was *Time Travel for Dummies*. But both books seemed to be saying that whenever multiple possibilities exist, the universe splits, and all possibilities occur. So there really cannot be a paradox. Cannot be a loop. If he were to rescue Shel, it would simply create a new universe in which Shel had survived the fire, and that was all there'd be to it.

So you plan to rescue a friend, and it causes a heart attack. Who could believe that?

What he really wanted to do was to go back and put the question to Michael Shelborne again. But he couldn't without letting him know what had happened. And there was no way he could bring himself to do *that*. At least not yet. Maybe later, when his own emotions had subsided.

In the end, he did nothing.

CHAPTER 34

"I took no pleasure in his death, Trainor."
"I know that, Achilles, but it could not have mattered
     to Troilus."
"Yet his blood—"
"—Is on your hands."
"So much death to preserve the pride of Menelaus."
"Indeed. But take heart. He died defending those he loved.
     You could have given no greater gift."
"Nonsense. I could have brought a cask of wine."
"Yes. But let us pretend it is not so."

—SOPHOCLES, *ACHILLES*

DAVE was outside raking leaves when a black car pulled up.

Two people, a man and a woman, were sitting inside. They opened the doors, got out, and started up the walkway.

The woman was taller, and more substantial, somehow, than the man. She held out a set of credentials. "Dr. Dryden?" she said. "I'm Lieutenant Lake." She smiled, a neutral gesture that purveyed no warmth. "This is Sergeant Howard. Could we have a few minutes of your time?"

"Sure," Dave said, wondering what it was about.

Sergeant Howard was a wiry, angular man who came up to Dave's shoulders. He had dark skin and features screwed up into a permanent frown. His expression implied he was being nice even though Dave was probably guilty of something.

He opened the front door, and they all went inside. Lake sat down on the sofa while Howard shoved his hands into his pockets and took to wandering around the room, inspecting books, prints, computer, whatever. "Can I get you some coffee?" Dave asked.

"No, thanks," said Lake. Howard managed a smile but shook his head no. The lieutenant crossed her legs and leaned forward. "I wanted first to offer my condolences on the death of Dr. Shelborne. I understand he was a close friend of yours?"

"That's correct," Dave said. "We've known each other a long time."

She nodded, produced a leather-bound notebook, opened it, and wrote something down. "Did you have a professional relationship?"

"No. We were just friends."

She seemed to expect him to elaborate.

Dave lowered himself into an armchair. "May I ask what this is about? Has something happened?"

Her eyes locked on him. "Dr. Dryden," she said, "Dr. Shelborne was murdered."

Dave's first reaction was to laugh. But she was dead serious. "You can't believe that," he said.

"I never joke, Doctor. Someone attacked the victim in bed, battered him seriously enough to fracture his skull and break both arms. Then he set fire to the house."

Behind Dave, the floor creaked. Howard was still moving around. "That can't be right," he said. "It was a lightning bolt, wasn't it?"

"There *was* a lot of lightning, and we can't tell whether the place actually got hit. But it's irrelevant. Somebody dumped gasoline on the ground floor and set it ablaze."

"*Gasoline?* I just don't believe it."

Her eyes never left him. "Who'd want him dead?"

"Nobody had any reason to kill Shel. He had no enemies. At least, none that *I* know of. It would probably have been a burglar, wouldn't it? A break-in?"

"Burglars don't usually attack occupants in bed. Or burn the house down." She pressed her index finger against her lips. "The killer broke into his desk, as well. Pried open one of the drawers."

"The bottom drawer?"

"Yes. How'd you know?"

Think fast, Dave. "It was where he kept his spare cash."

"Who else would have known that?"

"I don't know."

It was of course where Shel kept the other converters. *Someone else was in on the secret!*

"How much cash did he keep on hand?"

Dave shrugged. "Just small bills. Walking-around money. It wouldn't have been worth a break-in. Certainly not killing someone."

"You'd be surprised how little a life can be worth, Doctor. Would there have been anything else in that drawer?"

"I don't know."

"Well, whatever the killer was looking for, he found it."

"Why do you say that?"

"The other drawers were untouched."

My God. A maniac loose with a converter.

"Are you okay, Dr. Dryden?"

"Yes. Yes, I'm fine." His heart was pounding.

"You look pale." She frowned, and he could see her make a decision. "Doctor, why don't you tell me what the thief was after?"

Sure. Shel had a time-travel device in there. "I've no idea," he said.

"Okay. The fire happened about 4:30 A.M. Friday morning. I wonder if you'd mind telling me where you were at that time?"

"At home in bed," Dave said.

"And you were here all night, right?"

"Yes," he said, and added, unnecessarily, "asleep."

She nodded.

"You're sure about all this?" asked Dave.

She kept writing. "There's really no question that it was arson. And murder."

Dave was beginning to feel guilty. Authority figures always made him feel guilty.

"And you can't think of *anyone* who'd want him dead?"

"No."

She tapped her notebook with her pen. "Do you know if he kept any jewelry in the house?"

"I doubt it. He didn't wear jewelry. As far as I know, there was nothing like that around."

Dave started thinking about the gold coins that they always took when they traveled. A stack of them had been stashed in a shoe box in Shel's bedroom closet. (Dave had more of them upstairs in the wardrobe.) Could anyone have known about them? He thought about mentioning them. But they'd be hard to explain. Best keep quiet. And it would make no sense that he knew about a lot of gold coins in Shel's shoe box but had never asked about them.

Her eyes wandered to one of the bookcases. It was filled with biographies and histories of the Renaissance. The eyes were dark and cool, black pools that seemed to be waiting for something to happen. She tilted her head slightly to get a better look at a title. It was Ledesma's biography of Cervantes, in the original Spanish. "You speak Spanish?" she asked.

"Yes. More or less."

"Did he also speak Spanish, Doctor?"

"Shel had *some* facility."

Howard had gotten tired poking around. He circled back, picked out a chair, and sat down. "Dr. Dryden," Lake continued, "you live alone?"

"That's correct, Lieutenant."

"And you were alone in the house Thursday night?"

"Yes, ma'am."

"I take it there's no one who can corroborate any of this?"

"No. There was nobody here." The question surprised him. "You don't think *I* did it, do you?"

"We don't really think *anybody* did it, yet."

Howard caught her attention and directed it toward the wall. There was a photograph of Shel, Helen, and Dave, gathered around a table at the Beach Club. A mustard-colored umbrella shielded the table, and they were laughing and holding tall, cool drinks. She studied it, and turned back to him. "What exactly," she said, "is your relationship with Dr. Suchenko?"

"We're friends."

"Is that all?" She canted her head, and he caught a hint of a smile.

"Yes," he said. "That's all."

She made another notation. Glanced around the room. "Nice house." It was. Dave had treated himself pretty well, installing leather furniture and thick pile carpets and a stowaway bar and some original art. "Not bad for a teacher," she added.

"I manage."

She closed her book and began to button her jacket. "Thank you, Dr. Dryden." He was still numb with the idea that some-one might have murdered Shel. He had never flaunted his money, had never even moved out of that jerkwater town house. Possibly he'd come home from somewhere, and they were already in the house. He might even have been using the converter. Damn, what a jolt that would have been: return from an evening in the nineteenth century and get attacked by burglars. So they'd killed him. And burned the house to hide the murder. No reason it couldn't have happened that way.

Dave opened the door for the two detectives. "You will be in the area if we need you?" Lake asked. He assured her he would be, and that he would do whatever he could to help find Shel's killer.

It had been painful enough believing that Shel had died through some arbitrary act of nature. But it enraged him that a thug who had nothing at all to contribute would dare take his life.

HE attended a Monday evening memorial service for Shel at St. John's Methodist Church. Jerry was a member of the con-gregation, and had arranged things for his brother, who hadn't paid much attention to churches. Jerry was there, of course. And a few cousins and uncles, and some other people Dave didn't know. The preacher invited those who wished to speak to come forward, and they did. They described a stray cat Shel had taken in, and his two seasons as coach of the Little League Panthers. A member of the local Humane Society said how generous he'd always been both with time and money.

Dave remained silent. He would have liked to say a few words for his lifelong friend. But he didn't dare get started talking about Shel because he wasn't sure he wouldn't finish at the Library of Alexandria. Or with Molly Brown.

Helen was there, too.

When it was over, he took her to Strattmeyer's, and they had a couple of drinks while she looked listlessly out at the passing traffic on the Expressway. They exchanged all the usual clichés about how they couldn't believe he was gone, how there'd never be another like him, how it just seemed impossible.

"I saw him Thursday night," she said.

"I'm sorry, Helen." He didn't know what else to say.

"We were going to get married."

"I'm not surprised to hear it. He loved you, Helen."

"The police have been around to talk to me."

"They were at my place, too."

"They think it was murder. Dave, I can't believe that. Who'd have wanted to take his life?"

"I don't know. I don't buy it. It's a misunderstanding somewhere. It'll get straightened out."

But he *wasn't* dead. Not really. He's alive in 1931, he's alive in New York on V-J Day, and in the Lamplight back in Durham. Time travelers never die. Not really. And, in a way, we're all time travelers. Somehow, the entire temporal stream exists, but we're only conscious of a single moment. Is that how it is? That it isn't the *world* moving through the eons, but only our consciousness, like a light passing through a series of dark rooms? Or, maybe a better analogy, like an old-time film, in which only one frame at a time moves in front of the bulb?

He stopped with his second drink. Had to drive, and two was pretty much his limit.

"Are you going tomorrow?" she asked. She meant the funeral.

"Yes."

"I'll be glad when it's over."

CHAPTER 35

The weariest and most loathed worldly life
That age, ache, penury, and imprisonment
Can lay on nature, is a paradise
To what we fear of death.
                    —WILLIAM SHAKESPEARE, *MEASURE FOR MEASURE*

DURING the funeral, Dave kept thinking how Shel would appear at any time, walk up and say hello, ask whether he and Katie would like to join him and Helen for dinner. One of the curious phenomena associated with sudden and unexpected death is the inability to accept it when it strikes those close to us. People always imagine that the person they've lost is in the kitchen, or in the next room, and that it requires only that we call his name to have him reappear in the customary place. Dave felt that way about Shel. They'd spent a lot of time together, and, with the advent of the converters, had shared a unique experience. When the dangers and celebrations were over, they normally came back through the wardrobe.

Shel stood up there now, just outside the bedroom door, his face emotionless.

Dave froze.

Shel advanced to the top of the stairs and looked down. "Hi, Dave."

"Shel." Dave could barely get the word out. He hung on to the banister, and the stairs reeled. "Shel, is that you?"

Shel smiled. The old, crooked grin that Dave had thought not to see again. Some part of him that was too slow-witted to get sufficiently flustered started flicking through explanations. Someone else had died in the fire. It was a dream. Shel had a twin.

"Yeah," he said. "It's me. Nice funeral."

"You were there."

"Yes."

"I didn't see you."

"I didn't exactly stand up front." They stared at each other. "You should try it sometime, watching people throw flowers on your coffin."

Somewhere, far away, he heard the sound of a train.

"I'm sorry," said Shel. "I know this must be a shock."

An understatement of sorts. Shel walked across the landing. Dave's heartbeat picked up. Shel came to the top of the stairs and started down. Dave started to back up, to make room. Shel grabbed his arm so he didn't fall. His hands were solid, the smile very real.

"What the hell's going on?" Dave said.

Shel's eyes were bright and sad. He slid down into a sitting position and dragged Dave with him. "It's been a strange morning," he said.

"You're supposed to be dead."

He took a deep breath. "I know. I *am* dead, Dave. The reports of my death seem to be accurate."

Suddenly it was clear. "You've come back from *down-stream*. Or *up*stream. Who the hell cares? You're alive."

Shel nodded. "Yes." He drew his legs up in a gesture that looked defensive. "You sure you're okay, Dave?"

"I've been trying to get used to this. To the idea that you're gone. Or *were* gone. Whatever."

Shel took a deep breath but said nothing.

"You're using the converter now."

"That's right."

"So when you go back—"

"—The house will burn, and I'll be in it."

For a long time neither spoke. "Don't go back," Dave said at last.

"I don't see how I can avoid it."

Ridiculous. Dave's mind filled with images of lightning strikes and burglars in the night and the charred remains of Shel's desk. "Stay the hell away from it. What have you got to lose?"

"It's not that." His voice sounded tight. And there was a hunted look in his eyes. "I have no intention of going back there. But I'm not sure it's *my* call."

"That makes no sense, Shel."

"It *happened*, Dave. You know that, and I do. Somehow, I'm going to wind up in that fire." For a long moment, he simply sat on the staircase, breathing. "They found me in the bed."

"Yes. I know."

"I don't believe it." Shel was pale and his eyes were red.

"They think you were murdered."

He nodded. Said nothing. They made their way back down into the living room and dropped into armchairs.

"What happened, Shel? Do you have any idea who it could have been?"

"None." His head sank back and he stared at the ceiling. "I was downstream, looking at stuff. And I did what we always said we wouldn't do. No matter what."

"You looked at your bio."

"Yes." He shook his head. The heating system came on with a thump. Dave thought how he had to get it fixed. Shel got up after a minute and walked over to the liquor cabinet. "Mind?"

"No. Go ahead."

"You want anything?"

"Rum and Coke would be good."

He mixed the drinks, brought them back, and gave one to Dave. "I couldn't help it." He fell back down into his chair. "I read how I was one of two sons of Michael Shelborne. That I'd been in public relations. And that I'd died in a fire on Friday, September 13, 2019. The fire wasn't caused by lightning. It was deliberately set. Perpetrator never caught. That was all they had to say. Oh, and that my father vanished under mysterious circumstances."

"I'm sorry, Shel."

He sighed. "Goddam it, Dave, I can't believe this is happening."

Dave tried his drink. There was too much rum. "I don't know what to say."

"It's a scary thing to have the story of your entire life lying at your elbow. And it amounts to two lines."

"'This is what comes of traveling alone." Dave was annoyed. "We agreed not to do that."

"It's done. And if I hadn't, I'd be dead now." He was pale, frightened. He buried his forehead in his palms. "What the hell am I saying? I *am* dead."

"You're here."

"And I'm also in the graveyard."

"What are you going to do?"

"I don't know." He seemed lost. *"It's waiting for me back there."* His breathing was loud.

"Don't go back to the town house," Dave said. "Stay here."

Shel seemed not to have heard. "It must have been burglars."

"They broke into the desk. Into the bottom drawer."

"Well, that's what burglars do."

"You're sure nobody else knew? About the converters?"

He just stared out of those dazed, blank eyes. "Nobody else knew. But at least I'm warned. Maybe I should take a gun back with me."

"Maybe."

Avoid the irreparable act.

"Anyway," he said, "I thought you'd want to know I'm okay." He snickered at that.

"Don't go back at all," Dave said. "With or without a gun."

"I don't intend to."

"Good."

"If it drops me in the Atlantic, so be it." It was supposed to be a joke, and he laughed, though Dave remained silent. "Dave, I'm scared."

"I know."

"At some point, for one reason or another, it's going to happen." He finished his drink. "Maybe I get drunk. Maybe I lose my mind. Maybe I just decide to get it over with. Whatever it is—"

"Let it go, Shel."

"Easy for you to say."

"I'm sorry."

"It's knowing the way of it," he said. "That's what tears me up."

"Just stay here," Dave said again. "You're safe here."

Shel shook his head. "I appreciate the offer, Dave."

"But . . . ?"

"Nothing like watching your own funeral to remind you how valuable sunlight is. And that you don't have it forever. I've got a few places to go. People to talk to. Then, when I've done what I need to, I'll think about all this."

"Okay."

"I've got a place downstream. I'm going to stay there."

"Really?" said Dave. "Where?"

"Center City." He didn't elaborate, so Dave didn't push. Shel picked up the glass, drained it, wiped his lips. "Are they sure it's me? I heard the body was burned beyond recognition."

"The police checked your dental records."

"They matched?"

"Yes."

His brows came together. "Do me a favor, Dave. Make sure they actually *did* the identification. Maybe they thought there was no question it was me, and they just put that out there but didn't really bother. Okay?"

"Okay. I'll make sure."

He got up, wandered around the room, touching things, the books, a bust of Plato, a table lamp. He paused in front of the picture from the Beach Club. "I keep thinking how much it means to be alive. You know, Dave, I saw people out there today I haven't seen in years." He played with his glass. It was an expensive piece, chiseled, and he explored its facets. "When is the reading of the will?"

"I don't know. They may have done it already."

"I'm tempted to go."

"To the reading?"

"Why not?" He managed a tight, pained smile. "I could wear a black beard and reveal myself at the appropriate moment."

"You can't do that." Dave was horrified.

Shel laughed. "I know. But by God I'd like to." He shook himself, as if he were just waking up. "Dave, truth is that I know how I'm going to die. It's different from the simple knowledge that you won't live forever."

Dave said nothing.

"But it doesn't have to happen until I'm ready for it." He looked past Dave, out the window.

"I think you need to tell her," Dave said gently.

His expression clouded. "I know." He drew the words out. "I'll talk to her. At the proper time."

"Be careful," Dave said. "She's already been through a lot."

"Yeah."

"You okay?"

He nodded. Dave thought he might say something like *Not bad for a dead guy.* But he let it go.

CHAPTER 36

He has gone, left, cleared out, bolted.

—CICERO

THE critical question was whether they had in fact buried Adrian Shelborne, or whether there was a possibility of mistaken identity. Neither Dave nor Shel knew anything about police procedure other than what they saw on TV. So, in the morning, Dave set out to pursue the issue.

He started with Jerry, who seemed annoyed that Shel had died, almost as if he had in some way brought it on himself. "I shouldn't speak ill of the dead," he told Dave. "He was a decent man, but he never really made his life count." That was an echo of what Shel had said, but the meaning was different. Jerry thought in terms of a professional reputation and the attendant compensation. He sat behind a polished teak desk. An India rubber plant in a large pot stood by a sun-filled window. The furniture was expensive, padded with leather, ponderous, exuding a sense that whatever went on in the office was significant. Plaques covered the walls, appreciations from civic groups, corporate awards, various licenses and testaments. Photos of his two children were prominently displayed, a boy in a Little League uniform, a girl nuzzling a horse. His wife, who had left him years earlier, was missing.

"Actually," Dave said, "I thought he did pretty well."

"I don't mean money, Dave. But it seems to me a man has an obligation to live as part of his community. To participate in community functions. To help out. To belong to, say, the Optimists. Support one of the churches."

"I've a question for you," Dave said.

"Go ahead."

"In a case like this, how thoroughly do the police check the identity of the victim? I mean, it's Shel's house. He's the only one in it. So I was wondering if they might figure who else could it be? And maybe they just don't bother going further."

Jerry shook his head. "The cops are usually pretty careful about that sort of thing, Dave. Now understand, criminal law isn't my field, but they'd be crazy simply to make assumptions in a situation like this. They'd be opening themselves up to all kinds of liability. Which is why they check the dental records."

"They *said* they did. But is there a chance they might not have gone to the trouble? Because they were already sure?"

"No. Believe me, it's no trouble. And they're not going to risk lawsuits and public embarrassment. If they say it was Shel, you can believe that's who it was."

"I'm sorry to hear it."

He shrugged. "It's the way life is sometimes." He rose, signaling that the interview was over.

They walked toward the door. "You know," Dave said, "this experience has a little bit of déjà vu about it."

Jerry paused with his hand on the knob. "How do you mean?"

"There was a language teacher at Princeton, where I got my doctorate. Same thing happened to him. He lived alone, and one night a gas main let go and blew up the whole house. They buried him, then found out it wasn't him at all. He'd gone on an unannounced holiday to Vermont, and turned his place over to a friend. They didn't find out until several days after the funeral."

Jerry shrugged. The colossal stupidity loose in the world was no surprise to him. "Unfortunately," he said, "there's not much chance of that here."

DAVE probably shouldn't have tried to see how Helen was doing because his own emotions were still churning. But he called her from a drugstore, and she said yes, she'd like to see him, and suggested lunch. They met at an Applebee's on City Avenue.

She looked worn, dazed, and her eyes were bloodshot.

Nothing in his life had been quite as painful as sitting with her that day, seeing those raw emotions and knowing that, had it been *Dave* who'd died, she'd have been sorry but would have gotten over it easily enough.

The conversation was full of regrets, things not said, acts undone. She was as soft and vulnerable as Dave had ever seen her. By all the laws of nature, Shel was dead. Was he still bound to keep his distance? He wondered how she would react if she knew Shel was probably in Dave's kitchen at that moment, making a submarine sandwich.

He wanted to tell her. There was a possibility that, when she *did* find out, when she got past her anger with Shel, she'd hold it against *Dave* as well. He also, God help him, wanted to keep Shel *dead*. It was hard to admit to himself, but it was true. He wanted nothing more than a clear channel to Helen Suchenko. But when he watched her bite down the pain, when the tears came, when she excused herself with a shaky voice and hurried back to the ladies' room, he could stand it no more. "Helen," he said, "are you free this afternoon?"

She sighed. "It's my afternoon off. Just as well. People get nervous around weepy doctors. I'm free. But I'm not in the mood to go anywhere."

"Can I persuade you to come out to my place?"

She looked desperately fragile. "I don't think so, Dave. I need time to myself."

He listened to the hum of conversation around them. "Please," he said. "It's important."

* * *

THE gray skies sagged down into the streets, and all the head-lights were on. Helen followed him in her small blue Ford. He watched her in the mirror, playing back all possible scenarios on how to handle this. *He's not dead, Helen.* Leave out the time-travel stuff, he decided, at least for now. Use the story he'd told Jerry as an example of how misunderstandings can occur. And then bring him into the room. Best not to warn *him*. God knows how he'd react. But get them together, present him with a fait accompli, and you will have done your self-sacrificial duty, Dave. You dumb bastard.

He pulled into his driveway, opened the garage, and rolled inside. The rain had grown even more intense. Helen stopped behind him, and hurried out of her car. "This way." Dave waved her into the garage.

"Glad to be out of that," she said, with a drenched smile. "Dave, I can't stay long."

"Okay. We'll only need a minute."

The garage opened into the kitchen. He unlocked the door but stopped to listen before going farther. Everything was quiet inside. He stood back so she could enter and closed the door behind her, making no effort to muffle the sound. He switched on the kitchen light, then led the way into the living room. "About Shel—" He raised his voice a notch.

"Yes?"

"This is going to come as a shock."

She frowned. "You're not going to tell me he was already married."

"No. Nothing like that."

A white envelope lay on a side table, with Dave's name on it, printed in Shel's precise hand. He snatched it up, but not before she'd seen it.

"Just a list of things to do." He pushed it into his pocket. "How about some coffee?"

"Sure. Sounds good."

"It'll have to be instant." He went back out into the kitchen and put a pot of water on the stove.

She followed. "Do you always do that?" she asked.

"Do what?"

"Write yourself notes?"

"It's my to-do list. It's the first thing I do every morning."

She got two cups down. "What's going to come as a shock?"

"Give me a second," he said. "I'll be right back." He slipped out and opened the envelope.

Dear Dave,

I don't know how to write this. But I have to think about what's happened, and figure out what I need to do. I don't want to jump the gun if it's not necessary. You understand.

I know this hasn't been easy for you. But I'm glad you were there. Thanks.

Shel

P.S. I've left most of my estate to the Leukemia Foundation. That will probably generate a half dozen lawsuits from my relatives. But if any of those vultures shows signs of winning, I'll come back personally and deal with them.

Dave read it a half dozen times. Then he crumpled it, pushed it into his pocket, and went back to the kitchen.

She was looking out the window. Usually, Dave's grounds were alive with blue jays and squirrels. But none of the critters was in sight at the moment. "It's lovely," she said. Then: "So, what's this about?"

"Son of a gun," he said. "I went out to get it, and I forgot." He suggested she relax for a minute "while I get something." He hurried upstairs in search of an idea.

The wardrobe also functioned as a small museum. It held items brought home from their travels, objects of inestimable value, but only if you knew their origin. It had a sextant designed and built by Leonardo, a silver bracelet that had once belonged to Calpurnia, a signed folio of Jean Racine's *Andro-maque*, a pocket watch that Leo Tolstoy had carried while writing *War and Peace*. There were photos of Martin Luther and Albert Schweitzer and Pericles and Francesco Solimena. All more or less worthless.

He couldn't bear to give Calpurnia's bracelet to Helen without being able to tell her what it was. He decided instead on a gold medallion he'd bought from a merchant in Thebes during the fifth century, B.C. It carried a serpent's likeness. An Apollonian priest had insisted it was a steal. At one time, he'd said, it had belonged to Aesculapius, the divine doctor, who had been so good he cured the dead. He'd backed up his statement by trying to buy it from Dave, offering six times what he'd paid for it.

He carried it downstairs and gave it to Helen, telling her that Shel had wanted him to be sure she got it in case anything happened to him. She glowed and turned it over and over, unable to get enough of it. "It's exquisite," she said. And the tears came again.

If that thing had possessed any curative powers, Dave could have used them at that moment.

RAIN filled the world. Gradually, a murky curtain descended on the windows, and the world beyond passed from view. "I think we're going to get six inches before this is over," he told her. The Weather Channel was saying two.

He put on some music. She stood by the curtains, enjoying a glass of Chablis. They'd started the fire, and it crackled and popped comfortably. David added Mozart and hoped the storm would continue.

A pair of headlights crept past, out on Carmichael Drive. "I feel sorry for anybody who has to get around in this," she said.

"Stay here."

She laughed. "That wasn't a hint, Dave. Thanks, anyhow. But when it lets up, I have to get home."

They talked inconsequentials. She had composed herself,

and Dave wanted to believe it was his proximity. But he had no real chance. Even if Shel were safely in his grave, he was still the embodiment of too many memories. The decent thing to do would be to fade out of her life, just as Carmichael Drive, and the trees that lined it, were fading now.

She talked about a break in the weather so she could get home. But Dave's luck held. The rain continued to pour down, and they stayed near the fire. Dave was alone at last with Helen Suchenko, but it was a painful few hours. Yet he would not have missed them.

The Weather Channel reported that the storm system stretched from New York as far south as Baltimore. Rain would continue through the night.

What had she said? *"I feel sorry for anybody who has to get around in this."*

Dave was out in it. And on that night, shelter looked far away.

SHE talked about Shel. She'd shake her head as if remembering something, then dismiss it. She'd veer off onto some other subject, a movie, a nephew who was giving the family trouble, a medical advance that held hope for a breakthrough against this or that condition. There were a couple of patients she was worried about. (She did not name them, of course.) And she had to deal with a few hypochondriacs whose lives were centered on imaginary illnesses. She revealed that Katie had told her he was leaving teaching at the end of the semester. How did he plan to support himself? He said he was going to buy and sell art.

"I didn't know you knew anything about that."

"Ah, me proud beauty," he said, drawing out the last syllable, "there's a lot about me you don't know." He added that he'd miss teaching, which wasn't at all true. But it was the sort of thing people expected you to say.

Jerry's observation about Shel was probably at least equally true of himself. *Dave had never really made his life count.* The teaching hadn't done anything for him. He'd never been that good at it. Students didn't crowd into his classrooms the way they did for, say, Marian Crosby. No student had ever told him how he'd changed her life. Or inspired her to read the classics in the original.

What Dave had come to realize was that, without Shel, he lacked a sense of purpose, a reason to exist. The last year had provided a new dimension to his life. Selma had changed him. As had Aristarchus and the Library. As had Ben Franklin. He'd come to understand what it meant to *live*. And it was all upstairs, in recordings of conversations with Voltaire and Charles Lamb and Herbert Hoover and Aristotle and H. G. Wells. Those dialogues would make the damnedest book the world had ever seen, commentaries by the principal actors, the people on civilization's front lines, reporting on their dreams, their frustrations, their follies. *The Dryden Dialogues.*

But it would never get written.

At seven minutes after six, the power failed and the lights went out. The timing was perfect because Dave had just finished making dinner. He lit a couple of candles, and they sat in the flickering light and made jokes about how romantic it was. If the clouds had not dissipated, at least for those few hours they had receded.

Afterward, they retreated with their candles into the living room. The music had been silenced, so they sat listening to the fire and the rain. Occasionally, Dave glanced at the upstairs bedroom, half-expecting the door to open. He tried to plan what he would do if Shel suddenly appeared on the landing.

Eventually, the storm eased, and the power came back.

Helen obviously didn't want to leave. "But tomorrow's my day at the hospital. Have to be in early." She got up and got her wrap out of the closet.

"You okay?"

"I *will* be," she said.

DAVE tried to imagine what he would feel if he were in Shel's place. Knowing what the future held.

Where was Shel now?

Dave wanted to find him, to talk sense to him. To make sure he didn't do anything foolish. Like using the converter to go back to the town house and confront what waited.

Or, possibly, try to end it himself.

So where might he be? He remembered the night at Lenny Pound's when they'd made the list of what they wanted to do with the converters. And recorded the suggestions in Shel's notebook. Mark Twain's steamboat. Kit Carson. Leonidas.

There'd been one, in particular, that had lit Shel up.

Michelangelo.

CHAPTER 37

Power, like a desolating pestilence,
Pollutes whate'er it touches; and obedience,
Bane of all genius, virtue, freedom, truth,
Makes slaves of men, and, of the human frame,
A mechanized automaton.

—PERCY BYSSHE SHELLEY, *QUEEN MAB*

DURING the summer of 1496, a young and unknown Michelangelo arrived in Rome, looking for work. We could do him a favor, Shel had said, magnanimously. It would upset nothing, he'd get some money and some encouragement, and we would have the satisfaction of knowing we'd made a contribution to his career. And we could probably acquire one or two souvenirs along the way. The ultimate, Dave thought, in lawn sculpture.

They had not gotten around to it. And that meant Dave had a likely place to look for Shel.

This was the Rome of Alexander VI, a pope who brooked neither heresy nor opposition. It was a bad time for the True Faith, a few decades after the fall of Constantinople, when Europe had given sanctuary to armies of scholars from that benighted land. The scholars had repaid the good turn by unleashing the Renaissance. It was a dusty, unimposing Rome, still medieval, still brooding over lost glory. Dreary, bootstrap houses lined the narrow streets, themselves sinking into the rubble and ruins of imperial times. The hilltops were occupied by churches and palaces. More were under construction. The fortress of Sant'Angelo, containing Hadrian's tomb, dominated the banks of the Tiber. The western approaches to the city were guarded by the old Basilica of St. Peter, the predecessor of the modern structure.

Dave by now was a master at tracking down people he wanted to find, even in cultures that didn't have a phone book. In his clerical garb, he went directly to Pietro Cardinal Riario, portraying himself as acting for a man who hoped to buy salvation by making a substantial donation to whatever church project the Cardinal would recommend. Riario is, of course, known to history for his early support of Michelangelo, and for his occasional homicidal tendencies.

The future artist, the Cardinal said, was living in modest quarters not far from the Tiber. When Dave arrived, an hour later, he was not at home, but his landlord directed him to a dump site. There he found a young man seated atop a low hill at the edge of the facility, contemplating heaps of trash and rubble.

He was ordinary-looking, with clear, congenial features and handsome dark eyes. He was so absorbed in the scene around him that he didn't see Dave coming. "Hello," Dave said casually, following his gaze across the piles of debris. "It's a dismal prospect, isn't it?"

He looked up, surprised. "Hello, Father." He sounded preoccupied and probably hoped the priest would move on. "Yes," he added, "it is."

Gray smoke drifted out of the mounds. Carrion eaters wheeled overhead.

Dave sat down beside him.

"See that?" The young man pointed at a broken column. "That's what's left of the Forum."

Two men approached, wheeling a cart loaded with trash. They said hello as they passed, and proceeded along the crest of the hill. "Tell me," Dave said, "are you Michelangelo Buonarroti? The sculptor?"

He brightened. "Indeed I am, Father. Why do you smile?"

The men with the cart stopped and tilted the vehicle's contents into the dump.

"I've heard you are talented. But you must already know that. I'm looking for a friend. He said he was coming here to give you a commission."

Michelangelo got to his feet. "I have not yet established myself. But I'm happy to hear my reputation is growing. Your friend, is he a priest also?"

Dave was not sure how Shel might have presented himself. "He is, but he works among the poor and often dresses accordingly."

The young man's brow wrinkled, and he looked as if he had just made a connection. "Is your name David?"

That startled him. "Why do you ask?"

"I was given a message for David. Are you he?"

"Yes."

"That is odd."

"What is?"

"He did not say you were a priest. Just to be sure there is no mistake, what is your friend's name?"

"Adrian," David said.

"*Father* Adrian."

"Yes. That is correct. *Father* Adrian. And the message?"

"It's back at the house, Father. It came by courier two days ago. Would you care to walk with me?"

It was a warm, still afternoon. The sun was high and bright, and the sky filled with clumps of white cloud. "How long have you been in Rome?" Dave asked.

It was Michelangelo's turn to be surprised. "Only a few weeks," he said. "How did you know I had just come?"

"You're better-known than you realize, young man. What are you working on now?"

"Not very much, I'm afraid. Only Cardinal Riario sends me assignments. I am very much indebted to him."

"But you *do* have a commission from Father Adrian?"

"Oh, yes. But I have not yet begun on it. He wants two sculptures."

"What are they?"

"He asked me to do an Athena for him. In her role as protector of the city. And Hermes. As healer. But I haven't been able to decide yet what form either should take."

Dave took a couple of pictures, doing it as unobtrusively as he could. But Michelangelo saw the gooseberry and asked what it was. "A relic," Dave replied.

His house was one of a group of nondescript structures crowded around a muddy courtyard. It was halfway up a low hill, just high enough to glimpse the Tiber, which also looked muddy.

A workshop was visible at the rear of the house. While Michelangelo retrieved the message, Dave stuck his head inside. It was damp and smelled of wet stone. Tables, benches, and shelves were made of planks. A small piece of Carrara marble with a child's head just emerging was set atop a pair of boards on the floor. It might be, he thought, the *Sleeping Cupid*, long since lost.

He took more pictures. Children played in the courtyard, screaming and shrieking, and he wondered how it was possible for genius to function amid such bedlam.

Michelangelo reappeared and handed over a sealed yellow envelope with DAVID DRYDEN printed on it. "It does not indicate you are a priest," he added. "It is why I was confused."

"Thank you, Michelangelo. I've enjoyed talking with you." They shook hands, and it was one of those electric moments you get to enjoy if you're a time traveler. Then Dave gave him a gold coin and watched his eyes go wide. "See you finish his commission properly."

"Oh, I will, Father. You may be sure."

Dave waited until he was out of the neighborhood to open the envelope. The message read:

DAVE, COME AT ONCE. I AM IN THE BORGIA TOWER. ACCUSED OF HERESY OR SOME DAMNED THING. THE GUARDS CAN BE BRIBED.

SHEL

* * *

SHEL'S converter must have malfunctioned. Or someone had taken it from him. Otherwise, the authorities could not have held him. So there was no point going directly after him. Dave had to make a stop first.

He went back to Shel's town house, about 1:00 A.M. on the night of the lightning strike. There was no particular reason for that time, except that he wanted to avoid running into Shel. Maybe that would create a problem in the time flow, and maybe not, but he thought it best to avoid any unnecessary twists in the sequence of events.

He emerged in the living room. The storm that had set in that night was raging. And it seemed odd to be standing once again in the house that, he knew, would become a smoking ruin in a few hours.

He walked into the den and went straight to the desk. It occurred to him that he should come back here later to find out who murdered Shel. But he wasn't sure he'd have the stomach to stand by and watch that. Still, it was hard to see how he could justify *not* doing it.

Deal with it later.

The key to the desk was kept in a cup, along with some paper clips and rubber bands. The cup, with its Phillies logo, stood on one of the bookshelves beside a framed photo of Shel, Jerry, and their father.

Dave looked in the cup. No key.

Why was he not surprised? Nothing goes well when you're in trouble. But he needed to get the spare unit.

He dug through the clips and rubber bands. Stood on his tiptoes and checked the shelf.

Damn.

It wasn't on the desktop. Wasn't on any of the side tables. Wasn't on the floor.

He could have gone further back, maybe a few weeks, but he didn't want to risk running into Shel and thereby setting up a paradox. So he went into the kitchen and searched the cabinet drawers, where he found bottle openers, bags, tacks, plastic clamps. And a hammer and a couple of screwdrivers.

He carried the tools back to the desk and pushed the larger screwdriver into the space between the top of the bottom drawer and the frame. It was a tight fit, and he had to hammer it in. Outside, a siren sounded over the rumble of the lightning. It got louder for a few moments, passed, and began to fade.

The drawer started to give way. He gave it a final bang, and the frame broke apart.

He started to replay his conversation with Lieutenant Lake: *"The killer broke into his desk, as well. Pried open one of the drawers . . . Whatever the killer was looking for, he found it."*

"Why do you say that?"

"The other drawers were untouched."

He pulled the drawer out. And there was the third converter. The one that Michael had been using. The one Dave thought a thief had taken.

He slipped it into his cassock. Then, just to be safe, he used its hem to wipe his fingerprints from the hammer, the screwdriver, and the desk.

Then it was time to go.

THE Vatican, even at that remote period, was an architectural marvel. Pilgrims filled its courts and streets. The sacred buildings clustered behind crenelated walls and the Tiber, a sacred camp besieged by worldly powers. Dave looked up at Old St. Peter's, in which Pope Leo III had crowned Charlemagne; passed San Damaso Courtyard, which still hosted jousting tournaments; and paused near the library to get his bearings. The Borgia Tower was an ominous fortress guarding the western flank of the papal palace, paired with its military-appearing twin, the Sistine Chapel. Guards patrolled the entrance. He went up to the front door, as if he had all the reason in the world to be there. A sentry challenged him. "Your business, Father?" he asked. He wore a blue uniform, and he carried a dagger and a small axe.

"I am the confessor," Dave said, "of Father Adrian Shelborne, who I believe to be a visitor here."

The guard was barely nineteen. "Have you been sent for, Father?"

His manner implied that if Dave didn't have an invitation, he would not be admitted. And his instincts told him that, despite Shel's assurances, a bribe would not work. Not with this boy. He was too new. "Yes," he said. "The Administrator asked me to come." He was trying to remember influential names in this Vatican, but his mind had gone blank.

"Ah." He nodded. Smiled. Thought about it. "Good. Please come with me, Father."

They entered the Tower. He led Dave into an anteroom, asked him to wait, and disappeared through a side door. The anteroom was decorated with a Domenico Ghirlandaio painting. It was a scene from the Last Judgment. A God who looked much like Jupiter approached his throne in a sun-bright chariot, while angels sang and humans cringed or celebrated, according to their consciences. Dave was tempted to make off with it and come back later for Shel.

The sentry reappeared, trailing a sergeant. "You wish to see Cardinal Borgia?" he asked.

"No," he said quickly. That depraved monster was the last person Dave wanted to see. "No, I wish to visit Father Shelborne. To hear his confession."

"Ah." The sergeant nodded. It was a noncommittal nod, putting Dave in a holding pattern. He had cold, flat eyes, too close together. His teeth were snagged and broken. He had a broad nose, and a long scar ran from his right ear across the jaw to his lip, where it caused a kind of permanent sneer. Not his fault, Dave thought, but the man could not have managed a smile without scaring the kids. "Father, surely you realize where you are. Father Shelborne would not be denied the sacraments *here*."

Dave pressed a gold coin into his hand. "If you could see your way clear, *signore*."

The sergeant slipped it deftly into a pocket without changing expression. "He must have very heavy sins, Father."

"I would like only a few minutes, if you please."

"Very well." He straightened his uniform. "Let me see what I can do." He led the way deep into the building. Walls were lined with frescoes and paintings, likenesses of figures from both classical and Christian mythology, renderings of Church Fathers and philosophers and of the holy saints.

They mounted four flights of stairs and passed into chambers even more ornately decorated than those on the lower floors. Then the sergeant deposited him in a room with an exquisite statue of St. Michael, wings spread and sword drawn. Not a good omen.

"I'll just be a minute," he said. He went back out into the corridor. But Dave had plenty of time to admire St. Michael, and he was beginning to think about looking for assistance when the sergeant returned. "Sorry you were kept waiting, Father," he said. "Please follow me." And they were on their way again, down a long corridor, up another flight of stairs, and through a chapel. Finally, they paused outside a paneled door. He knocked, and the door opened into a well-appointed study.

A young man sat behind a large, ornate desk, making notes on a sheet of paper. A muscular priest stood on either side of him. He was about Michelangelo's age. But *this* youth wore a Cardinal's red garments. And that revealed who he was.

"Thank you, John," he said to the escort. The sergeant withdrew, closing the door softly. The wall behind the Cardinal was dominated by a variant of the papal seal. And a crucifix. Several thick books were stacked on a table to his left. One lay open. The only light was provided by a set of windows hidden behind heavy drapes, and a pair of oil lamps.

This was Cesare Borgia. *Don't drink the wine.* Appointed to the College of Cardinals by his father, Pope Alexander VI. My God, what had Shel got himself into?

Borgia smiled pleasantly, crooked his index finger, and signaled Dave to approach. "Good afternoon, Father ... ?"

"David Dryden, Eminence."

The Cardinal's lips were full and sensuous. The eyes were dark and detached, the nose straight, the jaws lean. He wore a constant smile, rather like a cassock, something to be taken off and put on. "Dryden." He tasted the name. Let his tongue roll around on it as if he might swallow both it and its owner. "Your accent is strange. Where are you from?"

"Cornwall, Eminence." Good a spot as any. "I am a poor country priest."

"I see." He placed his fingertips together. The hands were long and thin and had not seen the sun recently. "Somehow you do not look the part." Dave bowed slightly, as if he'd been complimented. "You wished to see Father Shelborne?"

"If possible, Eminence. I am his confessor."

His teeth were straight and white. "And where did you take orders, Father?"

"St. Michael's." David inserted pride into his response. Good old alma mater.

"In Cornwall?"

"Yes." He tried not to hesitate. What sort of priest has no idea where his seminary is?

"We've had other visitors from St. Michael's recently," Borgia said. "It has a magnificent view of the Umber, I understand?"

Where in God's name was the Umber? "Actually," he said, "it is the rolling hills of Cornwall that attract the eye."

Borgia considered the response. "And how do you stand on the matter of the Waldensians?"

The Waldensians were men who gave away all their money and traveled the roads of southern Europe helping the poor. By their example, they had embarrassed the more powerful members of the Church and had therefore been branded heretics. "They should commit to Mother Church," Dave said.

"Quite so." Cesare's tone sharpened. "Obviously, you are a man of piety, Father. But tell me, where does a country priest get gold with which to bribe my guards?"

"I had not intended it as a bribe, Eminence. I thought rather, in the tradition of the Faith, to share my own largesse. I have come recently into good fortune."

"What kind of good fortune?"

"An inheritance. My father died and left his money—"

Cesare waved the story away with a gesture that was almost feminine. "I see." The two muscular priests came to attention. "Who is paying you, Dryden? The French?"

"I'm in no one's pay, Eminence. I mean no one any harm." The Cardinal glanced at the priests. A signal. They came forward and took hold of Dave's arms and did the equivalent of a patdown. It was not gentle. One came only to about Dave's eyes, but he looked like a linebacker. The other was younger, trim, athletic, with a cynical smile. He was the type who, in a later age, would have been at the Y every day playing squash. The linebacker saw the converter attached to Dave's belt and removed it. The squash player found the other one, hidden in Dave's cassock. They held them out for Cesare, who took them, did a quick inspection, and placed them on the desk. They found Dave's gold and gave that to him also. Then they stepped back.

Cesare smiled at the coins and dropped them on his desk. It was the converters that held his interest. He held one close to an oil lamp and examined it. "Father," he said, "what *are* these things?"

Dave had a feeling the relic story wasn't going to sell here. "They're candlestick holders," he said.

"Candlestick holders?"

"Yes, Eminence."

"Show me how it works." He gave it back to Dave, who thereby received another chance to get clear.

"It's not completed yet. It still needs a saddle."

"You are, I assume, referring to a *socket*."

"Yes, Eminence. In Cornwall, we call them saddles."

"I see." He smiled. It was actually a benevolent smile. "May I ask why you are carrying two nonfunctional candlestick holders?"

"They were designed by my father. He died recently and—" He was flailing, and Cesare glanced at his associates, and they all roared with laughter. Cesare first, then the others.

When they subsided, Dave tried to finish: "—I was hoping to complete them. In his honor."

The Cardinal signaled him to return the converter. He hesitated, gave it back. Cesare placed it on the desk, beside the other one. Then he opened a drawer, from which he withdrew a third unit. Shel's. He laid it beside the others. "They seem to be three of a kind," he said.

"He is my cousin, Eminence."

"This one also has no socket."

"Yes. It is the most difficult part of the project."

"And you both carry these *things* in honor of your esteemed father. I am touched." His smile widened and snapped off. "David Whatever-your-name-is, let us be clear on one point. Unless you are honest with me, I will have to assume you and your friend are agents of a foreign power and beyond reclamation. If I am forced to that conclusion, I will then have no choice but to deal with you accordingly." He came around the side of the desk.

"Where is Father Shelborne?" Dave asked.

Cesare stared at him momentarily, then turned his eyes toward the door. The squash player opened it, went outside, and returned with Shel. He was dirty, bruised, covered with blood. He sagged in the arms of two guards.

Dave started toward him, but the linebacker and the squash player got between them. Shel's eyes opened. "You don't look so good," Dave said, still speaking Italian.

Shel tried to wipe his mouth, but the guards held both arms tight. "Hello, Dave. Good to see you."

Dave turned back to Cesare. "Why have you done this, Eminence?"

The Cardinal's eyes glowed with an inner light. "You have courage, Father, to come here and interrogate *me*. But I don't mind. We know your, ah, *cousin*, is a heretic. He is probably also a spy and an assassin. A *would-be* assassin."

"I tried to get an audience with His Holiness," Shel muttered.

"That was stupid," David said in English. "Why?" Alexander VI was the Borgia pope, a womanizer, a con man, a murderer, the father of Lucrezia and Cesare. "Why would you want to see *him*?"

"Seemed like a good idea at the time."

The linebacker drove a fist into Dave's stomach, and he went to his knees. "Please confine your remarks to *me*," said Cesare. "Now perhaps you will tell us why you are here. The truth, this time."

"Eminence," Dave gasped, "we are pilgrims."

Cesare sighed. "Very well." He glanced toward the windows.

The squash player looked at Dave with a resigned expression. He went to the windows—there were three—and drew the curtains apart. Dave looked out onto a balcony, bordered by a low wall. The middle window was actually a door, which he opened. They were several stories high.

Shel could see out over a large section of Rome. The river wasn't visible, but houses and streets were. And they were a long way *down*.

Shel's guards dragged him across the floor and hauled him outside. "Wait," Dave cried. "Don't—!"

Shel yelped. The guards held his arms and lifted him onto the wall while Dave tried to get past the two priests. Cesare seemed not very interested. "Have you anything to say, Father Dryden?"

"Yes. You're right, Eminence. We are French spies."

He nodded. "As I thought. Now perhaps you will tell me who sent you?"

"Monte Cristo."

"I'm not surprised." Cesare's thin lips smiled. "What was your purpose? To attempt the life of His Holiness?"

"No. Most certainly not. We hoped to sow political discord."

They leaned Shel out into the air. "I don't think I heard you correctly. Did you say you were here to kill the Pope?"

"Yes. Yes, that is why we were sent."

"Very good. I'm glad you've decided to be honest." Cesare gestured, and they brought Shel back inside. "I assume everyone here heard his admission?"

Shel glared at Dave. "Idiot," he said in English. "They'll kill us now."

Cesare sighed. "Take them away," he told the guards.

"Wait," Shel said. "Perhaps Your Eminence would care to allow us to make a contribution to the Church."

"In exchange for my intercession at your trial?" He looked interested. "You have more gold to bargain with?"

"I have access to a substantial sum." Dave watched, certain that Cesare could not be conned. They would simply take everything, and they would still end in the hands of the Inquisition.

"And where is this substantial sum?"

"Nowhere, just now—" It was as far as he got. Cesare nodded, a barely perceptible movement of head and eye, and one of the priests knocked him to his knees.

"Please do not waste my time," he said.

Shel struggled to speak. "I have no wish to do so, Eminence. You have the transmuters on your desk."

"The *what*?"

"The transmuters. They convert lead to gold."

The Cardinal looked at Dave to see how he was receiving this news. Dave tried to appear displeased, as if Shel had just given away a secret. Cesare picked up one of the converters. "Such a device," he said, "would do much to spur the mission of Mother Church."

"Would you like me to show you how it works, Eminence?" Shel tried to get to his feet, but a guard held him tightly.

"I think not. I would prefer that your friend show us." He motioned Dave to come forward, gave him a lead paperweight, and the converter. "Father Dryden, make us some gold."

The lead weight was a disk-shaped stone, with an image of St. Gabriel appearing to the Virgin.

Dave set the converter to take him downstream one minute. He adjusted the lead weight as though he were positioning it. "That looks about right," he said. Then he smiled at Cesare to be sure he had his attention and pushed the button.

The room and its occupants froze. They became transparent and faded out. When they reappeared, one minute later their time, the tableau had changed dramatically. Cesare's face was twisted with shock. The guards had released Shel and were cringing near the door. The linebacker was blessing himself, and the squash player, eyes wide, had retreated well away from where Dave had been standing. Shel, finally, had gotten to his feet.

Someone screamed Satan's name. The linebacker thrust a crucifix in Dave's face. Dave pushed him away and turned to Cesare, who was equally aghast. "You abuse your power, Eminence," he said. He scooped up the coins they'd taken from him and the remaining converters. He handed one to Shel. They were by then alone with the Cardinal, who did not seem to want to come out from behind his desk.

Dave reverted to English: "You all right, Shel?"

"Yeah." He was shaking his head, trying to clear it. "It's almost been worth it."

Dave smiled nonchalantly at Cesare, whose pale expression contrasted sharply with his red robes. "I'll see you in hell, Eminence."

Shel clipped the converter onto his belt. "I just realized," he said. "I didn't get my sculpture."

"Forget it. Let's go home."

One of the guards had recovered his nerve, gotten a poker somewhere, and came back into the office. Shel pushed the button and faded out. Dave followed a moment later. But when he materialized in the wardrobe, he was alone.

CHAPTER 38

Go, Stranger, tell the Spartans that we lie here obeying their orders.

—EPITAPH ON THE MONUMENT AT THERMOPYLAE

DAVE kept looking. He tried Kitty Hawk, North Carolina, in December 1903, and watched the Wright Brothers launch their flying machine. Unfortunately, there was no sign of Shel. Moreover, neither Orville nor Wilbur had any recollection of being approached by anyone resembling Adrian Shelborne. Dave thanked them and, thoroughly intimidated, excused himself, making no effort to engage in the casual conversation that Shel had always tried to initiate. Well, they *were* busy. But that wasn't the reason he hadn't tried. It was frustrating. He'd faced down Cesare Borgia and his thugs, but he couldn't find his voice with the world's first pilots.

He'd learned from the hunt for Michael Shelborne that it was necessary to look for an event rather than a person. Other than the comet of 1811, which wasn't going to do him any good, Dave had two events, but he wasn't enthusiastic about going near either.

Leonidas and his Spartans.

And Socrates on his last day.

Thank God Shel had shown no interest in the Little Bighorn.

HE found him on the road to Thermopylae. It was rough country, all cliffs and valleys, with scattered trees and occasional grass and lots of bare ground.

Shel looked good. Much better than Dave had expected. He was tanned. Fit. Almost a man on vacation.

"Shel," Dave said. "How you doing?"

"Dave." His voice was gentle, sober. East of them, armed soldiers were surveying the landscape. "Is that really you? What are you doing here?"

"Looking for you."

"Why?"

"I wanted to make sure you were all right. When are you going to come home?"

He shook his head. Looked toward the soldiers. "They're the Thespians," he said. "They'll die alongside the Spartans."

"Shel—"

"Dave, I'm okay. But I'm not going back."

"All right."

"There's nothing for you to worry about. I'm not going to do anything crazy." The appearance of an overall well-being faded. A haunted look came into his eyes.

"Helen would want me to say hello."

"Yeah," he said. "I guess she would. How is she?"

"She's all right."

"She find anybody yet?"

Dave looked at him a long moment. "It's only been a couple weeks. I think she'll need more time."

"You haven't told her?"

"No. I brought her to the house the day you were there. When I *thought* you were there."

"Oh."

"I was going to let you explain it."

"Dave, let it go, okay? Just let it go."

"Shel, it's not going to happen. You aren't going to wind up in that grave. You know that as well as I do."

"I *don't* know it." He took a deep breath. "Look, let's just not talk about it, okay? I know you want to help, but the best thing you can do is leave me alone."

"Shel, she misses you. If you can't bring yourself to go back after her, you don't deserve her."

That brought a long silence. The wind blew. Soldiers, walking past, not really marching but simply strolling, looked their way curiously.

"I'm trying to live my life," Shel said. "Do you know how long it's been for me since I watched the funeral? *My* funeral? Two years. Two years I've had to deal with this. Two years of wondering how it's going to happen. I don't even know for sure whether I *can* go back. There might really be some sort of cardiac principle. If I show up back in Philly, *your* Philly, I can't be sure I won't get hit by a lightning bolt. And I know how crazy it all sounds. But..." He couldn't go on.

Cheering broke out from the Thespians. New squadrons had appeared and were filing into the pass, their armor dusty. The Thespians got louder, yelling and clashing swords against shields. The newcomers responded in kind.

"It's the Spartans, I think," said Shel.

"Okay." Dave didn't much care. "I just wanted to be sure you were all right."

"I'm fine."

"They don't look like guys you'd want to pick a fight with," said Dave.

"I wouldn't think so."

"All right." He threw up his hands. "I don't particularly want to hang around here for the bloodletting." He turned away as if he were going to travel out.

"Don't," Shel said. "Dave, try to understand. I'm scared of this." His eyes were bleak.

"I know."

"Eventually, somehow, I'm going to wind up in that house. In that grave."

* * *

DAVE towered over the Spartans. Even Shel was bigger than most. They shook hands with a few. Wished them well.

"By the way," Dave asked him, "how did you land in the dungeon?"

Shel frowned, not seeming to understand. "What dungeon?"

Dave needed a moment. Then he realized that Shel was younger here than he had been in Rome. For him, the Vatican incident had not yet happened. "Never mind," he said. "You'll find out soon enough."

"Well. I'm pleased to know that when it happens, whatever it is, you'll be there to rescue me." His expression changed as a thought struck him. "You *did* rescue me, right?"

PEOPLE accustomed to modern security precautions would be amazed at how easy it was to approach Leonidas. He accepted the good wishes of his visitors and observed that, considering how big they were, especially Dave, they would both have made excellent soldiers. "Although"—he smiled at Dave—"I'm afraid you'd make a prominent target for the archers."

He had dark eyes and was in his thirties. He brimmed with confidence, as did his men. There was no sense here of a doomed force.

Leonidas knew about the road that circled behind the pass, the one that would eventually allow the Persians to get to his rear. But he'd already dispatched troops to cover it. "The Phocians," said Shel, when he and Dave were alone. "They'll run at the first onset."

Leonidas invited them to share a meal. They talked about Sparta's system of balancing executive power by crowning two kings. And whether democracy could really work in the long run. The Spartan hero thought not. "Athens cannot hope to survive indefinitely," he said. "They have no discipline, and their philosophers encourage them to put themselves before their country. God help us if the poison ever spreads to us."

Later, over wine, he asked where they were from, explaining that he could not place the accent.

"America," said Dave.

He shook his head. "It must be far away. Or very small."

They each posed with him and took pictures, explaining that it was a ritual that would allow them to share his courage. Sparks crackled up from the campfires, and the soldiers talked about home and the future. Later, Dave traded a gold coin to one of the Thespian archers for an arrow. "I'm not sure that's a good idea," Shel said in English. "He may need the arrow before he's done."

But they both knew better. One arrow more or less would make no difference. When the crunch came, the Thespians would refuse to leave their Spartan allies. They would die, too. All fifteen hundred of them.

But history would remember only the Spartans.

CHAPTER 39

To sail beyond the sunset, and the baths
Of all the western stars, until I die.

—ALFRED, LORD TENNYSON, "ULYSSES"

THE sensible thing to do would have been simply to leave it alone. Let Shel go. If he wants to wander through the ages, let him. But Dave knew that, if he did that, Shel would, in some manner, come back, or be carried back, to the town house on that Thursday night in mid-September. Before it burned.

He needed Helen. If it was at all possible to find a way to bring him home and sidestep the cardiac principle, he had to have her help.

The house had burned September 13. He pulled up the newscasts. Here was the town house, a charred ruin. And excerpts from a police statement that there'd been one fatality, a Dr. Adrian Shelborne. Then, two days later, another statement that the victim in the town-house fire had been bludgeoned to death.

One of Shel's cousins had posted pictures at her Web site, photos of Shel as a boy, Shel at ten in a rowboat with a fishing pole, Shel with his father feeding a camel in the shadow of the Great Pyramid. And here was Shel in a high-school cap and gown. And with his prom date, whose name Dave had once known but had long since forgotten.

Shel at Princeton. Shel getting his doctorate. Shel sitting in a tree. Shel showing off his Toyota to a girlfriend.

And, finally, pictures of the funeral. The preacher. The coffin, supported above the open grave. The mourners. Helen was visible. And Jerry. But not Dave.

The drive home afterward was seared into his mind. He remembered the intersections, the people on the streets, people living as though nothing had happened. He'd kept the radio on, to put a voice in the car. Peace talks had broken down somewhere. Domestic assaults were up or down. Couldn't remember which.

And there'd been that strange story out of California. The pileup on one of the freeways.

And two people stealing a body out of the wreckage.

Incredible.

At first, the aid workers had assumed they'd been trying to help. Panicked people doing what they could. Had to be. What other explanation was possible?

There was one.

DAVE called Helen at home—it was a Saturday—and left a message. An hour later, she called back.

"Are you free this afternoon?" he asked. "I have something to show you."

"Okay," she said.

"Dress casually."

When he got to her place, instead of escorting her to his car, he suggested they go inside for a moment.

That, plus the briefcase, got her curiosity up. "Sure," she said.

She lived in a sixth-floor condo above City Avenue. It was tastefully furnished, and a picture of Shel occupied a side table. They sat down opposite each other. "I've been doing some traveling," said Dave.

"Really? Where?"

He set the briefcase down on the sofa and opened it. She looked at the converters. "What are they?"

"An invention of Shel's father."

She picked one up. "It looks like a Q-pod."

"It's a time machine."

That provoked a broad grin. "Seriously."

"Helen, Shel and I have been traveling in time."

"Come on, Dave. You want to talk to me or not?"

"I'm not kidding."

She sat back and nodded. Right. Of course. Why hadn't she thought of it herself?

"It's true," he said.

"Dave—"

"If you'll allow me, I'll do a demonstration."

She frowned at it. Looked at her watch.

"All right," Dave said. "Let me show you." He handed her one of the converters. "Can you attach it somewhere? To a pocket or something? There's a clip on back."

"You're *serious*."

"Humor me."

She took a long, deep breath, put it into a pocket in her slacks, and fastened it. "Okay. Now what?"

"Stand."

He got up. She looked at him uncertainly, and stood.

"Ready?" he asked.

"I suppose. We aren't going back to play tag with dinosaurs, are we?"

"Laugh if you like."

"If you haven't noticed, Dave, I'm not laughing."

"Okay. There's a large black button at the top. When you push it, the room's going to fade. Don't be alarmed when it does. Within a few seconds you'll be somewhere else." The skeptical smile was gone. Her eyes held him in a frightened gaze. She was beginning to wonder if he'd lost his mind. "Ready?"

She nodded, mouth open. Said nothing.

He fastened his own converter to his belt. "One. Brace

yourself." That brought the smile back. But it was less self-assured this time.

"I'm braced."

"Wrong choice of words. Two. I'll be with you."

"Glad to hear it."

"Three."

She hesitated. Pressed the button, and he immediately followed suit. The living room began to grow dim. She stiffened. The walls and furniture faded to a green landscape with broad lawns and gas streetlamps. The lawns and lamps became solid, and she staggered out of the fading aura. He caught her as she started to fall.

"Welcome to Ambrose, Ohio," he said. "We've gone upstream. Into the past. It's 1905." She was making odd murmuring sounds. "Teddy Roosevelt is president."

"Not possible," she said. Eyes wide, she was looking at the sky, at clusters of trees, at a nearby town, at the dirt road underfoot, at a railroad station. "Can't be happening."

Dave had been there once before, with Shel, when Thomas Edison was supposed to pass through, but they hadn't done their research thoroughly, and he didn't show up. It was a pleasant little town with tree-lined streets and white picket fences. Straw hats were in favor for men, and bright ribbons for ladies. Down at the barbershop, the talk would be mostly about the canal they were going to dig through Panama.

Birds sang, and in the distance the clean bang of church bells started. He helped her across a set of railroad tracks, and they stopped in front of a general store.

She leaned against him, trying to shut it out.

"It takes a little getting used to," Dave said.

"This is crazy." People were burning leaves, talking over back fences. Cabbage was cooking somewhere. A single car, an open coach, really, with its engine mounted in the rear, moved noisily past them and crossed the tracks.

"How long?" she said.

"How long have we had these?"

"Yes."

"For almost a year. Shel's father invented it."

"Okay." She was in a state of near shock.

"He went back to see Galileo." Dave waited for her to laugh. She just kept looking straight ahead. A couple of people came out of a drugstore, looked their way, then turned in the opposite direction.

"But . . . ?" She seemed unable to manage a sentence.

"The device got wet, and he was stranded. He's still there."

"Where?"

"In the seventeenth century."

"Then he's dead."

"It's complicated."

They found a café and went inside. Helen lowered herself into a chair near the window. "I can't believe this is really happening."

He described what he and Shel had been doing. Told her about Michael's determination to stay where he was. The waitress came, and they ordered coffee.

"It's hard to believe any of this," she said. "Even with that sitting in front of me." She indicated the street scene outside the window. A couple of guys were passing in a horse-drawn cart. Signs on the walls advertised cigarettes and Coca-Cola.

"There's something else you should know."

"Wait. If we can really travel in time, we can go back and see Shel."

Her eyes pleaded for the response she needed.

He reached across the table and took her hand. "He's not dead."

"What?"

"You and I had lunch at Applebee's Wednesday. And afterward, we went to my place."

"Yes?"

"It wasn't so I could give you a Greek medallion."

"Why, then?"

"Because Shel had been there earlier that morning."

Her eyes slid shut.

"I wanted you to see him. But he'd gone by the time we got there."

"He's alive, and you let me go through that funeral?"

"I didn't know then, Helen. Not any more than you did. I assumed he was dead, and that was the end of the story. But he showed up at the house."

"All right," she said at last, "where is he now?"

"I don't know, Helen. Lost in time, somewhere."

"So who's in the cemetery?"

"He is."

"But you're saying he's still alive."

In a way, he'll always be alive. "Yes. He's still out there. But he won't come back."

She was visibly struggling to grasp the situation, and to control her anger. "Why didn't you tell me?"

"I didn't know how."

Her face had grown pale. When he'd finished explaining, her eyes looked empty. "You can take us back, right?"

"Home? Yes."

"Where else?"

"Anywhere. Well, there are range limits, but nothing you'd care about."

On the street, a couple of kids with baseball gloves hurried past. "And he thinks it's inevitable that he'll eventually get put in that graveyard?"

"Yes."

"I don't understand why he would."

"There seems to be a force that doesn't allow paradoxes." He told her about Ivy, and about Shel falling into the ocean.

"So what do we do?"

"I don't know whether we should do *anything*. With this crazy logic, he may be right. I wouldn't go back either to get hit in the head and thrown into a fire. Would you?"

"No," she said. "I guess not."

"I have an idea how we might be able to resolve things, though," Dave said.

"Hold on a second. Start with this: Do we have any idea at all where to find him?"

"I know some places to look."

"Will you take me to him?"

"Yes. I think he needs you."

A horse-drawn carriage clopped past. Helen stared at the quiet little buildings. White clapboard houses. "Nineteen-five," she said. "Shaw's just getting started."

CHAPTER 40

There was a young lady named Bright
Whose speed was far faster than light;
She set out one day
In a relative way
And returned on the previous night.

—*PUNCH*

MARK S. Hightower had been Shel's dentist for years. He operated out of a medical building across the street from the University Hospital, where Helen had interned and still served as a consultant.

Dave had met Dr. Hightower once. He was short, barrel-chested, flat-skulled, a man who looked more like a professional wrestler than a dentist. But he was soft-spoken and, according to Shel, a guy who was great with his patients.

Helen and Dave, in a taxi, pulled up in front of a brownstone building. The doctors' names—there were four of them—were posted on shingles. Hightower was on the first floor. A sign in the window read: WE CATER TO COWARDS.

Dave asked the driver to wait, and, carrying a converter in a laptop bag, went into the office. One patient and a guy who was probably a salesman were seated in the reception room while two people on TV discussed the latest misadventure of a prominent actress. The receptionist looked up from behind a glass panel. "Hello," she said, opening a window and sliding the sign-in sheet toward him.

"I'd like to make an appointment."

"Are you having a problem, Mr.—?"

"McCloskey. I'm new in Philadelphia. I just wanted to get a routine checkup."

She nodded, gathered some papers, and pushed them in his direction. "Fill these out, please."

"Thank you." He started toward one of the chairs, laid the papers on a side table, then turned and went back to the window. "Excuse me. Do you have a washroom?"

She pointed at a double door. "Through there, and on your right."

The doors opened into a corridor. He could hear a drill in back somewhere, but the corridor was quiet. He took the converter out of the laptop bag and went into the washroom. It was empty. He moved himself forward ten seconds. Got a reading on the location of the washroom so he could come back to it later.

He washed his hands and returned to the waiting room. "I'm sorry," he said to the receptionist, "but I think I came to the wrong place. This isn't Dr. Vester's office, is it?"

"No," she said. "This is Dr. Hightower."

"Oh. I'm sorry for wasting your time." He returned the papers and went outside.

Helen looked his way. "How'd you make out?"

"Okay."

CHAIN-REACTION collisions have become an increasingly dangerous occurrence on limited-access highways around the world. Hundreds die every year, thousands are injured, and property damage runs well into the millions. On the day that Shel was buried, there had been a pileup in California. It had happened a little after 8:00 A.M. on a day with perfect visibility, when a pickup rear-ended a station wagon full of kids headed for breakfast and a day at Universal Studios.

Helen and Dave materialized well off the highway moments after the chain reaction had ended. The road and the shoulder were littered with wrecked vehicles. Some people were out of their cars trying to help; others were wandering dazed through the carnage. The morning air was filled with screams and the stench of burning oil.

"I'm not sure I can do this," Helen said, spotting a woman bleeding in an overturned Ford. She went over, got the door open, and motioned Dave to assist. The woman was alone in the car. She was unconscious, and her arm looked broken.

"Helen," Dave said, "we have a bigger rescue to make."

She shook her head. No. This first.

She stopped the bleeding, and Dave got someone to stay with the victim. They helped a few other people, pulled an elderly couple out of a burning van, stopped a guy who was trying to move a man with two fractured legs. But Dave was unhappy. "We don't have time for this," he pleaded.

"I don't have time for anything else."

Sirens were approaching. Dave let her go, concentrating on finding what they'd come for.

He was in a blue Toyota that had rolled over several times before crumpling into a tree. The front of the car was crushed, a door was off, and the driver looked dead. He had bled heavily from a head wound. One tire was spinning slowly. Dave could find no pulse.

The guy was about the right size, tangled in a seat belt. When Helen got there, she confirmed that he was dead. Dave cut him free with a jackknife. EMTs were spreading out among the wrecked cars. Stretchers were appearing.

Helen could not keep her mind on what they were doing. "Your oath doesn't count," David said. "Not here. Let it go."

She looked at him desperately.

They got him out of the car, wrapped him in plastic, and laid him in the road. "He does look a little like Shel," she said in a small voice.

"Enough to get by."

Dave heard footsteps behind them. Someone demanded to know what they were doing.

A big, beefy EMT.

"It's okay," Dave said. "We're doctors."

Helen looked down at the body. "He's dead," she said by way of explanation.

The EMT looked annoyed. "We could use your help up ahead."

"On our way," said Dave.

As soon as he was gone, they put on plastic gloves. Dave attached one of the converters to the victim's belt and pushed the black button. They watched him fade and vanish. "So far, so good," he said. "I was afraid it would be like the cushion."

"What cushion?"

"It's a long story," he said. "I tried to use a converter on one, but it didn't work. Maybe it needs to be attached to someone."

Dave followed the body. The highway carnage grew transparent and was replaced by the washroom in Dr. Hightower's office. The corpse was slumped on the floor. He detached the converter from it and took it back to Helen. Moments later, they returned. Helen had a laptop.

HIS name was Victor Randall. They found pictures of an attractive woman with cropped brown hair seated with him in a porch swing. And two kids. The kids were smiling at the camera, one boy, one girl, both around seven or eight. "Maybe," Helen said, "when this is over, we can send them a note to explain things."

"We can't do that," Dave said.

"They'll never know what happened to him."

"That's right. And I don't think there's any way around it."

There was also about two hundred cash. Later, he would mail that back to the family. He dragged the body out of the washroom and laid it in the corridor. "Okay, Helen," he said, "your ball."

Using penlights, they began an inspection. A half dozen rooms were designated for patients. Dave followed her from office to office, not really knowing what they were looking for. But Helen did one quick turn down the passageway, stopped in a room at the far end, and pointed at a machine tucked away in a corner. "This is it," she said. The manufacturer's label said it was an orthopantomograph. "It's designed to provide a panoramic X-ray."

"Panoramic? What's that?"

"Full mouth. It should be all we'll need." The records were maintained in manila folders in an interior office. Helen found Shel's, thumbed through it, and took out a disk. "Okay," she said, "we caught a break."

"What's that?"

"The results are on individual disks."

She explained how it worked: The person being X-rayed placed his forehead against this plastic rest and his chin in the cup-shaped support. The camera was located inside the cone over here, which was mounted on a rotating arm. The arm and cone traversed the head, like this, and produced a panoramic image of the teeth. The only problem was that the patient normally stood during the procedure.

"We'll need six to eight minutes to do it," said Helen. "During that time we have to keep him absolutely still. Think you can manage it?"

Dave nodded. "I can do it."

"Okay." She checked to make sure there was a disk in the machine. "Let's get him."

They carried Victor to the X-ray machine. At Helen's suggestion, they'd brought along some cloth strips, which they now used to secure the body to the device. It was a clumsy business, and the corpse kept sliding away from them. Working in the dark complicated things, but after about ten minutes, they had him in place.

"Something just occurred to me," Dave said. "Victor Randall already has the head wound."

Her eyes closed momentarily. "You're suggesting the arsonist didn't hit Shel in the head after all. You know, I'm beginning to think it's going to turn out to be the lightning strike at that."

A mirror was mounted on the machine directly in front of where the patient's face would be. Helen pressed a button, and a light went on in the center of the mirror. "They would tell the patient to watch the light," she said. "That's how they're sure they've got it lined up."

"How are *we* sure?"

"What's the term? 'Dead reckoning'?" She punched another button. A motor started, and the cone began to move.

Ten minutes later, they took the disk out, leaving Victor in place until Helen could be sure they had good pictures. She inserted the disk into the laptop, brought up the picture, and handed it to Dave without looking at it. "What do you think?"

The entire mouth, uppers and lowers, was clear. "Looks good to me."

She took a deep breath. "Plenty of fillings on both sides. Let's see how it compares."

They went back to Shel's folder. "He goes to the dentist every three months," she said. (Dave couldn't help noticing she still talked about him in the present tense.) She checked the dates on the disks and removed one. "These are the results of his most recent checkup." She put it in the computer and brought up a panoramic picture, like the one they had just taken, and several smaller photos of individual sections. "I think they call these 'wings,'" she said. "But when they bring a dentist in to identify a body, they do it with *these*." She indicated the panoramic and compared Shel's with the one they'd just made. "Well—"

"What?"

"They don't look much alike in detail. If they ever get around to comparing Mr. Randall's panoramic with Shel's wings, they'll notice something's wrong. But it should be good enough to get by." She transferred the data, everything except the panoramic, from Shel's disk to Randall's.

A car pulled up outside.

Helen put Shel's panoramic disk in her pocket, marked his name on the Randall disk, and placed it in the folder.

Dave heard a siren. Getting louder. "Helen, I think we may have tripped an internal alarm."

"Probably."

"We have to go."

"All set." She replaced the folder and closed the file drawer just as the siren arrived and shut off. Blinds covered the windows, but rotating lights leaked through.

More car doors and voices. Out front and in the parking lot.

They retreated to the back and began taking Victor down from the X-ray machine. Meantime, they heard keys in the front door. "It's taking too long," Helen whispered.

The door opened. A flashlight shone in. A voice said, "Police." Then the door swung wide, and more beams appeared. The plan had been that David would take the corpse directly to the town house, remove the converter, and return with it for Helen. But time was becoming a problem.

The body came free and fell into his arms as the police started down the corridor. Dave began to attach Helen's converter while she wiped off the headrest and checked the floor to be sure no blood had been spilled. Then she and Dave turned off their penlights.

The passageway lights came on.

"We don't have time," she whispered. "We're going to have to leave the body." She inserted a fresh disk into the X-ray machine.

"We can't do that."

"Have to. No choice."

Maybe there was.

The cops ordered them to come out into the passageway. "Where we can see you. And get your hands up."

"Helen." A new voice, in the dark.

Dave's voice. A second Dave's voice.

Damn. It had worked. The second David held a converter out for an astonished Helen. "Take it. Quick."

Dumbfounded, she looked from one to the other, then grabbed the laptop.

The voices were right outside the door.

David activated Victor's converter, watched him fade, and followed. The darkened dental office went away, and he was back in the den at the town house, standing beside the desk. Victor's body lay on the floor.

Helen, still in a state of near shock, appeared, followed

instantly by the second David. She stared at one. Then the other. Leaned on a side table. "Are you twins?"

"No."

"What's happening?" she asked. "Where'd *he* come from?" But she wasn't sure which *he* she was referring to.

The two Davids laughed. Then the one who'd come in with the body removed the converter and set it to return to the point of departure.

"Where are you going?" asked Helen.

"Back to rescue you." He grinned. "I'll arrive a couple of minutes ago."

"I don't understand."

"Take care," he said.

"Wait."

"Got to go." He hit the button.

And he was back, watching himself bend over poor dead Victor, trying to decide what to do.

"...Have to leave the body," said Helen, while inserting a disk into the orthopantomograph.

The David who was about to attach the converter to the body shook his head no. "We can't do that."

"Have to," said Helen. "No choice."

"Helen." He couldn't see her well in the dark. But he heard her gasp. He pressed the converter into her hands, the one he'd removed from Victor back in the town house. "Take it," he said. "Quick."

She got it into her hands. Almost dropped it.

Dave and the body went away as lights went on and two police officers burst into the room, guns drawn. Helen started to fade, and Dave pressed the black button.

THEY were all back in the living room.

Helen gawked at him. At both of them. "Are you twins?"

The David who'd been with Helen was in the process of removing the converter from Victor Randall. "No," he said. He lifted the unit and reset it. Looked briefly at his other self, and smiled. "Got to go."

And he went away.

"Is he coming back?" asked Helen.

Dave smiled. "He already did." She looked pale. "You okay?" he asked.

"I think I have a headache."

CHAPTER 41

O, call back yesterday, bid time return.

—WILLIAM SHAKESPEARE, *RICHARD II*

LIGHTNING glimmered in the curtains. Shel's heating system came on.

Helen looked at the body and at the staircase. "We should have brought him in on the second floor."

"I didn't have the coordinates."

"It's only fifteen feet *up*."

She was right, of course. Dave made the adjustment for the converter, attached it to the body, and punched the button. It faded, and when they went upstairs they found him on the landing. "Which bedroom is Shel's?" she asked.

He almost told her that he thought *she'd* know. But he decided she wouldn't think it was funny.

There were three bedrooms, but it wasn't hard to pick out his. Pictures of their old high-school baseball team, plaques acknowledging his outstanding work for Carbolite, a pile of books on the side table.

Dave turned back the sheets, hauled the corpse onto the

bed, and dressed it in Shel's pajamas. When he'd finished, they put his clothes into a plastic bag.

They also had a brick in the bag. They went downstairs and got the keys for Shel's car out of the Phillies cup. They'd debated just leaving the clothes to burn, but neither wanted to leave anything to chance. Despite what one might think about time travel, David understood that what they were doing was forever. They couldn't come back and undo it, because they were *here*, and they knew what the sequence of events was, and you couldn't change that without confronting the cardiac principle.

They borrowed Shel's Toyota. It had a vanity plate reading SHEL, and a lot of mileage. But he had taken good care of it. They drove down to the river. At the two-lane bridge that crossed the Narrows, they pulled off and waited until there was no traffic. Then they went out to the middle of the bridge, where they assumed the water was deepest, and threw the bag over the side. Dave still had Victor Randall's wallet and ID, which he intended to burn.

They returned Shel's car. By then it was 3:45 A.M., thirty-eight minutes before a Mrs. Wilma Anderson would call to report a fire at the town house. Dave worried whether they'd cut their time too close, that the intruder might already be inside. But it was still quiet when they returned to the house and put the car keys back in the cup.

They locked the place, front and back, which was how they'd found it, and retired across the street behind a hedge. It was a good night's work, and they waited now to see who the criminal was. The neighborhood was tree-lined, well lighted, quiet. The houses were upper-middle-class, fronted by small fenced yards. Cars were parked in garages or on driveways. Somewhere in the next block, a cat yowled.

Four o'clock.

"Getting late," Helen said.

Nothing moved. "He's going to have to hurry up."

She frowned. "What happens if he doesn't come?"

"He *has* to come."

"Why?"

"Because that's the way it happened. We know that for an absolute fact."

She looked at her watch. 4:01.

"I just had a thought," David said.

"We could use one."

"Maybe you're right. Maybe there is no firebug. Or rather, maybe *we* are the firebugs. After all, we already know where the fractured skull came from." And he knew who had broken into the desk.

She thought about it. "I think you're right," she said.

"Wait here," he told her. "In case someone *does* show up."

"Where are you going?"

"To get some gas."

David left the shelter of the hedge and walked quickly across the street, entered Shel's driveway, and went back into the garage. There were three gas cans. All empty.

He needed the car keys again. He used the converter to get back inside and retrieved the keys. He threw the empty cans into the trunk of the Toyota.

There was an all-night station on River Road, only a few blocks away. It was one of those places where they concentrate on keeping the cashier alive after about eleven o'clock. He was a middle-aged, worn-out guy sitting in a cage full of cigarette smoke. A toothpick rolled relentlessly from one side of his mouth to the other. Dave paid in cash, filled the cans, and drove back.

Helen helped. It was 4:17 when they began sloshing gas around the basement. They emptied a can on the stairway and another upstairs, taking care to drench the bedroom where Victor Randall lay. They poured the rest of it on the first floor, and so thoroughly soaked the entry that David was reluctant to go near it with a lighted match. But at 4:25, they touched it off.

They retreated across the street and watched for a time. The flames cast a pale glow in the sky, and sparks floated upward. They didn't know much about Victor Randall, but what they did know was maybe enough. He'd been a husband

and father. In their photos, his wife and kids had looked happy. And he got a Viking's funeral.

"What do you think?" asked Helen. "Will it be all right now?"

"Yeah," Dave said. "I hope so."

DAVE'S first act on returning to the base time, Saturday, September 21, eight days after the fire at the town house, was to destroy Victor Randall's wallet and driver's license.

Then he used the converter to travel to Randall's house. He left ten thousand dollars in the mailbox.

He and Helen spent some time planning how to get the news to Shel. The Socrates event seemed like their best bet. "Do it tomorrow," she said. "I'm going home to crash for a while. This has been too much excitement in one day for me."

They were at his place, and she had just started for the door when they heard a car pull up. "It's a woman," she said archly, looking out the window. "Friend of yours?"

It was Lieutenant Lake. She was alone this time.

The doorbell rang.

"This won't look so good," Helen said.

"I know. You want to duck upstairs?"

She thought about it. "My car's out there. There'd be no point."

The bell rang again. David opened up.

"Good morning, Dr. Dryden," said the detective. "I wonder if you can spare me a few minutes?"

"Sure. Come in, Lieutenant. Where's your partner?"

She smiled. "We've been busy." She took a deep breath. "I have a few questions for you."

"Of course."

Helen came into the living room, but the lieutenant did not look surprised. "Hello, Dr. Suchenko. It's good to see you again."

Helen nodded. "And you, Lieutenant. How are you?"

"Fine, thanks." Lake cleared her throat and addressed

Helen. "I wonder, Doctor, whether I might have a minute alone with Dr. Dryden."

"Sure." Helen got her jacket from the closet. "I should be on my way anyhow." She patted Dave's shoulder in a comradely way and let herself out.

"Doctor," said Lake, "you've said you were home in bed at the time Dr. Shelborne's home burned. Is that correct?"

"Yes. That's right." When she'd asked her questions before, Dave had been annoyed. Now he felt queasy. Now he was, in a sense, the perp.

"Are you sure?"

The question hung in the sunlit air. "Of course. Why do you ask?" He could read nothing in her expression.

"Someone answering your description was seen near the town house at the time of the fire."

"It wasn't *me*." Dave immediately thought of the man at the gas station. And he'd been driving Shel's car. With his vanity plate in front just in case anybody wasn't paying attention.

"Okay. I wonder if you'd mind coming down to the station with me, so we can clear the matter up? Get it settled?"

"Sure. Be glad to." They stood. "Give me a minute, okay? I need to use the washroom."

"Certainly," she said. There was one on the first floor, and she waited while he went into it.

He called Helen. *"Don't panic,"* she said. *"All you need is a good alibi."*

"I don't *have* an alibi."

"For God's sake, Dave. You've got something better. You have a time machine.*"*

"Okay. Sure. But if I go back and set up an alibi, why didn't I tell them the truth in the beginning?"

"Because you were protecting a woman's reputation," she said. *"What else would you be doing at four o'clock in the morning? Get out your little black book."* The problem was that Dave didn't *have* a little black book.

CHAPTER 42

That old bald cheater, Time.

—BEN JONSON, *THE POETASTER*

DAVE had been reasonably successful with women, but not so much that he needed to organize a data center. Not to the extent, certainly, that he could call one with a reasonable hope of finishing the night in her bed. Except maybe Katie, who would do it as a favor, but he didn't want to involve her in this. What other option was there? He could try to pick somebody up in a bar, but you didn't really lie to the police in a murder case over a pickup.

Well, he'd have to come up with something. Meantime, he would need his car keys. He came out of the washroom, apologized to Lieutenant Lake for the delay, got his keys, and started out with her. "Oops," he said. And stopped, patting his rear pocket.

"What's wrong?"

"Let me get my wallet."

He went upstairs, into his bedroom, and used the converter to return to the night of the fire, to Thursday evening, when he'd been out with Katie. It was about seven hours before the town house burned.

He came back down into the den and let himself out. The garage, of course, was empty. He used the converter again to move forward to 12:30. He was home by then, and the lights were out in his bedroom.

He held his breath while the garage door rolled up. But everything stayed quiet. He opened the car door as quietly as he could, slid behind the wheel, started the engine, and backed out into the street.

HE wasn't going to find a credible woman wandering the streets, so he pulled over to the curb beside an all-night restaurant to think about it. He was in a run-down area lined with crumbling warehouses. A police cruiser slowed and eased in behind him. The cop got out, and David lowered the window. "Anything wrong, Officer?" he asked. The cop was small, black, well pressed.

"I was going to ask you the same thing, sir. This is not a safe area."

"I was just trying to decide whether I wanted a hamburger."

"Yes, sir," he said. Dave could hear the murmur of the police radio. "Listen, I'd make up my mind, one way or the other. I wouldn't hang around out here if I were you."

Dave smiled, and gave him a thumbs-up. "Thanks," he said.

The policeman got back into his cruiser and pulled out. David watched his lights turn left at the next intersection. And he knew what he was going to do.

HE crossed over into New Jersey and drove south on Route 130 for about a half hour. Then he turned east on a two-lane. Somewhere around two thirty, he entered a small town and decided it was just what he was looking for. Its police station occupied a drab two-story building beside the post office. The Red Lantern Bar was located about two blocks away, on the other side of the street.

He parked in a lighted spot close to the police station, walked to the bar, and went inside. It was smoky and subdued, reeking with dead cigarettes and stale beer. Most of the action was near the dartboard.

He settled in at the bar and commenced drinking scotch. He stayed with it until the bartender suggested he'd had enough, which usually wouldn't have taken long. But that night his mind stayed clear. Not his motor coordination, though. He paid up, eased off the stool, and negotiated his way back onto the street.

He turned right and walked methodically toward the police station, putting one foot in front of the other. When he got close, he added a little panache to his stagger, tried a couple of practice giggles, and lurched in through the front door.

A man with corporal's stripes came out of a back room.

"Good evening, Officer," he said, with exaggerated formality and the widest grin he could manage, which was then pretty wide. "Can you give me directions to Atlantic City?"

The corporal shook his head. "Do you have some identification, sir?"

"Yes, I do," Dave said. "But I don't see why my name is any business of yours. I'm in a hurry."

"Where are you from?" His eyes narrowed.

"Two weeks from Sunday." David looked at his watch. "I'm a time traveler."

LIEUTENANT Lake was surprised and, Dave thought, disappointed to learn that he had been in jail on the night of the fire. She said that she understood why he'd been reluctant to explain, but admonished him on the virtues of being honest with law-enforcement personnel.

When she'd left, he called Helen. "Let's go rescue your boyfriend."

CHAPTER 43

Bare ruin'd choirs, where late the sweet birds sang—
> —WILLIAM SHAKESPEARE, SONNET 73

"THE question you are really asking, Simmias, is whether death annihilates the soul." Socrates looked from one to another of his friends.

Simmias was young and clear-eyed, like most of the others, but subdued in the shadow of the prison house. "It is an important matter," he said. "There is none of more importance. But we were reluctant—" He hesitated, his voice caught, and he could go no further.

"I understand," said Socrates. "You fear this is an indelicate moment to raise such an issue. But if you would discuss it with me, we cannot very well postpone it, can we?"

"No, Socrates," said a thin young man with red hair. "Unfortunately, we cannot." This, Dave suspected, was Crito.

Despite Plato's account, the final conversation between Socrates and his disciples did not take place in his cell. It might well have begun there, but they were in a wide, utilitarian meeting room when Helen and Dave arrived. Several women were present. Socrates, then seventy years old, sat at ease on a wooden chair, while the others gathered around him in a half circle.

"I don't see him," Helen said, seconds after they'd entered.

Neither did Dave. That was a surprise. Shel had indicated several times that he wanted to participate in the final Socratic discussion.

Socrates was, at first glance, a man of mundane appearance. He was of average height, for the time, and clean-shaven. He wore a dull red robe, and considering the circumstances, he maintained a remarkable equanimity. And his eyes were extraordinary, conveying the impression that they were lit from within. When they fell on Dave, as they did from time to time, he imagined that Socrates knew where he'd come from and why he was there.

Beside him, Helen writhed under the impact of conflicting emotions. She had been ecstatic at the chance to see Shel again. When he did not arrive, she looked at Dave as if to say that she had told him so and settled back to watch history unfold.

She was, Dave thought, initially disappointed in that the event seemed nothing more than a few people sitting around talking in an uncomfortable room in a prison. And speaking Greek, at that. It was as if the scene should somehow be scored and choreographed and played to muffled drums. She had read Plato's account before they left. Dave tried to translate for her, but they eventually gave it up. She explained that she could get most of the meaning from her prior knowledge and the nonverbals. "When?" she whispered, after they'd been there almost an hour. "When does it happen?"

"Sunset, I think."

She made a noise deep in her throat.

"Why do men fear death?" Socrates asked.

"Because," said Crito, "they believe it is the end of existence."

There were almost twenty people present. Most were young, but there was a sprinkling of middle-aged and elderly persons. One wore a hood. His beard was streaked with gray, and he had intense dark eyes. He gazed sympathetically at Socrates throughout, and periodically nodded when the philosopher hammered home a particularly salient point. There was something in his manner that suggested a young Moses.

"And do all men fear death?" asked the philosopher.

"Most assuredly, Socrates," said a boy, who could have been no more than eighteen.

Socrates addressed the boy. "Do even the brave fear death, Cebes?"

Cebes thought it over. "I have to think so, Socrates."

"Why, then," asked Socrates, "do the valiant dare death? Is it perhaps because they fear something else even more?"

"The loss of their honor," said Crito.

"Thus we are faced with the paradox that even the brave are driven by fear. Can we find no one who can face death with equanimity who is *not* driven by fear?"

Moses stared at Helen. Dave moved protectively closer to her.

"Of all men," said Crito, "only you seem to show no concern at its approach."

Socrates smiled. "Of all men," he said, "only a philosopher can truly face down death. Because he knows quite certainly that the soul will proceed to a better existence. Provided he has maintained a lifelong pursuit of knowledge and virtue, and has not allowed his soul, which is his divine essence, to become entangled in concerns of the body. For when this happens, the soul takes on corporeal characteristics. And when death comes, it cannot escape. This is why cemeteries are restless at night."

"How can we be sure," asked a man in a blue toga, "that the soul, even if it succeeds in surviving the trauma of death, is not blown away by the first strong wind?"

It was not intended as a serious question, but Socrates saw that it affected the others. So he answered lightly, observing that it would be prudent to die on a calm day, then undertook a serious response. He asked questions which elicited admissions that the soul was not physical and therefore could not be a composite object. "I think we need not fear that it will come apart," he said, with a touch of amusement.

One of the jailers lingered in the doorway throughout the

long discussion. He seemed worried, and at one point cautioned Socrates against speaking too much, or getting excited. "If you get the heat up," he said, "the poison will not work well."

"We would not wish that," said Socrates. But he saw the pained expression on the jailer's face, and David thought he immediately regretted the remark.

Women arrived with dinner, and several stayed, so that the room became more crowded. In fact, no doors were locked, and no guards, other than the reluctant jailer, were in evidence. Phaedo, who is the narrator of Plato's account, was beside Dave. He whispered that the authorities hoped profoundly that Socrates would run off. "Davidius," he added, "they did everything they could to avoid this. There is even a rumor that last night they offered him money and transportation."

Socrates saw them conversing, and he said, "Is there something in my reasoning that disturbs you?"

Dave had momentarily lost the train of the discussion, but Phaedo said, "Yes, Socrates. However, I am reluctant to put my objection to you."

Socrates turned a skeptical gaze on him. "Truth is what it is. Tell me what disturbs you, Phaedo."

He hesitated, and Dave realized he was making sure of his voice. "Then let me ask," he said in a carefully neutral tone, "whether you are being truly objective on this matter? The sun is not far from the horizon and, although it grieves me to say it, were I in your position, I also would argue in favor of immortality."

"Were you in his position," said Crito, with a smile, "you would have taken the first ship to Syracuse." The company laughed together, Socrates and Phaedo as heartily as any, and the strain seemed broken for the moment.

Socrates waited for the room to quiet. "You are of course correct in asking, Phaedo. Am I seeking truth? Or trying to convince myself? I can only respond that, if my arguments are valid, then that is good. If they are false, and death does indeed mean annihilation, they nevertheless arm me to withstand its approach. And that, too, is good." He looked utterly composed. "If I'm wrong, it's an error that won't survive the sunset."

Simmias was seated immediately to the right of Moses. "I for one am convinced," he said. "Your arguments do not admit of refutation. And it is a comfort to me to believe that we have it in our power to draw this company together again in some place of God's choosing."

"Yes," said Crito. "I agree. And, Socrates, we are fortunate to have you here to explain it to us."

"Anyone who has thought about these issues," said Socrates, "should be able to reach, if not truth, at least a high degree of probability. And I would add, whatever validity may attach to our speculations, that the critical lesson to be taken away from this hour is that the lives we know are not forever. Live well. Enjoy what time is given you. It is a magnificent gift."

Moses seemed weighed down with the distress of the present calamity. Still, he continued to glance periodically at Helen. Now, for the first time, he spoke: "I very much fear, Socrates, that within a few hours there will be no one left anywhere in Hellas, or anywhere else, for that matter, who will be able to make these matters plain."

"That's *Shel*'s voice," Helen gasped, straining forward to see better. The light was not good, and he was facing away from Helen and David, his features hidden in the folds of his hood. Then he turned and looked openly at Helen, and smiled sadly. His lips formed the English words *Hello, Helen*.

She was getting to her feet.

At that moment, the jailer appeared with the poisoned cup, and the sight of him, and the silver vessel, froze everyone in the chamber. "I hope you understand, Socrates," he said, "this is not my doing."

"I know that, Thereus," said Socrates. "I am not angry with you."

"They always want to blame *me*," Thereus said.

No one spoke.

He set the cup on the table. "It is time," he said.

The rest of the company, reluctantly, one by one, following Helen's example, got to their feet.

Socrates gave a coin to the jailer, squeezed his hand, thanked him, and turned to look at his friends. "The world is very bright," he said. "But much of it is illusion. If we stare at it too long, in the way we look at the sun during an eclipse, it blinds us. Look at it only with the mind." He picked up the cup. Several in the assemblage started forward, but were restrained by their companions. Someone in back sobbed.

"Stay," a woman's voice said sternly. "You have respected him all your life. Do so now."

He lifted the cup to his lips, and his hand trembled. It was the only time the mask slipped. Then he drank it down and set the cup back on the table. "I am sure Simmias is right," he said. "We shall gather again one day, as old friends should, in a far different chamber."

SHEL swallowed Helen with his eyes. "I did not expect to see you again," he said.

She shivered. Peered intently at him. "Shel."

A smile flickered across his lips. "It's good to see you, Helen." He stood silhouetted against the moon and the harbor. Behind them, the waterfront buildings of the Piraeus were illuminated by occasional oil lamps.

"Where have you been?"

"To more places than you might easily imagine. But if you're asking where I live, I'm in Center City, Philadelphia."

"Why didn't you contact us?" demanded Dave.

"Not *your* Philadelphia. A more distant one." He still looked like a man in pain. "Dave, you seem to have become my dark angel."

Dave stared back at him. "I'm sorry you feel that way."

A gull wheeled overhead. "Socrates dies for a philosophical nicety," said Shel. "And Shelborne continues to run from his assigned fate. Right?"

Helen was trembling. "I'd do the same thing," she said.

"As would we all. Isn't that right, Dave?"

"Shel." They shook hands. Embraced. While Helen kept

her distance. "I suspect we would. But you don't have to run any longer."

Shel managed a smile. If only it were so.

"It's true," said Helen.

"What do you mean?"

"The grave has been filled, Shel. It wasn't you."

CHAPTER 44

A friend is a second self.

—CICERO

DAVE'S first act, when he got back, was to return the converter Helen had used to the sock drawer.

He came back without her. Shel invited her to go home with him. He didn't say where home was. But she'd gone. He had a new, improved model of the converter, and it had carried them both off. A few days later, Dave heard that Helen had canceled her membership in the Devil's Disciples. That same afternoon, word came that she'd closed her medical practice.

When he tried to call her, a recorded voice informed him that the number was no longer in service. She'd moved out of her condo, which had gone up for sale. There was no forwarding address.

Then one afternoon in November he came home to find a greeting card on his dining-room table. The card showed a pterodactyl in full flight, with the inscription MISS YOU. He opened it:

Dear Dave,

Shel and I are having a wonderful time. We have a pent-house on the Parkway near the end of the 21st century. He's talking about going on a grand tour. Maybe we will live near the Parthenon for a while, or possibly Paris during the 1920s. I have never been so happy. And I wanted to thank you for making it possible.
   I will never forget you, Dave.

                                        Love,
                                        Helen

P.S. We left something for you. In the wardrobe.

They'd left the *Hermes*. They had positioned it carefully under the light, to achieve maximum effect. It looked good.

He stood a long time admiring the piece. But it wasn't Helen. The house filled with echoes and the sound of the wind. He hadn't realized how much he'd miss her.

DAVE suspected that his friendship with Shel largely grew out of the fact they'd been opposites in so many ways. Where Shel was cautious, Dave could be reckless. Dave was not the guy, he'd once said, who would keep his mouth shut while Hitler was speaking. The difference in their sizes was striking. When they traveled together, Helen had once commented, they looked like a comedy team. While Dave got emotionally connected with every woman in his life, Shel was an all-or-nothing guy. The woman on his arm was either simply someone to keep him company or the love of his life.

Dave fell in love with everybody.

Another area in which they differed: Shel was perfectly content using the converter and traveling alone across the centuries. Dave had been along because of his language skills, and because a second person served as a safety factor. Shel had never said that, of course, but there was certainly some truth to it. Dave, on the other hand, could have been talking with Marcus Aurelius, but he wouldn't have enjoyed it nearly as much had Shel, or *someone*, not been there to share the experience. Consequently, with Shel and Helen both gone, he decided his time-traveling days were over.

He hadn't been satisfied simply carrying a conversation with Hemingway. He'd wanted to ride in the ambulance with him, to go chasing German submarines with him at the outbreak of World War II. But he didn't want it badly enough to actually *do* it. At heart, Dave was shy. He would never have gone to say hello to Tom Paine and Ben Franklin and Molly Pitcher and the rest of those people.

He got bored with his career as an art dealer and started looking for a new line of work. The State Department was interested in employing him as a translator, and the CIA contacted him about coming on board. They wouldn't tell him what they wanted him to do, other than that they would put his language skills to good use. He never found out how they knew he was available.

He discovered he couldn't just sit on the front porch. But none of the jobs appealed to him. He didn't want to spend the rest of his life parked in an office. It was hardly an appropriate career for a man who had talked with Voltaire and challenged Cesare Borgia.

In the end, he told Katie. Told her everything. And he needed to take her somewhere to provide proof.

So Katie showed up, and he took her to Ambrose, Ohio, as he had Helen. At eleven o'clock on a beautiful September morning in 1906. She loved the place. They hung out there much of the day, watching the trains roll through, drinking coffee at Sadie's café, and sitting in the town square.

"Where would you like to go next?" he asked. "What would you like to see?"

At first, she was reluctant to move out of the twentieth century. They watched Abbott and Costello perform in a vaudeville show, took in a Fred MacMurray comedy during World War II in downtown Philadelphia, and hit some of the pubs during the Jazz Age. Katie came immediately to love the experience. "Oh, Dave, look at the trolley car." "Dave, if we're going to come here, I'm going to have to expand my wardrobe." "Dave, I *love* Benny Goodman."

Their first trip outside the safety zone was to Tombstone, Arizona, in 1881, where Dave got lucky and ran into Calamity Jane again. Katie lit up Wyatt Earp's life for a few days. They met Virgil Earp and Doc Holliday, and rode a stage coach from Fayetteville to Fort Smith. After that, there was no holding Katie down.

BUT, for Dave, there was still something missing. And eventually he figured out what it was.

At the end of a long night in Tiberius's Rome, they'd decided to try a Roman bath. It became a fairly risqué experience for two people from Philadelphia. The bath grounds were home to a statue of a female warrior, which they'd paused to admire on the way out. She was complete with helmet and sword. It was well past midnight when they stood before it beneath a full moon. "It's magnificent," said Katie.

"It's Minerva."

"I'll bet," she said.

When they reappeared at Dave's place, Katie commented that Americans had lost the ability to enjoy themselves.

"We watch television," Dave said.

Her eyes were shining. "So what's for tomorrow night?"

"You make the call, Katie."

"Me? I don't know what's out there. If you want, I'd be content to go back to the bath."

"What would your mother say, love?"

"I think she'd want you to produce another one of those Q-pods." She squinted at him. "You okay, Dave? That wasn't too much for you, was it?"

"No. I'm good."

"So why—?"

"Why what?"

"You don't seem very turned on by the evening."

"Yeah." He sat down, and she dropped onto the sofa beside him.

"What's the problem?"

Dave still wanted to tell the world. Conversations with Caesar. An evening with Attila. (Well, no, that had never really happened.) Lunch with Abner Doubleday.

"Lunch with *who*?"

"Never mind. Look, Katie, it kills me to have done all this stuff and not be able to do anything with it."

"I know," she said. "I'm sorry. I don't know what to advise."

"I've been thinking about it."

"And?"

"The only thing I can think of is to use the material. But put it in novel form. Tell the story. The *whole* story. As if it were fiction."

"That's not a bad idea, Dave. Can you *write* a novel?"

"With what I've seen? Are you kidding?"

"Then do it," she said. "Otherwise, you'll never have any peace. Do you have a title?"

"I thought maybe *Time Travelers Never Wait in Line*."

"That's cute."

"It's true."

"I suppose it is."

"But you don't like it?"

She shrugged. "It's *cute*. I don't especially like *cute*."

"You have a better one?"

"Ummm. If I were doing it—"

"Yes?"

"I'd call it *Minerva by Moonlight*." She sat for a minute, waiting for a reaction. But none came. "Is there something else?" she asked.

"Yes," he said. "I have a promise to keep."

CHAPTER 45

The end crowns all,
And that old common arbitrator, Time,
Will one day end it.

—WILLIAM SHAKESPEARE, *TROILUS AND CRESSIDA*

OCTOBER 1, 1950, was a pleasant, sun-filled day. A crowd had overflowed Ebbets Field in Brooklyn for the season-ending showdown between the charging Dodgers and the Phillies, whose seven-and-a-half-game lead, during the previous two weeks, had shrunk to a single game.

The score was tied 1–1 in the bottom of the ninth, and the Dodgers had runners at first and second with nobody out when Duke Snider rifled a line drive single to center.

Down front in a box seat, Michael Shelborne stood up with the crowd. *They* thought the winning run was coming home as Cal Abrams rounded third. But Michael knew better.

Richie Ashburn threw a strike, and catcher Stan Lopata blocked the plate and made the tag. The crowd roared its disapproval, and somebody behind him said, "Hey, we've still got two on."

Michael leaned over, smiled at his son, and spoke under his breath: "It won't matter, kid."

* * *

IN 1934, Helen sat on the enclosed deck of their recently pur-
chased Cape Cod villa, looking out at the ocean, which was
bright and sun-swept and looked as if it went on forever. Like
time. This was a Helen that Dave would have been slow to
recognize. She was thirty years older, and if she had aged
well, she was nevertheless no longer the loose-limbed beauty
he had known.

There was movement behind her, and she turned to see
Shel and his father materializing within a pair of auras. Shel
had long since shed the beard.

"Hello, Dad," she said. "How'd the game go?"

Michael laughed, gave her a hug. "As if you didn't know."

Shel handed her a box of popcorn. "For you, love," he said.

She kissed him. "Dinner in about forty minutes."

Michael looked out at the Atlantic. "What have you been
doing all day, Helen?"

"Watching the kids." A sailboat was tacking with the
wind. It was carrying two boys. Teenagers.

"The Kennedys?" Michael asked.

"Yes," she said.

Michael studied them for a moment. Joe and Jack. "It's
good to see them enjoying themselves," he said.

EPILOGUE

ASPASIA showed up for the Riverside Theater's opening-night performance of *Achilles*. She was accompanied by Rod Connelly, who was an instructor at the Starlight Dance Studio, and by Harvey Barnard and his wife, Amanda.

Riverside had a full house. It was not necessarily an auspicious start because Riverside *always* had a full house, and it was a small theater. Rod, of course, knew the claims that had been made for the source material, and, as one would expect, he didn't believe a word of it. Furthermore, he had made no secret of the fact that he'd come principally to please Aspasia. "I've seen a couple of Greek plays," he said, with evident distaste. "They took my high-school class to see one, I forget what it was, but I couldn't make heads or tails of it."

The other one had been staged at the University of Pennsylvania years before. And, though Rod didn't directly say so, it was clear that his presence once again had been to please a young woman. Or maybe to impress her. In this latter instance, at least, he remembered the title, if not the dramatist. It had been *The Acharnians*. By, of course, Aristophanes.

Rod was adamant about people who'd send somebody an armload of Greek literature. "They won't tell you who they are. That means they're con artists. Trying to get away with something. If I were you, I wouldn't have had anything to do with these things."

Harvey's attitude wasn't much more positive. "It's just too good to be true," he said. Amanda cautioned him with stern looks to be careful. Don't hurt Aspasia's feelings.

Aspasia didn't really believe it either. Still, she *wanted* to believe. And it was an exhilarating experience to settle into her seat, open the program, and see the title, *Achilles*, and, where the byline would normally be found: *Thought to be by Sophocles*.

And there was the cast, Trainor, Polyxena, Paris, and Apollo, and, of course, Achilles, actually about to come alive.

Riverside was a theater-in-the-round. They had good seats, up close. The stage was decked with plants and dominated by a doorway. The program identified it as the exterior of Apollo's chapel outside Troy.

THE lights came on, and the chorus began a dolorous chant. Achilles made his entrance.

As the show proceeded, Aspasia tried to be skeptical. Achilles was perhaps too trusting of his longtime enemies, Polyxena too ready to give in to her lover's determination to risk everything in a meeting with Paris. Trainor, the priest, might not have been sufficiently respectful of the greatest of the Greek warriors. But she could find no fault with Paris. He was utterly torn between what he perceived as his obligation to the slain Troilus, and to Troy itself, and his repugnance at betraying his sister and ambushing a victim who trusted him.

During the climax, he enters, with a longbow over one shoulder, and tries to opt out. "What if the bolt does not take him down?" he asks the audience, while presenting an arrow for their inspection.

He is on the verge of abandoning the effort when Apollo steps out of the shadows. "I am with you," the god says. "Have no fear."

And, as Achilles enters the chapel, the audience sits riveted.

THE play ends with Trainor kneeling over Achilles' body while Paris retreats into the darkness. Polyxena produces a knife, which she will use on herself. The chorus closes out, and, for a few moments, after the last actor has left the stage, the audience is mute. Gradually, people begin to applaud.

When the actors came back to take their bows, the members of the audience were out of their seats cheering.

"Not bad," said Rod.

Harvey admitted that *Achilles* had been "very effective."

"But it proves nothing," said Aspasia.

"It doesn't prove," he said, "that it was written by Sophocles, but who cares? It's like arguing about who wrote Shakespeare. What really matters is that we have a previously lost work, or we've discovered another brilliant playwright. Take your pick."

Ahead, in the crowd, there was a familiar face. One she hadn't seen in years.

"Dave," she said. "Dave Dryden. How are you?"

He broke into the same relaxed smile she remembered. "Aspasia. It's good to see you. How've you been?"

"Couldn't be better. What did you think of the show?"

"Not bad." He was with a young woman and a tall, silver-haired man in pinstripes. "Katie," he said, "this is Aspasia. We were in graduate school together at Princeton." He squeezed Katie's wrist. "We're old friends."

"Princeton's getting to be a long time ago," Aspasia said. "Hello, Katie."

They shook hands, and Dave turned to the man in the pin-striped suit. "This is another old friend," he said. "Aspasia,

Ari. He's a librarian." Then he switched to Greek. "Had it not been for her, Ari, tonight would not have happened."

"He doesn't speak English?" she asked.

"No. Not yet."

Aspasia smiled, offered her hand, and responded in Greek. "Ari," she said, "I'm delighted to meet you."

Citations:

Warning:

The epigraph at the head of Chapter 34, attributed to Sophocles, is of course simply a happy hoax, intended to catch the unwary.

The new novel of the fantastic unknown
by the Nebula Award–winning author
of *Time Travelers Never Die*

Jack McDevitt

ECHO

AN ALEX BENEDICT NOVEL

Eccentric Sunset Tuttle spent a lifetime searching
in vain for forms of alien life. Twenty-five years
after his death, a stone tablet inscribed with cryptic symbols is revealed to be in the possession
of Tuttle's onetime lover, and antiques dealer Alex
Benedict is anxious to determine what secrets the
tablet holds. It could be proof that Tuttle discovered what he was looking for.

To find out, Benedict and his assistant embark
on their own voyage of discovery—one that will
lead them directly into the path of a very deter-
mined assassin who doesn't want those secrets
revealed.

M725T0610